SUSAN ANDERSEN

ALL SHOOK UP

AVON BOOKS
An Imprint of HarperCollins*Publishers*

This is a work of fiction. Names, characters, places, and incidents are products of the author's imagination or are used fictitiously and are not to be construed as real. Any resemblance to actual events, locales, organizations, or persons, living or dead, is entirely coincidental.

AVON BOOKS
An Imprint of HarperCollins*Publishers*
10 East 53rd Street
New York, New York 10022-5299

ISBN: 0-7394-1329-5

Printed in the U.S.A.

This is dedicated, with love,
to the women around Sue's table,
for years of laughter, conversation, and spectacular meals.

To
Mildred and Mom,
Monica and Jenny,
Tara and Renee,
Sari and Karen,
Lucille and Thelma,
Neesa and Rachel
and, of course, Sue herself

And to girls who wear glasses

—Susie

Prologue

Dru Lawrence's uncle Ben came to the monthly meeting armed with a police report on J.D. Carver. "He's clean," he said, slapping it down on the long, rustic conference table. "He hasn't been arrested as an adult, and his juvenile record is sealed."

"You needn't sound so disgusted, darling," Aunt Sophie said, reaching across the table to pat his hand before she snagged the report to read for herself. "That's very good news."

But Dru could understand where her uncle was coming from. Star Lake Lodge had been a family-owned business for four generations, and they'd all been shocked right down to their flip-flops to discover that Great-aunt Edwina had left her share of it to an outsider. And an *urban* outsider, at that. Edwina had been an absentee co-owner for so long, leaving them to run it as they'd seen fit for so many years, Dru had nearly forgotten it wasn't theirs alone.

"Maybe," she said slowly, "Carver's just stopping by to get a peek at what he inherited. He probably won't even stick around—and we'll end up sending his checks like we did Edwina's."

"I wouldn't count on it, hon," Uncle Ben said. "I got the impression from his terse note that he's ready to settle right in and take up the reins."

Sophie suddenly pushed back from the table and walked over to the open window. She bent in front of it and held the neckline of her blouse open to catch the breeze blowing the green-and-tan gingham curtains into the meeting room. Dru got up and went to the built-in oak buffet against the far wall. Reaching past a collection of native baskets, she picked up a pitcher of water and splashed some into a glass. She carried it over to her aunt, stopping along the way to align an oil painting of snow-covered birch trees with the other landscapes that adorned the barnwood-paneled wall.

"I don't know much about Carver," Dru admitted as she resumed her seat. "Except that he was one of Great-aunt Edwina's 'boys.' To tell the truth, I don't even remember her all that well, aside from bits and pieces." Edwina had been like Dru's parents, a sometime visitor who'd flown in and out of her life. She'd known her great-aunt mostly as a sophisticated, soft-spoken summer drop-in, here for one week each August and then gone again, back to her plush home in Seattle.

Sophie rolled the glass back and forth against her temple and smiled in fond reminiscence. "You would have liked her, if you'd gotten to spend a little more time with her." She returned to the table and gave the report a delicate nudge with her fingertips. "I always admired Edwina a great deal. And J.D. was special to her. He was the first boy she ever took in."

"And the one she fretted over having mismanaged," Uncle Ben added.

"I do remember that!" Dru straightened. "At least I remember sitting at your kitchen table as a kid while you grown-ups visited, and I remember her worrying over the way she handled some boy. The boy with her father's watch."

"That was J.D."

"I got the impression she cared for him a lot."

"Yeah, she did. He's pretty much the reason she got into taking care of all those troubled kids." Ben sighed. "Edwina had excellent instincts about people. And I guess when it comes right down to it, the shares were hers to do with as she wished." He looked at Dru. "Soph and I aren't as hands-on around here as we used to be, though, hon, so you're the one who's gonna have to work with J.D. on a day-to-day basis. What's your vote on all this?"

"Well, contesting the will is pointless—from everything I've heard, Great-aunt Edwina retained her full mental capacity right up to the day she died."

"The woman was sharp as a tack," Ben said.

"Then I don't see where we have any choice but to respect her wishes."

"I agree," Sophie said. "And if we're going to do this, let's do it right and give J.D. a warm welcome."

"Of course," Dru added dryly, "I also think I deserve a huge raise for taking on a new headache."

Ben looked up from his notes, peering at her over his reading glasses. "We'll definitely look into that—at next month's meeting. This month, though, we've got a big problem. The repairs needed around here are mounting up. We've got to find a way to hang on to competent workmen."

1

The gas gauge on J.D. Carver's vintage Ford Mustang read "Empty" when he arrived in Star Lake, Washington, one day ahead of schedule. But then, it never read anything else—the needle had been stuck there since he'd bought the car in '93. The car's trunk held a few of his favorite power tools, a tool chest, and a fully loaded carpenter's belt. The backseat held two table saws. He also had an antique gold watch in his pocket, an old canvas army duffel containing everything else he owned in the world, and a raft of emotions he'd give a lot to deny sitting heavy in his gut.

His life back in Seattle had gone to hell. It was his own fault, but knowing that didn't help. His friend Butch he didn't even want to think about right now. And Bob Lankovich, the man who'd given him his start in construction—and through whose company's ranks J.D. had risen to become foreman—was in prison. J.D. didn't want to think about Bob, either. *Or* his idiot son, Robbie.

He was just tired of the whole freaking mess—the threats, the being a pariah. In Rat City, for chrissake. How could anyone do anything bad enough to be a pariah in a neighborhood known as Rat City? His unexpected inheritance from Edwina Lawrence was nothing if not timely. It was an excellent time to get out of town.

He laughed without humor. Of course, Edwina was just another can of worms. He ought to open a damn bait shop—between her, Butch, and the Lankovich mess, he was ass-deep in worms.

J.D. rubbed at the tension knotting the back of his neck. He was pretty much down to his last option. He'd given up his studio apartment, sold the tools he couldn't fit in the car, and cleaned out his bank account. There was nothing left for him in the city where he'd grown up, and nowhere to go if this didn't work out. So he planned to make it work, come hell or high water.

He pulled up in front of the fieldstone-and-timber lodge that he now had a half interest in, and parked the car. Then he simply sat there for a moment, breathing in the rich scent of evergreens and lake. Reaching into the watch pocket of his jeans, he stroked a finger over Edwina's father's gold timepiece, which she had left him along with her share of the lodge.

The same watch she'd once accused him of stealing.

More than Robbie Lankovich's threats or J.D.'s disillusionment over Butch's collecting on a debt he'd always known would one day *be* collected, Edwina's ancient betrayal still had the ability to bother him.

He snorted softly. *Bother*. There was a nice, understated way of putting it.

It still had the power to twist his gut into a mass of knots, and that wouldn't do. Climbing out of the car, J.D. shouldered his duffel and stared up at the imposing shingle-roofed fieldstone porch that ran across the entire front of the inn.

It was bad enough that he still allowed a childhood injustice to color his life after all these years. But right now, he particularly needed to focus his concentration.

Because five would get you ten that he was about two minutes away from a no-holds-barred dog fight with Edwina's relatives over the share of this lodge that she'd bequeathed him.

Dru thanked the front-desk clerk and hung up the phone. Oh, God, he was here. She straightened in her chair, aware of her heart rate bumping up a notch. J.D. Carver was out in the lobby. He wasn't supposed to be here until tomorrow.

She'd believed she was fully reconciled to the new situation. She'd honestly thought she was prepared to meet Edwina's beneficiary and welcome him into both the business and the Lawrence clan. But if the sudden, apprehensive tripping of her pulse was anything to go by, she'd merely been fooling herself.

Standing, she checked to see that her sleeveless white polo shirt with its discreet lodge logo was neatly tucked into her walking shorts, then smoothed her hands over the crisp hunter-green material that skimmed her hips. She took a deep breath and blew it out. Okay, she was ready. She just wished he hadn't arrived early; it destroyed their plan to greet him as a family.

Dru squared her shoulders. Big deal; she'd just have to tough it out on her own. She'd been meeting and greeting people professionally since she was sixteen years old. Besides, Aunt Soph and Uncle Ben were just over at the cabin they'd reserved for Carver's use, putting on a few finishing touches to make him feel at home, so she'd have backup shortly. *Not* that she'd need it. She headed for the lobby. *Just think of him as a long-lost cousin.*

Easier said than done, Dru decided a few moments later as she looked at the man squatting in front of the massive fieldstone fireplace. Even from the back, he didn't look like her idea of a cousin.

He appeared to be one supercharged mass of muscularity—from the spot where his dark hair brushed the tanned skin of his neck, right down to his work-boot-clad feet. A pristine white T-shirt stretched across wide shoulders and clung to the narrowing wedge of his back until it disappeared into a worn pair of jeans that hugged his muscular thighs and butt. Her heartbeat inexplicably picked up.

She cleared her throat. "Mr. Carver?"

He twisted to look at her over his shoulder. His dark eyebrows met over his nose, and for just a moment he seemed to still. But it must have been her imagination, for he said in a neutral tone, "Don't call me mister. My name's J.D." He rose to his feet in one smooth, powerful movement.

He was downright intimidating at his full height when faced head-on. His T-shirt hugged the planes of his chest and the six-pack of muscles in his abdomen; it stretched thin over his biceps. Energy poured off him in almost palpable waves. Dru took a reflexive step back.

Then she caught herself and thrust out her hand. "J.D., then. And I'm Dru Lawrence. I'm the general manager here." Looking up into his eyes, she discovered that what she'd mistaken for brown was actually a dark hazel-green, ringed with an even denser green. "Welcome to Star Lake Lodge."

Nerves zinged when he wrapped his callused hand around hers and shook it firmly, and it was all she could do not to jerk free. What was the *matter* with her? She'd met plenty of well-built guys before, for heaven's sake—it wasn't like her to act like a high school girl confronted with the star jock. Resisting the urge to rub her hand down her shorts to remove the heat that lingered when he relinquished his grip, she dragged her *think cousin* advice to the forefront of her mind and mustered up a courteous smile.

He indicated the fireplace with a jerk of his square chin and didn't bother smiling back. "That andiron is nearly in two pieces. It needs to be pulled out and soldered back together."

Good God, the man certainly didn't lack brass—he hadn't even been here ten minutes and already he was offering criticism? An uncharacteristic impulse to invite him to kiss her rosy-red cheeks—and she wasn't talking the ones she could feel glowing with temper here—surged up Dru's throat. "I'll make a note of that," she said evenly, and forced another smile. "Is this your bag?"

She'd already bent to pick up the canvas duffel when his hand whipped the bag out from under her nose. Stuffing her own hands in her shorts pockets, she straightened. Smacking him would *not* be an auspicious way to start off the partnership. "I'm sure you'd like to freshen up after that long road trip. I'll show you to your cabin."

"Dru!" Sally Jensen, their front-desk manager, rushed up. She flashed an apologetic smile at J.D., got hung up gawking at his chest for a moment, then dragged her gaze back to Dru.

A genuine smile quirked Dru's lips for the first time since she'd clapped eyes on her new partner. Whew. For a moment there she'd thought she was sliding into something risky, and she didn't *do* risky. Clearly, J.D. Carver was simply one of those men who elicited strong female reactions—she probably would've had more to worry about if she *hadn't* noticed his hunky body. "J.D., this is Sally Jensen, our desk supervisor. Sally, J.D. Carver, the new part-owner."

J.D.'s dark eyebrows drew together, but Sally had already turned back to Dru. "Brian Kebler just called in sick."

"Wasn't he scheduled to take a party of water-skiers out today?"

"Yes, the Jacobsen clan at three o'clock. I've already tried to get a replacement from the backup list, without any luck. If you can't think of anyone else I can call, we're going to have seven disappointed kids."

"How about Monica White? Is she working the lunch shift today? She's been driving boats since she was old enough to see over the steering wheel, and she expressed an interest once in filling in."

"I'll check to see if she's here. If she's not, I'll give her a call at home to see if she can come in. But what do I do if she's unavailable?"

"Comp the kids an ice-cream party in the Eagle's Nest."

"Okay; that might work. Thanks." Sally spun on her heel and hustled off.

"Oh, Sally, wait." When she turned back, Dru said, "Make Uncle Ben Plan B instead of the ice-cream party. He might be available if Monica can't do it. If neither of them are free, though, go to Plan C."

Sally flashed her a thumbs-up.

Dru turned back to J.D. and found him watching her with those aloof hazel eyes. He had a strong blade of a nose, the bridge of which looked as if it had been broken more than once, and a wide mouth with a full bottom lip. "Are you ready?"

He shouldered his duffel and nodded curtly.

"You're not exactly Smiley the Social Hound, are you?" Oh, shit, where had that come from? Generally she was diplomacy personified, but something about this guy just breezed right past the guards she normally placed on her tongue.

His gaze did a fast slide over her, then returned to her eyes. "Depends on the situation."

Dru shrugged and headed down the hallway to the wing exit. It was no skin off her tush if he never smiled. Maybe he had bad teeth or something.

Which didn't quite explain why she felt so over-heated.

Injecting an almost military erectness into her posture, she coolly informed him, "Star Lake Lodge has been in business since 1911." Dru opened the door to the stairwell. "It has thirty-one rooms, including four suites, and we have eight cabins, seven of which are available this summer. The one we've prepared for you was put out of commission this past winter when it sustained storm damage." It most likely would've remained closed had they not been pressed for a place to put him up. In recent years, repairs and maintenance had turned into their largest headache, since craftsmen who could handle the jobs were scarce around here. "I'm afraid the porch roof is still a mess."

J.D. shrugged. "I can live with that." He pulled his gaze away from the sway of her hips as she preceded him down the interior staircase, and focused instead on the fat, glossy brown braid that hung down her back. "I expected you to just stick me in a room somewhere." Like in the cellar, maybe.

She spared a glance over her shoulder. "This and the ski season are our busiest times, which means we're booked to near capacity. That means you'd be forced to move from one room to another every couple of days, which isn't a whole lot of fun. We want you to be comfortable."

Yeah, right. He was suspicious as hell of do-gooders. Dru's fine, upstanding great-aunt had seen to that.

Not that he'd been perfectly content before Edwina Lawrence had barged into his fourteen-year-old life and turned it upside down. Bouncing from foster home to foster home was less than ideal for any kid, but at least there had been a pattern to his life; he'd understood the rules. And rule number one had been: don't get too comfortable. For sooner or later—and usually it had been sooner—he'd be out on the street again.

Not getting your hopes up was the first rule of survival, but Edwina had been different, and it had sucked him in, lulled him into forgetting a lot of hard-won lessons. She'd chosen him—he hadn't been foisted on her by an overworked social worker. And the fact that she was unlike anyone he'd ever known had been a seduction all on its own.

They'd met the day he'd tried to steal her purse. It had been one of his stupider moments, but he'd listened to his friend Butch's pitch of easy money and had given in to the lure.

The fragile-looking little old lady had taught him that crime didn't pay, though. Not only had she hung onto her purse, she'd gotten a good grip on him to boot. The only way to break loose would have been to hurt her. When Butch had taken off running, leaving him to face the music on his own, J.D. had heard the mental clang of barred doors slamming shut, and thought he was headed to juvie hall for sure.

But instead of turning him in to the cops, the way any right-thinking individual would have done, she'd taken him home. Then she'd made arrangements to foster him, and had offered him the run of her place.

He'd fallen in love with her that day.

She'd taught him there was an entire world far removed from the decaying streets and alleyways of the inner city, which was all he'd known up until then.

But what she'd offered with one hand she'd taken away with the other, at the very moment he'd finally relaxed his guard and begun to believe he was worthy of the clean new life she offered. And where once he had idolized her, he'd begun to bitterly resent the very breath she drew.

Shit. J.D. nearly tromped on Dru's heels as he blinked the past back where it belonged—*in* the past. *That was twenty years ago, ace. Get over it.*

Dru pushed open the outer door at the bottom of the stairs and the evergreen-laden scent of the country rushed in.

"You mentioned a ski season?" he said. "I didn't see any lifts around here." And although this was an alpine lake area, it wasn't the type of terrain he associated with ski resorts.

Dru glanced at him over her shoulder, and the blue of her eyes was electric in the sunlight. "That's because we feature cross-country skiing. See that trail-head over there?" She pointed to a hiking trail that disappeared into the woods down the side of the mountain. "That's called Treetop, and it connects us to over a hundred kilometers of trails that can be hiked and biked in the summer or skied in the winter."

She casually touched his forearm, and a muscle under his skin jumped as if he'd received an electric shock. Face carefully expressionless, he stepped away, slanting a quick look at her.

"Come on," she said, clearly oblivious. "Your cabin is down this way." She began to head toward the lake.

J.D. rubbed at the band of heat left behind by her touch. What the hell was that all about? He'd like to blame it on the fact that he wasn't accustomed to being touched, but that didn't explain the similar jolt he'd gotten when he'd turned around and seen her for the first time in the lobby. His initial reaction had been: *want it.* She'd looked so soft and round, standing there. Round eyes, round cheekbones, round breasts, round ass. He didn't understand it—hadn't then, didn't now. She was pretty enough, in a subtle outdoorsy, girl-next-door sort of way. But she sure as hell wasn't his type, so that covetous shock of awareness seemed out of place.

Rat City didn't imbue a taste for subtle or girl-next-door, and he liked his women brassy. Big hair, big tits, clothing spray-painted on to show every curve.

Watching her stride down the trail in front of him in her shorts and Keds, J.D. tried to figure out what had caused that uncharacteristic craving. He had to admit she had a body that would probably be dynamite in tight clothing. But it didn't take a genius to see she wasn't the type to wear it. She was too . . . fresh-faced. She had that silky, swingy hair, those freckles across the bridge of her nose, those big, guileless, startlingly blue eyes. He'd bet his last buck she wasn't a woman to hang out in bars, waiting for some stud to come along and buy her a drink, like the barflies he associated with. She looked more like one of those happily-ever-after, put-the-ring-on-my-finger types.

They rounded a curve in the trail and the lake was suddenly laid out in front of them in all its splendor. Shaped like a Christmas stocking, it was placid and blue. The sounds of kids splashing and laughing, the *sprong* of a diving board, and the occasional shrill blast of a lifeguard whistle cut through the silence of the woods.

"There's a roped-off swimming area and a float around the next bend," Dru said over her shoulder. She veered onto a short spur trail, and a moment later they emerged from the sun-dappled track into a small clearing, across which stood a cabin with half its porch roof missing. A man who looked to be in his mid-fifties sat with one hip perched on the railing, smoking a cigarette, while a little boy in a Star Wars Phantom Menace T-shirt wielded a light-saber against an imaginary foe.

The kid saw them first and his face lit up. "Mom!" he yelled and, the plastic light-saber clattering to the floor of the porch, launched himself off the steps. A second later he hung like a monkey from Dru's front, skinny legs around her waist, grimy hands linked behind her neck as he leaned back to give her a huge, goofy grin.

"Whoa, you're getting way too big for this." Staggering under his weight, she nevertheless grinned back and kissed him on the nose.

It was a scene like a hundred others J.D. had observed as an outsider looking in. Crossing his arms over his chest, he watched mother and child and congratulated himself on his acumen. *There you go, bud. All that's missing here is the carpool-mobile.*

It doesn't get any further from your type than this.

2

Supporting the warm weight of her ten-year-old son by linking her hands in the small of his back, Dru looked over Tate's head at her uncle. He was extinguishing his cigarette, and the fact that he'd been smoking in front of Tate could mean only one thing. "Aunt Soph having a menopause moment?" Her normally easygoing aunt's moods had been erratic for the past several months, and they'd all learned to get out of her way when one was upon her.

"She's hot-flashing, Mom," Tate said. "And when Grandpa Ben told her she'd missed one of the cobwebs on the ceiling, she said, 'How would you like this dust mop up your—' "

"Tate!"

"I wasn't gonna say it, Mom." But he clearly relished the idea.

"I got him out of there before she actually completed the sentence anyway," Ben assured her.

"But I know what she was gonna say," Tate said with a grin that showed his adult front teeth. "She was gonna say buttho—"

"Don't *even* think you're going to slip it by me by attributing it to someone else, bud."

"Dang." With another big-toothed grin, he unhooked his legs and hopped down. Turning back toward the porch, he caught sight of J.D. and stopped dead. "Hey. I'm Tate. Who're you?"

"I'm sorry, J.D.; where are my manners?" Hard as it was to credit, Dru had actually forgotten him for a moment. "This is my son, Tate. Tate, this is Mr. Carver."

"Just J.D.," he corrected her and thrust out a callused hand to Tate. "How's it goin', kid?"

"Goin' cool." Tate took the proffered hand and immediately began grimacing mightily, which told Dru he was doing his best to grind J.D.'s knuckles to dust. He simply loved the adultness of shaking hands, but they couldn't seem to convince him that a firm grip was all that was necessary for a perfectly manly handshake. He understood the concept when it came to women, but just let a man stick his hand out and Tate immediately turned it into a test of his machismo.

Since J.D. hadn't exactly proven himself to be Mr. Congeniality, she hurriedly said, "And this is my uncle, Ben Lawrence. J.D. got in a day early, Uncle Ben."

"I see that." Ben walked over to join them. "Tate, quit trying to crush his hand—we've talked about this before. Go stick your head in the door and tell your grandma that J.D. is here." He tousled Tate's silky brown hair as the boy turned to do his bidding. "Be prepared to duck in case she's still on the warpath, slick." His gaze followed the boy until Tate swooped his light-saber up off the porch on his way to the front door; then he turned to J.D. and offered his own hand. "Welcome to Star Lake Lodge."

Dru watched the two men as they took each other's measure. Her uncle was older and not as fit as J.D., but he was still damn fine-looking for his age. He'd spread a little around the middle, and his shoulders weren't as muscular as they once were. But his hair, though mostly gray now, was thick and wavy, and his brown eyes crinkled at the outside corners when he smiled, which he did often.

The same certainly couldn't be said for J.D. He exchanged handshakes with the sober impassiveness Dru had seen since his arrival. He answered her uncle's questions civilly enough, but didn't volunteer so much as an extra word that might make the introductions go more smoothly. He all but bristled with no-trespassing signs, and for some reason it put her back up. Luckily, Tate and Aunt Sophie emerged from the cabin before she forgot herself and said something unforgivably snide.

The fact that she was even tempted to do so brought Dru up short. What *was* it about this guy that tested all the control she'd worked so hard to perfect? This knee-jerk desire to provoke a reaction out of him was not good.

"Grandma Sophie's herself again," Tate announced

cheerfully as he pulled his great-aunt by the hand toward the group in the clearing. "I don't think she wants to put the dust mop up Grandpa Ben's bu—"

"*Tate!*"

Clearly unfazed by the exasperated warning that came from three separate throats, he gave an unrepentant shrug and pinned his honorary grandmother in place with his laser-blue eyes. "Well, you don't, do you?"

"No," Sophie agreed dryly. "I can safely say that impulse has passed." She walked up to her husband and slid her arm around his waist. Patting his chest with her free hand, she murmured contritely, "I'm sorry, Ben."

"I know you are, babe." He wrapped his arm around her shoulder and hugged her to his side.

Dru was aware of J.D. next to her, still and watchful, and she tried to see her aunt and uncle as they must appear through his eyes.

She'd lived with them so long she could see them only through her own, but she was struck as always by the closeness they radiated. It was simply part of their nature to gravitate together whenever they were in the same vicinity. It wasn't an excluding relationship, though—their natural warmth extended to everyone they cared about.

Dru's parents had been restless souls who'd traveled the four corners of the earth. One of her earliest memories was of them parking her with her aunt and uncle so they could go off to see the world and try something new and exciting. When she'd begun school, she'd always dreaded that moment when the bus let her off at the corner. She'd never known who, if anyone, would be there to meet her. Sometimes it had been one of her parents, but more often than not, it'd been a neighbor picking up her own child, or sometimes no one at all. Long before her parents had died in a hot-air-balloon accident in the Andes when she was nine, Sophie and Ben and Star Lake Lodge had come to represent security to her.

She smiled at the familiar sight of Sophie leaning against Ben. At fifty-one, her aunt looked closer to forty, and her milkmaid voluptuousness and vivid coloring still had the ability to turn the heads of men twenty years her junior. It might have been intimidating if not for the ready warmth of her smile.

Sophie smiled now as she stepped out from under the drape of Ben's arm and extended both hands to J.D. "Welcome," she said, grasping his much-larger hands in her own. "I'm sorry I wasn't there to greet you when you arrived. Dru, honey, did you show him the back road so he can bring his car around to unpack?"

"No, but we can do that now if he'd like." Dru raised an inquiring eyebrow at J.D.

His muscular shoulders hitched beneath the white T-shirt that strained to contain them. "That's not necessary," he said brusquely. "I've got everything I need right here." He nodded at the canvas duffel bag resting on the ground a few feet away.

Sophie smiled brilliantly. "Fine, then. Would you like some time alone to unpack and get settled in?"

"Yeah, that would be good." He hesitated for a moment, then added, "Thanks."

"We'll leave you, then. Tate! Come along, darling."

He came running. "Can I go swimming now? It's almost three, and that Dean kid in two-eleven said he was gonna go swimming then."

Dru glanced back as she followed her son and aunt and uncle down the trail. J.D. still stood where they'd left him, his hands thrust in his jeans pockets and his mouth broody. He looked a little lonely as he watched them go, almost . . . lost.

Suppressing a snort, she whipped around and caught up with Tate, who was slashing the air with his plastic light-saber and talking ninety miles an hour to Sophie and Ben. *Yeah, right.*

If that little bit of fantasy didn't qualify for Fanciful Thought of the Day, she didn't know what did.

J.D. tossed his duffel on the queen-sized bed and began to unpack. The cabin was compact, with its one bedroom, one bath, tiny kitchen, and combination living-and-dining room that was divided by an arch with built-in bookshelves. It had all he needed, though, and someone—Sophie Lawrence, he would guess—had even left a vase of flowers on the small table out in the dining room and another one here on the bedroom dresser. His gaze kept drifting to it. Something about that homey touch got to him.

The cabin had been built back in the days before deforestation was a household word, and he got caught up in sheer admiration for the craftsmanship that had gone into the tongue-and-groove walls, the hardwood floors, and the fir-door-and-window jambs and lintels. Then he turned his attention back to emptying the bag that sat on the faded patchwork quilt of its stack of white T-shirts, underwear, jeans, shave kit, and a few of his more cherished tools.

The canvas duffel was collapsing in on itself by the time his fingers brushed the stack of letters on the bottom. Slowly, he drew the bundle out and stared down at Edwina's spidery handwriting on the topmost envelope.

He didn't know why the hell he'd kept her letters all these years. He hadn't even bothered to open them after reading the first few that had caught up with him, since he'd known good and well what they would say: that Edwina had forgiven him.

For something he hadn't done, which had been pretty goddamn generous of her. Angered anew by the reminder of an old injustice, he threw the rubber-banded bundle into the wastepaper basket next to the nightstand and stomped out of the room.

A minute later he was back, fishing it out again. God only knew why—he'd be a much happier man if he could simply leave that part of his life in the trash bin where it belonged. But he couldn't seem to let it go. He threw the letters back in the duffel, slung the bag onto the shelf above the hanger rod in the closet, and shut the door.

But out of sight was not out of mind. He pulled Edwina's father's gold watch out of his pocket and ran his thumb over its etched cover. Pressing his thumb on the minuscule catch on its side, he snapped the cover open and stared blindly at its face, seeing only scenes from the past. Trying to shake off the unwelcome memories, he clicked the timepiece closed again and tucked it back into the watch pocket of his jeans. The first time he'd seen Edward Lawrence's watch was the day that Edwina had taken him into her home. The watch had lain on a leather-edged blotter on an antique desk in the study off the hallway.

Unfamiliar with that style of timepiece, he'd been drawn to it over and over again. He'd thought it looked like something that would belong to a rich guy, which he'd found totally cool. More than that, though, its age and sense of history had beckoned like a Lorelei luring sailors onto the rocks—though he would have been hard-pressed to verbalize what he'd so admired about it.

Only as an adult had he realized that it had been the watch's continuity, the fact that it had been in a single family for two generations, that he'd found so awesome. He'd been a throwaway kid who'd never known his father and whose mother had found feeding her drug habit more important than keeping custody of her son, and he was just whacked by the idea of a family not only hanging onto its kids, but saving pieces of its individual lives to pass down to them. Until he'd moved in with Edwina, he'd never possessed a single thing that was his alone, let alone something given him by an ancestor.

Edwina had changed all that, and for several months it had been like living in his most closely held fantasy. She'd treated him the way he'd imagined real kids were treated. Which had made the betrayal all the more bitter when Edward's watch had suddenly disappeared and she'd all but accused him of taking it. He hadn't taken kindly to that, and as ridiculous as it was, the ghost of that outrage lingered on like nuclear waste with an infinite half-life.

So if there was one thing he knew for damn sure, it was that even though the Lawrences *seemed* like a decent family, nobody just relinquished their rights to valuable property with the cheerfulness they'd just displayed. He slammed out of the cabin and headed up the trail to the lodge.

They had to be up to something. And he planned to find out what it was.

The front-desk clerk had just warned Dru that J.D. was headed for her office when the door opened and he walked in. Watching him close it behind him and turn to face her, she said into the phone, "The package beat the message, Joy, but I appreciate the attempt. While I have you on the line, would you tell Housekeeping that I'm making up my order and need their report by this afternoon? There's a lag time on the coffee packets for the rooms, so I particularly need to know about that." She settled the receiver back in its cradle and marked a check next to "Housekeeping."

Then, ignoring her increased heart rate, she rose and plastered a pleasant smile on her face. "Hello, J.D. Did you come to be shown the road to your cabin?"

"No. I came to be shown the books."

His remark was so unexpected that she simply blinked at him. "Excuse me?"

"The books. Ledgers that record all the financial data of an enterprise. I'm sure you've heard of them."

"I know what books are," she said with hard-won

composure, and came out from behind the desk. "I'll get them for you right away." She headed for the cabinet.

"Both sets."

Her spine snapped erect and she swung back to face him. "I don't know what type of business you're accustomed to dealing with, Mr. Carver, but Star Lake Lodge has one set of books, period, and those are meticulously kept."

He took a large step forward, and her office suddenly shrank down to a single wall comprised of his shoulders and chest. She tilted her chin up, but took an involuntary step back, then was furious that he could intimidate her so effortlessly. When he promptly took another step forward, she stood her ground. "Are you planning on stalking me around my office?" she inquired coolly. Then she lost it. "Who the hell taught you your manners, anyway? It certainly couldn't have been Great-aunt Edwina."

A muscle ticked in his jaw. "No, the lesson I learned from Edwina was that talk is cheap, and in the end there's only one person I can depend on—myself."

"Indeed? You'll have to excuse me if I don't cry big, sloppy tears over how misused you were. Because it seems to me that Edwina's talk wasn't all that cheap—for here you are, aren't you? Half-owner in our lodge."

He took another step closer. "And that bothers you, doesn't it, sweetheart?"

She deliberately chose to misunderstand. "That you're bad-mouthing the woman who made it possible?" She ignored her reaction to his proximity this time and thrust her chin up. "Yes, I can honestly say I find that rather tacky."

For a moment those don't-fuck-with-me eyes of his went hot with some emotion Dru couldn't pin down, and she felt a burst of triumph that she'd managed to push one of his buttons. It was only fair, considering he seemed to have a natural facility for pushing all of hers.

Then his eyes went cool and distant. "Well, see, that's the thing about us lowlife types," he growled, stepping forward again. "Tacky is mother's milk to us, and we live for the opportunity to get something for nothing." He ran a rough-skinned fingertip down her cheek, leaving a streak of heat in its wake.

Dru jerked her head back, but he just moved in closer. "And we don't particularly care who we have to step on to get it, either," he said in a low voice. "You might want to keep that in mind." His thumb rubbed her lower lip open, but he drew his hand back before she could slap it away. Giving her a slow once-over, he smiled insolently, and she saw that he didn't have bad teeth at all. They were maybe the slightest bit crooked—but very white and strong-looking.

The moment she dragged her gaze back to his eyes, he lifted an eyebrow. "The books?"

Blood thumping furiously in all her pulse points, Dru stalked over to the cabinet and pulled out the ledgers. A moment later she slapped them in his hands. "Here. These cover the past three years. Don't spill food on them and don't lose them."

"Guess that means I'd better not eat my peas with my knife again, huh?"

Embarrassed by her own snide rudeness, she resumed her seat, snatched up a pencil, and tapped it impatiently against the desktop, hoping to give the impression of a woman too busy for this nonsense. "Just be careful with them."

"Yes, ma'am." He gave her a bumptious salute and, with surprising grace for someone wearing several pounds of boot leather on each foot, strode out of the office.

Dru remained fuming at her desk long after he had gone. Things between her and J.D. were shaping up like Trouble with a capital *T*, but she had a bad, bad feeling that his being aggravating as all get-out was the *least* of her problems. She was more worried about the way she felt every time he was near.

Oh, man, she didn't like this; she didn't like it one damn bit. The only other time she'd responded to a man with this sort of gut-level reactiveness had been with Tate's father. It hadn't been nearly as visceral with Tony, either, and just look where *that* had led.

She'd been eighteen years old and away from the lodge for the first time since coming to live with Sophie and Ben when she'd met Tony. College had been exciting and full of promise. She'd felt like such an adult, and when she'd fallen for Tony at the end of her freshman year, she'd thought life just didn't get any better than this: first time out of the gate, and already she'd found her one true love.

For the end of that school year and all of her sophomore year, she and Tony had been inseparable. They'd done everything together: studied, played, talked, and laughed. And they'd made love—Lord, how they'd made love! The only thing they hadn't done was argue, and she would have sworn theirs was a match made in heaven. Then, on the last day of spring finals, she'd discovered she was pregnant.

She'd also discovered that heaven wasn't the place where this match had been made. For the next day, Tony was gone.

She'd been left to berate herself as ten kinds of a fool. She could hardly believe she'd been so careless and that all her dreams were dust as a result. She'd been laid low with morning sickness, scared over how it was going to affect the rest of her life, and terrified to tell her aunt and uncle.

Except for three agonizingly long weeks, however, it hadn't occurred to her not to tell them. During those weeks, while bitterly resenting the baby she carried, she had given serious consideration to having an abortion. It had seemed like the most practical solution: one that would keep Sophie and Ben from ever knowing how irresponsible she had been, and restore her life back to its even keel. But when she'd thought about it emotionally . . .

She'd girded her loins and told her aunt and uncle she was going to be a mother.

They were wonderful. She'd dreaded seeing the disappointment in their eyes, but they'd given her their wholehearted support without a single remonstrance for the foolish risk she had taken, or for the gossip she'd created in tiny, backwoods Star Lake. And Tate was the love of her life—she'd never regretted her decision to raise him herself. But it hadn't been a walk in the park, and she now knew better than to take careless risks. Her life was never again going to get turned upside down the way it had been eleven years ago.

So she didn't care how hot J.D. Carver was, or how he made her heart pound and her bones go weak. He wasn't going to just waltz in here and screw up the nice, safe life she'd made for herself and her son.

3

Dru's uncle stepped out of the gift shop just as J.D. passed by. Both stopped, and J.D. braced himself when he saw Ben glance at the stack of financial ledgers that he carried. But Ben merely said, "Settling in okay?"

J.D. nodded.

Ben slid his hands in his pockets and studied the younger man curiously. "So, the lawyer who read Edwina's will said you were in construction?"

"Yeah."

"This is a busy time of year for that industry. Did you have any trouble getting away?"

"No." J.D.'s laugh was short on humor. "The company I worked for folded when its owner went to prison."

"Ouch. What'd he do?"

"Substituted a whole lot of substandard material to save himself a few bucks."

Ben winced. "Nasty business. So how'd they catch him? Somebody blow the whistle?"

"Yeah." J.D. looked him in the eye. "Me." Lankovich had subbed inferior materials on an astounding number of projects, it turned out, but J.D. hadn't known about the others at first. It was discovering his boss had subbed materials on the job *he'd* headed, making his painstakingly built building unsafe, that had driven J.D. to turn him in.

Watching Ben's jaw drop, he said defensively, "I didn't *want* to turn the guy in—Lankovich was good to me, and he gave me my first shot in construction. But it was either that, or live with the consequences if people got hurt or even killed because I kept my mouth shut."

"I'm not judging you, son. You did the right thing, which isn't always the easy thing. I imagine you must have made a lot of people proud, though."

J.D. couldn't prevent the rude noise that slipped up his throat. "In my part of town, you don't rat out your employer, so what I made a lot of people was angry. Lankovich's kid, who fancies himself a real hard-ass, made it his mission in life to make me pay. Most everyone else froze me out."

"I'm sorry," Ben said sincerely. "That must have been tough."

Hell yes, it'd been tough. Robbie Lankovich had dogged his every move, and men J.D. had thought were friends had turned their backs whenever he came near. He'd never been in a position like that before, and hoped he never would be again. But he only shrugged. "Yeah, well. Shit happens."

"So did the kid who fancied himself a wise guy find a way to make you pay for turning in his father?"

"No." His smile was colder than an Arctic wind. "He gave it his best shot, but his pretensions are a hell of a lot more impressive than his abilities."

They exchanged stilted conversation for a few moments longer before J.D. edged away. He took the financial books into the Eagle's Nest, a small combination bar and cafe at the end of one the corridors off the lobby. It was a two-tiered room suspended over the valley, with long, floor-to-ceiling windows that provided a breathtaking view where the mountain dropped away. It also boasted a small balcony, tucked into the angle where the windows wrapped around the corner, but the French doors leading to it were taped off with an UNDER CONSTRUCTION sign. That immediately drew him, and he saw that the balcony's entire front railing had broken off. He tested the knobs on the doors, wanting a closer look, but the doors were bolted.

"It's locked for safety considerations, sir," said a voice behind him, and J.D. turned to see the man who had been behind the bar earlier.

"We had a record snowfall last winter," the bartender said as he gathered a couple of plates and glasses and swabbed down a nearby table. "Caused that section to give way."

"My guess would be it didn't take much. Looks like the wood was rotted."

The bartender nodded. "Between snow season and

spring and fall rains, it doesn't get much opportunity to dry out, so most of the railings and deck surfaces are replaced every couple of years. Can I bring you something from the bar, sir?"

"Yeah, I'll have a Corona."

The man went back to the bar and J.D. grabbed a table near the windows. It was too late for the lunch crowd and too early for happy hour, so he had the place to himself. He nodded his thanks when the beer was delivered a few moments later, then opened the oldest ledger to start tracking the lodge's financial history.

He found it hard to concentrate, though, because his mind kept wandering back to Dru. He wasn't sure if he had won that skirmish between them or lost it. He wasn't exactly the smoothest act in town when it came to women, but he'd never had one look at him as if he were the last standing Neanderthal, either. He had to admit, though: it had given him a primitive satisfaction to rattle her cage.

And where the hell had that come from?

He'd gone to her office with every intention of having a businesslike conversation. But then she'd given him that phony smile, and with an instinctive *screw tact* combativeness, he'd jumped straight on the offensive. When she'd looked at him as if he'd just crawled up out of the gutter and made that crack about his tackiness, his last good intention had gone up in a ball of flame.

She was no pushover, though. He'd thought she would be, had thought that he could utilize a little time-honored Rat City physical intimidation to back her down. But those big round eyes and soft, round body ought to come with a truth-in-advertising disclaimer—because she hadn't hesitated to call him on it. And except for that one backward step, she'd demonstrated her willingness to duke it out right where she'd stood, toe-to-toe with him.

And suddenly his quest to find out what the hell she and her relatives were up to had turned into something that felt a helluva lot like foreplay.

He straightened in his seat. *Jesus, man, are you out of your mind?* He'd been blowing smoke when he told her he lived to get something for nothing, but that's exactly what he'd been given—and how often did *that* happen to a guy like him? He planned to make this opportunity work for him. Playing I-know-I-can-make-you-want-it-as-much-as-I-do games with his new partner was not the way to go about it, and he was *not* screwing this up.

God knew there was nothing left for him in Seattle. Not even Butch, who had always been the closest thing he'd had to family.

And yet . . .

Standing, J.D. dug his phone card out of his wallet and walked over to the pay phone by the rest rooms. Even if things weren't the same between them, he should at least let Butch know where he was, and give him a number in case the cops needed to get in touch with him.

He and Butch had gone through the foster system together when they were kids; they had even occasionally ended up in one of the group homes at the same time. But it was out on the streets, where they'd both spent far too much time, that they'd gotten to know each other best. And just before J.D.'s sixteenth birthday, Butch had saved his ass from a headlong spill off the roof of a building they'd been messing around on.

It didn't matter that the game responsible for the near-accident had been instigated by Butch; it was understood that, from that day forward, J.D. owed him. Their corner of the city had rigid codes about these things, and it wasn't uncommon for a running score to be kept of who owed what to whom. The law might be an unwritten one, but it was ironclad.

So J.D. had appreciated all the more that Butch had never tried to collect on their old debt. It was a rare quality in their neighborhood, and it had always meant a lot to J.D. that his friend hadn't even seemed to realize he *had* a marker that could be called in at any time.

Then, last week, Butch had disabused him of the notion.

J.D. almost hung up the phone then and there, but dogged perseverance made him punch out the remaining two numbers. It wasn't like he hadn't always known, somewhere in the back of his mind, that his credit could be called in at any time. But he'd still felt disillusioned when Butch actually did it. It changed the tenor of their friendship.

Dammit, this was a mistake. J.D. started to hang up, but the phone at the other end of the line was picked up. "Yell-oh!"

Suddenly hearing Butch's voice raised a morass of conflicting emotions, and for a moment J.D. didn't say anything. Butch had always been so many things that he was not. He was a fun guy to be around, for starters.

Even as a kid, he'd been quick with a joke and even quicker with ideas for entertaining ways to pass the time. Grown up, he'd maintained a knack for making people laugh that J.D. envied.

He was one of those guys to whom people just naturally gravitated. Women *loved* his ass, and it didn't seem to matter that he was married to the Psycho Bitch from Hell, who'd snatch any woman bald-headed she caught throwing so much as a sideways glance his way.

"*What?*" Butch's impatient voice broke into his reverie. "You got something to say, spit it out. I don't have time for this sh—"

"Hey," J.D. said. "It's me."

"*J.D.*?"

"Yeah."

There was an instant of dead silence. Then: "Where the hell are you, man? I tried to call you, but your line's been disconnected, and when I went by your crib it looked deserted, but I couldn't tell if that was permanent or if you were just out for the day."

He sounded agitated, and J.D. heard rustling and crackling over the line. He could picture Butch pouring his change from hand to hand, the way he did when he was nervous.

A small kernel of unease unfurled in J.D.'s gut. "I gave the place up—it was time for a change."

"Yeah? So where are you?"

There was something just a bit too anxious about the inquiry. "What's wrong?"

"Huh? Ain't nuthin' wrong," Butch replied, speaking too fast. "You dropped outta sight and I'm just wondering where the hell you've gotten yourself off to, is all."

Like hell. They went weeks without seeing each other and Butch had never given a damn before. "You're up to something, Dickson. What is it?"

"Nothing!"

"Has it got anything to do with that business with the cops?" The business that had changed their friendship forever? J.D.'s gut knotted more.

"Hell, no; that's all taken care of."

Then it was a woman. "You've stepped in some kind of shit—I can hear it in your voice. You might as well tell me what it is."

"Ain't nothing to tell. Jesus, what's your problem, Carver? A guy shows a little concern when his buddy disappears, and suddenly he's up to something? What kind of shit is that?"

"You know I'm gonna find out, so why don't you just save us both the time and trouble and—"

"Where the fuck are you, Carver?"

"Hot on the track of whatever it is you're trying to hide," J.D. snapped back, responding to the tone. He banged the receiver into its hook and stalked back to his table.

Shit. He should have listened to his instincts—calling Butch was a big mistake. He'd hoped once he talked to him the simmering resentment that had filled him since last week would disappear, but he was even more pissed than he'd been before.

Butch had his flaws. Mostly they were minor, but he had one that was a killer: he wasn't good at accepting responsibility for his own actions. Nothing was ever his fault.

It had been that way as long as J.D. could remember, but usually it was over little stuff: a reprimand at work, a fender bender or speeding ticket, an argument with his wife. Last Tuesday, though, Butch's inability to own up to his mistakes had led to his calling in J.D.'s marker. Reliving it one more time merely took yet another layer of shine off their former friendship, but like a tongue to a broken tooth, J.D. just couldn't leave it alone.

Butch opened the door to his apartment, and J.D. peered past him into the living room. "Gina *is* working late tonight, right?"

His friend grinned, his handsome face creasing in amusement. "Why is everyone always so anxious to avoid Gina? So she gets a little cranky. Big deal."

J.D. snorted. "Saying Gina is a little cranky is like saying pit bulls are a little tenacious. That woman is a hundred and twenty pounds of pure mean, and you know it."

"A hundred and fifteen. You don't even wanna let her catch you adding weight on her." He nodded at the sack in J.D.'s hands. "That beer?"

J.D. reached in and pulled a bottle out of the six-pack, then handed the bag over. He dropped down on the couch while Butch continued into the kitchen. Popping off the top, he took a pull and said, "You know, I've never quite understood why you married her. You two are so different."

The refrigerator door slammed shut. "Hey, what can I tell you? It's a love match."

J.D. snorted. "More like a fight to the death, if you

ask me. I hope to hell flirting was all you were doing with Kittie Lockrill at The Tug the other night, because if Gina ever catches you screwing around on her, you're a dead man."

Butch shrugged and turned on the television set. They propped their feet up on the coffee table and settled in to watch the Mariners game.

J.D. attended to it with only half his attention. The rest was tied up trying to think of a way to tell Butch about his unexpected windfall from Edwina. Ordinarily he would have said something immediately, but he'd learned of the inheritance during Lankovich's trial, when he'd been a very unpopular man in their neighborhood. And since Butch was out of work because of J.D.'s actions, neither bragging about his sudden good fortune nor trying to explain why he felt conflicted about it seemed like a smart idea.

He was mulling over ways to bring it up, and brooding over Robbie Lankovich still dogging his footsteps, making all those stupid-ass threats for turning in his father, when a knock sounded on the door. Butch backed toward it without taking his gaze off the screen. As he pulled the door open, his attention was on Alex Rodriguez coming up to bat, but J.D. straightened at the sight of the two visitors.

He'd spent too many years on the streets not to recognize a cop when he saw one. And though he hadn't broken any laws since he was a kid, he still had a knee-jerk distrust of them.

"Yeah?" Butch demanded disinterestedly, then groaned as A-Rod's first hit flew into the foul zone.

"Butch Dickson?"

"Yeah, who wants to know?" He turned and looked at them for the first time. "Oh, shit. Cops. Whaddya want?"

They stepped inside without waiting to be invited. "We need to know where you were this afternoon, Butchie boy," said the older one. "At four o'clock, when someone answering to your description robbed the One Stop over on Ninth."

"Hey, go hassle somebody else. Do I look stupid to you? If I was going to rob a convenience store, I sure as hell wouldn't pick one in my own neighborhood." Arms stiff and his hands in his jeans pockets, Butch hunched his shoulders. "Besides, I cleaned up my act. I haven't been in trouble for years now."

The younger detective looked around the apartment, and J.D. looked around himself, trying to see it as a stranger might. One thing he'd give Gina credit for, she'd fixed the place up nice.

The cop clearly agreed. "Pretty spiffy digs for someone with no visible means of support," he said.

Butch turned on him. "Fuck you. My wife works full-time, and I had a good job until my employer went belly-up month before last. I've been collecting unemployment while I look for a new job."

"Is that what you were doing at four this afternoon?" the older cop demanded. "Collecting unemployment?"

Butch gave him a flat-eyed stare. "This is a trick question, right?"

"Where were you at four, Dickson?"

"Right here," Butch shot back. He jerked a thumb at J.D. "With him."

J.D. didn't so much as blink an eye, but everything inside him stilled. What the hell was this? He hadn't shown up until five. Oh, Christ, what had Butch gotten himself into?

Then he pulled himself up short. Since when did he let the cops make him jump to a hasty conclusion? Maybe Butch wasn't the most accountable guy in the world, but he *had* stayed out of trouble since J.D. had gotten him the job at Lankovich's six years ago. And like he'd told the cops, he wasn't stupid enough to knock over a store he used on occasion. He was probably just trying to save himself the hassle and expense of having to prove his innocence through the legal system.

In any case, the look Butch turned on him reminded J.D. that he owed him. So when the cops demanded to know if that was a fact, that he and Butch had been together during the stated time, he shrugged and said, "Yeah." But anger and a sense of betrayal gnawed at his gut with dirty little rat teeth.

"Thanks, buddy." Butch danced back into the living room after he'd slammed the door behind the cops' departing backs. He grinned as if he and J.D. had pulled off the scam of the century, then made a face when he noticed that J.D. didn't share his jubilation. Shrugging, he went to get himself another bottle of beer out of the fridge. "You want one?" he called.

"No."

Butch flopped on the couch a moment later and raised his beer in a salute. "Here's to outfoxing the pigs."

J.D. just looked at him.

"What?" Butch demanded in exasperation. "C'mon! You pissed that I called in your marker? You owed me, bud."

And it bothered J.D. more than he could say that his friend had been keeping score all these years, after all. He felt like the greenest sort of rube for believing Butch was better than that. "Yeah," he said shortly, contemplating the last inch of beer in his bottle. Then he looked Butch in the eye. "We're square now, though."

J.D. thought about that now as he eyed the noisy group who'd just entered the Eagle's Nest and were busily admiring the spectacular view. He remembered the sinking feeling he'd gotten in his gut at the giveaway signals that Butch was hiding something. J.D. hadn't demanded to know if Butch had robbed the store; he really hadn't wanted to know.

For then he'd have had to do something about it—and he hadn't known how the hell to reconcile doing the right thing with a gut-deep conviction that he was honor-bound to repay the old debt.

All bets were off, though, when late that night he'd heard on the news that a store clerk had been shot during the robbery and was in critical condition at Highline Hospital.

He'd tracked his friend down the next day and demanded to know what the hell he'd been up to. And that was when Butch had confessed that he'd been with Kittie Lockrill that afternoon. "But, J.D.," he'd said plaintively, "how the fuck was I supposed to tell that to the cops? You know damn well it'd get back to Gina—and if she finds out, I can kiss my dick goodbye. Compared to her, Lorena Bobbitt is filled with the Christian spirit of forgiveness."

J.D. had been frankly relieved. In the twelve hours between learning that someone had been injured and talking to Butch, he'd wondered if his friend could have done it. He hadn't truly been able to envision it, because Butch had never been the violent type, but he *was* impulsive—and that sometimes led him to rash acts. It was good to know that Butch was only stepping out with some hot-pants Kewpie doll, stupid as that was.

Being all too familiar with his friend's facility for lying, however, he'd gone to see Kittie to verify Butch's story. When it checked out, J.D. had packed up and left town with a clear conscience.

He'd kept to himself the news of his inheritance and the fact that he was leaving Seattle to claim it. It was probably dog-in-the-mangerish to blame Butch for collecting on the debt, but his doing so had severed a crucial tie between them. J.D. hadn't known him half as well as he'd thought he had.

So there just hadn't seemed to be all that much left for him in Seattle.

J.D. packed up the ledgers and headed for his car. He needed to move, and while driving down the mountain to the town of Star Lake, he did his best to put the past out of his mind. He bought some provisions at a grocery store called the Pack 'n' Save, then stopped at the lumberyard and picked up material to repair the cabin roof.

He drove back up the mountain and found the road that led behind the cabins. Minutes later he'd parked the Mustang behind his new home and transferred the contents of thc car into it.

Shortly after seven, the silence drove him out again. He was accustomed to the sounds of neighbors and traffic, airplanes and sirens. All this peace and quiet was making him twitch.

It sure smelled good up here, though. The aroma of meat roasting on a barbecue wafted from one of the other cabins, and heading down the path toward the dock Dru had mentioned, he breathed in the verdant, green scents of the forest. He appreciated the lack of carbon monoxide fumes that painted the city air with such heavy-handed brush strokes this time of year.

It was quiet in the woods surrounding the lake. The placement of each cabin had been planned for maximum privacy, and if anyone occupied the one he passed, he didn't see them. No voices carried on the wind and no kids pounded along the trails that wound in and out of thc trees edging the lake. He felt as if he had the entire area to himself.

He stopped at a long, narrow dock that jutted out from shore. Rowboats were tied up along one side of it and two jet boats were moored on the other. Hands in his pockets, he walked to the end, enjoying the creak of wood and the dock's slight sway beneath his feet. The boats on either side bobbed gently with the movement.

Out on the lake, at an angle to the dock, was a float

with an elevated lifeguard chair and a high-and-low diving tower. It rocked slightly on the mirror-smooth lake, and J.D. caught a glimpse of two swimmers who had clearly just abandoned it. When he turned to follow the direction of their progress, he saw the tip of another dock just beyond a forested jut of land. That was probably the dock the kids used to swim to and from the float, since the one he stood on had the boats. It didn't seem prudent to mix swimmers with boaters.

Though he had no burning desire to talk to vacationers, J.D. stepped off the marina to check out the other dock. If he was going to be part of this resort, he needed to know how everything worked.

Rounding the curve of land a minute later, he stepped onto the second dock, then stopped dead.

For standing at the end of the dock, with her back to him as she bent over to dry her legs with a thick towel, and her head raised to watch her son swim the last few yards to the dock, was Dru Lawrence.

4

She wore a faded black tank suit with red piping. Except for its high-cut legs and racer-back, it wasn't at all distinctive. The material had certainly seen better days, but when he looked at the curve of her nice round butt, it wasn't the snags roughening the fabric that held his attention. His fingers flexed and his palms itched like a bad case of nettle poisoning. Damn, he didn't understand this attraction at all. Rubbing his hands down the thighs of his jeans, he cleared his throat.

She jumped slightly and whirled to face him. "You startled me!"

Lake water ran in rivulets from her soaked braid; her nipples, hard from the cooling evening air, poked against the wet cloth that stretched over the fullness of her breasts; and J.D. really wished he'd slipped away while he'd had the chance.

That put his back up. Big deal, so she had a nice set. He was a red-blooded guy; it was his job to notice these things. All it meant was that he should have gotten himself laid before he left town—because he wasn't about to mess up this opportunity over a few stray hormones. And he sure as hell wasn't cozying up to any woman without knowing what the hell she and her family were up to.

As if she's interested in cozying up to you, anyhow. J.D. nearly snorted. He doubted a woman could *be* more oblivious. She gave him roughly five seconds' attention for every fifty-five devoted to watching Tate's progress toward the dock.

Then a thought hit him like a sledgehammer between the eyes. "So where's *Mr.* Lawrence?" he demanded. Funny that it had never occurred to him she might be married. Considering she had a kid and all, that was pretty dumb.

"Uncle Ben?"

"Your husband, sweetheart."

"Oh. Him." Her laugh was short and surprisingly cynical for someone he'd pegged as a little Suzie Homemaker. She looked him dead in the eye. "Doesn't exist—*sweetheart.*"

Good.

Shit. What was he—crazy? He had no business feeling that little surge of satisfaction. He shoved his hands in his pockets. "Gone with the wind, huh?"

"So long ago, his memory is dust." She tilted her head to one side and suctioned her palm against her ear until a little trickle of water ran out. "There, I can hear again." Then she shrugged. "Which, considering the charm of your conversation so far, may or may not be a good thing. Do you actually have a purpose for being here, or are you just out skulking around?"

"I don't skulk, honey; I'm familiarizing myself with the area. I take it this is the dock the guests use to swim out to the float?"

"No, actually, that's the one with the boats. Aunt Sophie and Uncle Ben live up there." She indicated a log house that he hadn't even noticed atop a small bluff. "This is the family dock." She raised an eyebrow at him. "You obviously missed the 'Private' sign."

Yeah, he'd been too busy admiring her butt. Jerking his attention back to the matter at hand, he said with some disgust, "You let kids swim from the same dock where you've got boats taking off?"

She'd turned back to keep an eye on Tate as he swam the last few feet to the dock, and J.D. couldn't prevent himself from checking her out one last time. His gaze had cruised midway down the long length of her legs when she shot him an annoyed glance over her shoulder and said, "You know, for someone who's not even been here a full day, you sure seem to have a lot of problems with the way we run our business. It's a wonder we ever managed to limp along without you."

He took a step forward. "Excuse the hell outta me. It doesn't take a mental wizard to know that jet boats and swimmers are a tragedy waiting to happen."

"Which is exactly why every day, from seven in the morning until seven at night, the swimming area is blocked off with ropes and fluorescent floats, from the dock to the nearest corner of the raft, and from the raft's other corner to that tree sticking out over the water.

The morning lifeguard strings it out and the afternoon lifeguard brings it back in. Had you looked a little more closely, you would have seen that the ropes and floats are stored in the rowboat at the end of the dock."

Ignoring him, she leaned down to extend a hand to her son. "Hey, Tate! I think you broke your record."

J.D. watched as the kid clambered up on the dock and shook off like a wet dog, flashing his big grin. "I think so, too. Hi, Mr. Carver."

"J.D.," he corrected him.

The kid's grin did the impossible and grew even brighter. "Hey, J.D. You gonna go swimming? Where's your suit—you got it on under your jeans? Or are you plannin' to skinny-dip?"

"You're such a Nosey Parker!" The smile Dru bestowed on her son nearly matched his for sheer wattage. Wrapping a big towel around Tate's shoulders, she curved herself against his back and hugged him to her front. "You writing a book or something?"

"Yeah, kiss my bum, and we'll call it a love story!" Tate flashed her a smile both cheeky and wary over his shoulder, clearly pleased with his own daring but unsure how it would be received.

Dru gave his head a tough noogie. "Tate Lawrence! Do you kiss your mother with that mouth?" Then she laughed, spun him around, and planted a swift kiss on his lips.

"Mom!" He swiped the kiss away. "Jeez, not in front of J.D.!"

"Pffft. J.D.'s been kissed by his mother. C'mon, gimme a smooch. Give in to the dark side, Luke."

Tate laughed and skipped away. "No way! And I'm not *Luke* Skywalker, Mom; I'm Anakin."

"Oh, well, pardon me. I lost my head there for a moment."

J.D. couldn't remember his mother ever horsing around with him, and he could count on one hand the number of kisses she'd bestowed on him. Watching Dru and her kid, he felt his gut knot up. He had a sudden urge to get the hell out of there.

The dock creaked just as he turned to go and he looked up to see Ben approaching. The older man smiled easily. "Hey," he said. "You all come on up to the house. Soph's made crème brûlée, and you know what will happen if she has to eat it all by herself."

Dru was very happy to see her uncle. He was exactly what the doctor ordered—an added barrier between herself and the heart-pounding, sweaty-palm feelings J.D. Carver generated in her without even trying.

Picking up the towel Tate had dropped, she wrapped it with studied casualness around her hips to cover up her butt, which she'd always regarded as too big. Being half naked in front of a fully dressed male was a tough way to feel on top of one's form, especially when one was on the plump side and the man in question didn't have a superfluous ounce of fat on his entire body.

She was relieved when J.D. said, "I'll get out of your way and let you get to your dessert," and started for shore.

But Uncle Ben put out a restraining hand when the younger man started to walk past. "Don't run off, son. You're invited, too."

Dru could have groaned aloud. She racked her brain but couldn't come up with a single snappy remark that would discourage J.D. without making herself look like an inhospitable bitch.

"Yeah, J.D.," Tate chimed in. "You can't miss Grandma Soph's crème brûlée. It's the best!"

J.D. still looked as if he planned to refuse. Dru prayed for it, tried for all she was worth to access some telekinetic powers to influence him in that direction. Then he glanced her way, and she just knew that her feelings must be on her face, for he suddenly flashed those white teeth at her in a feral grin, shrugged, and said, "Sure. Why not?"

Damn. Damn, damn, damn! She bared her own teeth back at him and insisted he precede her when he stood aside as they filed off the dock. She'd put up with his company because she had no other choice and because, her recent behavior to the contrary, she really was an adult. Double-dyed damned, though, if she'd allow him to walk behind her while she trailed puddles of water and swished her big old butt in his face as they climbed the trail up to Ben and Sophie's house.

There were simply some places where a woman had to draw the line or seriously question her own intelligence.

On the other hand, having him go first meant she had to watch *his* tush flex as he climbed the short trail ahead of her. God, life was unfair sometimes. It wasn't bad enough that his mind was small and tight—his butt had to be, too? Even all covered up, it didn't take a genius to see it was one of those hard-as-concrete numbers with the sucked-in cheeks. She'd kill to have one half so nice.

Aunt Sophie met them at the door. "Oh, thank goodness you were available. Hello, darling," she said to Tate, catching a flying peck on the lips before he raced past her, headed for the back of the house and the television set. "Come in, come in! J.D.! I'm so glad you're here to help us eat the crème brûlée I made. I told Ben if I had to eat it all by myself he was a dead man."

"Why?" J.D. asked. "Did he hold a gun to your head and force you to make it?"

Ben choked and Dru simply gaped at J.D., stunned. They'd all grown accustomed to tiptoeing around Sophie lately to avoid setting her off. Not that there was any predicting what would do so; the things one might suppose would anger her often didn't faze her in the least, while the most innocuous remarks could send her into the red zone.

But Sophie merely laughed. "I didn't say it was rational, dear. My uncertain temper these days is the uncharming by-product of my rampaging hormones. Or perhaps that's *failing* hormones; I've never gotten it quite straight. In any case, killing Ben is something we want to avoid at all costs. I'm rather fond of the man, so thank you for coming."

Then she turned to Dru. "Drucilla, you're covered in goose bumps. Go put on something warm."

"*Drucilla*?" J.D. said incredulously. "Someone actually named you Drucilla?"

Dru's hands hit the towel tied low around her hips. "Oh, like J.D. is the name for the millennium," she snapped back. "What does it stand for, anyway—juvenile delinquent?" She raked her gaze over him in a head-to-toe once-over. "From what I've heard, that would certainly be appropriate."

"Drucilla!" Sophie stared at her as if she'd suddenly grown fangs.

The appalled wonder in her aunt's voice recalled Dru to her manners, and to the fact that she and J.D. weren't the only ones in the room—something she'd momentarily forgotten. She blinked. And just when the heck had they gravitated so close to each other? Suddenly aware of the heat radiating off his large body, she took a giant step back.

"I apologize," she said grudgingly. "That was exceedingly rude. Excuse me, won't you? I'll just go throw on some clothes."

She felt his gaze like hands running up and down her body. "Don't feel you have to do so on my account," he said, and even though his tone was perfectly respectful, she still managed to read all sorts of innuendo and suggestiveness into his words.

With a meaningless social smile, she pivoted on her bare heel. What was *wrong* with her? You'd think she'd just gotten out of junior high school. Closing the door of the guest room behind her, she leaned back against it for a moment. She had to quit being so damn reactionary. It wasn't as if he were some troublesome guest who would be gone in a day or two.

Dru went to the chest of drawers where she kept a revolving supply of clothing. Maybe he'd get bored with country living and go back to the life he knew best. At least that's what she fervently hoped as she pulled out a pair of jeans and a T-shirt.

She peeled off her bathing suit and stepped into the jeans, tugging them up her damp legs. Maybe, if she was very, very lucky, J.D. would grow tired of playing innkeeper and agree to have his checks sent to him. Then she could reclaim the serene life she'd built for herself and Tate.

And that's exactly what she told her best friend later that night on the phone. After she'd put Tate to bed, she'd tried to settle down as she picked up his toys and wiped crumbs off the breakfast bar that divided the kitchen from the living area of the spacious attic apartment at the lodge. But the dormered ceilings, which usually made her feel comfily tucked in, seemed to close in on her, and not even the magnificent view of wooded hills rolling down to the valley worked its soothing magic. Tracking down the cordless phone receiver to the rag rug beneath the antique coffee table, she picked it up and punched out Char's number.

She and Char had met on the swim float the summer before she'd moved in permanently with Ben and Sophie. Although opposites in many ways, the two girls had hit it off the moment they'd met, when Dru had seen Char doing handstands off the low board into the water and demanded to be taught how to do it. Char was her closest friend, her confidante, and her lifeline to sanity when life turned crazy. Which it'd certainly done with a vengeance today.

She poured out her concerns the moment her friend picked up.

Char's snort carried clearly over the telephone line. "So let me get this straight. The new partner turns out to be one-hundred-proof testosterone in construction boots—a guy who in less than twelve hours has managed to get your juices flowing for the first time in it's-been-so-long-I-can't-even-remember—but you think if you're lucky, he'll go back to where he came from? *Hel-lo*! Wake up and smell the pheromones, Drucilla Jean. You've been on ice way too long as it is."

"Hey, I *like* being on ice—it sure beats making a major ass of myself." Dru walked over to the tiny window seat and tossed its brightly patterned pillows to one end in order to make room for herself. "I'm telling you, Char, I get around this guy and I don't even recognize myself. Remember that little stoolie Sandy Heston, back in the sixth grade? The one who was forever tattling to the teacher? That was me tonight. One minute we're all sitting around the table, and Carver's practically licking his damn bowl—not to mention sucking up to Auntie Soph over how good the crème brûlée is."

Okay, that wasn't fair, but she couldn't bear to think of the look on his face as he'd scraped his ramekin clean—as if he'd never known such a taste sensation existed. He probably *hadn't* had the easiest time of it growing up, and when he'd seen everybody looking at him and simply said, "This is great," to Aunt Soph, the pinch of empathy she'd felt had scared the hell out of her.

"And?" Char demanded when the silence went on too long.

"And the next thing I know, I'm ratting him out over his complaint about the dock." She flopped onto her back and drummed the fingers of her free hand on her stomach. "As if I hadn't already told him exactly what the deal was."

"That was mature."

"Tell me about it. I looked even more adult when J.D. told them, cool as you please, that while I had explained the arrangement, he still felt there should be a sign spelling out the exact rules and regulations, with a warning that swimmers proceed at their own risk."

"I, uh, hate to say this, cookie, but that's not such a bad idea."

"I know," Dru agreed glumly. "Ben and Sophie thought it was brilliant, for legal purposes if nothing else. So naturally J.D. came off looking all grown-up and rational, while I looked like the whiny little stool pigeon I was." Her heels hung over the edge of the window seat and she toed off her flip-flops. "It didn't help that I wasn't wearing any underwear."

"Why, did he stare at your boobs or something?" Char's sigh filtered down the line. "I wish someone would stare at mine, but some of us are more mammary-challenged than you well-endowed types."

Dru made a rude noise. "And when we're both sixty, yours will still be perky, while mine will probably be down around my knees. My heart bleeds for you."

"*Did* he stare at 'em?"

"No, it wasn't that. I doubt he even noticed. It was more—I don't know—he was so together, and my hair was wet, my boobs kept shifting back and forth every time I *breathed*, and my big butt was spread out all over the chair."

"Stop that. I should be so lucky as to have enough boob *to* shift, and your butt is not big."

"Well, it sure felt that way without my undies. I felt vulnerable, okay? Kind of an awake version of that caught-naked-in-public dream. I could have used the armor of my silkies and a blow-dryer."

"I understand that. For me, it's lipstick. Give me a tube of Estée Lauder, and I can face just about anything. But what about him? What kind of underwear do you suppose he wears? Tightie-whities or boxers?"

"My guess would be none."

"Oooh," Char breathed. "Ya think?"

"If his attitude is anything to go by. He acts like such a swinging dick, you'd think he has to kick it out of his way with every step he takes."

"Damn. But, Drusie, if you don't think he was wearing any underwear, either, shouldn't that have you feeling less uncomfortable?"

"No, it's that attitude thing again. I felt big and blowzy. *He* was probably busy congratulating himself on what a big one he has."

"I have *got* to meet this guy. You think he might need a massage?"

"His ego sure as hell doesn't. But I imagine you're talking about a *real* massage, right?" Which Char provided at the lodge four days a week.

Char's voice sounded wistful. "It'd sure be nice to deal with some real muscle for a change. All I've gotten lately is soft tourist bodies."

"Well, hey, who knows? He'd probably eat it up with a spoon, the way he did the crème brûlée, so if you wanna take a run at him, be my guest."

"You know better than that, Dru."

Dru stared at the receiver with blank surprise. She and Char had made a pact back in junior high school never to horn in on the other's relationship with a guy—and panic bloomed that her best friend thought that was what J.D. had the potential to be. "It's not like that!"

"Uh-huh."

"It's not, Char. I don't even like him."

"Yeah, that must be why your heart pounds every time he's around, huh? Dislike."

"Dammit, Char," she began in exasperation, but a sleepy voice interrupted her.

"Mom?"

She sat up, peering around at Tate, who stood ruffle-haired in the doorway. "Hey, baby, what are you doing up?"

"Gotta go?" Char inquired. "We'll talk tomorrow."

Dru turned off the phone and, getting up, set it back in its stand on the end table. "Can't sleep?"

"I hadda pee." A huge yawn escaped him. "Then I heard you talkin'. I thought someone was here."

"I was just talking to Char."

Tate nodded and yawned again.

"You ready to go back to bed?"

"Uh-huh." He shuffled in front of her down the short hallway to his room. A moment later he climbed onto the mattress and flopped down on his back. He immediately rolled onto his side.

Dru pulled the blankets up around his shoulders and leaned down to give him a kiss. " 'Night, sweet pea. Luva-luva you."

"Love you, too, Mom," Tate murmured. Before Dru

had straightened, he was once again sound asleep.

Leaving his door open a crack, she went back into the living room. She flipped on the television to a Seattle channel for the news, but after hearing about an oil spill in the straits, the mutilation of a horse in Arlington, and the death of a cashier who had been shot during a convenience-store robbery last Tuesday, she snapped it off again.

She had problems of her own. Hearing those cheery little tidbits didn't help.

5

Butch hung up the phone receiver and threw himself back on the couch. Taking a pull from the beer bottle in his hand, he thunked his feet on the coffee table. Gina always went ballistic when he did that, but she wasn't home to see him, so what the hell.

Where the fuck was J.D.? The man Butch had shot in that farcical robbery last Tuesday had died yesterday, and his alibi was out doing God knew what, God knew where.

Dammit, how was it possible for everything to turn to shit so freaking fast? It wasn't like he'd *meant* to shoot the guy or anything—that old pistol had been in his glove box for years, stuffed under wads of fast-food-joint napkins. It was the last remaining link to his wild-child years, and he'd kept it around not because he'd ever expected to use it, but for the protection it represented.

He hadn't set out to knock over the convenience store, either. He'd just been so damn tired of being broke and having to listen to Gina rag on and on about what a deadbeat he was these days, and why the hell wasn't he out there beating the pavement looking for work now that Lankovich, that crook, had closed his doors. So sheer impulse had made him dig the gun out of the glove compartment when he'd stopped at the store for a six-pack. Damned if he was going to beg his old lady for beer money again.

He hadn't intended to actually *use* the gun, but the idiot behind the counter just had to play hero. It was his own damn fault Butch had to shoot him; anyone with half a brain knew you were supposed to just hand over the money. But nooo, he'd argued about it in his lousy English; then he'd reached under the counter. Hell, how was Butch supposed to know a gun hadn't been under there? That's what anyone would have thought—and there was no way in hell he was gonna let some minimum-wage-earning towelhead get the drop on him.

Even so, he hadn't meant to squeeze off a round. But Jesus, not one frigging thing had gone the way it was supposed to go that afternoon, and his finger had simply convulsed with nervous tension against the trigger. The next thing he'd known, the guy was spinning backward and collapsing against the shelves of cigarettes behind him. And there'd been blood—great fucking amounts of bright red blood—all over the damn place.

Now he had to do something about J.D., before J.D. heard about it and got it into his head to do something irretrievably stupid. The more Butch thought about it, in fact, the more he realized that whatever he ended up doing would have to be permanent.

Shit. It gave him a headache just thinking about it. They'd been buds forever, him and J.D., and he liked him; he really did. But J.D. had always had that inconvenient moral streak running through him. Butch laid the blame for it on the old broad who'd taken him in that one year. But the bottom line was that J.D. would never understand about what he'd done.

He knew exactly what would happen: the minute J.D. caught wind of the store clerk's death, either he'd expect Butch to come clean about Kittie so the cops could talk to her and clear his name once and for all, or he'd double- and triple-check her story himself. And Kittie wasn't exactly the brightest bulb in the marquee. If J.D. grilled her hard enough, Butch wasn't sure he could trust her not to fold right in the middle of the story he'd fed her.

And hell, if it came down to a choice between friendship or twenty-to-life in Walla Walla, there was no fucking contest. He was real sorry about it, but that was just the way it went. And he wasn't about to sit around twiddling his thumbs until he was taken by surprise, either. Especially after that phone call—he'd almost crapped when J.D. phoned practically on top of his hearing about the store clerk. He'd tried to trace the call, but that had gotten screwed up too. Just when he was about to hit *69, Gina had rung up to let him know she was catching a drink with a friend after work.

Sometimes life just sucked.

He knew J.D. too well. The man was a frigging pit bull when he wanted information. Much better to make a preemptive strike against him than wait around for J.D. to get wind of this new development and "help" his ass right into the slammer.

Trouble was, he didn't know where his old buddy had gotten himself off to. The temporary job he'd taken was finished; chances were he'd picked up work out of town. Or maybe he'd just moved across town and Butch would run into him down at the union hall.

But he wasn't gonna sit around on his ass counting on that. He climbed to his feet and hunted down his car keys. It was time he put out a few feelers and found out who the hell knew where J.D. was.

J.D. stood barefoot on the dew-dampened front porch, scraping crème brûlée off the oval sides and bottom of the white ribbed custard dish Sophie had sent home with him last night. He licked the last of the dessert off his spoon. Damn, this stuff was good. With a regretful look at the empty container, he walked back into the cabin, held the dish under a running tap, and scrubbed it clean. He knocked back the last of his coffee and rinsed that cup out as well. A moment later he brushed his teeth, then finished dressing and let himself out of his cabin.

It wasn't nearly as quiet this morning as it had been last night. He barely dodged three noisy pubescent boys who barreled around a blind corner in the lake trail, and already shrill voices from out on the water pierced the air. Reaching the dock, he saw the fluorescent floats Dru had lectured him about bobbing on the lake's placid surface from dock to float, and kids churned the water between the two berths. One rowboat remained in the roped-off area, one was tied up at the float, and the rest had been moved to the motorboat side of the dock.

He continued on to the Lawrences' private dock and climbed the short switchback trails to the oversized log cabin on the bluff, where he saw Sophie in one of the flower beds that framed her front porch. Her back was to him and a small pile of weeds to her right testified to her activity. At the moment, however, her gardening gloves lay in a heap by her right hip and her bottom rested back on her heels while she vigorously flapped her shirttails, exposing half her back. He cleared his throat. "Hey."

She jumped and swore. Swinging around to face him, she snapped, "What are you, a damn cat? Give a gal some warning!"

"Sorry," he said mildly. He watched her drop the shirttails and blot her face with the back of her hand. Her face was flushed.

Then she dropped her hand to her thigh and sighed. "No, I'm sorry," she said and struggled to rise to her feet. He stepped forward to assist her as she admitted, "I was having another hot flash, but that's no reason to take it out on you. I'm jumpy as a bowlful of Mexican beans these days, and bitchy to boot."

He couldn't help but grin. "You call that bitchy? In my neighborhood, we'd call that downright hospitable. I ought to introduce you to a woman named Gina Dickson someday. Now, *she* has bitchy down cold."

She blinked at him in silence for several seconds. "Wow," she finally said. "You should do that more often."

"Huh?" Had they skipped to a different frequency here?

"You should smile like that more often. You've got a terrific smile."

He felt it drop away from his face. Dammit, he hadn't come here to get all chummy. Until he knew more about these people, that would be plain stupid. He thrust the little custard dish out at her. "Here."

She took it. But when he immediately turned away, she snapped, "Oh, get the stick out of your rear. Come sit on the porch with me and have a cup of coffee. Contrary to what you seem to believe, we're not the enemy. And if you truly think we are, then wouldn't the prudent thing be to infiltrate our camp, to learn what nefarious schemes we plan to hatch?"

Okay, so now he felt like a raving paranoid. That didn't mean they still weren't out to get him. All the same, he turned back, climbed the porch steps, and said gruffly, "That crème stuff was really great. You cook like that all the time?"

"I used to. I'm a pastry chef," she said and patted the old wicker rocker next to hers. When he'd seated himself, she gently set her own chair to rocking. "I used to be the evening pastry chef in the restaurant here, but last year Ben and I decided to cut way back on our hours to get an idea of how we'll handle retirement. So now he only does the buying for the gift and sport shops, and I bake the breads for the restaurant and the Eagle's Nest, and occasionally a few of the desserts. I miss it sometimes, and every now and then I get a wild hair to whip something up."

She leaned forward to pick up a cup from a tray on

the small wicker table, and held it under the spout of a thermos pump. Fragrant steam wafted in the slowly warming morning air as she handed him the coffee. "How are you settling into your cabin?"

"Fine."

"I apologize for the porch roof. We've had a great deal of difficulty in the past couple years finding and keeping reliable help for the repairs. The most competent workers invariably end up leaving for Wenatchee or Seattle."

"Not a problem." He shrugged. "I picked up the materials to fix it while I was in town yesterday. I'll get started on it as soon as I figure out what I'm going to use to cut the wood. I didn't bring my circular saw."

"You'll fix it?" The smile she flashed him was so warm, he quit rocking and blinked. "Oh, my God, you're the answer to a prayer. I'm not sure what a circular saw is, but Ben has all sorts of power tools in the garage. It's never locked. And be sure to keep track of your receipts, dear, for reimbursement."

Tate burst into the yard just then, followed an instant later by Dru. J.D. straightened in his seat. She looked crisp and efficient this morning in her neat shorts, polo shirt, and Keds, but he got a glimpse of the image he'd taken to bed with him last night: Dru braless and barefoot, with damp, rumpled hair and flashing eyes.

Tate raced up the steps. "Hey, J.D.! We didn't know you were here, did we, Mom?"

J.D. didn't miss the irony in her voice when she stopped at the foot of the stairs, looked up at them, and replied, "No, I can honestly say we didn't know."

Or you wouldn't have come anywhere near here, would you, sweetheart?

"So what am I, darling, that I don't even rate a hello?" Sophie demanded. "Chopped liver?"

"I was gonna say hi, Grandma, but I got sidetracked when I saw J.D. was here."

"And you're always pâté in his book, anyway," Dru assured her.

"Oh, well, *pâté*. That's all right, then. For a minute there, I was afraid I was the stuff they turn into cat food."

J.D. watched the two women grin at each other.

"Can I watch the big screen for a while, Grandma?"

"That's entirely up to your mother."

"Mom?" Tate showed her a winning smile.

"I suppose. Keep in mind that we won't be staying long, though. I don't want to hear any whining about being pulled away in the middle of a program."

" 'Kay." The screen door slammed behind him as he ran into the house.

Sophie turned her attention back to Dru. "I'm surprised to see you this time of day—but delighted, needless to say. C'mon up. Would you like a cup of coffee?"

"No, thanks; I'm afraid I don't have the time. I've actually come to beg a favor."

"What's that, dear? Oh, but first, I don't believe you've said hello to J.D."

Rocking back on her heels, hands thrust in her shorts pockets, she leveled a cool-eyed gaze on him. "Hello, J.D."

"Drucilla," he said, and watched with satisfaction as

her eyes narrowed at him, becoming a great deal less cool in the process.

She tilted her face up to her aunt. "Would you watch Tate for me for a couple of hours? Candy canceled at the last minute, and I've got a walk-through with that conference-site committee for the Spokane Dentists Association."

"When?"

"Now, actually. The representatives are due in about twenty minutes."

"Oh, darling, I'm sorry. I have an appointment at ten with Dr. Case, to go over some new strategies to get these damn mood swings and hot flashes under control. And Ben went to Wenatchee for the monthly Gun and Rod meeting; he won't be back until tomorrow morning. Maybe . . . let me think . . . oh, dear, who could we get to fill in?" Then a brilliant smile lit her face. "I know!" She turned to J.D. and his gut did a little twist. "Didn't you say you were going to work on the porch roof this morning, dear?"

"You are?" Dru demanded at the same time that he said warily, "Yeah?"

"Well, there's our solution. Tate can stay with you; he's a good little helper. And it will only be for, what did you say, darling, two hours?"

"Yes, but—"

"Perfect," Sophie said with satisfaction.

J.D.'s rocker came to a dead halt. "I don't know about perfect," he said flatly. "You've only known me for one day. You want to leave a ten-year-old kid in my care? Hell, for all you know, I could be a card-carrying member of Pedophiles R Us."

Sophie laughed. "Don't be ridiculous, dear."

"He's not being ridiculous," Dru said. "We *don't* know him from Adam, and I don't know that I want to entrust my child into his keeping."

Though she was only agreeing with what he'd said, for some reason it put his back up. "Oh, get a grip," he snapped. "I don't lust after little boys, and I'm not going to hurt your kid. I don't have a lot of experience with boys his age, but we can sure as hell muddle along on our own for a couple of hours."

"And what are your other options, darling?" Sophie inquired with gentle reason.

"I could always—" Dru looked at her watch. "No, I guess I couldn't." And after all, his police record *had* been totally clean. She blew out a gusty sigh. "All right, fine." Tacking on a grudging "Thank you," she climbed the porch steps and pulled open the screen door, poking her head into the house. "Tate, I'm going back to work. You're going to stay with J.D. for a little while."

"Cool," came the distracted reply from the great room. The volume on the television rose a notch.

"I can tell he's real concerned," J.D. said, deadpan. Then he shrugged. " 'Course, I haven't gotten him alone yet."

Dru stopped dead and J.D. could practically see sparks from the electric-blue gaze she locked on him. "Don't even joke about that," she snapped. "I'm taking a huge step here, leaving my son with someone I barely know. I'll be damned if I'll listen to any sick wisecracks on top of it."

Because he could see she was genuinely upset and he would've killed for a mother with half her concern when he was Tate's age, he said, "Yeah, okay. I'm sorry. Go do your sales thing. We'll be fine."

"Don't screw up," she commanded and, turning on her heel, crossed the yard with long-legged strides. A moment later she'd disappeared down the switchback trail.

He slowly unclenched, muscle by muscle. He'd never met anyone who could turn him into one big nerve ending with so little effort the way that woman could. Blowing out a breath, he turned to see Sophie observing him. "I guess I'd better not screw up." Somehow he managed to keep his tone light.

She rewarded him with an approving smile. "She might sound a tad overprotective—"

He snorted. "She sounds downright hostile."

"Perhaps. But you must understand that Tate's the light of her life."

"Yeah, I'd have to be an idiot not to have figured that out." He rose to his feet and stood looking down at her. "I guess I'd better go collect the kid and let you get ready for your appointment." Squaring his shoulders, he sternly slapped down the consternation that nudged him at the thought of having sole responsibility for Tate for the next couple of hours. What the hell did he know about ten-year-olds? It'd been a long time since he'd been one.

As if she'd read his mind, Sophie said briskly, "I've been in the inn business for nearly thirty years, and it's taught me to be a pretty good judge of character. You'll do fine, dear."

J.D. found Tate stretched out on his stomach on the floor in front of the television set. "Time to go, sport."

"Ten more minutes, okay? The show's still on."

"Didn't I hear you promise your mom you wouldn't use that excuse if she let you watch TV?"

Tate shot him a toothy grin over his shoulder. "Yeah, but that was her. I didn't promise you—"

"Turn off the tube, kid. We've got a porch roof to build."

"No foolin'?" Tate hit the remote and the screen went dark. He jumped to his feet. "Let's go!"

They stopped by the garage and J.D. selected a number of tools, including a Skil saw, which sent Tate into a paroxysm of delight.

"Can I saw something?" he demanded, dancing around J.D. as they made their way back to his cabin. "When do we get to cut something?"

"Later," J.D. said. "First we have to get rid of the damaged portions. Then we'll build a framework."

It felt good, getting back to doing what he did best. He'd always found building satisfying, whether it was starting from scratch or taking something old and defunct and transforming it into a thing of function and beauty. As birds called to each other from the trees and the sun rose higher over the clearing in front of the cabin, he tore off the destroyed sections of the roof and tossed them down into the yard. Tate collected them and carted them to the spot J.D. had designated, stacking them in a pile.

By the time he swung down from the roof, sweat had spread wet patches under his arms, across his chest and stomach, and pooled in the small of his back. He pulled his T-shirt over his head and tossed it aside. Amusement tipped up the corners of his mouth when

Tate immediately followed suit, exposing a narrow, perfectly dry little chest.

"You're doing excellent work," he said, wiping a trickle of sweat out of his eyes with the back of his forearm. "Let's take a break, whaddaya say?"

Tate swiped his arm across his eyes. "You bet."

J.D. opened the refrigerator a few moments later and looked inside. He glanced over at Tate. "So what d'ya think, kid—a beer?"

Tate's eyes lit up and he offered that big-toothed, megakilowatt smile. "Sure!"

J.D. fished out a couple of Thomas Kemper root beers and popped the tops. He handed one to Tate and clinked the neck of his own bottle against it. "Here's mud in your eye, sport."

They brought their drinks out into the yard and sat on the grass in the sun. J.D. took a deep swig from his bottle, then lay back and closed his eyes, cradling the cool glass against his bare stomach. He felt Tate do the same and couldn't prevent the wry smile that tugged at the corner of his mouth.

They lay quietly for several moments. Then Tate said, "J.D.?"

He was aware that the kid had sat up and was now looking at him, but he kept his eyes closed. "Yeah?"

"Are you a bastard?"

J.D. jackknifed to a sitting position, cold anger coursing through his veins. He pinned Tate in the cross hairs of his displeasure. "Is that what your mother says I am?"

"No!" Tate scrambled back. His pop bottle tipped over and rolled twice, root beer glugging out into the grass. His eyes grew huge, but although his chin trembled once, he thrust it out in a way that reminded J.D. of the kid's mother. "It's w-what I am, and I just thought maybe, uh, you were, too."

J.D. froze. *Good going, Carver. Maybe you oughtta take that temper down to the swimming area, where there's a whole bunch of little kids you can terrify.*

"I'm sorry," he said gently and reached out to right the pop bottle. He winced when Tate flinched away, and carefully extended the drink to him. "I am sorry, Tate. I shouldn't have snapped at you."

" 'Kay." A beat of silence went by; then Tate said tentatively, "That's the first time you've said my name."

"Huh?"

Tate settled himself cross-legged and took a sip of his root beer, visibly regaining his usual ebullient confidence. "That's the first time you've called me Tate. Usually you say 'kid.' "

"Is that a fact?" J.D. studied the boy. "What the hell makes you think you're a bastard?"

"I heard Kathleen Harris say it once to Marylou Zeka when I was down at the Pack 'n' Save in town, and when I asked Mom what it meant, she said that was just a rude word for ignorant people to label me because she wasn't married when I was born." He tilted his head to one side. "So are you? A bastard like me?"

"I've been called one often enough, but my folks were actually married." And he was still reeling that Dru hadn't been. "For about five minutes, that is," he amended. "You know, don't you, that there are a lot worse things you could be? Your mom's crazy about you, and so are your grandma and grandpa."

Tate shrugged, as if that were a given. "Sure."

"Well, I hope you appreciate it, because that's not exactly small spuds, kid. I might as well have been a bastard, because my father is just a name on a birth certificate to me. He and my mom were both drug users and he disappeared before I was even old enough to remember him."

"Yeah, my dad did that, too. He left when he found out Mom was going to have me. Mom says he was just a kid himself, and that sometimes kids panic at the thought of that kinda responsibility."

Pretty damn generous of her to make excuses for the guy, considering the jerk had left her high and dry to shoulder the share of both parents.

Tate wiggled his butt into the grass. "Uh, J.D.?"

"Yeah?"

"Don't tell Mom I told ya that, okay? When I told her what Mrs. Harris said, she explained about my dad leavin' because he was scared and all, but she looked kinda sad."

"Your secret's safe with me, buddy." J.D. rose to his feet and extended a hand to pull Tate to his. "I saw a glass-recycling container in the mudroom. Let's go toss our bottles in it. Then what d'ya say we take a few measurements, so we can get down to the serious business of cutting wood?"

6

Dru rose from one of the leather love seats bracketing the fireplace and shook hands with the delegates from the dentists' association. She calmly watched as they filed past the long, timber front desk and out through the front door, but the minute it swished closed behind them an exultant smile spread across her face.

Jenna, the banquet coordinator, whooped. "Way to go, Dru! I've never seen a conference sold so smoothly."

Dru shrugged, but the grin didn't leave her face. "This place sells itself. Where else you gonna find views like this to go along with such an impressive package of meeting rooms, meals, and activities? Especially during ski season."

"Throwing trail passes for their families into the package was brilliant, though."

"Yeah, I thought that was pretty good, too." Dru laughed and reached out to squeeze Jenna's arm. "That array of menu samples you set up in the conference room certainly didn't hurt, either. Good job."

Moments later she was headed up the trail to J.D.'s cabin, still jazzed on the satisfaction of a job well done. How blessed she was to have a career she loved so much.

Arriving at the clearing, she swept her gaze across the area—and spotted J.D. Carver without his shirt on.

She stopped abruptly, as if an invisible force field had dropped out of the sky in front of her. Heart rate racing like an Indy 500 contender, she licked her lips several times in a futile bid to get back a little of the moisture that had left her mouth.

Bare, J.D.'s tanned shoulders looked even wider than they had in his ubiquitous white T-shirts. His back was long, damp, and muscular, and it tapered beautifully down to the sweat-soaked waistband of the jeans riding low on his hips.

He swiveled to plant a knee on a board braced atop a long sawhorse, and muscles bunched and elongated in his arms and back as he leaned forward to mark it with a pencil. He stuck the pencil behind his ear, and a tangle of dark hair shone in his armpit when he raised his arm higher to swipe perspiration from his forehead. Dru caught a glimpse of the silky hair fanning his chest; then he shifted slightly and she gawked like a schoolgirl at the fuller view it afforded her, helplessly tracking the narrowing growth pattern of dark hair down his hard stomach.

He slid the board out until the mark he'd made lined

up with the end of the sawhorse, the end hanging out beyond it. When he suddenly jerked his chin in a peremptory, c'mere gesture, she jumped guiltily. But he wasn't even looking in her direction. Tate trotted down from the porch, where—to her eternal shame—she hadn't even noticed him. He slid under J.D.'s bowed stomach and chest, his back to the man's front as he assumed an identical posture of one knee on the sawhorse, the other foot planted on the ground. He leaned forward to brace his left hand on the board just before the end of the sawhorse, and Dru smiled at the serious expression on his face. He must be in heaven to be included in such a guy activity.

Then J.D. bent the elbow of his braced arm, dipped, and came up with a round-bladed, jagged-toothed saw in his free hand. Tate wrapped his hand around the handle, J.D. covered it with his own, and with a press of his finger against the trigger, the saw suddenly roared to life.

Dru's spine snapped straight. What the hell was he thinking? Tate was *much* too young to be handling hazardous power tools. A scream of outrage roared up her throat, but she bit it back, terrified it would startle her son and cause him to jerk his braced hand forward into the path of the screaming teeth that were passing a mere hairsbreadth away from his fingertips. The instant the lumber tumbled to the ground and the saw whined into silence, however, she shot across the clearing.

Tate, who had hopped down to pick up the piece of wood, saw her first. "Hi, Mom! We're rebuilding the porch roof." J.D.'s head snapped up, but Dru hadn't the first idea what he was thinking as he watched her approach.

Her inclination was to snatch her son to her and inspect him head to toe for injuries. But she forced a few deeps breaths and reached for a measure of calm, then plastered a smile on her face. "I can see that. But J.D. is going to have to get along without your help for a while. I want you to run along to your grandma and grandpa's."

"But, Mom—"

"Now."

"Aw, *man*." He kicked at the grass, but accepted the shirt J.D. swept up off the ground and extended to him.

"You did good work, Tate. Thanks for the help."

Tate's smile was dazzling. "Yeah, it was major cool. Thanks for the beer."

"*Excuse* me?" Oh, this just kept getting better and better.

Except for a sulky look, Tate ignored her. "Bye, J.D.," he said and loped across the clearing.

He'd barely disappeared from view before she swung around and confronted J.D. "What the *hell* is the matter with you?"

He climbed the porch stairs in one huge stride. Infuriated at being ignored, she followed directly behind him, dogging his footsteps so closely she all but tromped on his bootheels.

He grabbed his T-shirt off the railing and swiped it across his chest and arms to remove the sweaty coating of sawdust that covered his torso. He tilted his head slightly when she began to impatiently tap her foot. "Aside from my failure to bring about world peace, you mean?"

"Don't you get smart with me, Carver! I leave you alone with my son for two lousy hours, and—"

"Twenty-five minutes," he interrupted. "I know. But you don't have to apologize. I'm not griping about the overtime, even if it was unscheduled."

Frustration made her growl deep in her throat. "You're unbelievable! If Auntie Soph and Uncle Ben hadn't raised me better, I'd pop you one for pulling stunts like that with my son."

His dark eyebrows rose. "I take it you have a problem with my baby-sitting skills?" He had the unmitigated nerve to give her a slight smile, and Dru's blood pressure soared. "I think I did a pretty damn fine job myself. Tate does, too."

She took a hot step forward, and jabbed him in the sternum with her finger. "You call giving a ten-year-old beer and letting him play with power tools a *fine job*?" Her drilling finger underscored her ire on practically every other word. "If I were a man, I'd—"

"If you were a man, sweetheart, you wouldn't get away with half the shit you already have." He grabbed the offending finger in his fist and held it away from his chest. "Don't go poking at me; I don't take kindly to it."

In pure, unthinking fury, Dru, who had never hit another human being in her entire life, swung her free hand at him.

The next thing she knew, both her hands had been captured, and she was being whirled around and thrust against one of the porch posts. Surrounded by the scent of hot, overworked male, she was aware of the hard-skinned hands pinning her wrists above her head, the muscular forearms bracketing hers, the big body preventing any kind of retreat. But more than any of that, it was the fierce expression in his dark hazel-green eyes that pinned her in place.

"Listen, sister," he said, thrusting his face close to hers. "You put your hands on me again, you damn well better have friendly intentions." He pushed back slightly and frowned. "And for the record, I've been a construction foreman for more than a dozen years. If there's one thing I know how to do, it's instruct guys in the use of power tools."

"Tate isn't a *guy*, you troglodyte, he's a little boy!"

"Hell, yes, he's a little boy—and if you'd been paying the least bit of attention instead of reacting like a hysterical mama bear with a threatened cub, you would've seen that I was directing the saw, not Tate."

"That would have been so comforting if he'd lost a finger," she snapped. "They were within *centimeters* of that big blade!"

"They were behind mine! I would've had to buzz off my own fingers before that blade came anywhere near Tate's, and trust me, lady, I've been handling machinery too damn long to make that sort of rank beginner mistake."

Her heart pounded and her blood thundered through her veins, and she wanted to argue and rage and call him a liar. But she couldn't truly remember the exact placement of their hands; she'd only known that Tate's had seemed much too close to that whirring blade. "Fine," she said through her teeth. "I'll give you the benefit of the doubt and agree that's true."

"Mighty damn big of you."

"Yes, it is." She thrust her chin up, only then fully realizing how close they stood. The sudden awareness increased the throb of her already racing pulse and, furious, she added, "But there's still the matter of the beer."

"Oh, for chrissake, Drucilla. I gave him *root* beer."

"Root beer?"

"Yes. I'm not half the lowlife you seem to think I am—hell, I doubt anyone could be. Not to mention that only an idiot feeds booze to a little kid." Releasing her wrists, he pushed back and gave her a look of disgust. "And that, lady, is something I have never been."

Her arms dropped to her sides. Okay, she felt like a total fool. Her full-steam-ahead righteousness had fizzled into the humiliation of knowing she'd jumped to an insulting, ill-thought-out conclusion. Rubbing her wrists, she looked at him. Energy radiated off his powerful body and something in his eyes made her heart pound and her breath come short, and it made her want to berate him further, to vilify him for a number of reasons, not all of which had to do with her son.

But one thing was clear; she'd accused J.D. of being careless with her son when she didn't actually know that to be a fact. Hell. She'd rather smooch a snake, but she was going to have to apologize. Her lip curled in distaste.

She *hated* being wrong.

Watching her watch him as if he were some ravaging beast that had somehow been allowed to wander into her civilized world, J.D. had a sudden urge to give her a demonstration of just what an animal he could be. The very idea hauled him up short, and he took a smart step backward, thrusting a hand through his hair.

Holy hell. Where did this shit keep coming from? He'd never been a man who got off on forcing his attentions on women, and he sure as hell didn't understand why this woman could so easily short-circuit his good sense. Tense and angry because he was still hungry for any excuse to lay his hands on her, he turned away.

"J.D., wait," she said.

He didn't look back. "So you can tell me again how I've screwed up? I don't think so."

"No," she said, but he didn't wait to hear the rest. He headed for the door, needing to get away and give all these roaring hormones a chance to settle down.

"Dammit, Carver," she snapped and grabbed his arm. "Will you let me apolo—"

A savage sort of satisfaction burst through him, and whirling back, he backed her against the porch post again. "I warned you not to touch me," he growled. "You can't say I didn't warn you."

Then he clamped his mouth down on hers.

Her mouth was open in surprise or in protest—he wasn't sure which, and at the moment, he didn't honestly care. All he cared about was that her lips were soft and full as they cushioned his as if made for that specific purpose, that the warm inner cavern of her mouth was slick, and that her tongue was moist and sweet as he plunged his in to lick up all her flavors.

And then, oh, God, yes, *there*. With a soft yearning sound, her tongue tangled with his, and he groaned when her hands came up, hot skin against hot skin, to clutch at his shoulders. He pressed her up against the post with his body, and made another rough sound in his throat at the feel of her breasts flattening against his chest.

Seconds, minutes, or hours later, he lifted his head and stared down at her slumberous eyes and swollen mouth. Licking his bottom lip, tasting her there, he canted his head to a new angle and kissed her again, his mouth widening over hers, his tongue dancing deeper. She made a soft little sound low in her throat and slid her hands up to cup his neck. Her legs shifted slightly apart.

His head reared back. "*Yes*." Breathing like a racehorse at the end of a long stretch, he changed the angle again and then plunged back into the kiss. God, she tasted good. He couldn't get enough. He skimmed his hands down her back and insinuated them between her body and the post, sliding them onto the lush curve of her butt. Sinking his fingers in, he pulled her up onto her toes and bent in order to line up the soft cotton seam of her shorts with the worn denim fly that was doing its best to contain his hard-on.

"Oh," she said against his lips and he rocked his hips. "Oh!" Tugging his head back, she panted, "Oh, God. We shouldn't be doing this."

"I know," he agreed. But he tightened his hands on her butt and pulled her closer, pressing against her insistently. He watched with satisfaction as her eyes drifted closed and her hands urged him closer; then he lowered his mouth again and kissed her until they both teetered on the edge of control.

A small background sound tugged at the last bit of sanity still clinging to his consciousness. He wanted to ignore it, but something in its tone pulled at him. He cracked open one eye.

And saw Tate standing frozen across the clearing, mouth agape, staring at them.

"Shit!" His breath sawing, J.D. yanked his hands off the kid's mother and leaned back. Fingers tense, palms braced on the post over Dru's head, he held himself a stiff arm's length away and stared down at her, struggling to find a semblance of his usual control.

"Hmmm?" She blinked up at him with drowsy confusion. "What?" Reaching out, she lazily traced her forefinger in a zigzag pattern down his chest.

J.D. gritted his teeth against his body's reaction to her touch. "Tate," he said, and jutted his chin in the boy's direction.

Her hand dropped to her side as if she'd just snagged a thirty-pound fly ball out of the air. "*No.*" Taking a deep breath, she turned to look out at the yard. With a moan, she immediately rolled back, her eyes closing. "Oh, my God. What am I supposed to tell him?"

But she didn't wait for J.D. to offer a solution. Taking a deep breath, she exhaled and forced him to step back as she pushed away from the post. Turning away from him, she went to stand at the head of the shallow set of steps. "Tate? Honey? What—?"

"Grandma and Grandpa weren't home." Tate came closer, but stopped by the sawhorse at the foot of the stairs. Stuffing his hands in his pockets, he toed a clump of sawdust and shot them curious glances from beneath his lashes. "You guys were kissin', weren't ya?"

J.D. realized the post had prevented the kid from seeing them as clearly as he'd first feared, which was probably a damn good thing. He sucked in a breath, half expecting to hear Dru tell Tate they'd been practicing their mouth-to-mouth resuscitation.

But she merely said, "Yeah," and he realized that he'd be smart to quit underestimating her. She apparently didn't lie to her son.

Tate eyed them with more overt interest. "How come?"

Now, *there* was a good question. J.D. still couldn't believe he'd gone crazy like that. He wished to hell that he hadn't, because now instead of wondering what she tasted like, he knew—and it was dangerous, dangerous knowledge indeed.

Face all alight, Tate answered his own question. "You must really like each other, huh?"

The kid looked as if he were envisioning a brand-new daddy, and J.D.'s gut cramped. But when Dru immediately said, "No!" his eyebrows drew together. No? That sure as hell wasn't what it'd felt like when she'd been holding onto him, kissing him back. He would have said she liked him just fine.

Dru's cheeks grew pinker by the moment. "That is, what I mean to say is that we don't *dislike* each other, it's just . . . um, we only just met yesterday, and . . ."

Clearly impatient, Tate demanded, "Then how come you were kissin'?"

Yeah, lady, I'd like to hear an explanation for that myself.

He could all but see the heat waves that radiated off her face. "Well, see, it's been a long time since I've kissed a man," she said. "So I guess I just wanted to see if I still remembered how."

He was a frigging *experiment*? What had she been doing, an analysis of the kissing techniques of city slickers versus their country brethren? Or maybe she'd been indulging a hankering to experience a guy from the wrong side of the tracks. Some women got off on slumming.

"So did you, Mom? Remember how?"

"Oh, yeah," J.D. interjected. "She remembered just fine. If she'd remembered any better, in fact, I'd be crippled." He bared his teeth at Dru when she shot him a glance meant to drop him in his tracks. That little session up against the post sure as hell hadn't been one-sided, and he'd be damned if she got to pretend that it was.

Dru wrapped her arm around Tate's narrow shoulders and abruptly instructed him, "Say good-bye to J.D." Then she whipped him around.

"But—" Tate didn't get the opportunity to say more before she headed for the spur trail across the clearing. Swept along at her side, he craned a look back over his shoulder. "Bye, J.D."

"Yeah, so long, kid." Hands in his pockets, he watched Dru's braid swish against her back as she disappeared with her son into the woods. "And I wouldn't get too comfortable if I were you, sweetheart," he advised under his breath as he turned back to his interrupted project. "Because I have a feeling this thing between you and me is a long way from over."

* * *

"Don't give me a hard time," Dru ordered Char as she came back into her living room after tucking Tate into bed. Ever since Char had dropped by, her son had been regaling her not only with his own adventures, but with Dru's as well. Dru knew her friend was probably a seething cauldron of curiosity by now—curiosity she would just as soon not address. "Whatever this afternoon's madness was between me and J.D., it's over now. Completely. Totally."

Char grinned and scooped her Marilyn Monroe blond hair behind her ears. She lounged against the corner of the couch, hogging most of the space with her stretched-out legs. "So you really were kissing the hot new guy? And Tate caught you?"

"Yes. It wasn't one of my brighter moments, obviously." Dru dropped down on the opposite end of the couch and swiveled to face Char, hugging her knees to her chest and resting her chin on her kneecaps. "As you can probably tell, Tate's fascinated by the idea, and he seems determined to spread it all over Star Lake. *Just* what my reputation needs—they've barely gotten over the fact that I never married Tate's daddy."

"Do you really care what a few small minds gossip about?"

"I do if it affects Tate. But kissing is pretty tame stuff, so even if it does get around, it should blow over fast enough. What I really hate is the thought of disappointing my aunt and uncle."

"Don't be silly. Ben and Sophie love you to death."

"I know they do. But jeez Louise, Char, I met this

guy *yesterday*." She regarded her friend. "Do you think if I offered Tate a hundred bucks I could keep him from blabbing to Aunt Soph?"

"Not a chance."

"That's pretty much my gut feeling, too," Dru agreed glumly. "And we both know forbidding a kid to do or say anything only makes it that much more appealing." Squeezing her temples between the heels of her hands, she gave her friend a morose look. "It's official, then—I'm screwed."

"Certainly sounds as if you could be, if that's what you really wanted. Some women have all the luck." Char's brown eyes glowed with interest. "So c'mon, tell me. How did you and Mr. Construction come to be kissing?"

"Good question. It all started when I needed a babysitter and Aunt Sophie saw J.D. as the answer." She explained the circumstances that followed. "And the next thing I know, he's pushing me up against the porch pillar and kissing me senseless," she concluded.

"He's good, I take it?"

Dru shrugged. "He was okay." *Liar, liar, pants on fire.* Every hormone in her body stood at attention merely *thinking* about that kiss.

It scared her to death.

Char knew it, too, but she just smirked knowingly over the glass of iced tea she'd raised to her lips. "Tate sure seems to like him."

"I know. I think it's because J.D. lets him do all that guy stuff that I don't know diddly about. I'm telling you, Char, if I hear "*J.D. says*" one more time, I'm afraid I'll do something violent."

"So where do you and the hunkmeister go from here?"

"Absolutely nowhere." On that much, at least, Dru was unequivocally clear. "I was curious, but my curiosity's been satisfied. End of story."

"Uh-huh." Char shook her head in disgust and nudged Dru's thigh with her bare toes. "You're an idiot, Drucilla Jean."

"That pretty much goes without saying," Dru agreed. "But not for the reasons you think, I bet."

7

The following afternoon Sophie heard the screen door creak open, then slap closed with the homey sound of wood against wood. She looked up, even though the front door wasn't visible from her work station in the kitchen. A smile curved her lips when Ben's voice called out, "Soph! I'm home. You here, babe?"

She came out of the kitchen, drying her hands on a towel and feeling the lightness that always lifted her heart whenever she saw her husband after even the briefest separation. "Hi!" She strode into his open arms and laughed when he swung her off her feet in a circle. "How was your meeting?"

"Okay. Marv Peterman was more long-winded than usual, which I didn't think was possible, but overall it was pretty decent. Henry was there. I asked him to look into that partnership we talked about for Dru."

"Oh, good. God knows she's earned it. This thing

with Edwina and J.D. really drove home the fact that she's overdue some recognition for all the hard work she's put into the lodge—drawing a paycheck just doesn't cover it. Does Henry think he can get a third of our share drawn up for her by her birthday?"

"He wouldn't make any promises, but he said he'd look into it and get back to us by the end of the week at the latest. But enough about everyone else." He bent his head to nuzzle her neck. "How's my best girl?"

"Umm." She tilted her head to afford him easier access. "Fine. I missed you." Arousal stirred and she pressed closer. She and Ben had shared an intense physical attraction from the first day they'd met. Some of the intensity had naturally faded over the years, but recently the unthinkable had happened: her sex drive had hit the skids entirely. The sudden loss was one more side effect of what Ben ironically called her "celebration" of womanhood.

Reluctantly, she pulled back. "Damn. I hate to call a halt to this, considering I'm horny for the first time in what feels like forever, but I've got the restaurant's bread in the oven, and it's due to come out in"—she consulted her watch—"seven minutes."

Ben slid his hands down to her rear and gave her a squeeze. "I can be a real fast worker."

"Not that fast you can't, bud. Your best time in the twenty-eight years I've known you is something like thirteen and a half minutes."

"Yeah?" He grinned. "Well, eliminate all that foreplay bullshit you women insist on and I bet I could show you a brand-new personal best."

She sighed and laid her head on his shoulder. "Oh,

Ben, I miss it. I miss *this*. You've been so great with all my ups and downs, but I'm tired of feeling like an alien is inhabiting my body. I want me back."

"So do I, babe. Especially the sexually demanding you."

His plaintive tone made her laugh, and she hugged him. "Well, I don't know," she teased. "It's sorta relaxing not to be at the mercy of my sex drive for a change."

He gave her that great big, *God, I love you* smile that had first won her heart more than a quarter century ago, and she found herself smiling back as fatuously as she ever had at twenty-three. "But seriously," she said, "Margaret did say I'd get it back once the worst of this has passed, although it may never be quite as strong as it was."

Ben laughed. "Whose is?" He watched as she suddenly ripped her T-shirt from the waistband of her shorts and began flapping its hem with enough vigor to make her cream satin bra play peekaboo. It would have been humorous if he hadn't seen the telltale flush that climbed her throat and face. Some days she got as many as four or five hot flashes an hour, giving her no rest. "What else did Margaret say? She have any new strategies for getting this under control?"

"She's going to start me on vitamin E and some progesterone cream that I'm supposed to rub into my skin." Sophie made a rude noise. "That'll make a huge difference, I'm sure. I don't know, Ben, maybe I should just go back on the Premarin."

"Not with the history of breast cancer in your family—it's too risky."

"At least it worked! God, I'm so tired of these hot flashes and losing my temper at the drop of a hat. I hardly recognize myself some days. I've lost it but good around Tate a few times already. I'm going to end up scarring the child's psyche."

It was Ben's turn to make a rude noise. "Tate lives for the opportunity to hear a dirty word he can repeat. Since his mama rigorously monitors his television and movie viewing, you're the best entertainment going."

Sophie suddenly brightened. "Ooh. Speaking of Tate, he came visiting this morning with some *very* interesting news."

"Yeah?" The timer went off on the convection oven, and Ben followed her into the kitchen, watching as she efficiently transferred golden-brown loaves of bread to the marble countertop and reloaded the oven with a new batch.

"Oh, yes, indeed." She closed the oven door, set the timer, and tossed the pot holders on the countertop. "Seems Tate caught J.D. going at it with our Drucilla against one of the porch pillars."

"What?" Mellow good humor disintegrating, Ben's spine snapped straight, and he pushed away from the doorjamb he'd been leaning against. "I'll kill him."

Sophie laughed and grabbed his arm. "Easy, boy. He was only kissing her, and from what Tate said, it doesn't sound as if she was fighting him off."

"Holy shit, Soph." He squeezed the tense muscles at the back of his neck. "He's been here, what, a lousy forty-eight hours? That's a little too damn fast to start making time with my niece."

"How long did you know me before you kissed me, Ben?"

"Hell," he began indignantly, "I knew you for a good, uh—"

"Eight hours tops, sport. And how long before we made love?"

"That was different!" He didn't even want to think about Dru in that context.

"No, darling, it was exactly the same."

"We don't know squat about this guy."

"We didn't know anything about him when we decided to honor Edwina's wishes regarding the lodge, either, but we decided to go along with it."

"That's hardly the same thing as standing by while he slaps the moves to our baby!"

"Oh, honey, she's not a baby, and frankly, I think it's high time some man riled up her hormones again. She's been so damn careful not to step outside the boundaries since Tate was born, and it's just not natural. She needs more of a life than she's allowed herself. And I like J.D., Ben. He has every excuse to be bitter and disenfranchised, but he's a decent man."

"He's sure as hell a suspicious one—the way Dru said he's going over the books, you'd think our primary goal in life was to rob him blind. And I bet he's pretty damn quick to use those big fists of his to settle an argument."

"Which wouldn't be surprising, given the way he was brought up. But I bet he's not as quick to use them as he is to use the threat of them. Being a construction foreman means overseeing a lot of men, many of whom, I imagine, only respect someone who can physically intimidate them. I certainly can't picture him getting violent with a woman, though. I also have a hard time envisioning him just going off half cocked for no good reason. He might be a little rough around the edges, but he strikes me as steady. And God knows he's honest."

"How the hell do you know that?"

"Have you heard him hesitate to speak his mind, whether it's something we want to hear or not?" She took his shrug as agreement and added, "And he seems to have a good mind. Besides, I like the way he looks at Dru."

"I know I'm going to regret asking this, but what way is that?"

"Oh, my." She came over to slide into his arms and hug him around the waist. "Like he'd like to eat her up with a spoon the way he did my crème brûlée."

He moaned, and Sophie laughed. "It's not that bad, darling. I know you still think of Drucilla as your little girl, but watch her. She's come alive the past couple of days, and that's such a pleasure to see." She kissed his throat, humming deep in her own. "I do believe I'm beginning to recapture that sexy feeling again."

"You're just trying to distract me."

She wiggled against him. "Is it working?"

"Oh, yeah." He walked her backward toward the hall that led to their bedroom. "Like a charm."

J.D. closed the current year's financial ledger and set it atop the journals from the previous two years on the kitchen table. Tipping his chair back on two legs, he crossed his arms over his chest while he stared up at the ceiling.

Okay, so the Lawrences hadn't cooked the books. But no one was as friendly as they'd been without a reason. In his experience, everyone wanted something—and he'd sure as hell like to know what it was that Ben and Sophie wanted from him.

Not to mention Drucilla. And the pitiful truth was that she could probably get whatever she desired, if she ever kissed him again the way she had yesterday.

The chair legs thumped down on the wooden floor as he sat up straight. He'd told himself he wasn't going to think about that. It had been a fluke—the moon aligned with Jupiter or some such shit—that had put him and Dru in the same spot at the same time when emotions were running high on both sides. He was glad Tate had shown up when he had. It had saved them from making a mistake they'd both regret.

Yeah, right. He shoved to his feet.

Okay, he wanted in her pants. *Badly*. But a fuck was all it would be, and she was definitely one of those "make love" kind of women—which was to say, not his kind at all.

Sex for him was purely recreational. It could be fun; it could be slow and lazy or down-and-dirty fast and furious. But in the end it boiled down to one thing only: your basic, no-frills fornication.

Once upon a time, he'd looked for love. But not in recent years. A guy only had to have his teeth kicked down his throat a couple of times before he wised up.

So he'd gotten lucky for about five minutes yesterday, but the odds against that happening again were pretty steep. There was no sense wasting time thinking about it. He gathered up the books and let himself out of the cabin.

He didn't know what the Lawrences' game was, but he knew the only way to beat them at it was to learn everything he could about the lodge—its ins and outs and how it was run. Knowledge was power, and he planned to do what he always did in a new situation: suck up every bit of information he could unearth.

Several moments later he knocked on Dru's office door. He could hear her laughing and, filled with a sudden inexplicable impatience, he barely waited for her soft "Come in" before muscling through the door.

She and a showy blonde sat on either side of her desk, and as they both turned to look at him, Dru's laughter faded. The blonde regarded him with interest, but Dru looked at him as if he'd bulled his way in where he had no business being. His shoulders hunched up slightly.

So, big deal. Like being an outsider was something new.

"Hello," the blonde said, exposing a deep set of dimples.

She was his type of woman: flamboyant makeup and hair, flashy fingernails, friendly smile. "Hey, there."

"J.D., this is my friend Char McKenna," Dru said, and his attention was immediately diverted from the blonde's eye-catching attributes to Drucilla. Her prettiness was a subtler thing: shiny hair, a sprinkling of freckles, and those dark-lashed vibrant blue eyes. It didn't make a damn bit of sense that she could make him forget the other woman was even in the room.

"Char's our masseuse here," she told him. "Char, J.D. Carver. You know what he is."

Char choked and J.D. scowled at Drucilla. What the hell was that supposed to mean?

Dru gave him a cool smile to disguise the surge of heat his abrupt appearance had elicited. For just an instant, she'd been thrown back into that kiss that she'd spent far too much time denying meant a darn thing. Taking a deep, quiet breath, she eased it out. "Is there something I can do for you, J.D.?"

Oh, baby.

She could practically *hear* the words as he gave her a very male look, one corner of his mouth tipping up. Glancing over, she caught Char pursing her lips in a silent whistle and fanning herself with her fingers, and Dru cursed her own hyperactive imagination as she envisioned all manner of things she could do for him. Damned if she'd be reduced to stuttering and acting like a flustered virgin, though. She raised her brows inquiringly.

"Yeah." The slight smile and animal heat disappeared, and he dropped the ledgers he'd borrowed on her desk. Straightening, he stood, hands on his narrow hips, and regarded her with level eyes. "Put me to work."

"What did you have in mind?"

"Anything that pertains to the joint. I want to learn it all."

That was fair enough. As a part owner, he should know every aspect of the business. "Okay." She thought for a moment. "Do you have a pair of sneakers?"

"Huh?"

"Sneakers. Do you—"

"I heard you. I just don't see its relevance to teaching me the business."

"I'm going to put you to work at the front desk. It's where every guest's stay begins, so it seems an appropriate place to start. But it requires you to wear the uniform." She indicated her own outfit. "We can supply you with the shorts and polo shirt, but we don't provide shoes."

"I'll go to town and pick up a pair." He turned to Char and gave her one of his rare white smiles. "Nice meeting you." Glancing back at Dru, he pinned her in place with the intensity of his regard. "I'll be back in a half hour or so."

Dru couldn't have said why that struck her as more warning than promise.

The door closed behind him, and Char sagged back in her seat. "Whoa. Be still, my heart." She gave Dru a look. "And you said kissing him was *okay*? I'm surprised we didn't have to air-vac you to the Harborview burn unit in Seattle." She stared at the door consideringly. "I wonder if he has a brother."

Laughter that felt suspiciously like hysteria exploded out of Dru's throat. "I don't know. I'll be sure to ask."

Amusement was the farthest thing from her mind, though, after Char had left and she waited for J.D. to return. The sport-shop employee who'd put her on hold came back on the line to ask for a clarification on the information she'd requested, and Dru brought the phone receiver back up to her lips again.

"Yes. Size large on the shirt and I'm guessing a thirty-four waist on the shorts. You do? Great. Thanks, Joe. I'll be right over to pick them up." She reseated the receiver and rose to her feet. How on earth had her nice, organized life grown so chaotic so fast? She felt as if everything were spinning out of control.

After letting the front desk know where she could be found, she stepped into the sport shop. It rented equipment and sold trail passes, ski clothing, and related accessories during the ski season, then rented boats and sold summer sportswear, including the lodge logowear, in the summer.

Joe was discussing a reservation for a water-ski party with two guests when she entered, so she straightened a stack of T-shirts and neatened the sunglasses rack while she waited. When she turned back from inspecting the display window, he caught her eye and pointed to the folded shorts and shirt that sat at the end of the counter. She walked over to pick them up, initialed the slip that he slid over to her without interrupting his conversation with the guests, and headed for the door.

She nearly ran smack into J.D. For some reason it irritated her to see him pull back from the imminent contact as briskly as she did.

"Sally said I'd find you over here."

"Yes. I was getting you this." She thrust out the garments. His hand was a shock of warm, rough skin as it slid across hers to take the clothing. She cleared her throat. "You can change in the men's rest lounge if you want." She indicated the wide hallway across the lobby. "It's across from the game room on the other side of the elevator. I'll meet you at the front desk when you're ready."

Five minutes later Dru saw him striding up the hall toward the lobby, and she stared. She'd seen him only in jeans and white T-shirts, and he looked almost dressed up in the crisp cargo shorts and polo shirt. The fresh-off-the-rack whiteness of the shirt made his arms and throat appear particularly bronzed, but his legs were only lightly tanned, probably from his working in jeans all the time. They were muscular and hairy, though, and she was hard-pressed to pull her gaze away.

But somehow it was his socks, not the stunning fitness of his body, that really got to her. They were dingy, which was exacerbated by the brand-new brilliance of his tennis shoes, and there was just something sort of . . . lonely about them. She could picture him in a laundromat all by himself, stuffing everything willy-nilly into one load. It really brought home the fact that he'd been raised pretty much on his own, kicked from place to place. A warm kernel of tenderness unfurled inside her, and stretched toward him like a blossom to the sun.

Dru came to abruptly. Oh, no. No, no, no, no, *no*. He wasn't a motherless child, and hadn't been for a long time. He was a fully grown man who was long on opinions and short on charm, and she wasn't about to offer to wash his socks for him. Good God—what was the matter with her?

He walked up to her. "Everything fits. You have a good eye."

She eyed the slight gap at his waist. "The shorts look a little big."

"They're fine. My waist is a thirty-three, but it's a difficult size to find, so I usually buy thirty-fours and have a little extra breathing room." He shrugged. "No biggie."

"Fine. Now, about your socks—"

He looked down in surprise, then shocked her by flashing a crooked grin. "Sorry about that. This pair somehow got in with a load of jeans. I usually wear them for work. Want me to go get a pair that are actually white?"

Okay, that proves it, Drucilla Jean—you're an idiot.

She couldn't make herself smile back. "They should be fine for one day. You'll be behind the desk."

God, she couldn't believe she'd had that come-and-let-me-mother-you moment. If she'd thought about it for a few lousy seconds instead of reacting with sappy emotionalism, she would have remembered that his T-shirts were always dazzlingly white.

Well, fine. She became all business. "You're all set, then. Put your stuff under the counter here, and let me find Sally so you can get started."

8

J.D. pulled out his watch and checked the time. Blowing out an impatient breath, he clicked it shut and stuffed it back in his pocket. It was only ten minutes later than the last time he'd checked, and he still had an hour to go before he'd be free of the front desk. The good news, though, was that he'd be free of it forever.

He'd never realized that days could drag on so long. If he could just hold on these final sixty minutes, he intended to loosen some of the knots in his neck by putting in an hour or two rebuilding the railing around the Eagle's Nest balcony. If there was one thing he'd learned in the six days he'd manned the front desk, it was that he'd go nuts working at a job that kept him confined and inactive.

Not to mention dealing with the public. He'd had to grit his teeth against his basic nature all week. Some of the guests gave new meaning to the word "rude," and his natural inclination was neither to simply take it nor to turn the other cheek. That went against every precept for survival he'd ever had drummed into his head.

Thank God he had the weekend off for good behavior before he started in a couple of new divisions next week. At a meeting with Dru, he'd been given a list of all the departments, and they'd hammered out a schedule for him for the next several weeks. Starting Monday, he'd split his time between the ground maintenance crew and learning the workings of the elegant restaurant. Of the two, he had no doubt about which he'd like best.

The phone rang. Sally was chasing down information for a guest, which left him to answer it. Damn. He could run any power tool ever invented, but this phone system made him feel like an idiot. It rang again. Lights blinked on the myriad buttons, and he punched one as he picked up the receiver. "Star Lake Lodge."

"Ben Lawrence, please."

"I'm sorry, Mr. Lawrence isn't available. Can I take a mess—"

"Damn, I've already tried him at home. How about Dru? Is she around?"

"Yeah, sure, let me put you on hold for a second." But when he looked down, Dru's line was blinking. "Nope, I'm sorry. Looks like she's on the phone. Can I take a message?"

"Yes. This is Henry Briggs. Tell Ben I'm sorry it took so long to get back to him, but I finally got that information he wanted, if he'd like to give me a call."

"Got it. Henry Briggs. Sorry. Has your information. You can call back."

The man laughed. "You're a bit different from their usual front-desk type, aren't you?"

"So I've been told." J.D. looked down at the blanks on the pink message slip. "Does Ben have your number?"

"Yes."

"Okay, then. I'll see that he gets the message."

Briggs thanked him and wished him a good day.

The entrance doors opened, and two women entered. One was elderly with lavender hair and large, crusty diamonds on her fingers and ears; the other was middle-aged with defeated shoulders, wearing an expensive-looking but unflattering dress. The old lady had a querulous, carrying voice as she gave her companion step-by-step directions and warnings regarding the suitcases the younger woman juggled. J.D. rang for a bellboy, then braced himself, recognizing trouble when he saw it.

"Good afternoon, ladies," he said when they came up to the desk. "Welcome to Star Lake Lodge. How can I help you?"

"How *may* I help you, young man."

"You could tell me the name your reservation is under."

The middle-aged woman's lips curled in a slight smile, but the older woman straightened in affront. "I wasn't asking how I could assist you, you imbecile. I was correcting your abominable Engl—"

Something of what he felt must have shown in his eyes when he lifted his gaze to meet hers head-on, for she abruptly cut herself off and drew back slightly, bristling.

"Manion," the middle-aged woman said in a soft voice. "The reservation is under Mrs. Roberta Manion. I'm her daughter, Estelle."

"I hope you enjoy your stay, Ms. Manion." Smiling at her caused her to blink rapidly, and since it wasn't his aim to make her nervous, he dropped his gaze to the keyboard, where he hunt-and-pecked out their name. A second later the information he sought appeared on the screen. "Here we go. You're in the Timberline Suite." He selected the appropriate envelope of keys and information from its cubby and slid it across the countertop to Estelle.

The old lady reached out and snatched it before her daughter could pick it up, and swallowing the hot words that rose in his throat, J.D. completed the check-in process. Looking up, he saw the bellboy approaching and swallowed an oath as well.

He wished to hell it was anyone but Sean. It was the kid's first job and he was still easily flustered. An old barracuda like Mrs. Manion was unlikely to add to his confidence.

But it couldn't be helped, so he introduced the young man to the two guests. "He'll help you with your luggage, ladies. Sean, Mrs. and Ms. Manion will be staying with us in the Timberline Suite." He turned to the women and indicated the small suitcases Estelle had brought in. "Do you have more luggage in your car, or is this it?"

"Of course we have more luggage," the elder Manion snapped. "We're going to be here for a month."

"Come with me," Estelle interjected softly to Sean. "I'm parked out in the valet drive."

J.D. didn't know whether to be relieved or to curse when the old lady immediately followed in their wake, complaining with every step she took. God, give him a crew of belligerent construction workers any day.

Only moments after the doors had closed behind them, J.D. heard Roberta Manion's voice rise in fury. "Shit!" He vaulted the counter and pushed through the doors.

Sean had retrieved the luggage from a late-model Mercedes, hauled it up onto the wide, covered porch, and was stacking it on the luggage cart in accordance with the old woman's commands. As J.D. approached, she demanded that the bellboy rearrange a piece, and if the strained patience on Sean's face was anything to go by, it wasn't for the first time.

"No," she snapped as he set it down. "I said I wanted it here. *Here*, you see?"

"Yes, ma'am." Ears red, he moved the piece to the place that she indicated on the luggage trolley. Unfortunately, just as he went to set it down she slapped the cart's hanging post in irritation, and the cart wheeled away from him. The piece of luggage tumbled to the ground.

"Oh! You stupid, incompetent boy! Look what you've done! I'll see you fire—"

J.D. had had enough. "If you find so much disfavor with Sean's work, Mrs. Manion," he said, stepping forward, "perhaps you ought to do it yourself." Giving the kid's shoulder a brief, encouraging squeeze as he passed, he squatted and swept up the case, arranging it on the cart with swift efficiency.

"Why, you rude hooligan! I'll see you fired, too."

"*Mother*," Estelle whispered in mortification, but J.D. slowly rose and stared down at the old lady.

"You're welcome to try. You might find it a little difficult, however, since I own part of the place. And Sean here works for me, so it won't be possible to terminate his employment, either." He rolled the newly arranged cart to the bellboy. "Here you go. See them to their room." Turning to Estelle, he said, "I'm counting on you to see that your mother behaves herself with him."

He heard about it, of course. It was too much to hope that the old woman wouldn't complain, and with only two minutes left on the clock, he was called into Dru's office.

"Are you totally crazy?" she demanded before he'd even cleared the door. Spine poker-straight, arms crossed militantly, she glared up at him.

"Possibly." He crossed his own arms over his chest and looked at her. Her cheeks were pink and her eyes so electric they all but shot sparks. "Depends on who you're talking to, I imagine."

"*I've* been talking to Roberta Manion." She relaxed her aggressive posture, clearly deciding that sweet reason would be more effective than an outright attack. "Listen, I know she can be rather difficult—"

"*Rather* difficult? That little old lady could give lessons to a piranha. The way she chewed up Sean, I half expected to see her spitting out his bones."

"That's no reason for you to exacerbate the problem by being rude in return. Star Lake Lodge prides itself on its exceptional service. We didn't get that reputation by telling our guests that if they don't like the way we do something, to go do it themselves."

Hell, you would have thought he'd goosed the old broad rather than offered a simple suggestion. He liked Dru in her attack mode a hell of a lot better than being talked to as if he were some sixteen-year-old who needed to be shown the error of his ways.

Before he could dispute her claim, however, she said, "Since this is your last day on the front desk, I was able to calm Mrs. Manion by assuring her you would no longer be manning it. And I comped her and Estelle dinner in the restaurant, so this particular incident has been smoothed over. But in the future, J.D., please keep in mind that—"

"You did *what*?" Raw, hot fury shot through his veins, and he reached her desk in a single stride. Slapping his hands down without regard to the stacks of paperwork, he leaned foward aggressively and felt a spark of satisfaction when she drew back. "And just where does Star Lake Lodge stand when it comes to its employees? Is no abuse too gross, as long as the guest is happy?"

"Of course not. Don't be ridiculous."

"What the hell is so ridiculous about it? Roberta Manion called Sean stupid and incompetent. She threatened to see him fired because he fumbled one of her cases after she smacked the damn cart away. She browbeat the kid, and you're fucking *rewarding* her by comping her to a free meal in your precious four-diamond restaurant?"

She shot to her feet and leaned across the desk in turn. "Don't you use your foul language with me, J.D.

Carver! You're not on a construction crew any longer."

"The *hell* with my language!" Only a scant half foot separated their faces, and he thrust his nearer still. Spreadsheets skittered to the corner of the desk and accordioned to the floor. "What kind of message does that send to our employees?"

"My God, your gall just recognizes no bounds, does it? They're not *our* employees, you—" She snapped her mouth shut, apparently realizing her mistake, and J.D. gave her a feral smile.

"Oh, yeah, sweetheart, they are. Yours and mine and Auntie and Uncle's. In fact, I'm not all that certain about the 'you' part of this equation. If I'm not mistaken, *you're* my employee as well." He saw her eyes narrow and her cheeks flushed a deeper rose. The pulse in the hollow of her throat thumped fifty miles an hour, and his smile grew even more barbarous.

"I don't pretend to have your expertise in this field," he said, "so I sure don't intend to mess with that reputation for fine service you're so friggin' proud of. I can even swallow a great deal of rudeness from the guests and still say, 'Yes, ma'am; thank you, ma'am.' But understand this, Drucilla." He leaned in until their noses were a millimeter apart. "I'll be damned if I'll stand by and watch some old battle-ax whose manners are yellower than her diamonds terrorize a kid who's knocked himself out to uphold the lodge honor."

She surprised him by slowly straightening and nodding, the anger draining from her expression. "It's possible I may have acted rashly simply because you were involved in the complaint," she conceded.

"What?" He clapped a hand to his heart in feigned amazement. "You didn't find it difficult to believe I might have been rude to a guest without provocation?"

"Not even for a second." She picked up the phone and punched a two-digit number. "This is Dru," she said a moment later. "Please send Sean to my office."

The bellboy knocked a moment later, and came in with an apprehensive look on his face when Dru bade him enter.

She offered him a seat, and as soon as he'd perched on the edge of the visitor's chair, she said, "I owe you an apology."

"Ma'am?"

"You've probably heard by now that I comped Mrs. Manion and her daughter to dinner in the restaurant. I'm sorry, Sean. I failed to obtain all the facts before I did so, and as J.D. has so rightly pointed out, that amounts to rewarding her for abusing you."

"Oh, uh . . ."

"J.D. told me what Mrs. Manion did, and how you handled the situation. I assume that she continued to be verbally abusive when you took their bags to the suite."

Shifting uncomfortably in his chair, Sean clearly didn't want to admit any such thing and perhaps be labeled a complainer. Then a way to put a positive spin on the situation must have struck him, for he brightened. "Ms. Manion gave me a huge tip."

"Good for her. It sounds as if you earned every penny of it. I'd like to give you a two-hour water-skiing party as well, as both an apology and a thank-you for handling a difficult guest in a professional manner.

Call Joe in the sport shop and set up a time that works for you and your friends."

"Oh, wow. Thanks, Dru. Thanks, Mr. Carver."

"J.D.," he reminded him.

"Yeah, right—J.D. Thanks."

He left the office, and J.D. watched as Dru called the sport shop to alert Joe to the arrangements. This keeping-his-distance business would be a hell of a lot easier if she'd clung to her superior attitude instead of turning reasonable on him. There was probably a subversive reason behind her sudden about-face, but he couldn't figure out what. Something, no doubt, designed to drive him away.

Or perhaps just to drive him crazy.

He thought about that rapid pulse he'd seen fluttering in her throat, and the urge he'd had to lick it, to feel it throbbing beneath his tongue. Swallowing a curse, he left the office before he did something irrevocably stupid.

It wasn't until he'd unwound with some straightforward carpentry on the Eagle's Nest balcony that he remembered the message for Ben. Damn. Reluctantly forgoing the lure of a cold beer and some sports talk with the bartender, he cleaned up his work area, then went to collect the message slip from the front desk.

Sally looked up in surprise when he approached. "Hey, J.D. I thought you were long gone."

"Look who's talking. What are you still doing here? You putting in overtime?"

"In a way. Cheryl had a late appointment in town, so I agreed to stay for a couple of extra hours." She eyed the tank top, jeans, and boots he'd changed into and the carpenter's belt slung around his waist. "Looks like you've been working on that railing again."

"Somebody has to."

She grinned. "Not only are you a world-class fix-it guy, but word has it you're now our hero of the hour as well."

"Huh?" What the hell was she talking about?

"Your defense of Sean. It's the talk of the employee grapevine."

"You're kidding." He stared at her in amazement. "How come? I didn't do anything."

"Mrs. Manion has been a thorn in the help's side for fifteen years. It warms the cockles of our hearts to hear that you went to bat when she started in on Sean. He worships you now, of course."

J.D. shifted uncomfortably at the thought, but it warmed him a little, too. "Why do the Lawrences put up with her, if she's such a pain?"

"Oh, you get some like that sometimes. Most of the guests are sweeties, but a few can be pains, and fewer still, thank God, turn out to be *royal* pains. It doesn't take much stretch of the imagination to figure out which category Roberta Manion fits into, but she brings in a ton of money. She books suites, eats in the restaurant, and drops a bundle in the gift shop." Sally smiled wryly. "And, of course, Estelle tips really well."

"Crazy damn business, if you ask me."

Sally laughed. "It is that."

J.D. collected the message slip and headed out, feeling inexplicably cheerful. A hero, huh? How about that.

Passing the dock a few minutes later elicited an outright laugh. The new sign was up, and a flash of pride, knowing it was his suggestion that had brought it into being, warmed him more effectively than a straight shot of a hundred and twenty proof.

The lake was quiet and still, with blue shadows starting to stretch out over the water. It was just after seven, the lifeguards were gone, and except for a couple in a rowboat headed for shore, the area was deserted. He really was going to have to break down and buy a pair of swim trunks one of these days so he could give the water a try.

Or, what the hell—maybe he'd wait until dark some night and go skinny-dipping. He hadn't done that since he and Butch had taken a couple of girls out on an after-midnight foray on Lake Union back when they were teenagers.

Feeling downright mellow, he was almost inclined to concede that the Lawrences were exactly what they portrayed themselves to be. Hell, he'd never been around an actual, real-live functional family—maybe such things truly did exist.

The concept seemed to be reinforced when the first person he saw in the Lawrences' yard was Tate. Wearing nothing but a pair of faded swim trunks, the boy danced around the yard, dark hair flopping as he lunged and feinted and slashed his plastic light-saber through the air with unselfconscious abandon.

J.D. stopped to watch him. "Killing off the bad guys, Tate?"

"J.D.!" The light-saber fell to his side, and he raced over, his grin splitting his face. "Yeah, I was killing 'em all deader'n doornails." He stared up at J.D., blue eyes wide. "What is a doornail, anyway?"

"You got me."

The question must have been rhetorical, for Tate shrugged aside J.D.'s lack of an answer. "Didja come here to go swimming with us?"

"No, I came to give your grandpa a message."

"Oh. When you're done, you can come swim with us if you wanna. We're going to race to the float."

"That sounds real nice, but I don't have a suit." He sure wouldn't mind seeing Dru in hers again, though.

"Ya oughtta get one."

"You know, I was just thinking that very thing on my way over here. Maybe I'll run into town tomorrow and pick one up."

"I get to go to town tomorrow, too. Me and Billy Drooder are gonna hang out, and I'm spending the night at his house and everything."

"Sounds like fun."

"No foolin'. We get to rent videos to watch after dinner." He stepped closer and lowered his voice. "Don't tell Mom, but Billy's mom lets him watch PG-Thirteen."

"And that's a pretty cool thing?"

"Way cool. Don't tell Mom, though."

The corner of J.D.'s mouth quirked. "My lips are sealed, kid."

"About what?"

J.D. looked up to see Dru and Sophie and Ben coming down the porch steps. They all wore bathing suits, but Dru, he noticed with regret, had cutoffs over hers.

"Why are your lips sealed?" she demanded.

Feeling Tate's sudden tension at his side, he gave an

easy shrug. "If I told you, then they wouldn't be sealed very long, would they?"

"Do you have a question you need answered, Tate? You can ask me anything, you know." Dru frowned at J.D. "Tate doesn't have any secrets from me."

J.D. tried to swallow his snort, but couldn't totally suppress it. "What world do you live in? I might not be any kind of authority on family dynamics—"

Dru had a credible snort of her own. "That's a fact."

"—but I can tell you this much: the boy hasn't been born who tells his mother everything. You can relax, though. We aren't harboring any earth-shattering secrets. We were just talking guy stuff."

"Yeah," Tate chimed in. "Guy stuff."

She looked ready to argue, but Ben interrupted. "Is there something we can do for you, J.D.?"

He didn't sound nearly as friendly as he usually did, and J.D. looked at him in surprise. He hadn't even seen the man in over a week, so he didn't understand how he could have managed to piss him off. J.D. shrugged and fished the pink message slip out of his pocket. "It's more what I can do for you. You had a call from a guy named Henry Briggs this afternoon. He said—"

Ben snatched the slip from his hand. "Fine. Thanks. I'll take care of it."

Dru gave her uncle a funny look. "Henry Briggs? Isn't that your lawyer friend? What do you suppose he wants?"

"He's looking into something for your uncle," J.D. said, while sudden anger burned in his gut. Ben's lawyer—God, he was a chump. He stared at the

Lawrences as they stood in their cozy little family grouping. Hell, yes—a world-class chump to have imagined he'd ever be anything more than an outsider looking in. "And I guess it doesn't take a genius to figure out what that something is, does it?"

9

Dru watched a shaft from the lowering sun gild J.D.'s brown shoulders as he stalked across the yard. When she'd walked out of the house and seen him there so unexpectedly, her stomach had flip-flopped. It was still riled up, with equal parts sexual tension and the shameful jealousy she'd felt knowing Tate had just told him something he didn't care to share with her. Watching J.D. stride away in obvious anger made it roil even more. Forcing her gaze from his receding back, she turned back to her aunt and uncle in time to see Sophie smack Ben on the arm.

"Way to go," her aunt said.

"What on earth was that all about?" Dru demanded. "What did he mean, it doesn't take a genius to figure out what Henry's looking into?" Before she could explore the sudden suspicion blooming in her mind,

Tate tugged on her hand, and she looked down to see him staring up at her anxiously.

"Is J.D. mad at us?"

"Not you, slick," Ben said. "He's mad at me."

"How come?" Tate said at the same time Dru demanded, "Tell me you're not having Henry look into the feasibility of contesting J.D.'s claim."

"Of course not!" Ben thrust his hand through his hair. "I don't know how this train jumped its tracks so damn fast, but let's just slam on the brakes here. I'm having Henry look into something entirely unrelated to J.D."

"What?"

He froze for an instant, his face going blank. Then, avoiding her eyes, he said stiffly, "That's none of your business, Drucilla."

Sophie rolled her eyes, watching her husband go rigid at being caught unprepared, and her niece draw back as if he'd slapped her. She stepped forward to do some damage control.

"For pity's sake, you two. Drucilla, darling, we're having Henry research something for our estate planning. And, Ben, Dru is hardly a child—she's not going to come unglued at the thought of a death so far in the future."

"Whose death?" Tate demanded, and Sophie started. She'd forgotten that he was there.

"Your grandfather's or mine," she said matter-of-factly, then reached out to hug him to her when she saw his eyes go wide with incipient panic. "Neither of us plans to die anytime soon, darling. But an intelligent person always makes sure his estate is in order before he becomes old, ill, or incompetent."

"Oh. Okay. We oughtta tell J.D. that. Then he won't be mad at us anymore."

"He was never angry with you," Dru said. "Don't worry about him, okay? Let's just go swimming the way we planned—everything will be fine."

But Sophie observed the unconscious longing in her niece's eyes as she darted a glance across the now deserted lawn.

Sophie stifled her sigh. Really, this was just too vexing. The two of them weren't exactly fast out of the gate to begin with, but at least they'd been making some progress. Now that J.D. thought they were trying to cheat him out of his inheritance, though, he was bound to be even more guarded than usual. He wore that abundance of pride like body armor, and Drucilla was so relationship-shy, it would never even occur to her to make the first move.

Which left *her*. Ben would have a conniption if he thought she was meddling, but it was obvious Dru and J.D. were attracted to each other. They just needed a little shove to get them going in the right direction.

Sophie smiled to herself as she contemplated various ways to throw the two of them together. She'd utilize as many of those ways as it'd take until Dru and J.D. either settled the attraction between them once and for all or lost interest in each other entirely. Which she didn't think was very likely.

* * *

"Are you ever gonna get up off your damn butt and find yourself another job?"

Butch tapped his fingers against the phone resting on his stomach and looked up at his wife. The setting sun poured through the sliding door to the lanai, creating an angelic halo of light around Gina's well-teased hair.

He nearly grunted aloud. *There* was a comparison to make your eyes roll. Though her face was in shadow, he didn't doubt for a moment that she glared down at him. And angelic was the last thing the hands on her hips and the spike-heel-shod foot tapping an impatient tattoo suggested.

Instead of rolling his eyes, though, he narrowed them at her. "As a matter of fact," he said coolly, setting the phone aside and pushing back until he was leaning against the arm of the couch, "I just spent most of the afternoon trying to line up exactly that."

"Uh-huh." Her voice was so skeptical, a guy would've thought she'd heard it all before. "And what's your excuse for not having one this time?"

Jesus, she was a bitch. It was the very thing that had first attracted him to her, but sometimes she got a little above herself. And the truth of the matter was, he *had* accomplished something today—a couple of somethings, in fact. He'd finally come to a decision about J.D.

He'd decided to call off his search.

J.D. must have moved out of state or something, because he'd vanished into thin air. No one seemed to have a clue where he'd gotten himself off to.

Which meant Butch was officially in clover. J.D.

had just been reacting the other day—Butch admitted the way he'd handled the call coulda used a little more tact. Point was, though: if J.D. was out of state, he wasn't going to be looking into Butch's business. And chances that he'd hear of the clerk's death were pretty much nil. And *that* meant Butch didn't have to do something about it.

A sharp pain brought his attention back to Gina, who had bent over to poke him with one of her inch-long red talons. "I *said,* what's your excuse this time?"

He reached out and yanked her down to straddle his lap. "I don't need an excuse. I lined up some work on a project down by Safeco Field." Pulling up her skirt, he slid his hands onto her bare ass on either side of the thong that rode the division of her buttocks and, digging his fingers in, pulled her tight against his burgeoning hard-on. Gentle treatment was wasted on Gina, which was fine with him. He delivered a stinging slap to her bare rump. "It's only temporary, though, so don't get your hopes up."

Gina rose up far enough to claw open his fly. "Temporary works. Temporary is just fine. As long as you're finally doing something to earn your damn keep."

"Come *on*, Mom." Tate danced with impatience on the walkway fronting the lodge. "What are we waiting for, anyway? Billy's *expecting* me."

"I know he is, sweetie, but the air-conditioning unit for Cabin Four has finally arrived at Bronsen's, and Aunt Soph asked me to pick it up while we're in town."

"So let's go get it, then."

Dru felt a smile curve her lips. As if he cared one way or the other about an air-conditioning unit. He just wanted to get to town so he could play with his friend. "We need both a truck to haul it and some muscle to transfer it from the store to the truck, since Harvey Bronsen isn't as robust as he used to be. Aunt Sophie promised someone would be bringing the truck around any minute now."

Not that Dru couldn't sympathize with Tate's impatience—it was her day off, too, and she didn't feel like expending energy on the lodge. She hadn't expected to even get out of the car when she dropped Tate off at his friend's, and had dressed strictly for comfort in shorts that rode low on her hips and in a cropped tank that exposed her belly button whenever she raised her arms the least little bit.

For a few brief moments, after Aunt Soph had called with her request, she'd considered changing into her lodgewear to present a professional image at Bronsen's Hardware. Then she'd decided to hell with it. It *was* her day off, so everyone could simply take her as she was.

Tate hopped from foot to foot. "What's taking him so darn long?"

"For heaven's sake, Tate. We've been waiting less than five minutes. You're not late yet and Billy will still be there, so do us both a favor and take a nice, deep breath and settle down."

He not only took a deep breath, he blew it out in a loud sigh of impatience. But then the lodge truck rounded the bend and he brightened. "Finally! Here he comes!" He snatched his backpack up off the sidewalk and slung it over his shoulders, then strained toward the approaching truck like a compass needle to magnetic north. A huge smile suddenly split his face. "Hey, look, Mom, it's J.D.!"

"Ducky." A hot rush of blood flushed her throat and cheeks. Of all the volunteers Aunt Sophie could have drummed up, she'd had to enlist *his* help? Was there no justice in the world?

Dru squared her shoulders. Well, she would simply have to make the best of it, for it was a done deal now. Meeting J.D.'s dark-eyed gaze with a cool look of her own when he leaned over to push open the passenger door, she said, "Good afternoon."

"Hey, J.D.!" Tate's greeting was much more exuberant as he clambered up into the cab. "You gonna get a bathing suit while you're in town?"

"Yeah, I thought I might." The smile J.D. gave Tate faded when he gazed past him at Dru. He nodded briefly. "Drucilla."

"J.D." She swung up into the cab and pulled the door closed, grateful that her son was separating them.

Which only went to prove that old "Don't count your chickens" adage. For no sooner had she admonished Tate to buckle up than he turned to her.

"Trade places with me, Mom." Without awaiting a reply, he scrambled over her. "I wanna look out the window."

And that quickly, she found herself brushing shoulders with J.D. every time he reached to shift gears.

Luckily, the trip down the mountain was a short one. They were soon cruising along Star Lake's Main

Street, with Tate bouncing on the seat with increasing enthusiasm. Turning to Dru, he said, "I don't hafta go with you and J.D. to get the air conditioner, do I, Mom?"

Her lips curved up. "No, I think that would be more than we can expect your patience to bear."

They pulled into the Drooders' driveway a few moments later. The side door banged open and Billy burst out into the yard. Tate threw open the truck door while J.D. was still killing the engine, and the two boys raced toward each other, meeting in the middle of the yard in a full-body slam. The sheer force of it knocked the boys on their rumps in the grass, where they flopped, guffawing hysterically.

Dru shook her head and smiled ruefully. Sliding over on the seat, she leaned out the truck window and waved to Billy's mother, who had stepped out the door in her son's wake. "Better you than me," she called.

Mary Drooder laughed. "Oh, they'll be fine. We've got some activities planned for today and they're going to rent some videos for this evening."

Dru felt the tiniest twinge of concern. "About what they watch, Mary—"

"You haven't met J.D. yet, have you, Mrs. D.?" Tate interrupted, and something that sounded suspiciously like a choked laugh emerged from J.D. When Dru turned to look at him, however, his face was perfectly composed. He cleared his throat, and she decided he must have had a little tickle in it. Turning back to Mary, who had come up to the truck, she performed the introductions.

J.D.'s forearm brushed her breasts as he leaned past

her to offer his hand to Mary. To distract herself from the sudden rush of heat, she scrambled to remember what she'd begun to say before she'd been interrupted. Hadn't there been something that had sent up a red flag in her mind? Oh, yes, the videos. "About the videos the boys rent—"

"J.D. kissed Mom," Tate said. "On his front porch. He went like this." Tate mimicked a pose that looked horrifyingly carnal.

Every thought in Dru's head fled as a scalding rush of blood suffused her face. "Tate Lawrence!"

J.D. roared with laughter and fired up the truck's engine. "Enjoy those videos, Tate," he said and tipped his head at Mary Drooder, who stared at them in open-mouthed fascination. "It was nice meeting you." He put the truck in gear, and twisted to look over his shoulder as he backed out of the driveway.

"You think that was *funny*?" Dru could feel the blood throb in her cheeks as she sat staring blindly out the window in utter mortification. A bitter laugh escaped her throat. "But then, why shouldn't you? People will merely think you're quite the stud."

"Oh, lighten up, Drucilla. Nobody's going to brand you the slut of Star Lake just because I kissed you. The way you're carrying on, you'd think I screwed your brains out against that post."

"Don't call me that!" Somehow it was easier to concentrate on the way he invariably used her entire name—instead of calling her Dru like everyone else—rather than on the fact that the entire town of Star Lake would soon know they'd been kissing on his porch . . . and was quite likely to brand her exactly that.

To be fair, J.D. had no idea that she'd had Tate out of wedlock. She wasn't ashamed of the fact—not when it had brought her Tate. But she'd worked hard to prove to the people of Star Lake that she *wasn't* a young woman of loose morals. J.D. was probably the only person in town who didn't know her entire life history, and she'd really like to keep it that way.

He looked over at her. "Why not? Drucilla's your name, isn't it?"

"Yes, but hardly anyone calls me that." At least not anyone she was desperately trying to keep at a distance.

"Your aunt does." He shrugged. "Besides, I like it; it's different."

"No kidding it's different. It's ridiculous, is what it is, and if you want to call me that, then you have to tell me what J.D. stands for. It's not fair that you get to know my given name when I don't know yours."

"John David."

She made a rude noise. "Well, big whoop. That's a perfectly nice name." She'd been hoping for something even more unusual than her own. Then she shot him a suspicious look. "You're making that up, aren't you? It's probably really Jebediah Dorkal, or some such."

He downshifted into second as he approached the stop sign at Main, then eased on the brakes. Once the truck had rolled to a stop, he shifted onto one hip and fished his wallet out of his back pocket. He lobbed it into her lap.

She flipped it open and read his driver's license.

Sure enough, it read *John David Carver*. "Well, hell." She tossed the wallet back in disgust.

He snatched it out of the air and shoved it back in his pocket. A faint smile curving up one corner of his mouth, he tipped his head toward Main Street and said, "Which way to the hardware store?"

"Left."

Aside from a couple of terse directions, she didn't say anything else, and J.D. caught himself shooting sidelong glances her way. It was the damnedest thing, but he felt . . . good. That wasn't exactly a feeling he was familiar with, and, God knew, it didn't make a lick of sense. The Lawrences had practically handed him proof on a silver platter that they talked out of both sides of their mouths. They treated him like family with one breath, then contacted the family lawyer to cut him out of his share of the lodge with the other, and he was furious with the lot of them.

Except . . . Dru hadn't appeared to know anything about it. Had she known, she never would have given away the fact that the message was from Ben's lawyer.

But that was hardly cause to regard her as his new best friend. She'd been pretty clear that she considered him a pimple on the butt of humanity. So why was he sitting here next to her feeling so damn good all of a sudden?

Hell. He hunched over the wheel defensively. It was probably just because this beat being hounded to kingdom come by Robbie Lankovich. Or maybe it was because Dru had a mouth on her that he found semi-entertaining. For someone he'd pegged as a little Hetty

Homemaker, she was a constant surprise. She seemed constitutionally incapable of being anything but politeness personified with the lodge guests—but she sure as hell was fearless when it came to being rude to him.

Or maybe this feeling of happiness didn't have anything to do with her at all. Perhaps it was just residual amusement at the way Tate had played his mother to keep her from putting any restrictions on his viewing material. You had to admire the kid's killer instincts; he'd gone straight for the jugular.

They pulled up in front of the hardware store a few moments later. J.D. intended to get Dru's door for her, but he was only halfway around the back of the truck when she slammed the cab door shut behind her. She immediately set off for the store's front entrance, and he had to take a couple of giant quicksteps just to catch up. He arrived in time to reach out in front of her and open the door, then stood back and indicated with a wave of his hand that she should proceed him. She sailed through, giving him a look that a young queen might have given a peasant getting notions above his station. He bared his teeth at her and followed in her wake.

The store was doing a fairly brisk Saturday-afternoon business. Several men perused the goods on the shelves, one couple wrangled good-naturedly over paint chips, and three old men stood around a display of lighting fixtures, shooting the breeze.

Then J.D. and Dru walked down the main aisle, and the place went dead silent. J.D. found it slightly unnerving, and he thought for a moment that it must have something to do with those teaser shorts and not-quite-long-enough top Dru had on. Although her outfit was far from risqué, *he* was having a hard time keeping his eyes off the here-and-gone flashes of flesh as she moved. The momentary peek at the pale curve of her waist. The lush hint of hip.

Hell, it *rated* a moment of silence, if you asked him.

But when he made eye contact with the other people, he noticed that every eye in the place appeared to be on him.

Then conversations resumed as suddenly as they'd stopped, but on a quieter, more distracted level, and it was clear that nobody was willing to get so caught up in a discussion that he might miss out on something.

Dru seemed not to notice. She walked straight to the counter in the back of the store. "Afternoon, Harvey."

"Hey, Dru." A tall, thin man with a tubular nosepiece that led to a canister of oxygen nodded at her in a friendly manner, then thoroughly checked out J.D. "I imagine you're here to pick up the AC unit."

"Yes. Aunt Sophie said it finally came in."

"Yep. It's in the back. I can have Kev bring it out for you, if you'd like." He inclined his head toward J.D. "Or is that what he's here for?"

"Kev's back?" Dru's smile was so brilliant it made J.D. blink. "I thought he was some hotshot attorney in D.C. these days."

"He's taking a little time away. About your man here—"

"Oh! Yes! I'm sorry; I didn't introduce you, did I? This is J.D. Carver." She turned to him. "J.D., Harvey Bronsen. Bronsen's Hardware, as you've probably figured out, belongs to him." Turning her attention back to the proprietor, she said, "J.D.'s our new partner at the lodge."

It always took him by surprise when she publicly admitted his claim to Star Lake Lodge, but he kept his face impassive as the older man once again subjected him to a close scrutiny. Then Bronsen nodded and said, "I'll just go get that unit."

J.D. looked around while they waited. He was engaged in a stare-down with one of the geezers over by the lighting display when he felt Dru suddenly come to full alert next to him.

A deep voice exclaimed her name, and she said, "Oh, my God! Kev?" A tall man strode out of the doorway, flipped up the pass-through in the counter, and walked straight up to her, picking her up and twirling her around. Dru clutched his shoulders and laughed, and J.D.'s fists clenched at his sides as the heat of an uncharacteristic emotion roared hot and furious through his veins.

It was all he could do not to plant one in Kev-the-attorney's smiling face.

10

Dru had known Kev Bronsen forever. They'd gone through school together since the fourth grade, when Dru's living arrangements with her aunt and uncle had become permanent.

They'd never been more than friends, though, and it was pure relief to be swung around in a man's arms without having her face heat up or her heart pound out an erratic tattoo. She hugged him with sheer enthusiastic gratitude when he set her back on her feet. "It's so good to see you," she said and gave him a light peck on the lips.

A deep-throated sound like a dog's warning snarl caused her to step smartly back from her old friend, and she twirled around, her heart rate unaccountably jacked into hyperdrive. Then she felt like an idiot, for J.D. merely stood with his hands in his pockets, shoulders relaxed and his face perfectly noncommittal, as he observed the two of them.

Her own posture went ramrod-militant. Even if that territorial sound had come from him, what was she doing jumping like a nervous girlfriend trying to avoid displeasing her lover? She could kiss whomever she darn well pleased.

She dredged up her manners. "Kev, this is J.D. Carver. J.D., Kev Bronsen."

They regarded each other silently for a moment. Then Kev stepped around her and extended a hand to shake. J.D.'s hands remained firmly jammed in his pockets and he merely nodded. "Bronsen."

Dru wound her arm through Kev's when his hand dropped to his side, and she shot J.D. a glare. "Don't mind him," she said. "He prides himself on his lousy manners."

"Hey." J.D. shrugged. "Guy's gotta glory in his accomplishments."

"Not to worry, sugar," Kev said coolly. Stroking Dru's arm with a familiarity that was nearly sexual and not at all like him, he bared his teeth at J.D. "I know exactly what his problem is."

That was more than Dru did. She didn't like the way J.D.'s eyes narrowed and he suddenly straightened, or the combative light in Kev's eyes. What was it with guys and their eternal pissing contests?

She dropped Kev's arm and took a step that brought her midway between both men. "Lucky we're in a hardware store," she said. "It shouldn't be a problem to find a tape measure to determine who has the biggest one."

There was an instant of thunderous silence. Then: "She's pretty cute when she gets all testy, isn't she?" Kev said and reached for her braid.

Dru dodged his touch. The move backed her into J.D., and the hands he reached out to steady her when she stumbled over his big feet were hard and warm.

"You get that tape measure." His voice was a low growl in her ear. "And you won't ever give pencil-dick there another thought."

She leaped forward as if she'd been goosed. Dammit! This was supposed to be her R and R, and here she was getting all riled up. If she ruled the world, men would never be allowed on the streets on a woman's day off. She turned to Kev, who at the moment was only an increment above J.D. on her favor meter. "So what brings you home?" she demanded. "Are you here on vacation?"

"Nope. I've moved back."

"You're kidding—you couldn't wait to get out of town! It's all you ever talked about."

"Yeah, well." He rolled his shoulders uncomfortably. "Turns out big-city living wasn't all that I thought it would be."

"But aren't you an associate in some happening D.C. law practice?"

"Was. I left." He must have seen she was about to demand details, for he smiled slightly and said, "I'm not saying I'll stay here forever, Dru. But Dad's not in the best of health, and I didn't like some of my practice's practices, so to speak. It was a good time to come home."

"Speaking of your old man," J.D. interrupted, "I

haven't got all day. Where did he disappear to with that air-conditioning unit?"

"Probably out back, sneaking a smoke."

Dru stared at Kev, horrified. "He's on oxygen, and he's still *smoking*?"

He shrugged. "Might as well. His emphysema is pretty far advanced, so quitting at this point's not going to buy him much time."

"Blowing himself up by lighting matches around an oxygen tank could shorten it considerably, though."

"Yeah, well, that's Dad. But to be fair, he does unhook the canister and turn it off before he lights up."

As if he'd heard his name, Harvey banged through the back-room door, pushing the air-conditioning unit in front of him on a hand truck. He wheeled it up to Dru and slapped an invoice on the counter. "Here you go. Sign your John Hancock at the *X* there, and you're on your way."

She had just finished signing her name when a feminine voice said, "Rumors are flying fast and furious around town that you came in here with a good-lookin' guy."

Dru looked up to see Char sashaying down the aisle, and she smiled. "Hey, there. I was going to stop by to see you this afternoon, but my plans got changed when Aunt Soph asked me to pick up this AC unit we've been waiting on." Patting the box in question, she indicated J.D. with a tilt of her chin. "She roped J.D. into coming along to provide the muscle."

"And it's that very muscle that's got the whole town buzzing," Char said and flashed him her trademark flirty smile. But when she saw the man who stood slightly behind him, the humor dropped away from her face. "Well, wouldja look at what the dog dug up. You slumming in the old stomping grounds for a couple of weeks, Kev?"

"Hell, no," he said. "If I'd wanted to slum, I would've headed straight for your place."

"I see you haven't lost your charm," she said flatly. "When are you slithering back to the big city?"

Dru winced. Char and Kev had never gotten along. Their antipathy had been the bane of her existence back in high school, when she'd wanted nothing more than for them to like each other as much as she'd liked them both. She'd have thought that maturity would've lessened their hostility, but that didn't appear to be the case. "Kev's moved back, Char."

"Be still, my heart." The blonde pinned her gaze on him. "So where's the little woman and your two-point-five kiddies, stretch? Tucked up at your father's house?"

"Nope. The little woman left me for someone who didn't work sixteen hours a day, and the kiddies never happened. How about you? Manage to lasso a husband yet? Or is that what brings you here—the need for more rope?"

J.D. stirred beside Dru. "Much as I'm enjoying the Punch and Judy show," he said, "I have some other errands to run. I'll go wrestle this unit into the truck."

Dru never would have believed his company would be more appealing than Char's or Kev's, but she found herself saying, "I'll go with you—I've got a few errands of my own." She looked over at her friends, who had barely spared them a glance. The atmosphere between them was thick with tension. "I'll see you two later."

"Christ," J.D. muttered a few moments later as he squatted to get his arms around the heavy box. "Any more sexual friction between those two and the place'd go up in flames."

Dru felt her mouth drop open. She snapped it closed. "As usual, you've got it all wrong. They don't even *like* each other. They never have."

He rose to his feet, the muscles in his shoulders, arms, and back jumping to prominent relief beneath his T-shirt as he tussled the unit onto the bed of the truck. When he got it situated he looked at her, and his pitying expression set Dru's teeth on edge. "Whatever you say."

"It's not what I *say*, Carver. It's a fact."

"Uh-huh."

"Dammit, don't patronize—" She found herself addressing his back when he turned on his heel and walked away. "Hey! Where do you think you're going?"

"To get myself some swim trunks."

She strode after him. "So you just walk away in the middle of a conversation? I was talking to you!"

"Oh, was that a conversation? Sounded to me like it was gearing up to be a tirade." Without lessening his stride, he shot her a glance. "It's my day off, blue eyes—I don't have to listen to one of your lectures."

His day off? Digging her knuckles into her temples, she emitted a soft shriek of frustration.

That made him grin, a genuine smile of amusement

such as she'd seen directed only at her son. "You're an interesting woman, Drucilla."

"I can't tell you how happy I am to provide you with a moment of comic relief." She had to lengthen her stride to keep up with him as he headed for the Mercantile. "You could've bought a suit in the lodge's sport shop, you know."

His laugh was short and derisive. "Yeah, right. Have you looked at that stock lately? It sells Speedos, and that's it."

"What's the matter with Speedos?"

"Aside from the fact that they're butt-ugly and there's no way in hell I'm wearing one? Not a damn thing."

"Butt-ugly, huh? Hmmm. I'm so glad you took the time to share that thoughtfully concise evaluation with me. I'll make a note to order some boxer-style trunks—in case some of our guests are as unevolved as you."

He pushed open the door and stood back to let her precede him. "Unevolved. Is that what you call it when a guy doesn't care to squeeze his package into half an ounce of shrink wrap?"

She resisted the urge to drop her gaze to the package in question and tipped her nose up instead as she breezed past him. "For a guy who bragged he'd win the my-dingus-is-bigger-than-yours contest, I would've thought that'd be right up your alley."

"Only if I wanted to start a riot, sweetheart. Showcase the Natural Wonder like that and we'd have to call in the National Guard. Not to mention I'd never get a moment's peace again from the females in Star Lake."

She stopped dead in her tracks. "My God," she breathed in near admiration. "I have never *met* anyone with such incredible balls."

He shrugged modestly. "That's what I've been trying to tell you."

Okay, lousy choice of words. She willed her face not to turn red. When her willpower didn't have any noticeable effect, she deliberately dropped her gaze to the equipment in question. She studied it long and hard. Then she looked up into his hazel-green eyes and shrugged. "I've seen bigger and better."

But only in her dreams. The truth was, she hadn't seen the real deal in years. Stalking away, she made it around the end of one aisle and halfway down the next before collapsing against a shelf of bath towels.

Hands to her hot cheeks, she sucked air deep into her lungs and held it. Expelled it and sucked in some more in an attempt to catch her breath. She now knew he dressed to the left. And that his . . . package . . . was darn near as impressive as he claimed. Okay, *as* impressive. Especially when it'd started crowding his fly at her prolonged examination. The idea of seeing *that* in the honest-to-God flesh had the blood surging to her cheeks all over again.

But she'd strip naked and parade down Main Street before she'd massage his already huge ego by admitting it.

Not wanting to be caught hyperventilating among the bath accessories, she moved away from the shelf and went to grab a handbasket. As long as she was here, she might as well get a few of the toiletries she was running low on.

Cruising the aisles, she thought about the little bomb that J.D. had lobbed about Char and Kev. Could he be right? She'd love to reject the notion out of hand, but had to admit the desire probably stemmed from a knee-jerk need to say black when J.D. said white. And that was something she had to quit doing. Who would have believed, before he'd blown into her life, that she had it in her to be so reactive?

Now that the idea of Char and Kev striking sexual sparks had been raised, she had to concede it had a certain kind of logic. But wow. Wouldn't *that* set tongues to wagging if folks caught on. There was nothing Star Lake liked quite so much as its gossip.

More important, Dru wondered if either Char or Kev realized what they were doing . . . or if it was only she who had been so slow to catch on.

J.D. watched Dru stare at a display of toilet plungers and mutter to herself. When she turned away, he found himself tracking the sway of her hips and her long legs as she moseyed down the aisle. With a soft oath, he tore his gaze away and went back to the stack of swim trunks. He had to quit spending so much time looking at her. And he *really* had to quit messing with her the way he'd done earlier.

Back in high school, he used to watch the good girls—during class, in the hallways, on the campus. When they caught him at it, he wouldn't look away, getting a bittersweet sort of charge out of seeing them blush and scramble to get out of his range. The phase hadn't lasted long—he'd outgrown the need to fluster them long before he'd graduated. Yet here he was, reverting to his old ways.

He didn't know what it was about her. Partly, he supposed, it was that same old fascination with good girls rearing its ugly head. He'd figured out long ago *that* was a product of envisioning the sort of upbringing they'd had—the house, the yard, the mother and father who doted on them. And despite Dru's having Tate out of wedlock, he considered her one of them. There was just something sort of luminous about her. Something untouched.

Yet she refused to be pigeonholed, and every time he thought he had her securely pegged, she slipped out of the niche he'd assigned her. She was no pushover scrambling to stay out of his way. When she'd turned around and scoped out the Natural Wonder until it'd started unfurling—then told him she'd seen better—he'd been mighty tempted to crowd her up against the nearest solid surface, and hadn't particularly cared if it was horizontal or vertical.

He'd show her better.

He gave up the search for a pair of swim trunks as a lost cause. The stock seemed to consist of either blindingly neon, baggy to the point of ridiculous, or garish Hawaiian prints. The hell with it. He'd hack off a pair of jeans and call it good.

As he passed a postcard rack, he stopped to check out the selection. He'd washed his hands of Butch, yet he still found himself picking out a card for him. His shoulders twitched defensively. So big deal, it would cost him a quarter. He probably wouldn't even send it.

He caught a glimpse of Dru again over by the rack of women's bathing suits. She was holding up an animal-print tankini and still looked to be firmly entrenched in shopping mode, so he headed for the back of the store where he'd seen a tool aisle. He didn't expect much in such a catchall kind of store, but checking out tools was always good for killing ten minutes or so.

He tried not to speculate what Drucilla would look like in that suit.

The array of tools was pretty much what he'd expected, though there were a few good pieces mixed in with the usual low-grade imported stuff. He pored over the selection for a while, chose a five-eighths drill bit he'd been looking for, then went to see if there was anything worthwhile back on the endcap.

He hit paydirt.

The endcap display itself didn't hold anything of interest, but suspended from the ceiling against the back wall was a canoe. He stared at it, transfixed.

He'd always wanted a canoe. He and Butch had helped themselves to one from the Arboretum rental shed at the University of Washington once, and paddled around for a couple of the best hours of his life before being chased off by the rental shack's owner.

This canoe was not new by any stretch of the imagination. It was old and beat-up, but he didn't care. He wanted it. He headed for the front of the store.

Dru was talking to the clerk at the checkout stand, her purchases in a plastic bag that swung from one hand. For the first time since he'd clapped eyes on her, he barely spared her a glance. He focused on the woman behind the cash register. "How much do you want for that canoe back there?"

She blinked. "The canoe? That old one? Why . . . I

don't have the faintest idea. Let me call Fred." She came out from behind the checkout station and walked partway down the main aisle. "Fred!" she hollered. "Can you come up here?"

Moments later an older man with more tufts of hair growing out of his ears than his head trotted up the aisle. "What d'ya need?"

The woman, who had been inspecting J.D. while they waited, indicated him with a jerk of her thumb. "He wants to know how much for Davey's canoe."

"You're kiddin'." The man stared at J.D. "The thing's a wreck, son. I only put it up in the first place to humor my grandson, because he wouldn't believe me when I told him that no one in their right mind would ever buy it."

"I will."

Dru slid her hands in her pockets, the bag dangling from her wrist. "That still makes you half right," she told Fred.

J.D. ignored her. "How much?"

"Well, I can let you have it fairly cheap." Fred scratched his bald pate. "But you have to understand that I won't guarantee its seaworthiness."

"I'm a carpenter. I'll make it seaworthy."

"You ever work on a boat before, son?"

"No." J.D. shrugged. "But how hard can it be?"

The older man opened his mouth as if to argue, but Dru jumped in.

"Save your breath, Fred," she advised. "J.D.'s got the biggest ego the region's ever seen. When it comes to his carpentry, though, it's justified: he's already taken on a couple of jobs up at the lodge, and his work is spectacular."

J.D. looked at her in surprise. She was championing him? His amazement must have shown, for she shrugged and shot him a crooked smile of self-deprecation, as if she couldn't quite believe it herself.

He turned back to the shop owner. "Well?"

Fred shrugged good-naturedly. "Hey, if you want it, it's yours. My grandson will be thrilled."

J.D. grinned. "Yesss."

A short while later he looked up from carefully fitting the canoe into the truck bed next to the air conditioner and saw Dru watching him with a slight smile. Embarrassed to be caught stroking the boat, he growled, "What? You think I'm an sucker, don't you?"

"There's one born every minute, they say."

He narrowed his eyes at her. "Then this should give you a great big charge."

"Oh, it does. But not because I think you're such a sucker; that remains to be seen." She gave him a gentle smile. "I like to see people go after their dreams, and I got a charge out of seeing you get something you obviously want very much." She opened the passenger door and climbed in, leaving him staring after her.

Well . . . damn. How was he supposed to respond to that?

11

J.D. thought about her words off and on all that afternoon. He thought about them into the evening, and right through to the next afternoon, returning to them over and over again. Going after his dream, his ass—no one had a stupid boat as a dream.

The sun was hot on his shoulders and he heard the mellow tinkle of a wind chime someone had hung from his porch roof; contentment filled him as he used a block of sandpaper to stroke away cracked paint from the bottom of the canoe. Where did she come up with this shit? It was just a project to keep him sane when his next indoor job had him going stir-crazy.

He attacked a particularly rough spot on the canoe's surface, then tenderly slicked his hand in the sandpaper's wake to check for smoothness, thinking about where he'd take it out first. Maybe the far end of the lake, where it was mostly wilderness. He wondered if the tiny library up at the lodge had any books on boats. If not, maybe he should run to town and pick one up. It always paid to collect as much information as you could in order to do the best job possible. That wasn't pursuing a dream, it was simply common sense.

He was just thinking about knocking off for a while when Ben walked into the clearing. Shading his eyes, J.D. watched him approach. He set his sanding block aside and straightened.

Ben walked up, handed him a beer, then looked down at the canoe resting bottom-up between two sawhorses. "I heard you got yourself an old boat to fix up."

J.D. eyed him suspiciously. "So you thought you'd just mosey on over and offer me a little avuncular advice?"

"Nope." Ben twisted the cap off his own beer and lit a cigarette. "Sophie likes you, and it's upset her that you're pissed at us." He slid the lighter back into his pocket and met J.D.'s gaze squarely. "We've got this new saying around our place: when Sophie ain't happy, ain't *nooo*body happy. So I thought I'd mosey on over and clear the air."

"That's pretty ironic, considering what you're doing with that cigarette."

"Oh, Christ, don't tell me you're one of those. I've gotten so flippin' p.c. lately, I hardly recognize myself. I don't smoke in restaurants; I don't smoke in the car. I gave up smoking indoors period, and I even gave it up *outdoors* when Tate's around. Damned if I'm gonna give it up outside for you, too. Here, I'll move downwind. Is that better?"

"Much. Thanks."

"Don't mention it. Now, I came over here today to set the record straight. My contacting a lawyer had nothing to do with you or Edwina's bequest. Dru's—" He cut himself off and leveled a look at J.D. "This goes no further than you and me, capeesh?"

"Yeah, I get it."

"Good. Dru's turning thirty in a couple of weeks, and I contacted Henry Briggs to look into what it'll take to transfer a third of our shares to her and make her a partner in the lodge. Telling you in front of her would've spoiled the surprise."

J.D. thumped his beer bottle down on the sawhorse that held the upside-down canoe. Anger built with slow heat in his gut. "What do you take me for—a moron? There was something different in your attitude before I ever mentioned that phone call." He glared at the older man. "I wasn't hatched yesterday, Pops, so do us both a favor and don't try to blow smoke up my ass."

"You *are* a moron, Carver, if you think I don't have more balls than to sneak around behind your back, trying to contest your claim. My so-called attitude didn't have a damn thing to do with your inheritance from Edwina. It was because I'd heard you were messing with Dru!"

J.D. felt his jaw fall open and closed his mouth with a snap. "Messing with her! I didn't *mess* with her—I kissed her one time!"

"Yeah, well, she's my baby and—"

"You said she was going to be thirty!"

"I know how old she's gonna be," Ben roared. "You think that makes a damn bit of difference?" Then he took a deep breath. "When it comes to your own, you never quit worrying, okay?"

"Fine." J.D. shrugged. He added bitterly, "But what you're actually saying is that I'm not the kind of guy you want getting his hands down your baby's pants, right?" He'd known that we're-all-just-one-big-happy-family-and-you're-a-part-of-it-now routine was pure crap.

Ben took an incensed step forward but then caught himself. "You don't strike me as the type who's real big on commitment, that's the truth." He sucked in a final drag of smoke, then rubbed the paper tube of his cigarette between his fingers until the coal dropped out. Stepping on it, he pocketed the spent butt and gave J.D. a skeptical look. "Or are you going to tell me I'm doing you an injustice?"

"No, you've pretty much hit that nail right on the head. What does a guy have to do, though, before he can kiss your niece—sign a declaration of intent?"

Ben whispered a profanity. Thrusting his hand through his thick gray hair, he stared at J.D. "Now you sound like Sophie. I'm not saying what I felt was rational, all right? I'm just telling you that if you detected a change in my attitude the other day, that was why."

"Fair enough," J.D. agreed slowly, wondering where the older man expected him to go from here.

"I'll make you a deal," Ben said. "I'll stay off your case about Dru if you'll stop by and see Soph periodically. For some reason she's got a real soft spot for you." He suddenly smiled, a friendly, crooked one full of warmth. "Like I could ever put a halt to anything Dru wanted, anyway, once she got it into her head. As everyone loves to remind me, she's a grown woman with a mind of her own. I guess if she wants you kissing her, you're gonna be kissing her."

"You don't think I might have something to say about that decision?"

Ben gave him a who-are-you-trying-to-kid look, and one corner of J.D.'s mouth tipped up. "Okay, so if Dru wants me kissing her, I'll probably kiss her." The thought of her making such a demand made a place low in his gut go hard and tight. Then he got real. "If it's any consolation, though, neither of us plans to go there. That kiss was a fluke, pure and simple."

Ben snorted. "You just keep telling yourself that, sport." He killed off his beer and turned to go. "Stop by and visit Sophie," he commanded.

J.D. watched him until he disappeared down the trail. That was a first. The type of woman he usually kissed didn't tend to inspire male relatives into paying him a visit.

He shrugged and turned to pick up his tools and supplies, then headed for the cabin to clean up. Might as well take a break and go see if he could find some books on canoes and boat building.

As he passed his small dining room table a moment later, the colorful postcard he'd bought for Butch caught his eye, and he stopped to pick it up. He'd written, *Glad you aren't here,* across the back. Then, thinking of their conversation a few days ago, he'd added, *But I'm still expecting to see your face plastered on the six o'clock news any day now.* He had addressed it, although he'd probably never get around to buying a stamp for the thing. Because, while he'd written the first part of it as a joke, he actually *was* glad Butch wasn't here.

This place felt worlds removed from his old neighborhood and all the wheeling, dealing, and jockeying for position that went on there. It still seemed god-awful quiet at night, but he liked hearing birds instead of traffic during the day, and smelling growing things instead of the weary scent of defeat and exhaust. It was pristine in more ways than the merely physical, and he had no desire to see pieces of his old life corrupting it.

He propped the card back up against the vase of wilting flowers on the table and headed for the bathroom to wash up.

"Come in," Dru called in response to the knock on her door. She flashed Char a smile when the door opened, then turned to snatch her rolled towel off the couch. "I'm almost ready. Let me just find my sunglasses."

"Look at you!" Char stepped into the apartment. "I didn't know you'd bought yourself a new bathing suit."

"I got it yesterday after I saw you at Bronsen's. The seat was pretty well shot on my old one." And she didn't want J.D. to see her in it again. Shrugging the thought aside, she struck a pose. "So what d'you think?"

Char shook her fingers. "Ossky wow-wow."

A surprised huff of laughter escaped Dru. "I haven't heard that expression since your grandpa died."

"I know, but it's appropriate. What I can see looks fabulous. Drop your shorts and I'll give you my opinion on the whole look."

Dru laughed a deep belly laugh. "I'm sure glad

nobody's around to hear you say that—this is how rumors get started."

"And considering neither one of us has had a date in way too long, it probably wouldn't stretch people's imaginations a heck of a lot to jump to the wrong conclusion. So let me rephrase that. Show me your suit in its entirety," Char said in an affected, societylike tone, "that I might judge its overall appearance."

"I'll show you when we reach the dock. No sense stripping down now, since I'd just have to put my cutoffs back on again." She grabbed her sunglasses off the kitchen counter.

"I don't want to see your stupid suit, anyhow."

Dru laughed. "You're such a liar, McKenna. You're probably already planning how to find one even better so you can one-up me."

"Damn. There's something sort of spooky about being known that well."

They grinned at each other, then turned as one for the door.

A short while later they spread their towels out on pads on the end of the Lawrences' private dock. Char plopped down on hers, set out her water bottle, magazine, and sunscreen, then looked up at Dru, who was still shucking out of her cutoffs. "Where's Tate today?"

"He spent the night at Billy's and he's still there. Mary was going to bring him home earlier, but the boys were having such a good time, she called to ask if he could stay until dinner." Kicking her shorts aside, Dru twisted around to look at herself over her shoulder. "Okay, be honest—does this animal print make my butt look too big?"

"It's a tankini! I thought it was a one-piece. How chic. And no, you boob, it looks great. What is it with you and your butt, anyway? I wish I had half your curves."

"I wish I had half of 'em, too."

Char laughed and tossed her the bottle of sunscreen. "Here, get my back, will you?"

Dru knelt behind her and shook the lotion down toward the cap.

"I couldn't believe it when you just walked off and left me stuck with Kev yesterday," Char groused into her folded arms. "Thanks a bunch—some friend you are."

Dru, who had just poured the sunscreen into her palm, stared at her friend's back in amazement. "Are you serious? I told you I was taking off, and the two of you barely blinked. My God, I told J.D. he was wrong, but he had you guys pegged dead to rights. You and Kev were so focused on each other, I could have set off a *bomb* and you wouldn't have noticed."

Char rolled over. "What are you saying?"

"That the two of you were all caught up in some verbal foreplay thing."

"Are you *nuts*?"

"Quite possibly. But not about this." Resting back on her heels, Dru rubbed her hands together and applied lotion to her own arms. She met her friend's perturbed gaze. "The air between you was positively charged with electricity, Char. *Sexual* electricity. Have you had the hots for him since high school, or is this a new development?"

"I don't have the hots for him!"

"In denial, huh?"

"Dammit, Dru, knock it off. We just rub each other the wrong way. We always have; you know that." Char apparently didn't like the expression on Dru's face, for she added belligerently, "If you're so blessed eager to discuss hot attractions, what's the story between you and J.D.?"

"If you expect me to get all defensive on you, Char, I'll have to disappoint you. Because the truth is, I think I'm in deep, deep trouble—and that's not even counting the fact that Tate told Mary about J.D. kissing me, so the entire town is probably humming about it as we speak. I'm physically attracted to him, and that's hard enough to deal with. But now I keep seeing these hints that there's more to him than I thought."

"Like what?"

Dru settled back on her towel and started to apply sunscreen to her legs. "He's usually so darn controlled that it's hard to get a clue to what he's all about, but I'm catching glimpses of an honest-to-God person beneath that stony facade. Someone lonely, who hasn't had much given to him in his life. You remember how I told you he was with Aunt Soph's crème brûlée?"

"All I remember you saying is that he all but licked his bowl."

"I didn't mention how the look on his face while he ate it made me realize that his upbringing probably lacked a lot of the things you and I take for granted?"

"No. Funny how you kept that part to yourself."

"Yeah, well . . ." Dru shifted self-consciously on her towel. "Anyway, yesterday he bought that old canoe that's been hanging in back of the Merc."

"That wreck that belongs to Fred's grandkid?"

"Yeah. Except you would've thought it was a brand-new, shiny red wagon and that he was Tate's age, he was so thrilled." A brief laugh escaped her. "He'd probably wear pink frillies before admitting that, but it showed, Char, and it was all I could do not to haul him in and hug him to my breast."

Char lowered her sunglasses to look at her. "Would that have been so awful?"

"Hell, yes. It's a terrifying thought. I can't exactly trust my own judgment when it comes to men, can I? After Tony?"

"For heaven's sake, Dru, you were nineteen years old! You're going to be thirty next month—I think your ability to judge a man's character has probably matured by now."

"Yeah, you'd think so, wouldn't you? I'm sure it works that way for most people. But while I certainly feel *older* than I did when I was convinced Tony was my One True Love, I don't feel all that more mature."

"So, what, then? You aren't even going to take a shot at it and see where it might lead you? The worst thing that could happen is you might get laid."

"No, that would be the best thing that could happen. I remember *liking* sex, and it's gotta be like riding a bike—I'm sure it comes back to you no matter how long it's been. The worst thing would be that I've utterly mistaken the hints of vulnerability I think I've seen in J.D., and I'd get my heart stomped into the ground once again. I've spent too many years building a good life for Tate and myself to just rush to the edge of a cliff and blindly hurl myself into the emotional abyss."

"Great metaphor. A little pessimistic, perhaps, but very visual."

"Yeah?" Dru looked Char straight in the eye. "I freely acknowledge I'm terrified to risk my emotional welfare by pursuing a relationship with J.D. But at least I don't deny there's something there to *be* pursued."

That effectively ended the conversation, since Char wasn't willing to do the same. Still, Dru gave it extensive thought later, when she was alone.

Was she the worst sort of coward to not even try? Maybe J.D. did have the depths she was beginning to suspect he had. Tate sure was crazy about him, and Aunt Sophie seemed to like him a lot as well.

Of course, Tate was crazy about snakes, too; and Aunt Soph was a victim of her hormones these days, and therefore not the most reliable judge in the world.

For several moments she dreamily considered the seductive vision of J.D. in that carpenter's belt, repairing all the things around here that had long needed repairs. Then she pulled herself up short.

That was no reason to get involved with a guy who had trouble written all over him. There were plenty of fix-it guys right here in Star Lake whom she could hire . . . even if they weren't particularly reliable. Besides, J.D. was about a hundred and ninety pounds of heartache on the hoof.

So the smart thing would be to give him a wide berth until this fascination for him passed.

And she was nothing if not a smart woman.

12

Dru did a fairly decent job of avoiding J.D. for the next few days. She saw him working with the ground crew a couple of times, but fortunately those glimpses were few and far between, since she generally worked afternoons in the lodge and had left by the time his split shift started in the restaurant.

She heard about him, of course; it was too much to hope otherwise. Tate went to see him Monday morning to regale him with his adventures with Billy, and J.D. had let him stick around to help sand the canoe.

They discussed the boat's myriad details while they worked. Turned out it was constructed of edge-glued cedar strips that hadn't been properly cared for. J.D. talked sheer lines and keel lines to Tate, explained the finer points of bow stems, gunwales, thwarts, and the like. The two of them also carried on an ongoing debate as to whether the finished boat would look best painted red, black, or dark green. J.D. leaned toward red; Tate's vote went for the always macho black.

Dru knew all this because Tate related every blessed word, boundlessly and in faithful detail. If she heard that canoe's praises sung one more time, she just might scream.

Tonight, though, she was getting a break. Sophie and Ben had invited Tate to spend the evening with them, so it was their turn to pretend an interest in the never-ending "J.D. and the Canoe" stories. Perhaps that wasn't fair—Sophie most likely would listen with genuine interest. But Dru looked forward to a few hours' rest from having to hear about the man and his boat.

It was cause to celebrate, and she couldn't decide if that called for a trip to the Red Bull Saloon in town for a beer and a swirl around the dance floor, or for a nice stretch-out on the couch with a good book. She almost called Char to see if she had any plans for the evening, but she'd been surrounded by people all week. In the end she decided to make a bowl of popcorn and start that Janet Evanovich novel she'd had the gift shop order for her.

She was immersed in the story at eight o'clock when the phone rang. Laughing to herself over Stephanie's and Lula's antics, she stuck her finger in the book to mark her place and reached for the receiver. "Hello."

"Darling, it's me," Aunt Sophie said. "I'm sorry to break into your time alone, but we've got trouble over at the restaurant."

Dru swung her feet around and sat up, setting her book aside. "What kind of trouble?"

"Apparently the sous-chef's been hitting the sauce the entire shift, and is now quite drunk. Carlos is threatening to quit, and guess who's conveniently on hand to smooth things over?"

Oh, hell, J.D. was working at the restaurant. "I'm on my way."

Dru looked down at her tank top, jeans, and bare feet. There was no time to change, not as long as J.D. was their only hope of preventing Carlos from leaving. That, she knew from experience, called for diplomacy, flattery, and a little judicious flirting, none of which were exactly Mr. Charm's long suit. She slid her feet into a pair of sandals, pulled a denim shirt over her pink tank top to disguise her braless state, and hauled her loose hair out from beneath the collar, flipping it behind her to hang down her back.

As she ran down the three flights of stairs, she consoled herself with the knowledge that J.D.'s current stint was in the restaurant itself with the manager, not in the kitchen. The two divisions were run separately, each with its own hierarchy. So, really, how much damage could he do? By rights, he shouldn't even be involved.

She didn't see him in the restaurant when she arrived, though, and keeping her voice low, she asked the manager where he was.

"I'm sorry, Dru," he said. "When things starting flipping out of control in there, I tried to tell him we don't have any authority over the kitchen. But he said as part owner of this lodge, he damn well did."

She silently cursed. "How long ago?"

"Just a couple of minutes. After I called to alert Sophie to the situation."

"Okay." She blew out her breath. "You did the correct thing. So what about Greg? Is he as tanked as Sophie made it sound?"

" 'Fraid so."

"Great. Call Melinda and see if she can come in to take up the slack. Let me know immediately if that's going to be a problem." Then she strode with suppressed urgency toward the kitchen.

The moment she rounded the order station, the noise level escalated dramatically. Servers appeared in response to the buzzers attached to their belts, to pick up the round trays that contained their filled orders; others stopped to drop new orders off. Oven doors slammed, cooks yelled out their needs, and plates clattered as the kitchen crew pulled them off the rack beneath the heating lamp, to be decorated with the sauces and arranged on serving trays before being passed along to the chef to present his specialties. The pastry chef called for more melted chocolate for the paper cone he used to embellish a plate of assorted delicacies over at his table in the corner, and helpers squeezed between the appliances and the work stations as they ran to fill the various requests.

Conspicuously lacking in the cacophony were the chef's and sous-chef's voices. Ordinarily, they would be shouting out what they needed if an item wasn't conveniently at hand. Dru couldn't see Greg, but she spotted Carlos at the end of the stubby hallway by the screened back door, across the room.

And J.D., curse his hide, was headed straight for him.

Swell. Given J.D.'s steamroller people-management skills, she'd better do something pretty darn fast or she was going to be shy one highly creative, temperamental chef.

She shucked off her shirt as she threaded her way between the workers, and hooked it over an empty stool pushed up against the wall. Reaching into the low scoop of her tank top, she slid her fingers around to the outer curve of first one breast, then the other, and hauled everything front and center to maximize her cleavage. As she stuffed the hem into her waistband to keep the tank's neckline low, she heard Carlos speak.

"What you want?" he demanded with his customary arrogance, though his faint Spanish accent gave the words a musical flavor. "You don't belong here and I don't want to deal with you."

"That's tough," J.D. said, "because look around you, pal—I'm who's available."

Carlos drew himself up to his full height. "I am not your pal, señor, and this"—a wave of his hand indicated the activity around them—"is unacceptable. I cannot and will not work like this. How am I supposed to maintain creativity when my sous-chef is stinking drunk?"

"By doing the best you can in a bad situation."

"No. The conditions, they are impossible, and I don't put up with them. I am Carlos. I can get a job anywhere in the world just—like—that!" He snapped his fingers.

J.D. took a step forward, getting right in the other man's face. The chef was actually a little taller, Dru noticed, but that didn't stop J.D. from stating with flat menace, "I can break every bone in your body just like that, too—and don't think I'll hesitate to do so if you don't haul your high-strung ass back to work."

No, no, no, no, NO! Dru hurriedly propelled herself forward again. You had to stroke Carlos' ego; threats only made him dig in and defend his position.

Carlos thrust his head forward like an enraged bull until the two men literally stood nose to nose. Aggression rolled off them in waves. "You can certainly try, señor." He regarded J.D. with haughty disdain. "I welcome you to do so. Then, after I knock you on your scrawny gringo buttocks, I'll sue you for assault and battery. That is the American way, and I"—he slapped his chest—"am a naturalized citizen. I will enjoy owning a part of this lodge, knowing it was once yours."

The look on J.D.'s face was priceless. Dru would have loved a moment to savor it, but they'd all be better served if she stepped in before the two men's egos swelled any further. She could practically smell the testosterone from here.

Dru took a deep breath and strode up to squeeze between them. Both men immediately took a step back to make room for her. Ignoring J.D. at her back, she leaned into the chef. "Oh, Carlos, I was so *sorry* to hear about Greg," she said. "What on earth set him off?"

He looked at her down the length of his aquiline nose. "Who knows with that one? His girlfriend—how you say it?—discharged him."

"Dumped, you moron," J.D. said. "The term is 'dumped.' "

Dru stepped backward, bringing her foot down hard on his instep as she reached out to pat Carlos' white-jacket-clad arm. "That must have played *hell* with your creativity!"

"It was impossible," Carlos said, but his voice lacked the heat it held when he'd said the same thing to J.D., for his attention had gotten snagged by Dru's cleavage. Dragging his gaze away, he said a bit more forcefully, "I cannot work like this!"

"Of course you can't," she agreed. "Genius like yours calls for a sous-chef who'll help, not *add* to your already considerable stress."

A snort sounded behind her and she dug her heel more forcefully into J.D.'s instep. He wrapped his hands around her hips and moved her off his foot. His palms continued to cup her, and she pried at his fingers with one hand while stroking Carlos' forearm with the other. The chef began to scowl at J.D., and Dru swiftly raised both arms and languidly twisted her hair up, holding it anchored atop her head. J.D.'s hands dropped away, and Carlos' attention swung back to her.

"I can't bear to see your brilliance disrupted like this, so I've called in Melinda," she said and let her hair fall, smoothing her hands down its length. "She's an excellent sous-chef, and she'll give you the help you deserve."

"Perhaps." He eyed her with male appreciation, but his priorities were, as always, firmly entrenched in his career and sense of self, and he added haughtily, "But don't expect me to lift a finger until she arrives."

"Of course not. We'll just have one of the cooks prepare the orders that are already up." She looked at him hopefully. "Perhaps the customers won't notice?"

He stiffened with outrage. "The *line* cooks? I'll not have those cretins touching my dishes—the customers came to eat a Carlos Santiago creation!" He stormed back to his station, roaring directions to his crew.

"*Yes*!" Dru did a little victory wiggle, her hands pumping the air overhead. She felt great, absolutely great. She loved averting crises—it was so satisfying to figure out what a situation needed, and to do all she could to supply it.

Hard-skinned hands suddenly hauled her out through the screened back door and swung her around. She shook off the hair that had fallen over her eye, braced her hands against the lodge's exterior fieldstone wall at her back, and grinned up at J.D. "Smooth as ever, I see."

He slapped his hands on either side of her shoulders and scowled. "You're pretty damn pleased with yourself, aren't you?"

"Yes, I am." She nodded, feeling high and full of herself. "Very pleased. I circumvented what could have been a big-time mess. *I* did that. Not you, *me*."

"Yeah, by shaking your tits in his face. That was professional."

"As opposed to threatening to break his bones, you mean?" She laughed in his face. "Admit it, Carver. You're just jealous."

To her surprise, his face flushed. "I'm not jealous. I don't give a rat's ass if you want to shake—"

She poked him in the sternum. "You are *such* a liar. You're absolutely *green* knowing that my method worked, while yours blew up in your face." She laughed again, feeling excited and reckless. With a boldness she hadn't felt in years, she slid her hands up the front of his polo shirt, appreciating the hard heat of his chest beneath the soft material. "But don't worry," she assured him huskily, "because I have a consolation prize for you."

And, raising up on her toes, she kissed him.

She felt gutsy and in charge—which lasted all of thirty seconds while she pressed her lips to J.D.'s. She eased her tongue across the slick inner curve of his lower lip, and coasted it over the hard edges of his teeth.

Then he made a sound deep in his throat and his hands came up to twine in her hair. And suddenly she was held fast as his mouth devoured hers and his tongue took charge, leading hers in a dance of uninhibited, primal rhythms.

He tasted of man and heat and hunger, and she knotted her fingers in the material on either side of his shirt's button placket and held on tight, kissing him back. She wanted to wrest the lead back from his control, but she was too breathless and aroused to make the effort. So she simply poured her heart and soul into kissing him the best she knew how.

It was apparently enough, for when he suddenly tore his mouth away he was breathing hard. "*God*," he panted. "You drive me crazy. I want to take you every way there is, strip you down and—" Licking his lower lip, he gathered her hair in both hands and piled it atop her head, holding it there while he lowered his head. Dru leaned back against the wall as she felt his open mouth, hot against the underside of her jaw. She shivered as he slowly dragged his lips down her neck, then again when his tongue lapped against the pulse that hammered in the hollow at the base of her throat.

Then everything went dark as he released her hair and it slid over her face, blinding her. She brought both hands up to push it out of her eyes, and out of habit twisted it up and held it anchored atop her head.

"Yes," J.D. rumbled in approval. "Like you did inside. I wanted to do this then." He curved his hands around her breasts.

His palms were hot and his fingers hard-skinned as they pressed her breasts together, lifted them, then tightened around them until her nipples poked like missiles against the fabric of her tank top. He bent his head and caught one between his lips, sucking it to a fuller extension.

"Omigod!" Blistering sensation zinged from her nipple to that hot, achy core between her thighs, and her arms dropped to her sides. Wrapping her hands around the back of J.D.'s head, she arched her back, pushing the tip of her breast deeper into his mouth.

He transferred his attention to its mate, then raised his head and stared at the wet fabric that clung to the hard thrust of her nipples. Flattening his hands against her breasts' fullness, he massaged the resilient globes, his clever fingers curving to capture the overflow. He seemed to have difficulty dragging his attention away from the erotic contrast that thin pink cotton and her lightly tanned flesh made against the weathered darkness of his hands. But when he did look up, he apparently saw something in her face he liked equally as well, and his hands flexed. One corner of his mouth curved up. "Ah, you like that, don't you?"

Oh, God, yes. But he sounded so cocky and looked so sure of himself, while she could barely function and felt completely out of her league. It took every ounce of discipline she had to manage a casual shrug. "Yeah, it's okay."

He laughed, a genuine, teeth-flashing, head-thrown-back belly laugh. "You don't give an inch, do you?" He lowered his head and kissed her, hard and thoroughly. His hands slid away from her breasts and started tugging at her top, pulling it from her waistband. The next thing Dru knew, the thin cotton jersey had been shoved up under her arms and her breasts were bared to the evening breeze.

Before she could decide if she was embarrassed or too turned on to care, J.D. had ripped his own shirt free from his shorts and yanked it up to pull his arms out. He couldn't take it off over his head without breaking their kiss, so it dangled down his back as he hauled her against him. Her breasts flattened against his hard chest, and where bare skin pressed against bare skin, heat spread.

She wrapped her arms around his neck and reveled in the rub and glide of her smooth breasts against the hairy solidness of his chest as she undulated in little clockwise circles. J.D. made a rough noise deep in his throat and kissed her harder, his hands sliding around her back to press her closer.

Seconds, moments, eons later, one of his hands eased around her rib cage to insinuate itself between their bodies. He pulled back enough to cup her breast and they both stilled for an instant while the feel of his callused hand on her bare skin registered. Their lips drew apart, and hazel eyes met blue as they absorbed the powerful effect.

Then J.D.'s mouth clamped back down on hers, and the few coherent thoughts still left in Dru's mind dissolved. Her only awareness was his mouth, all hot suction and assertiveness, and his hands, rough-skinned but oh-so-gentle as they coaxed sensation after sensation from her body.

The feelings kept escalating, and he began to kiss his way over to her ear. His breath blasted hot and ragged down the whorls, and goose bumps rose in its wake.

"It's not enough," he said hoarsely. "Why isn't it enough?" He pressed a fierce kiss to the side of her neck. "I want to be inside you." He slid his hand between her legs in a devastating demonstration of where, fingers stroking. "God, Drucilla, I want to make lo—"

It took her a moment to realize he'd gone completely still. By the time it began to sink in that he was no longer kissing her with desperate urgency, his hands had slid from her body and he was withdrawing. Cool air rushed in where a second ago she'd been warmed by his skin, and she blinked up at him in confusion. "J.D.?"

He stared down at her naked breasts beneath the pushed-up tank top, and his hands clenched into fists at his side. "Pull it down."

"Excuse me?" She followed his gaze and saw herself, pearlescent in the twilight, her nipples damp and militantly erect. Flushing, she jerked her tank top into place. She looked up to see him wrestling his own shirt on.

Mortification set in as her blood slowly cooled. My God. It wasn't even fully dark, and they'd been going at it right outside the restaurant door, where anyone could have caught them. "Lucky no one decided to step out for a smoke break or needed to toss something in the Dumpster," she said shakily while she tucked her top into her jeans. "I'm glad one of us has some sense." *And wouldn't you know it had to be him.*

He paused with his hand down the front of his shorts as he adjusted his shirt. "You think I stopped because we're outside the restaurant?" His laugh was short and harsh. "That's good. I stopped, sweetheart, because I realized I was about to stick it to a good girl . . . and that never leads to anything but trouble."

A trickle of cold rolled down her spine. All that heat, those hints of tenderness she'd felt in his touch, had been . . . merely generic for him? Not only would anyone have served his purpose, but certain types would have suited him *better*?

"Good girl," she repeated slowly. "Let me get this straight: you didn't care about getting caught. You would have—how did you so eloquently put it?—'stuck it to me' had I not been a *good* girl?"

"In a heartbeat."

"And you stopped because you suddenly remembered I'm not your usual type."

He shrugged. "I've made it a practice never to mess with your kind. You always have expectations I'm not prepared to fill."

"My *kind*? What, you think if you get in my pants I'll expect you to marry me?" She laughed harshly. "Well, I hate to disappoint you, J.D., but I'm not as good as you seem to think. Tate's daddy never bothered to marry me and I thought I *loved* him. What makes you think I'd demand more of you?"

"I never thought you'd expect marriage," he said stiffly.

"What, then? You afraid I'll follow you around, panting for more? Or do you imagine you have some magical ability to ruin me for anyone else?"

"There's no 'imagine' about it." He suddenly leaned very close, his dark-eyed gaze burning into her. "One session with the Natural Wonder, sweetheart, and you'll never be the same."

She thought she caught a glimpse of something almost vulnerable in his eyes. But even suspecting that his boast was a smoke screen for another emotion, she couldn't help but react to it. She subjected him to a cool up-and-down. "Don't flatter yourself, *sweetheart*. That so-called Natural Wonder you're so proud of? They're a dime a dozen, and I can get the use of one anytime, anywhere. In fact, maybe," she said, pushing past him, "I'll go do that right now. Thanks for priming the pump—I'm sure whoever benefits will want to thank you, too." She stormed away.

It was a bluff, of course, and she knew she ought to go straight home. But she was too wired to be confined to her apartment, so she headed away from the lodge to the trail that led down to the lake. Of all the arrogant, conceited, *fat*headed braggarts—God, he was full of himself! As if one lousy roll in the hay would have her trailing after him like some pathetic puppy. She'd been fooling herself to think he had a redeemable, more vulnerable side.

Well, it would be a cold day in hell before he got another shot at her.

As she approached the boat dock, she heard soft, drunken singing. Greg, the sous-chef, sat with his back against one of the smooth pilings at the end of the pier, singing some country lament about love gone wrong and cradling a half-empty bottle of bourbon to his chest. She started to walk by, but then thought of what could happen when drunkenness and a lake were combined. She stepped onto the dock.

It swayed slightly beneath her feet as she made her way to where he slumped against the end piling. "Greg? You okay?"

The song broke off and he peered up at her. "Dru? Hey, girl." He blinked several times. "I'm kinda hammered."

"I can see that. Let me help you back to the lodge."

"Nah. Wanna shtay here."

"Sorry, I can't let you do that. You're in no condition to be on your own around the water. Take my hand; I'll help you up."

He gave her a loose, sad smile. "You're such a good girl."

"Yeah, I've been hearing a lot of that tonight. Come on. We'll find you a room or call you a cab."

"Call me deshtroyed," he said with great tragedy, and hiccuped. "Cathy broke my heart."

"Then she doesn't deserve you," Dru assured him, even though she'd never met the woman. She helped him to his feet, staggering under his weight when he suddenly threw an arm around her shoulder and stumbled for shore. His shambling gait sent them careening toward the edge of the narrow dock, and she threw her entire weight into getting them back to the safety of the center. Their zigzags caused the amber liquid in his bottle to slosh from side to side. "I'm sure she's an idiot and you're far too good for her."

"Don' know about that," he said sadly and brought the bottle to his lips, knocking back a belt. Lowering it a moment later, he swiped at his mouth with the back of his hand. "But I'll tell you thish. Man-woman lay . . . shunships really bite."

"They do indeed," Dru said with heartfelt agreement. "I'll drink to that."

13

A couple of days later Sophie knocked on the door of J.D.'s cabin. There was no answer and she tried again. When it, too, went unanswered, she transferred the arrangement of flowers she carried in her right hand to her left, which required a bit of juggling since it already held the set of bar clamps J.D. had requested. She tried the knob with her freed hand. It turned, and she eased the door open. "J.D.?" she leaned in to call. "Are you home?"

Obviously he wasn't, but she was here and didn't feel like making this trip twice, so she stepped inside, leaving the door ajar. She crossed to the dining table and shook her head at the dead flowers that still graced it. Men.

She set the bar clamps on the table and picked up the vase. A bright postcard that had been propped against it skittered to the floor and she stooped to pick it up.

Usually she considered postcards fair game, but because she already felt guilty about invading his privacy, she tossed it unread next to the clamps and carried the vase and fresh flowers into the kitchen. Remembering the other arrangement she'd put in the bedroom, she went to fetch that, too.

J.D. had refused the maid service that was available for the cabin, and looking around, Sophie could see why. The man was neat as a pin. Not one article of his clothing was tossed around and everything was exactly where she and Ben had arranged it the day J.D. had moved in. *Nothing* was out of place, in fact. It was kind of sad, how lacking in personal touches the place was. Except for a couple of books on canoes on the nightstand and that postcard, she could hardly tell anyone lived here. One would think J.D. had lived his entire life in a barracks.

She walked back to the kitchen, where she emptied the dead flowers, washed the two vases, and filled them with fresh water. She'd listened to enough of Edwina's stories to be familiar with J.D.'s background, but although she suspected emotional deprivation as a child, she didn't have a clue how his adult life had progressed. She'd go out on a limb, though, and bet it hadn't been one big, cozy blanket wrapping him up in warmth.

She knew she should keep out of whatever relationship he and Dru were forging, but she hadn't been kidding when she'd told Ben she admired the man J.D. had fashioned out of his less than ideal beginnings. Her eyebrows drew together as she divided her flowers between the vases. More than that, she knew Dru had strong feelings for him. Whether they were positive or negative was a tough one to determine, but ever since J.D. had entered their life, there'd been a spark about her that Sophie hadn't seen for a long, long time.

She'd give a bundle to know what had gone on between them the other night. The restaurant manager had confided they'd both disappeared for a while after the fiasco with the chefs . . . and only J.D. had returned. He'd added ruefully that J.D. had been touchier than a dog-bit tomcat—and his mood hadn't improved appreciably, for Sophie had heard reports of him snarling at people yesterday, too. Drucilla, bless her reticent little soul, was keeping her own counsel. But *something* had happened, because she tightened up every time J.D.'s name was mentioned. No doubt the two of them were putting extra effort into avoiding each other.

Sophie sighed as she stood back to admire her finished work. There. J.D. could stand a few homey touches to brighten up his life.

She knew in her heart that what would probably brighten it the most was her niece. The same went for Dru. Sophie had good instincts about these things, and if those two weren't so blessed relationship-shy, not to mention just plain stubborn, she'd bet they'd discover something pretty darn special together. Their obstinacy sparked her temper.

But then, most things made her short-tempered these days, she acknowledged ruefully as she put one of the fresh arrangements on J.D.'s bureau in the bedroom. The homeopathic stuff the doctor was having her try seemed to be helping, but not nearly quickly enough to suit her.

She carried the other arrangement into the dining room and set it in the middle of the table. Standing back, she eyed it critically, then reached out to tweak a few of the blooms until she found the right aesthetic balance. She spotted the postcard that had been propped against the dead bouquet and picked it up, restoring it to the way she'd found it.

She realized it was a generic Star Lake card, one that advertised the entire region. Well, for heaven's sake! This wasn't a card he'd received, after all—it looked like one he was getting ready to mail. She turned it over and read the back, her lips lifting in a slight smile at its brief, pithy sentiments. Good. He did have a friend.

He probably didn't realize he could ask for stamps at the front desk, and in typical male fashion would no doubt leave the card right here in the middle of the table until it turned yellow with age before he'd ever remember to buy the correct postage in town.

What the heck—she'd slap a stamp on it herself and take it to the registration desk to go out with the daily pickup.

She hesitated at the front door, glancing back at the table. She tapped the edge of J.D.'s postcard against her teeth as she considered her options. Okay, Dru and J.D. weren't children, and she ought not to butt into their love lives. But really, they acted as if they *were* kids sometimes.

So she was going to give them one more nudge. Then, she swore, if they failed to get their act together, she'd stay out of it for good.

She went back and picked up the bar clamps. J.D. was still welcome to them.

But she had a different delivery girl in mind.

J.D. noticed the flowers first thing when he came through the door following his stint with the ground crew that afternoon. Sophie had obviously been here to exchange them for the dead ones he'd been meaning to toss, and a little jolt of pleasure shot through him that she'd gone to the effort.

Then his eyebrows drew together. Because as nice a gesture as it was, she was pretty free about coming into his place uninvited. And, dammit, while he had a nice bunch of flowers, she still hadn't brought the clamps he'd requested. If that wasn't just typical of the entire Lawrence family. They were quick to give him things he never asked for, or even knew he wanted—but could they give him just one damn thing he specifically requested? Hell, no, they left him twisting in the wind every time.

He took a deep breath and expelled it. Okay, that was pretty much bull, and he was working himself into a fine lather over basically nothing. His nerves were a little raw, was all. So sue him.

Without the clamps, though, work on the canoe was out, since he needed to glue a few pieces together before he could proceed. Maybe he'd occupy himself by planing down the threshold to the front door. It had a tendency to stick in the mornings, when the heavy mountain dew caused anything made of wood to swell.

Dark clouds rolled in while he squatted on his heels in the open doorway to analyze the problem. It looked like rain, and hearing distant thunder over the Cascades, he rolled to his feet and went out into the yard. Gently, he lifted his canoe off the sawhorses and carried it up to the porch, where he carefully laid it down well under the cover of the roof. Then he walked back to the doorway and stared blindly down at the threshold.

Eventually he shook himself out of his reverie, swore, and went to get his wood plane. He hated to admit it, but he'd had a tough time concentrating on anything since the other night. He couldn't seem to get all those images and sensations out of his mind.

He brought the tool back and knelt in front of the doorway, leaning forward to apply the plane to the warped threshold. As shavings of wood curled up over the blade, his mind went right back to Dru, where it had been ever since she'd made that threat and stomped off.

She was driving him crazy. He couldn't concentrate, his sleep was all dicked up, and he'd been losing his temper right and left. And while he might never be a contender for Mr. Congeniality, he didn't usually snap people's heads off at the least provocation, either. But ever since she'd thanked him for priming the pump and told him she'd find someone else to put out the fire he'd started, he'd been tied up in one huge knot.

Jealous. Jesus Jake, he could hardly credit it, but he was so jealous he could chew nails. It was an emotion he'd never experienced in his life and he didn't like it. He didn't like it one damn bit.

Though he'd denied it at the time, he realized he was

jealous even before Dru had accused him of it after the incident with the chef. She'd raised her arms to lift all that shiny hair atop her head, and when he'd seen the sleek hollows of her underarms and the sides of her breasts exposed by the low-cut armholes in her tank top, it had hit him like a freight train, knowing that ass Carlos was seeing her like that, too. Worse, knowing Carlos was seeing her full-frontal, and that she'd done it deliberately to psych the guy into going back to work. The only saving grace was that she hadn't realized *why* he was jealous—she'd actually believed it was because she'd handled that self-satisfied jerk better than he'd been able to.

His problems should be so simple. It had eaten holes in his gut when she'd pushed past him and stomped off, saying cocks were a dime a dozen and maybe she'd just go find another one to finish the job. He'd started after her in a red-hot lather, only to be brought up short by the realization that he was still working. He'd never cheated an employer of an honest day's work in his life, and it wasn't until it was much too late to matter that he'd remembered he *was* the employer. By then, of course, she was long gone.

He was an idiot. A freaking idiot. He could have had her, and he sure as hell hadn't stopped because of any lousy scruples about her being some Goody Two-Shoes. He'd stopped because he'd almost blurted how much he'd wanted to make love to her. To make *love*. Jesus Jake. Two lousy weeks in this place and he was turning into someone he didn't even recognize.

The fact was, he was nursing a bad case of blue balls and had no one to blame for it but himself. Forget semantics—call what they'd been about to do fucking or call it making love, but what it boiled down to was one fact: they *had* been about to do it, and he'd let the opportunity pass him by. If he hadn't gotten all shook up over a stupid word, he would've finally satisfied this burning need to know what it felt like to be deep inside her. By now everything could have been back to normal. But oh, no, he'd had to . . .

The threshold he'd been planing faster and faster suddenly swam into focus, and he saw that he'd reduced it to about the depth of a toothpick. "Son of a bitch!" In a rare, unchecked fit of temper, he flung the wood plane out into the yard. If that wasn't just frigging great! Now he'd have to find a piece of wood to rebuild it, or he'd have the wind whistling through here like a goddam Kansas prairie. Of all the stupid, rank amateur, dumb-ass mistakes—

"That's what I like about you, Carver," commented a cool voice. "Your unquenchable cheer."

J.D.'s head snapped up and his heart began to thud against his rib cage. Dru walked toward him across the clearing. She was dressed in her usual work uniform of sleeveless polo shirt and walking shorts, but just for a second he got a flash of the image he feared was seared on his retinas for all time: hair tumbled, mouth red and swollen from his kisses, bare breasts thrusting up at him while a flush suffused her from chest to forehead.

His dick started to twitch to life, and swearing beneath his breath, he surged to his feet. He wasn't *even* going to go there. He'd burned that bridge and it was probably a damn good thing. It was time he got his ass back to a businesslike neutrality when it came to her. From now on, he was Switzerland.

And damned if he'd let himself wonder if she'd gone out and found another man after she'd left him the other night, either.

He surreptitiously adjusted himself before he crossed the porch and ambled down the stairs. He bent over to pick up the plane, then straightened to watch her traverse the final few yards. She had a pair of quik-grips in her right hand.

She held the bar clamps out to him. "Here. Aunt Soph said you'd asked for these and she'd neglected to bring them when she stopped by earlier."

"Thanks." She looked as though she were ready to turn right around and leave, and he heard himself explain, "I've got to glue some pieces back together on my canoe, so I needed these to hold it together until it dries."

"Hmmm." She couldn't have looked more disinterested, and once again she made as if to leave. But then she hesitated and glanced toward the canoe, which rested upside down on the porch, and at the pile of wood shavings where the threshold used to be. She gave the latter an unsmiling nod. "What are you doing there?"

"The door sticks when it gets damp, and my original plan was to shave a little off the threshold so it'll open and close more smoothly."

"Looks like you shaved off more than a little."

He shrugged. "I got carried away. Now I have to rebuild the damn thing."

"Is that why you threw your thingamajig?"

"It's a wood plane. And yeah." He rubbed his hand against the back of his neck. "Not very mature of me."

She simply stared at him.

"I was frustrated." And he was getting more frustrated by the minute. Dammit, did she have to be so damned distant? She talked to him as if he were one of the guests—so freaking polite, you'd never suspect they'd been all over each other the other night.

The thought hauled him up short. *Jesus, Carver, can you possibly be a bigger ass?* He acted as if she'd been the one to cut things off instead of him. No doubt she was behaving exactly the way she thought he'd prefer.

The way he *should* prefer . . . yet somehow didn't.

The truth was, he didn't have a clue to how to talk to her today. Yet he didn't want her to leave.

He made another attempt at conversation. "I notice the sous-chef is back at work. Did you decide to give him another chance, then?"

"Yes. I ran into him shortly after I left . . . um." Her gaze shifted away in her obvious discomfort at bringing up a reminder of their encounter; then she squared her shoulders and gave him a level look. "He was down by the lake and in no shape to be near the water or on the road, so I manhandled him up to the lodge and got him settled for the night in a spare room." Her shoulders hitched delicately. "He assured me yesterday that if he had any further problems, he wouldn't handle them by trying to drown them in a bottle, so I've put him on probation."

It was a perfectly polite recital of the facts—and it made him crazy. Would it kill her to inject the smallest *inflection* into her voice? It wasn't as if he were asking her to jump for joy or even *smile* at him—although she sure as hell was quick enough to smile at everybody else. Surely she could spare a meager hint of warmth. Was that asking so fucking much?

But then, why should he expect otherwise? She wasn't the great Edwina's relative for nothing. The Lawrences were real big on offering affection and then yanking it away just when you thought it might be safe to reach out for it.

J.D. drew himself up. "Well, I'm sure you've got things to do," he said flatly. "Don't let me keep you."

"What?" She blinked those intensely blue eyes at him. Then they went all frosty and she, too, drew herself up. "Oh. Yes, of course." She surveyed him dispassionately. "Good luck with your canoe and your thingamabob there." She waved vaguely at the pile of wood curls that used to be his threshold. Then she turned and walked away.

J.D. went back to work. It was quite a while before it dawned on him that if Dru had been busy settling in the drunken sous-chef, she probably hadn't had the time to carry through on her threat to find herself a stud. Good. He could just shelve this stupid-ass jealousy once and for all. Get back to his real life.

So why did he still feel like putting his fist through the nearest wall?

14

Butch stopped to pick up a six-pack of beer on his way home. It was celebration time. He'd just completed his last day on the current job and the next one didn't start until the middle of the month. So he had a couple of weeks to enjoy the summer weather, maybe go down to Alki and watch the girls in their bikinis inline-skate along the path fronting the beach. Life was good.

It would be a helluva lot better, though, if the family of the man he'd accidentally shot would quit agitating for their brother's case to be kept open. Unfortunately, it had been a slow couple of weeks, newswise, so the local stations kept running the damn story with updates on the family's sense of outrage. One of the younger, more militant members had even insisted it was a hate crime based on the store clerk's race.

What a crock of shit. It was a fucking *accident;* if

the clerk hadn't made that dumb move that looked as if he were going for a gun, he never would've been hurt. His stupidity was what had gotten him killed—he could have been frigging *purple* and it wouldn't have made a lick of difference. They oughtta just let him rest in peace.

But what the hell, it couldn't last much longer. Statistics were in Butch's favor—a more newsworthy story was bound to break any minute now; then today's filler would become yesterday's sound bite. Besides, it wasn't like J.D. had ever resurfaced, so even if the damn stations did squeeze another ounce of drama out of a story that had already been sucked dry, chances were he was already somewhere halfway across the country where he'd never hear it, anyhow.

Butch collected the mail from the row of mailboxes on the apartment building's first floor but didn't bother sorting through it as he climbed the stairs to his apartment. What was the point—all it ever contained was either bills or Gina's beauty magazines and catalogs. Mail was strictly her territory.

He let himself into the apartment and tossed the stack on the breakfast bar that separated the kitchen from the living room. He put the six-pack in the fridge, pulled out a bottle, and popped the cap. Grabbing a bag of chips from the counter as he passed by, he headed into the living room and turned on the tube.

He was still sitting there, a pile of greasy crumbs and a half circle of empty bottles on the coffee table in front of him, when Gina got home from work.

She took one look at the mess and snarled, "Dammit, Butch! Pick that shit up!" Without awaiting a response, she dropped her purse on the counter and continued on into the bedroom.

A few minutes later she reemerged, wearing skintight jeans and a red sweater. She scowled at the mess that still cluttered the table. "I told you to clean that up."

Butch slouched lower on his tailbone. "C'mon over here and make me."

She snorted. "Forget it. I'm not in the mood for a hump. And I'm not your fucking maid, either."

"Hey, who asked you to be? I'll clean it up when I'm done here."

"Yeah, right. I'll hold my breath waiting for that to happen. Your idea of cleaning up is carrying your mess into the kitchen and dumping it on the counter for me to deal with."

"Grouse all you want, babe." He folded his hands behind his head and smirked at her. "We both know you're just jealous because my job's finished and I'm on vacation. Well, tough. I'm in the mood to celebrate, and you're not gonna screw it up for me."

She shrugged and picked up the mail. Butch heard her mumbling under her breath over the bills as she sorted through them. Then she suddenly looked up.

"Hey, did you know J.D.'s east of the mountains?"

Butch froze, his beer bottle suspended mid-tip. He lowered it without draining the last sip, a queasy feeling commencing a slow roll in his gut. "J.D.'s still in the state?"

"Yeah, in the Okanogan, it looks like. I wondered where he'd gotten himself off to; I haven't seen him around lately. Here, he sent you a postcard." She flipped it in his direction, then rose from her stool. "I guess I oughtta figure out what to get out for dinner. Would it kill *you* to get it started once in a while? You get home before I do."

He wasn't listening. He got up off the couch to scoop the brightly colored postcard off the carpet, where it had landed a few feet away. Turning it over, he read the message. His legs went rubbery beneath him and he stumbled back to the sofa. He dropped down with uncoordinated abruptness, and for several long moments he simply sat on the edge of the cushion where he'd landed and stared at the card in his hand.

Eastern Washington? J.D. was just over the mountains in frigging eastern Washington? Where the hell was this Star Lake place, anyway? He'd never heard of it. The card said in the beautiful Okanogan, but *where*, exactly? That covered a helluva lot of territory.

Christ. He rubbed a hand over his face. He'd thought for sure J.D. had headed down to California, or maybe lit out east. East of the mountains had never even occurred to him. There was bupkes construction going on over there for one thing, and besides, Butch had visited that side of the Cascades once when he and J.D. had decided to try their hand at fishing, and he'd never understood why anyone in their right mind would want to go back. It was just one big wasteland, as far as he could see, all ugly brown terrain and sagebrush.

But I'm still expecting to see your face plastered on the six o'clock news any day now.

Ah, man. Every one-stoplight little town they'd stopped at on that trip'd had cable television, since without it reception was nonexistent. And on those cable TVs had been the three main Seattle channels, KING, KIRO, and KOMO.

Two of which were currently airing the brouhaha stirred up by the clerk's family.

Shitfuckhell. If J.D. caught sight of one of those reports, he'd be back so fast Butch wouldn't know what hit him. For all he knew, J.D. was on his way back over the mountains this very minute.

He shoved to his feet. He'd made one little mistake and he was sorry as could be about it, but it was over and done, and there wasn't one frigging thing that could be done about it now. He sure as hell couldn't raise the freakin' dead.

Well, damned if he was going to let J.D. screw up his life over some sorry-ass clown who didn't have the brains to put his hands in the air when a gun was aimed his way. Butch was going to find himself an atlas and see where this Star Lake town was located. Then he'd just have to take himself a little trip.

Timing was on his side, at least—he had a couple of weeks before his next job started, so he wouldn't have Gina riding his back because he'd cut out on work. His mistake was relaxing his guard in the first place—but he'd take care of it now. No way in hell did he plan to put up with having the constant threat of exposure hanging over his head. That was no way to live, and it was clear that the time had come to make his move. From now on, he followed the Golden Rule According to Dickson.

He'd do unto J.D. before J.D. had the opportunity to undo him.

* * *

Dru's office door banged open and Tate and Billy raced in. "We're tired of playing Ping-Pong," Tate said. "We're gonna go set up a fort in the woods."

She glanced out the window. It had been threatening rain since yesterday, but although dark-bottomed clouds boiled low in the sky, the rain still hadn't materialized. "Okay, but make me a map of where you plan to set up this fort so I can find you if I need to."

" 'Kay. Can we ask the Eagle's Nest to pack us a lunch?"

"If they aren't too busy. No pop, though. Ask them to throw in a couple of cartons of milk."

"Ah, *man*," he groused. But then he grinned at her and raced out as precipitously as he'd entered, Billy hot on his heels.

Dru smiled and shook her head. She got up to close the door they'd left wide open, then returned to the paperwork on her desk.

The intercom buzzed a short while later, and without taking her attention away from the report in front of her, she reached over to activate it. "Yes?"

"Dru, it's Sally. I've got a map at the front desk that Tate and his friend dropped off, and you've got a visitor. Do you have time to see Kev Bronsen?"

"Kev?" She straightened in her seat. "Yes, sure, send him in."

It seemed as if she'd just taken her finger off the intercom button when he opened the door and stuck his head in. "I hope this isn't a horrible time. I know I shouldn't interrupt you at work."

"Actually, I skipped lunch, so I could use a break." She smiled, genuinely happy to see him. They'd always had a wonderfully uncomplicated relationship. "Wanna go down to the Nest and grab a sandwich?"

"That'd be great."

Seated across from him at a small table several minutes later, she openly studied him. Kev had always been good-looking. Now he also possessed a sophistication and polish that he hadn't had as a teenager.

He thrust his long legs out in the aisle on the side where they wouldn't pose a threat to anyone walking by, tipped back his chair, and gave her a crooked smile. He raised his brows inquiringly when she continued to stare. "What?"

"I was just thinking how very big-city polished you look. Do we seem like rubes to you now?" They must, she thought as she took in his expensively barbered brown hair and the casual coupling of his fine-gauge cashmere sweater with a threadbare pair of Levi's.

"My first couple of years away, I probably would have said yes," he admitted with a shrug. "I was pretty full of myself then, and way prouder than it merited that I'd gotten out of here. But I've learned that people are pretty much people wherever you go, and a little of the basic decency you find in the folks around here goes a lot further in the long run than the surface sophistication of the city. Trust me, Dru, you scratch that, and nine times out of ten, you're gonna find some poor slob harboring a shitload of insecurities."

Because he looked disillusioned, she said with deliberate dryness, "I wouldn't be too quick to romanticize small-town folks, if I were you. Your memory can't be all that short, and not everyone around here is as decent as yours truly, you know."

He laughed. "Believe me, I haven't forgotten what a hotbed of gossip this burg can be." He studied her as thoroughly as she'd studied him. "For instance, rumor has it that you and Carver were kissing on his porch." He gave her a reproachful look. "I thought you had better taste than that."

"Please." Dru chortled. "This from the guy who chased Terry McMann for an entire year back in high school. Don't talk to me about *better taste.*"

"Hey, she had great tits and she was accommodating in the backseat of Dad's Chevy; it didn't get much better than that." He smiled reminiscently. "Whatever happened to Terry, anyhow?"

"She got religion and teaches Sunday school in Yakima. I heard she wears orthopedic shoes now, and has a passel of kids."

"Aw, *man*," he said mournfully, sounding spookily reminiscent of Tate when she'd told him he couldn't have pop for lunch. "What a waste." Then he smiled at her across the table. "I've missed you, Dru; it's really good to see you again. What do you say we go down to the Red Bull Friday night and show the rubes around here how to shake a leg?"

"That sounds like fun. I haven't been dancing in quite a while." Then she thought of the chemistry she'd witnessed between him and Char, and the vow she and her friend had made back in junior high school not to horn in on each other's boyfriends. "I'll have to get back to you, though. I've got Tate to consider."

"No problem. You know where I live—give me a call."

She tracked down Char later that afternoon in the tiny office that fronted the massage-therapy room. When she stuck her head inside the door, she saw her friend sitting with her feet propped up on an open desk drawer, reading a magazine.

It always gave her a kick to see Char in her work environment. Forget pale-faced, Birkenstock-wearing New Agers. The pale green lab coat was about the only concession Char made to her profession—her hair was as bouffant as always, her makeup vibrant, and her fingernails screw-me red. Dru knew her clientele was often taken aback upon their first introduction, but no one who'd ever had a Swedish massage by Char ever again thought twice again about her flamboyant looks.

Dru smiled. "Hey. You got a minute?"

Char tossed the magazine aside and dropped her feet to the floor, sitting up. "Sure, come on in. I've got the entire hour. My three o'clock canceled."

"Difficult to get rich that way."

"Tell me about it. On the other hand, it was Roberta Manion, and no matter how well her daughter tips, I'm always wrung out by the end of a session with her. I swear that woman would complain if you hung her with a new rope."

Dru laughed and pulled up the extra chair, breathing in the scents of Char's aromatic oils and enjoying the London Philharmonic as it purled Bizet's *Carmen* out of the overhead speakers. "I can't stay the whole hour, but Kev dropped by a while ago and I need to talk to you."

Char stiffened, her smile wiped away. "What on

earth does anything concerning that fool have to do with me?"

"He invited me to go down to the Red Bull Friday night, and I want to talk to you about it. It's not a date or anything," she rushed to add. "It would be strictly as friends, you understand, but I thought I should—"

"Drucilla Jean, you can have wild, unprotected sex with the guy for all it means to me." Char shrugged. "Although, as your friend, I'd have to question your judgment."

"Dammit, Char, why do you do that?"

Char looked at her warily. "Do what?"

"Why do you pretend you don't care anything about him?"

"Well, gee, let me think. Could it be because I *don't* care anything about him?"

You are so full of it. "If you say so."

"I do say so," Char said tightly.

"Okay. Then prove it."

"Excuse me?"

Dru looked her friend in the eye. "Prove it."

"And how do you suggest I do that?"

"Say you'll come to the Red Bull Friday night, too."

"Oh, yeah, that oughtta be fun. Kev and I get along so well."

"You don't even have to talk to Kev if you don't want to. Come for me."

"And put you in the middle? I don't think so."

"Let me get this straight—you're staying away for me?"

"Hell, yeah. And for me and Kev, too. I'm saving us all a stress-filled evening."

"Chicken."

Char stared. "What?"

"You heard me. You're nothing but a chicken."

"Is this where I'm supposed to stamp my feet and yell, *Am not, am not*? What are we, in grade school?"

"Baaawk." Dru cackled in her best chicken imitation. "Bawk-bawk-bawk-bawk-*baaaawk*."

"Oh, for crying out loud—*fine*. I'll come to the Red Bull Friday night." She gave Dru a look. "You do a lousy chicken call."

"Maybe." Dru rose to her feet. "But I do great double-dog-dare-ya psychology."

Wednesday morning, Tate showed up just as J.D. was applying the last coat of paint to his canoe.

"Oh, wow!" he exclaimed excitedly. "It's all done!"

"Almost." J.D.'s voice was muffled by the paper mask that covered his nose and mouth, and he waved Tate away when he got too close. "Stand back. Your mom'll have my hide if this ends up on your clothes, and I don't want you breathing these fumes." He continued to sweep the spray gun from the air compressor, applying candy-apple red paint in a carefully controlled layer from bow to stern.

"Oh, man." Tate all but danced in place. "Can I go out in it with you when it's ready?"

"Sure. Long as your mom or your grandparents say it's okay."

"They will. They let me go out in the rowboats all the time, so long as I wear my life preserver." Tate settled on the bottom step of the porch and watched J.D.

put the finishing touches on the paint job. He was silent for several moments, then said, "Mom's got a date."

J.D. stilled for an instant, then forced himself to keep directing the nozzle in wide sweeps in order to avoid any drips. But his teeth were gritted and his skin felt tight. "Yeah?" he finally said. "Who with?"

"I dunno. Some old friend. You kissed her," Tate said with sudden plaintiveness. "Are you gonna let her do that?"

"I don't really have a say in what your mother does." J.D. was glad to turn away from Tate as he cleaned his equipment, because he felt territorial and savage and not at all like his normal self, and he sure as hell didn't want to scare the bejesus out of the kid—which was what he'd probably do if Tate saw his face. For one of the few times in J.D.'s life, controlling his expression was simply beyond him.

"They're goin' dancing," Tate said glumly. Then he brightened. "But I get ta stay at Billy's again."

J.D. took a deeper breath and blew it out. "Well, there you go. Maybe you'll get to watch another PG-Thirteen movie. When's all this going down, anyhow?"

"Friday night."

"Huh. So where do people go to dance around here?"

"In that saloon down in town." Tate shrugged impatiently, clearly tired of the subject. "When do you think the paint will be dry enough to put the canoe in the water?"

"Friday or Saturday, I guess. I want to give it a couple of days to be sure it sets up. You think you could help me move it up on the porch without getting paint on your clothes?"

"Sure!"

Tate chattered away as they transferred the canoe onto the perch J.D. had made to keep it out of the weather, but J.D. only heard about one word in ten.

He'd have to find out what the name of that saloon was. Because, come Friday night, he planned to be there to keep an eye on Drucilla Lawrence and her *date*.

15

A drop of rain fell on Butch's head and he scowled up at the low bank of gun-metal clouds. Great. It wasn't bad enough that for two days now, he'd been prowling the streets of Star Lake—what there were of them—and he was no closer to discovering J.D. than when he'd arrived in the area Wednesday night. Now the skies had to look as if they were about to open up at any moment, too? That was all he needed, a downpour. That would just be the goddamn sprinkles on his cupcake.

He grabbed hold of his temper. Maybe he was overreacting a tad. The real problem was, he couldn't simply walk up to people and flash a picture or say, *Hey, have you seen a guy around here answering to this description?* He needed to be a little cagier than that.

To that end, he'd taken a room in a motel two towns away. The place was a dump, but it was the height of the tourist season and apparently not everyone harbored an aversion to the east side of the mountain range that he did, so it was the best he could do. Besides, he sure as hell wasn't about to book a room in the last-known place his prey had inhabited, even if there were rooms to be had. If things went down the way he planned, he didn't want people to connect him to J.D. in any way, shape, or form.

Of course, first he had to find him. J.D. could be anywhere in the area, and *that* was only if he hadn't merely been passing through in the first place.

If he *were* still around, there was a confusingly large number of places to check out—way more than Butch would have suspected. There was some fancy-ass lodge located about seven miles up the mountain, for instance, on the lake that the town was named after. Life should be so simple that he'd find J.D. there, but he wouldn't hold his breath. It didn't sound at all like J.D.'s kind of place. A more likely prospect was the smaller lakes and resorts that riddled the area, and unfortunately, there were dozens of those.

Star Lake might be a burg to him, but it was still the largest of the blink-and-you've-missed-'em towns in the area, so all the people who lived in a fifteen-mile radius shopped here—not to mention tourists looking for more entertainment than a resort store or a bait shop.

Not that there was a helluva lot more to be found in Star Lake, from what he could see. Butch looked at Main Street with a jaundiced eye. Except for one tavern that had *sawdust* on the dance floor, for chrissake, the whole town seemed to roll up the sidewalks at six o'clock.

One thing he'd give it: this part of eastern Washington was a lot prettier than the section he'd been in before. Big fucking whoop. Like a few stands of evergreens in the foothills of the Cascades could make up for the dearth of anything interesting to do . . . never *mind* a nightlife.

All the same, maybe he'd head back here tonight and grab himself a beer at the Red Bull Saloon. It was the weekend, after all, and even Hayseed Central beat cooling his jets in that ratty motel room. Who knew, maybe he'd hit upon some hot country honey in need of a thrill.

At least then the day wouldn't be a total loss.

It was Friday night and the Red Bull was hopping. Char pushed open the front door and was met by a cacophony of voices all speaking at once, plus a new out-of-town band playing a loud but pretty decent rendition of the Dixie Chicks' "Don't Waste Your Heart." Pausing to let her eyes adjust from the bright lights of the parking lot to the saloon's atmospheric dimness, she peered through a smoky haze tinted in patches of red, blue, and gold by the neon beer signs that lined the windows. She watched couples circle the dance floor for a moment, then turned to look for Dru.

And the Scourge of Star Lake.

She sighed, wishing she possessed that enviable ability to think on her feet—maybe then she'd have come up with a really brilliant excuse to avoid being roped into this. But Dru knew her inside and out, and that chicken taunt had guaranteed she'd put in an appearance, even though she'd arrived late. Spotting her friend and Kev on the other side of the dance floor but on this side of the bar, she reluctantly started toward them. They leaned toward each other over the table while Dru talked, and as Char approached, she saw Kev throw his head back and laugh.

Anxiety tightened her stomach. Damn. She didn't want to spend time in his company. They'd never gotten along worth a damn, and the ever-present tension between them didn't have a darn thing to do with sexual attraction.

Did it?

She straightened her shoulders. Of course it didn't. He just always made her feel so . . . inadequate. He had back in high school, and he apparently hadn't lost his touch. Whenever she was in his company, she felt as if she weren't quite pretty enough, smart enough, witty enough. Who in her right mind *would* want to spend time with someone who made her feel so lacking in every desirable attribute, who unerringly attacked her most basic sense of womanliness every time they met? She'd learned to attack first so she wouldn't look like some sorry-ass victim.

Well, the hell with it. She'd stay just long enough to satisfy her pride; then she was out of here. Skimming her fingers down the bare expanse of stomach between her top and the short denim skirt she wore, she adjusted the hip-hugger's wide belt as she strode up to the table. "Hail, hail, the gang's all here," she drawled.

Dru looked up at her, a smile lighting her face. "Hi! I'm so glad you're here. I was beginning to worry you wouldn't make it."

Kev's heavy-lidded gaze didn't make it any farther than her belly button.

She began to wish she'd worn something less revealing than her red lycra crop-top with this skirt, but shrugged the thought aside. This was exactly the sort of thing Kev excelled in—making her feel like poor white trash when she was actually dressed no differently from half the other women in the place. Even Dru, who could certainly do no wrong in his eyes, had on a long, gauzy, peach-colored dress that Char knew molded to her thighs when she moved. It was styled like an old-fashioned camisole on steroids, with a row of tiny pearlized buttons from the neckline to its calf-length hemline, and narrow straps culminating in a scooped neck that afforded glimpses of lush cleavage every time she leaned forward.

Char wished she had such grown-up boobs.

She pulled out a chair and sat down. No sooner had her butt touched the seat than one of the lodge guests came up and asked her to dance.

Silently blessing him, she flashed her biggest smile but said, "The next one, okay? Let me just grab a beer first."

He wandered away and she caught the waitress' eye as the woman wove her way between two nearby tables. The band launched into a new number, and she had to raise her voice to be heard when the woman came over. "A Corona and lime, please," she said and tossed her tiny purse on the tabletop. Then, ignoring Kev as if he simply didn't exist, she leaned into Dru. "The band's not half bad, is it?"

"No, they're pretty good. We were just commenting on that, weren't we, Kev?"

Over the next hour, Char danced with every man who asked her and flirted for all she was worth. Anything to get away from that table. She even put up with the tourist who got too familiar. She removed his hand from her butt and told him she wasn't interested in starting anything with him, but she did it with a smile. Ordinarily, she'd have cut his big-city-stud pretensions off at the knees with ruthless precision.

When she was forced to sit out the band's break, she watched Dru knock herself out trying to bring her and Kev into a three-way conversation. Unfortunately, neither she nor Kev was in a particularly cooperative frame of mind. They managed not to snipe at each other, but that probably had more to do with the decibel level than with their mutual respect for Dru. In fact, Char found herself growing increasingly resentful of her best friend.

It didn't make sense, and it probably wasn't fair, but she nevertheless felt angry, and wretched, and just sort of sick at heart as she watched Kev smile and laugh and flirt with her. Dammit, why had Dru insisted she join their date? She'd known perfectly well that mixing Char with Kev was like pouring gasoline on fire, but, oh, no, she'd just had to have her own way. Well, Char didn't appreciate feeling like a fifth wheel.

Which was probably why, when she saw J.D. Carver walk up to the bar, she got up and intercepted him. "Hey, there," she said as he turned away from paying for his beer. She rested her elbow on the bar and smiled up at him. He was big, hard, and unsmiling, dressed as always in his faded jeans and dazzlingly white T-shirt. "You here alone?"

He gazed down at her and nodded. "You?"

"Good as." She shrugged and tilted her head toward the table at the edge of the dance floor. "I'm here with Dru and her date."

J.D. looked beyond her, and she watched his eyes narrow the moment he spotted them.

Excellent. If nothing else, J.D. Carver was a man with an attitude, which ought to at least liven things up. "You know what they say, don't you, J.D.? That two's company, and three's a crowd? Well, I've been the one turning this shindig into a crowd. So come join us and help me even things up."

"Perfect." The smile he gave her, however, looked like trouble.

She didn't know whether to be worried or pleased, but—what the hell—opted for pleased. She was in a dangerous mood.

And since Dru had thrust her into the company of the one man she'd known perfectly well Char most wanted to avoid, it seemed only fair to return the favor.

Holy shit! Butch came to attention at his table in the far corner. J.D. was here—the freaking mountain had come to Muhammad.

He might not even have seen his erstwhile buddy if not for the blonde with the sweet navel. He'd been watching her since she'd first come in, wondering if he ought to make a move on her.

She was exactly his type, with her short, belly-exposing skirt and her tight red top that fit close as a tattoo and showcased those fine little teacup-sized tits of hers. He'd watched her flirt and dance with half the men in the joint, and had wanted to give her a whirl himself. But the guy with the other woman at their table had spent the past hour scowling at all the guys squiring her around the floor. When some joker had rubbed his hand down the blonde's ass on the dance floor, the man had come halfway out of his chair.

Butch didn't pretend to understand what the hell that was all about. The guy seemed to be with the brunette with the shiny hair and the nice set, but he looked about two minutes from coming unglued over the little blonde. What Butch *did* know was that he planned to keep a low profile while he was in Star Lake. And that meant giving the kinky little ménage à trois a very wide berth.

A good decision, as it turned out. Because there the blonde was, leading J.D. back to her table.

Butch leaned back in his chair and sipped his beer. Now that J.D.'s whereabouts were no longer in question, it occurred to him that he didn't really have a plan for disposing of his old friend without rousing suspicion.

Not to mention without having to come face-to-face with him.

Which might happen any minute now if J.D. took a seat on the side of the table that Butch would opt for—the one that would give him an unobstructed view of those two equally fine sets of knockers across the table. The side that would leave him directly in line with Butch's table.

Damn. He'd better get the hell out of here before

J.D. spotted him and screwed up his entire strategy.

He supposed he ought to go out to the parking lot and jockey his car around so he wouldn't be stuck when he needed a quick getaway. He'd seen the way people blocked each other in out there, and the smart money said he'd better find a spot from which to follow J.D. when the other man left. He needed to know exactly where his ole bud was staying.

Because once he had that information, he'd be in a much better position to come up with a plan to get rid of him.

Why me, God? Dru silently demanded as she watched Char and J.D. wend their way from the bar to the table. *Isn't it enough that my matchmaking turned out to be such a bust? I've already done a bang-up job of making myself and my two best friends miserable tonight—is it truly necessary to saddle me with J.D., too?*

Talk about overkill.

Her body, damn its hide, didn't seem to agree. But it obviously just wanted to get laid, so what did it know?

She shifted edgily in her chair and found herself sitting taller and pulling her shoulders back to display her breasts a bit more prominently. Her skin grew warm, her pulse quickened, and every nerve ending she possessed came alive with anticipation. To occupy her hands, which suddenly itched something fierce to touch that long, hard body drawing ever closer, she reached for her nearly full glass and drained it in one long swallow. An additional warmth she probably didn't need exploded in her stomach. That episode with J.D. outside the lodge's kitchen had clearly done a number on her. It was as if she'd been conditioned to his touch—because just one look, and she wanted him again. She wanted him bad.

Well, tough patooties, because she was stronger than a few renegade hormones. Struggling to keep from looking like an infatuated fool, she directed a cool smile at the couple as they walked up to the table.

"Look who I found at the bar," Char said, stroking her hand down J.D.'s arm.

"J.D.," Dru said, praying her impersonal smile wouldn't suddenly degenerate into a snarl. She was shocked at the unprecedented urge she had to break her best friend's fingers.

"Drucilla," J.D. replied, and his eyes were anything but impersonal as they touched upon her loose hair, her bare shoulders and chest, and lingered for the briefest moment on her cleavage. Then he forced his gaze away and gave Kev an abbreviated, cool nod. "Bronsen."

Kev's response was every bit as chilly. "Carver."

Without waiting to ask who was sitting where, J.D. circled the postage-stamp-sized table and set his beer down on it. He pulled out the chair that Char had been using all evening and dropped down next to Dru. Hands stuffed in his jeans pockets, he sprawled back in his seat, big shoulders encroaching on Dru's space, hard thighs spread wide, one leg pressing hers from knee to hip. Dru's temperature immediately skyrocketed into the spontaneous-combustion zone.

Char shrugged at having her place usurped and sat next to Kev. "Well, say, now," she said brightly. "Isn't this cozy."

Kev made an impatient move, as if prepared to push

back from the table, but Char ignored him as she'd been ignoring him all evening and leaned toward J.D. "Wanna dance?"

"Sure, why not?" He stood and waited for her to circle the table. Then, placing a hand lightly on the bare skin at the small of her back, he guided her to the dance floor.

Swallowing hard to rid herself of the bitter taste of a jealousy she'd love to deny, Dru looked at Kev across the table. "I feel like I should apologize. This isn't at all how I envisioned the evening going."

He shrugged. "You win some, you lose some." But his gaze barely left the dance floor. A couple of minutes later he stiffened, his eyes going bleak. "Christ, not the octopus again."

Dru turned to see what he was staring at. A man had cut in on J.D. and was dancing off with Char. Dru swiveled around as J.D. sauntered back to the table.

Presenting him with her back obviously didn't deter him in the least. Warm hands suddenly slid beneath the fall of her hair and he gathered it all together in a loose ponytail, which he used to tilt her head back. She looked up into his face, looming upside down over hers.

"Want to dance?" His voice was low, gravelly, and it sent hot shivers chasing down her spine.

She opened her mouth to refuse. "Okay."

Damn. Where had that come from? She shot an apologetic look at Kev, but he hadn't even noticed. All his attention was focused on the dance floor, so, with a shrug, she tugged her hair out of J.D.'s fist and rose to her feet.

They danced for about thirty-five seconds to the fast

number before the band concluded with a climactic flourish. The combo immediately segued into a slow, torchy ballad, and J.D. didn't bother to ask if she'd care to sit it out—he simply pulled her in, wrapped her in his arms, and commenced a slow, sexy sway in place.

All her bones immediately turned to butter, and with a soft sigh she slipped her arms around his neck and snuggled her cheek into soft white cotton where his chest curved into collarbone. Inhaling the scent of laundry detergent and man, she felt rather than heard the rumble of satisfaction that resonated in his chest. Then he bent his head and rubbed his cheek against the top of her head, and she closed her eyes in total surrender.

His arms pulled her closer yet, his hands tightening possessively, and he inserted a knee between her legs to execute a step that involved them in a full-body undulation. Interior muscles deep between her legs instigated a chain reaction of tight, achy little clenchings. She reminded herself of her stronger-than-a-few-renegade-hormones speech. It was a good, strong vow, noble even, and the type of oath a take-charge kind of woman would pledge.

So why did she suddenly doubt it?

Oh, man, she was in trouble. Big, big trouble. And she didn't even have the good sense to care. She was about five heartbeats too late to fight the feelings that swamped her every time she found herself in his arms.

16

Kev watched Char remove the octopus' hand from her ass twice before she suddenly pushed back, said something that made the man's mouth go hard, and stormed away. Instead of returning to the table, though, she headed for the door.

He half rose out of his seat, but the hand he'd planted on the table to lever himself up brushed a little tapestry drawstring bag that had been resting next to his elbow, and he lowered his butt back into his chair. She'd be back; there wasn't a woman alive who'd leave her cache of girly goods behind. When he looked up again, however, he saw the octopus exiting the bar in Char's wake, and he surged to his feet. He snatched up her purse, shoved it into his waistband, and headed for the door.

At first glance, the parking lot appeared deserted. Then he heard voices around the side of the building, and pivoting on his heel, he headed for the corner. The rain that had been threatening the past couple of days had finally arrived while they were inside, and it drummed against the Red Bull's shake roof and formed reflective pools on the black tarmac of the parking lot. Kev kept close to the saloon's lapboard siding beneath the overhanging eaves.

". . . nothing but a goddamn little tease," he heard an angry male voice say just before he reached the corner.

"How do you figure that?" Char's voice demanded. "Because I haven't jumped to avail myself of the services you're so hot to supply?"

"Hey, I could show you a real good time. I'm hung like a horse."

Kev turned the corner to see her backed against the wall, glowering up at the man towering over her. She made a rude noise. "You want to know what my definition of well hung is, buster?" she asked. "When there's no room between the noose and your neck. Now, back off!"

Instead, the man moved closer, dropping his hands from the side of the tavern, where they'd been caging her in, to grip her shoulders and yank her up on her toes. "Listen, you little bitch—"

Seeing those fingers gouge into her delicate flesh cranked Kev's temper into the red zone. "You heard her," he snapped. "Back off!"

Both heads jerked around to stare at him, and he had just enough time to note that Char didn't look all that thrilled to see who had come to her rescue.

"Who the hell are you?" the octopus demanded.

"The guy who's gonna ream you a new asshole if you don't get your hands off her."

The man spent a moment longer than Kev liked sizing him up, and Kev barked, "*Now*!"

"Yeah, big deal," the tourist said, dropping his hands and stepping back. "She's a frigid bitch anyhow." Turning on his heel, he stormed off into the rain.

Char lunged away from the wall as if she planned to go after him. "*Frigid bitch*? I'll show you frigid, you sonofabi—"

Kev reached out and snagged her chin in his hand, tipping her face up to his and studying every inch of it for signs of injury or trauma. "Are you all right?"

She sagged back against the wall. "Aside from the fact that this has been a crappy night altogether?" she asked and wearily raked her fingers through her hair. "Sure. I'm just peachy."

"Glad to hear one of us is. I think I aged ten years when I saw that guy with his hands all over you."

"Oh, right, like you give a great big rip about anything that happens to me." She slugged him in the shoulder. "Who do you think you're fool—ummph."

He'd caught her hand in his and lowered his mouth to hers to cut off her tirade. His intention was merely to offer a gentle, healing kiss to show her that not all men were animals.

But maybe that's exactly what he was, because his mouth had barely settled on the softness of her lips before heat exploded deep in his gut and he found himself pressing her back against the same wall he'd just rescued her from, offering her hot kisses that were wet, deep, and on the edge of control.

And for a few runaway heartbeats she kissed him back, too, her arms clinging, her right knee climbing up the outside of his thigh. But then her foot dropped down to the pavement and she shoved him away to stare up at him through narrowed eyes.

"No," she said flatly, a hand splayed against his chest to hold him off. "Huh-uh, no way. You're not leading me down that rabbit hole—I'm through with men."

He tried to catch his breath. "You don't kiss like you're through with men."

"Yeah, well, you caught me in a weak moment. From now on, though, the whole lot of you can just leave me to my own mechanical devices."

He laughed. "Don't you think that might get a tad lonely? And what happens when you run out of batteries? We men do have our uses, you know. I admit I can't offer you anything as impressive as Harry the Horse claimed—"

She garbled a laugh and, encouraged, he added, "But I bet I can make you laugh, and I know I can keep you warm when the nights get cold." His voice lowered. "And I can make you feel things that no mechanical device will ever come close to making you feel."

For all of ten seconds she stared up at him in interested speculation. Then her eyes went flat and suspicious again. "*Please*. Am I supposed to believe you're madly attracted to me all of a sudden?"

"There's nothing sudden about it, toots. I've been hot to get into your pants since junior high school."

"You are such a liar! You've always treated me as if I had all the sex appeal of Olive Oyl."

"Hell, yeah! I wanted *out* of this town! You never did, though, and I knew damn well you were the one person who could keep me here. I wasn't taking any chances."

"Uh-huh." She made a rude noise. "Do I look like I was born yesterday, Bronsen?"

"Nope. You look like a fully grown woman to me." He bent his head and burrowed his nose into her hair where it brushed away from her temple, inhaling deeply. "God, you smell good."

"Yeah? You wanna know what I smell, Kev? Pure, unadulterated bullshit." She picked up one of his hands and sniffed its fingers. "Yep. These are the hands slinging it, all right."

He laughed and scraped his teeth over her earlobe.

She shivered, but raised her hands to push him away.

"This is no bull, Charlotte," he whispered in her ear. "I wanted you then and I want you now. I'm just not tiptoeing around it the way I used to, and I'm not playing any more games to hide my feelings." He touched the tip of his tongue to the whorl of her ear and breathed, "You can believe me or not. But one way or the other, I'm going to wear you down."

"Don't hold your breath, buster." But she quit resisting. And when his head lowered further still to ply kisses down the side of her neck, she sucked in a breath and tilted her head back to afford him freer access.

Before he could feel too smug, however, she fisted her hands in his hair and pulled his head back. "How do I know this isn't just a case of if-you-can't-have-the-one-you-love-then-love-the-one-you're-with? Is that what this is all about, Kev? Did Dru turn you down or something?"

"I've never been interested in Dru that way and you know it." He felt a little ticked that she'd actually believe he'd play her off against her best friend. "I only asked her out tonight as a friend who wanted to have a decent time with another friend, and—" It suddenly struck him like a sledgehammer that he'd walked off and left that friend high and dry. "Oh, shit—Dru!"

He grabbed Char's hand and headed around the corner of the tavern. "Some true-blue bud I am," he berated himself as they reached the front door. "I was so intent on you that I can't even remember what she was doing when I took off. But I know Carver was right there to take advantage. And I have a bad feeling that I might have just thrown her to the wolf."

J.D. pulled out his pocket watch for the third time in the past eight minutes and consulted the time.

"You got a train to catch, Carver?" Dru demanded dryly.

He repocketed the watch and looked at her. Reaching out, he carefully brushed a strand of her silky hair behind her ear. "No. I'm just wondering how soon I can call Bronsen a deserter and drag you out of here."

Even in the hazy dimness, he could see her face turn pink, and not for the first time wished the band played more of those slow, belly-rubbing numbers. He wanted her back in his arms, wanted to smell again the scent of oranges from her shampoo, feel the softness of her skin beneath his hands.

"Kev will be back," she informed him firmly.

That's what he was afraid of, and he shrugged. "I want to take you home anyhow." He was tired of starting fires with her that had to be put out, of having to back away before this thing between them was given a chance to run its natural course. He'd never known such a hunger, and he wanted to feed it.

Hell, he wanted to *gorge* on it. Looking at her squarely, he didn't make the least attempt to hide his feelings.

She reached for her beer and drained it in one long swallow.

He watched her set her empty glass back on the table, then eyed the foam mustache that gulping down her beer had left on her upper lip. He started to lean forward, but caught himself.

Licking up that foam ought to be one of those things you could tease a woman about, one of those man/woman maneuvers that drove the mating dance. It was just another way to prime the pump.

Except his pump was already in jeopardy of blowing sky-high. One kiss, and he feared he'd clear the table with a swipe of his arm and lay her out on top of it. He reached over and gathered the foam off her lip with the tip of his forefinger, which he then brought to his mouth and sucked clean.

She shifted in her chair, leaning a little closer.

J.D. shoved to his feet. "Okay, I think you've been abandoned. I'd better take you ho—"

"Hey, sorry about disappearing like that," said Kev's voice.

Every red cell J.D. possessed howled in denial, and he slowly turned to face the man.

Kev held Char by the hand and was saying to Dru, "Char had a little trouble with a tourist. I'm going to see that she gets home safely. You ready to go?"

All J.D.'s territorial instincts reared up on their back legs, and he stepped in front of Kev, going chest to chest with him. "I'll take Dru home," he said flatly.

Kev responded with equal aggression. "Forget it, Carver. I brought her; I'll take her home."

"For heaven's sake, you two." Dru sat forward to see around J.D. "If the testosterone in here gets any deeper, Char and I are going to need life preservers."

Char voiced her agreement, and J.D. and Kev stepped back from each other.

Dru smiled up at Kev, and J.D. felt his gut clench. But then she said, "It's really not necessary to take me home." She reached out and gave Kev's hand a squeeze. "Both J.D. and I are headed up the mountain, so there's no sense in going out of your way. J.D. will see that I get home safe and sound. You do the same with Char."

Kev studied her. "You sure?"

"Yeah."

"Okay, then." He slid his arm around Char's shoulders, tucking her under his arm. "We're gonna take off."

"I'll talk to you tomorrow, Dru," Char said. She turned to J.D. and smiled. "It was good seeing you again. Thanks for the dance."

Then they were gone.

J.D. turned to Dru. "You ready to go, too?" If she said no, he was going to self-destruct.

She picked up her purse and stood. "Yes."

They were quiet on the walk out to his car, and an edgy, sexually aware tension seemed to consume every available bit of air in the Mustang from the moment they climbed into it. J.D. had driven halfway up the mountain when he couldn't take it any longer and suddenly pulled over onto an overlook. He set the emergency brake and turned to Dru.

"Damned if I'm going to try to nail you in the backseat of my car like some randy sixteen-year-old," he said, and hooking his hand around the back of her neck, pulled her to meet him over the console between the bucket seats. "But I have to at least have this." He clamped his mouth down on hers.

Her lips immediately opened to welcome him and a ragged breath escaped him as he eased his tongue into her mouth. There. God, yes, *there*. That was exactly what he'd needed—the taste of her, her always generous responsiveness.

Taking a deep breath, he pulled away before he could be tempted to talk her into the backseat of the car, anyway. Resting his forehead against hers, he asked, "Where's Tate tonight?"

"Spending the night in town with Billy again."

There is a God. "Will you come home with me?"

She studied him for a moment by the dim light of the instrument panel, then slowly nodded. "Yes."

He wasted no time getting the car back on the road.

He parked the Mustang behind his cabin a short while later and climbed out of the car. Too impatient to round the hood, he vaulted it instead and yanked open Dru's door, reaching in to assist her out of the car. Pressing her to him, he closed the car door with his free hand, then slid that hand around her waist to splay it over her hip. He bent his head down to hers and kissed her again. Within seconds his emotions had gone from zero to a hundred and twenty and he was pressing her up against the side of the car, more than willing to take her right where they stood.

But not only was it raining; every single encounter between them had been up against one hard vertical surface or another. He drew back, gently tucking her hair behind her ear. She was going to think he was a graduate of the slam-bam school of screwing if he didn't get a grip, so he was going to take it nice and slow.

Even if it killed him.

He stepped back and threaded his fingers through hers. "Come on in." He led the way around to the front porch and reached above the door's lintel for the cabin key. "You want another beer, or a cup of coffee or something?" The only illumination in the cabin was provided by a single light in the kitchenette.

Dru stepped inside and gave him a smile. "No, thanks," she murmured. She tossed her purse on the couch and turned to him, sliding her hands up his chest to his shoulders and raising on tiptoe to kiss him again.

Ah, man. He wrapped her up in his arms and straightened to his full height, causing her toes to dangle an inch or so above his feet.

He loved kissing her. Her lips were incredibly soft and tasted sweeter, fresher, than any other he'd ever kissed. He'd always thought that one woman's kisses were pretty much the same as another's, but he'd obviously been kissing the wrong women all these years, because Dru's lips were like no one else's he'd ever tasted.

A tiny frisson of unease wormed its way into his consciousness, and he eased his mouth away from hers and slowly lowered her back to the floor.

She slid down his front until her toes were perched on top of his boots. She blinked up at him with a sort of slumberous confusion, and when he looked down into her heavy-lidded blue eyes and saw the swollen condition of her lips, the just-rolled-out-of-bed disarray of her brown hair, his reservations dissolved as quickly as they'd cropped up. He slid his palms down her back to the fullness of her bottom, where his fingers curled to sink into the lush curves and pull her closer. The material beneath his hands felt thin to the point of nonexistence.

"I'm surprised you didn't start a riot tonight wearing this get-up," he said huskily. "You always go out in public in your underwear?"

She laughed. "It's a *dress*, Carver, not underwear!"

"Yeah? Where'd you get it—Miss Kittie's Shop for Wayward Saloon Girls? All you need are fishnet stockings, a ribbon around your neck, and a pair of old-fashioned, high-buttoned shoes to look like one of those girls back in the Wild West." He rubbed against her. "The ones all the cowboys wanted to take upstairs."

She slanted him a glance that nearly sent him into cardiac arrest and turned his erection into a five-alarm hard-on. "You strike me much more the city boy than cowboy type, " she said softly. "*Still . . .*" She stood on her tiptoes, pressed a kiss to the edge of his jaw, and whispered, "You want to take me upstairs, J.D.?"

Ah, man. He scooped her up in his arms and headed for the bedroom.

Butch had waited until he saw J.D. and the woman walk around to the front of the cabin before he risked climbing out of his car, which he'd parked down the lane. He eased the door closed behind him, then slipped down the dark road in their wake. After hearing the cabin door slam shut, he stood in the clearing to stare up at the dimly lighted cabin. Though barely able to see them through the front window, he saw enough to know they were making out. As he watched, J.D. picked the woman up and headed somewhere into the interior.

He'd sure like to know if this was J.D.'s place or the woman's. Guess he was stuck hanging around until he saw who left and who stayed.

What he'd also like to know, in the meantime, was what the frigging *hell* was going on around here. First, there'd been that guy at the tavern who'd appeared to be with the stacked girl with the shiny brown hair, but who'd clearly been lusting after the blonde. Then the blonde had picked up J.D. *Then*, while Butch was waiting in the lot for J.D. to emerge, he'd seen the other guy come out of the tavern in the wake of the blonde and later drive off with her. Now here was J.D.

with the brunette, looking in a great big hotter hurry to get into her pants than Butch had ever seen him.

He'd always thought small towns were dead boring, but *this* one looked like a freaking hotbed of revolving bedmates. What did they do—toss their damn keys into a hat? He supposed when there was no ready-made entertainment to be found, the natives just created their own.

He never in a million years, however, would have expected straight-arrow J.D. to be a part of it.

17

J.D. lowered Dru to the bed and followed her. His weight bearing her down into the mattress, he immediately picked up where they'd left off in the living room and kissed her with a ferocity that melted her into one large puddle of sensation.

Then his mouth was gone with a suddenness that left her blinking in confusion when he pushed up on one elbow. She watched, disoriented, as he reached for the lamp on the nightstand and switched it on. Propping himself back over her, he gazed down at her with his customary unsmiling intensity and trailed rough-skinned fingertips down her chest to the first button on her dress. "I don't intend to miss seeing an inch of you," he said, and for a man with such big hands, he was amazingly dexterous as his fingers slipped the first tiny button free of its loop and moved down to the next.

Oh, God, John David. I love you.

Heat exploded in her chest. *Are you crazy?* her alter ego demanded. How could she think anything so outrageous? She hardly even knew the man.

Except . . .

She knew he was patient with Tate and gave generously of his time whenever her son showed up on his doorstep. She knew he was quick to look out for those who lacked the power to look out for themselves. And that he talked tough, but often acted with contradicting gentleness.

She knew he made her feel like more of a woman than she'd ever felt in her life.

Well, there you go, then. You're simply confusing the promise of hot sex with true love.

Relieved to explain it away so neatly, she grabbed his wrists when he began to separate the two halves of her dress that he'd unbuttoned clear to her waist. "You first," she said, nodding at his T-shirt. "You're way overdressed."

Sitting up, he crossed his hands over his flat stomach and grabbed a double fistful of the white cotton. He pulled it from his waistband and up over his head in one economical move, muscles shifting smoothly beneath his skin.

She licked her lips as she stared up at him. His shoulders gleamed in the lamplight, his dark hair was tousled, and his eyes were heavy-lidded as he looked back at her. And Dru knew with sudden stunning clarity that there was much more than mere sex at work here.

Just who are you trying to fool, anyhow?

If sex was all she needed, why hadn't she availed herself of other men over the years? She'd always liked sex with Tony—and God knew there'd been numerous opportunities since then: a host of male guests who'd made it clear they'd be more than happy to stand stud service for her.

Yet time after time, she'd passed. The couple of times she'd accepted an invitation had proved rather than disproved her point. She feared she was one of those depressing women for whom love and sex went hand in hand. Because the few times she'd managed to convince herself she didn't need the former in order to be gratified by the latter, she'd been left feeling not only emotionally dissatisfied and incomplete, but also pretty darn sleazy.

Which was ridiculous—she *knew* it was ridiculous. Men certainly never felt this way about loveless sex. But that was the thing about feelings: they could be contrary and bullheaded and, right or wrong, they simply were what they were. Stern lectures to herself full of valid arguments had never talked her out of one yet.

But loveless sex wasn't the problem in this instance. She almost wished it were—but her heart was fully, completely wrapped up in J.D.

She prayed to heaven he didn't end up breaking it, but holding herself aloof to prevent being hurt wasn't a real option. So she might as well enter into this wholeheartedly.

And let the devil take the hindmost.

She reached up to touch J.D.'s chest. She really liked his chest hair; it was straight and fine and grew in an wedge from his collarbone to his waist. There was just something primordial and wholly masculine about soft hair covering all that hard muscle.

He sucked in an appreciative breath at her touch and closed his eyes for a second. Then they slid open again and he looked down at her. He touched a fingertip to the corner of her lip where it curled up in amusement. "What?"

"I was just thinking how very much I like this"—her hands stroked him from pectorals to waistband, pausing to explore the depth of his navel with a fingertip—"the way your body hair grows. And how glad I am that you're not one of those men with hairy shoulders."

His mouth crooked up on one side. "Yeah, it looks like *you've* got hairier shoulders than I do." Then he gently scooped the fall of her hair away from her face to pool on the quilt beneath her. "Nope . . . wait . . . I guess it doesn't grow there, after all."

She laughed. He'd never teased her before and her heart gathered the moment like a treasure to be stored away.

His fingers brushed over her collarbone and down her chest to the unbuttoned halves of her bodice. He peeled them back. "I want to see you naked." A hoarse laugh escaped him. "Big surprise. I've wanted to see you naked from the first moment I laid eyes on you." Unhooking her demi-bra, he peeled that open, too. Then he tugged the gauzy dress down, and when it caught beneath Dru's hips, he said, "Lift up."

The next thing she knew, she was lying there in nothing but a pair of satin-and-lace undies and skimpy leather sandals that tied at her ankles.

For a moment, J.D. simply stared. "God," he finally

breathed and traced the long crease where the outer slopes of her breasts rose away from her rib cage, brushed his fingertips down to the indentation of her waist, and then trailed them over the flare of her hips. Swinging a leg over her thighs to kneel astride her, he brought his hands up and touched all ten fingers to her chest with the sensitivity of a world-renowned violinist tuning his Stradivarius.

"You are"—he grazed his fingertips down her chest to the rise of her breasts—"so damn"—his hands tenderly spread wide to encompass the resilient globes—"magnificent." He closed his fingers, trapping her nipples between his knuckles and pressing the fullness of her breasts together.

An electrical current of sensation rode an invisible conductor to that place deep between Dru's thighs, and instinctively she raised her hips off the bed, but J.D.'s denim-clad thighs held her in a tight grip. A soft moan escaped her throat and he leaned down and kissed her, a full-throttle, pedal-to-the-metal kiss of hot, strong lips and cocksure tongue. And the whole time, those hard-skinned hands gently manipulated her breasts, pressing, shaping, massaging the fullness, trapping her nipples between his fingers and tugging.

Her hands slid restlessly over his chest, his shoulders, his stomach. Then she reached for his waistband.

J.D. groaned into her mouth but straightened and shifted farther down her legs to kneel out of reach. Dru opened her mouth to ask where he was going, but before she could utter a word he'd bent again and sucked her left nipple into his mouth. Another moan escaped her, this one even more heartfelt than the last, and she forgot everything except the look of his lean cheeks hollowing as he drew on her and the itchy, restless commotion inside that made her hips instigate a tiny bump and grind between J.D.'s gripping knees. "Oh, please," she whispered. "Please."

Suddenly, he was spreading her legs and stretching out on top of her, linking their fingers and sweeping her arms high over her head. The position arched her back, thrusting her breasts up, and his hard chest with its soft fan of hair crushed them as his hips moved and the inflexible length of his erection rocked and rubbed and teased between her legs. With a needy sound deep in her throat, she drew her knees back in order to feel him more fully, but even as she did so he pulled away again and shoved back to crouch between her legs, staring down at her and breathing heavily.

"J.D.!" she protested breathlessly.

Her knees were still drawn up toward her chest, and before she could lower her feet to the spread he ran his hands along the backs of her thighs to cup the cheeks of her bottom. He looked down at her with heavy-lidded eyes. "You've got the greatest ass I've ever seen."

A bark of laughter escaped her. "You liar. I've got a big butt."

"It's perfect—trust me on this. And *this*"—he smoothed his fingers over the satin-and-lace triangle that stretched between her legs—"God, this is sweet." His forefinger drew a line from the uppermost curve of her mound down to her cheeks. "Wet," he murmured and Dru followed his gaze to see the material rapidly dampening with each pass of his fingertip as it pressed ecru satin into the soft furrow between her legs.

Lightning rocketed through her, but self-consciousness spread heat across her face and down her chest, and she glanced up at him a little uncertainly. When his eyes met hers, though, she saw that they were hot and full of admiration, and her self-consciousness melted away.

Desire stamped its mark on his face as he watched his finger pressing the thin satin into feminine folds. "If that isn't the prettiest sight," he murmered; then his hand curled around the elastic band of her panties and pulled them down her legs. The next thing Dru knew, he had an unobstructed view of her most private parts. He licked his bottom lip and growled, "Ah, God. This is even prettier yet."

He reached out to touch her, but she scooted out of range, sitting back against the headboard. Almost more sensation than she could bear flared deep between her thighs, and she squeezed them together. "Take off your jeans," she demanded. "Things are a little unequal around here."

He climbed to his feet and peeled off his boots and socks. Then he reached for the waist button on his jeans.

Rolling onto her knees, Dru hooked the fingers of both hands into his waistband and gripped the band with her thumbs. She gave a tug, pulling him to the edge of the bed.

"Let me," she whispered and kneaded the backs of her fingers against his rigid abdomen. She unfastened the button and fumbled for the zipper tab, sliding it south. She watched as the teeth separated and slowly exposed a widening V of tanned skin that gradually gave way to paler flesh. A dark stripe of hair trailed down the hard muscles of his stomach and disappeared into the deeper shadows cast by his clothing. "No underwear," Dru said with a satisfied smile. "I *told* Char you probably didn't wear any."

He stared down at her. "You and Char discussed what kind of underwear I wear?"

"Sure."

"When was this?"

"I don't know—the first day, I think." She shrugged. "Maybe the second."

"Damn. I thought only men did that sort of thing."

She laughed. Then she eased his jeans down his hips, and her amusement over the uncharacteristically flustered look on his face abruptly disappeared. She swallowed dryly. "The Natural Wonder, I presume."

"In the flesh, ma'am. And very happy to make your acquaintance."

"I can see that." She glanced up at his face, then back down. "Happy, and *then* some."

His penis was long, thick, and dark-skinned as it rose from the thick thatch of hair at his groin. "It's been a long time since I've seen one of these in the adult form," she admitted. "And this is certainly very adult." She stroked a fingertip over its blunt head.

His penis jerked up against the hard wall of his stomach at the touch, then pointed straight out at her. She wrapped her hand around it and lightly squeezed, marveling at the contrast of its velvet-smooth surface to the rigidity beneath.

J.D. sucked for air. Holy Mary, Mother of— If he wanted to avoid a quick regression to caveman behavior, he'd better do something fast. She was destroying the last of his self-control.

He reached for the hand she'd wrapped around his dick, intending to peel her fingers away. Instead, he found himself wrapping his own hand over hers and directing it up and down his shaft for several strokes. Then, squeezing his eyes shut against the sensations, he did what he should have done right away and removed both their hands.

He had to slow the hell down before he went off like a teenager with his first woman.

He maneuvered them onto the bed and, lying on his side next to her, pushed up on one elbow to kiss her. Her mouth was so soft and sweet, and kissing it helped steady him. For several long moments he cradled her face between the thumb and fingers of his free hand and simply enjoyed the feel of her smooth skin, the taste and texture of her lips.

But both of them were much too far along to slow the pace for long. J.D. became aware of Dru's legs shifting restlessly, of her hips executing small, seeking thrusts. He lifted his head and stared down at her. "Tell me what you want."

"Love me?" she said. "Please, J.D.? I'm so . . . oh, God, I'm just so—" Her legs spread against the quilt. "I want you inside me."

His heart banged up against the wall of his chest, and he fumbled open the drawer of the bedside stand. He grabbed out a condom and put it on. Then he rolled to prop himself above her.

"Are you hot, Drucilla?" he whispered hoarsely. He reached down to ease his fingers into the slick delta between her legs and slide them up and down. The sight, the feel, of all that honeyed heat made him suck in a sharp breath. He expelled it with a gust. "Oh, yeah. You're hot, all right. And, God . . . so . . . wet."

She made a frantic noise in her throat and crooked her knees, letting them drop toward the bed and opening herself up to him. It broke J.D.'s control and he shifted over her, thumbing down his erection and lowering himself until he could rub its nerve-rich head up and down her slippery feminine cleft, once, twice, three times. It was like sliding against wet satin, and he couldn't wait any longer. Lining himself up with her opening, he pushed.

His penis slid into her an inch or two and they both arched and froze, staring at each other. Then, "Oh, God, *yes*," Dru said, and J.D. slowly pushed as deep inside her as a man could go. She closed tightly around him, and he had to grit his teeth against the urge to start banging away like a pile driver run amuck. Planting his hands on the mattress on either side of her shoulders, he stiff-armed himself away from her upper body and took slow, controlled breaths, pulling his hips back in increments, then thrusting them forward, pulling back and thrusting forward. Carefully, slowly.

So slowly.

Sweat began to roll from his hairline, and if the feel of his balls was any criterion, he suspected they might be turning blue. But, dammit, he would make this last for her.

Dru had no desire for it to last; she was teetering on the ragged edge as it was. So close—dear God, she was so very close—but not . . . quite . . . there. She tilted her hips up, inhaling sharply when all that hard heat stretching up inside her sank a little deeper, drove her a little closer to the precipice.

"Oh, *please*," she whispered. "A little faster. Please? Um!" His erection touched a place deep inside her that gave her an intimation of the ultimate sensations to come, but then it was gone, slowly sliding away. "A little harder, J.D.?"

He continued those long, slow, measured strokes.

Dru's hackles rose. Was he teasing her? Showing her how a city boy could turn a country girl inside out if he set his mind to it? She looked up into his face.

And saw that this was no tease.

The muscles in his arms and shoulders were locked and stood out in stark relief. His face, his neck, his chest, were drenched in sweat, and he looked as if he hurt somewhere way down deep at its most elemental level. His dark eyebrows were furrowed over his nose, his pupils were dilated as he stared blindly straight ahead, and his lips were drawn back from his clenched teeth in lockjawed tension.

She reached up and cupped his face in her hands. The muscles beneath her palms were like granite. "J.D.?"

It took a moment for her voice to sink in; then he looked down at her. His eyes suddenly focused and he started to lower his head to kiss her. Her hands tightened fractionally to hold him off long enough to ensure his attention. "Harder?" she murmured. She raised her head to press a soft kiss against his lower lip, then lowered it back onto the spread. "Please, John David, love me harder. I'm so close and—"

A growl reverberated deep in his chest as all the restraint he'd demonstrated up until now disappeared. His mouth slammed down on hers in a feverish kiss, and his hips began to pick up speed, pounding into her with emphatic, rapid-fire thrusts.

"Oh, my God," she breathed when he lifted his mouth off hers. His arms bent and his chest came down on hers, then his hands slid under her bottom and tilted her hips to a new angle. Every inward thrust he made hit against that sweet spot high up inside her, and she felt the coil of an approaching climax wind tighter and tighter yet. "Oh, my—J.D.? Oh, God, oh, God, *John David*!" His name emerged as a scream and her fingernails sank into his back as she suddenly exploded into a million and one particles, concentric bands of sensation clenching, clenching, clenching, clamping hard around the hard heat that forged a place for itself deep inside her.

"Oh, Jesus." J.D.'s voice was a low, hoarse rasp. "Oh, Jesus, I'm coming, Drucilla; I'm—" Pulling back, he slammed deep one last time, then groaned, a long, harsh, satisfied sound that wrapped itself around her heart. For several long moments, all his muscles froze solid.

Then he collapsed atop her.

She should have felt flattened—he was a big man and not exactly light as a feather. Instead, she gloried in his weight as it bore her down into the quilt. Sweat bonded them together everywhere they touched, and Dru wrapped her arms around his neck and stroked his hair, his neck, his shoulders.

I love you. She squeezed her eyes shut. *God, I do. I love you, John David Carver.*

She longed to say the words aloud, but didn't dare. The memory of his saying that doing it with a good girl led to nothing but trouble was still too fresh in her mind. She needed to play it cool, or he'd probably kick her out of bed so fast it'd make her head swim.

She tightened her hold on him and listened with satisfaction to the sound of contentment he made. So, fine, then. She would simply keep her *I love you* to herself for the time being.

But no one on earth could stop her from thinking it.

18

J.D. stretched out on top of Dru's round, soft body and tried not to think. Since he felt as though all his brain cells had ended up in the reservoir tip of his condom, that wasn't all that tough to do, at first. But once his heart quit thundering in his ears and he'd caught his breath, it was difficult not to make a host of unwelcome comparisons.

Never before, following even the hottest bout of sex, had he felt anything remotely close to the way he felt right now. Not merely this low, warm hum of sexual satisfaction, but . . . peaceful, too.

It was an odd word to use in conjunction with himself. And "cosmically fulfilled" would hardly be his first choice to describe his usual postcoital condition, but the truth of the matter was, that was how he felt. Or like some big old alley cat who'd just scored himself a nice, warm hearth and three squares a day. All he knew for certain was that sex with Drucilla felt a lot more like making love than his usual let's-screw-and-then-I-gotta-hit-the-road routine.

And it scared the bejesus out of him.

Because he'd satisfied all that rampant sexual curiosity he'd been harboring about her and had finally slaked a major case of lust—and that should have been the end of it.

Instead, he felt like starting all over again. He wanted to rebuild her arousal kiss by kiss, touch by touch, until he heard her breath catch in her throat and her voice beg for satisfaction. Until he felt her writhe beneath him and clamp down around him as she came.

Burying his face in her hair, he shivered, but it wasn't from the cold. When Dru murmured and tightened her arms around him, he eased his hands out from under her butt and wrapped her in his arms to hold her in return. Feelings he didn't want to examine too closely swamped him, making him edgier than that alley cat defending a hard-fought-for scrap of food from all comers.

He took a slow, deep breath and quietly expelled it. *Okay, Carver, get a grip,* he instructed himself firmly. *It's the situation that's making you feel this way. It's just the situation.*

For the first time since his brief stay with Edwina, he'd been given a piece of something to call his own—not to mention a place that was beginning to feel a bit like home, and people who at least gave lip service to treating him like family. Of course, he knew that feelings of belonging were unreliable at best and emotional security was a myth. His life had gone through some dramatic changes in the past few weeks. Add to that the fact that he'd never gotten it on with a woman like Drucilla before, and you had a righteous set of extenuating circumstances. Maybe she wasn't the goody-goody he'd originally thought, but she was still a good girl.

She sure didn't cling and scream and use her nails on you like a good girl—and you've got the welts on your hide to prove it.

He shoved the thought aside. Fine, forget about her being a good girl, then—he'd never gotten it on with a *mother*, at least not one who'd displayed anything close to Dru's caliber of parenting. She was a good mother, exceptional, really, and maybe because he'd never known what it was to have a mother like her to fiercely protect his interests when he was a kid, he had a reverence for the breed.

J.D. breathed easier. *That's* what made this seem different. He'd just never made lo—had *sex* with such a caring mother before. Some of the women he'd met in bars had had kids, of course, but they'd always seemed to have a lot less interest in what those kids were doing than in satisfying their own needs.

Or maybe more than anything else, this connection he felt with Dru had to do with her calling him John David. Nobody called him by his given name, and there'd just been something so . . . intimate about it. It had really gotten to him.

That was likely the reason he'd felt so tender toward Dru when they were making lo—fuc . . . having sex—all right, dammit, making love! He was man enough to admit it had felt like they'd made love.

But it wasn't like he was *in* love, or anything. That wasn't an emotion he believed in, at least not for himself.

Dru wheezed for air under him and J.D. pushed up on his forearms and looked down at her guiltily. "I'm sorry. Can you breathe?"

She sucked in a deep breath and let it out. "I can now. You're not exactly a lightweight, are you?"

He started to push back, but she looped her arms around his neck and held him in place.

"I didn't mean you should go," she said softly. "I like feeling your weight—as long as I can grab a breath every now and then." One of the sweetest smiles he'd ever seen crossed her face. "It's solid and nice," she said with the closest thing to shyness J.D. had ever seen from her.

His heart contracted. If he were a good man, he'd ease out of this relationship before she started putting too much stock in it. He wasn't a long-term-relationship kind of guy and never would be, and it was unfair to allow her to think that he was. The kindest thing he could probably do would be to give her a kiss, say, "Thanks, it's been fun," and then take a giant step back.

But he was neither a good man nor a kind one, and he didn't *want* to do that. At least not yet. She looked so pretty lying there beneath him with her rumpled hair and her swollen lips, with those siren breasts and that little waist, and he felt himself growing hard again inside her. He lowered his head to kiss her.

This time it was a friendly, lazy tussle of warm-skinned body rubbing warm-skinned body as they scrapped for position. Dru took him by surprise by rolling them over, then pushing up to sit astride him. "Queen of the mountain," she declared, and laughed, thumping her chest in triumph. Then she raised her hips and slowly lowered them again, and the smile slid away. He about went crazy seeing the heavy-eyed sensuality that took its place.

He did go nuts when she started in with that *Please, John David* stuff again. Hands gripping the lush swell of her hips, he rolled her back under him and thrust hard, fast, and furiously to another teeth-clenching climax. And when they were both limp with spent satisfaction, he pulled her into his arms and held her tight until exhaustion claimed him.

He awoke before she did in the morning. It was just after dawn and he'd had too few hours of sleep, but once he was awake, he was awake for good. The rain had stopped sometime in the night, and fingers of light edged around the shade covering his window. Raising his head off the pillow, he looked down at Dru nestled against his chest.

She looked soft and sweet and completely untouched by the sort of ugliness that had marred much of his life. In an unaccustomed fit of chivalry, he knew he had to come clean with her about his inability to sustain any kind of relationship. She was a decent woman and she deserved to know the truth so she could make an informed decision as to where she saw this thing going.

A cynical laugh got caught in his throat. Nowhere, that's where she'd see it go. Once she understood the kind of guy he was and the sort of relationships that were his norm, she'd be gone so fast he probably wouldn't see her for the dust.

The idea bothered him more than he liked to admit. But he assured himself that the ache in his gut was simply a knee-jerk reaction to being denied something—even if the person denying it to him was himself. Giving the situation a long, hard, realistic look, he decided the important thing was preserving some sort of manageable relationship—because even after things inevitably ended between them, they'd still have to work together.

So there was no sense in stringing it out until things got to the point where it was impossible to do even that.

J.D. was no longer in bed when Dru awakened. She stretched beneath the sheet with a soft groan that became more heartfelt as twinges in unaccustomed places made their presence known. Then she smiled, because, truly, what a fine time she'd had getting in this condition. Continuing to stretch, she rolled over.

She heard the bathroom door open, and a moment later J.D. walked into the bedroom. He had obviously showered and was already dressed in a fresh white T-shirt and jeans, although his feet were still bare. His cheeks and jaw had that gleam only seen on babies' bottoms and newly shaven skin, and he'd brushed his wet hair away from his forehead.

Dru sat up, tucking the thin sheet under her arms and ignoring the room's faint chill against her exposed back as she smiled up at him. Lord, but he was sexy. "Good morning."

He thrust his hands in his front pockets. "Mornin'."

His tone was agreeable enough and he even smiled at her, but there was something about his posture, a stiff wariness that caused a trickle of unease to roll down Dru's spine.

"What?" she demanded.

"We have to talk." He rolled his shoulders. "Look, Drucilla, it's been . . ."

"*Fun*?" she suggested flatly, and upon seeing the grimace of guilt that quirked his mouth, regarded him through narrowed eyes. Had she really been that mistaken? He'd seemed so involved, so careful and sweet with her, that she'd convinced herself he must surely care about her a little, too. But she was beginning to get a bad, bad feeling that she'd been fooling herself.

"No! That is, it *was* fun, of course—it was *more* than fun." Fists pressed to the bottom of his pockets, he hunched his shoulders up around his ears for a second as he stared down at her. "Shit. This is coming out all wrong." He gave her a look filled with regret. "Dru, last night was really great—"

"I get it, all right?" God, she couldn't believe she'd been such a chump. She climbed out of the bed, pulling the sheet free as she rose and wrapping it the rest of the way around her. Being naked in front of him was conceivable five minutes ago; it wasn't an option now. "Last night was great, but it's over. You've gotten what you wanted, and it's time for me to go back to my own place and leave you to yours." She spotted her panties on the floor and her dress draped over the dresser top, where J.D. must have picked it up off the floor and put it this morning. She scooped up the undies and headed for the dress, looking around for her sandals. "Don't worry. I'll be out of your hair in seconds flat."

Suddenly he was behind her, his arms wrapping around her to pull her back against him. She struggled to get free, but he tightened his grip and she immediately stopped. Damned if she'd engage in a wrestling match with him; this was humiliating enough as it was.

He rubbed his cheek against her temple. "I've never had a relationship that's lasted more than three nights running," he said in a low voice. "I don't believe in fairy tales and I'm not a man for love ever after."

It was both an apology and an explanation from a man Dru instinctively knew rarely offered either, and she twisted her head around in an attempt to see him. "Who asked you to?" she demanded, but most of her belligerence had drained away. His chest was warm against her back, his arms warm and strong as they wrapped around her waist. Some of the stiffness left her as she uncricked her neck to face front again and rest against him. "I'm not a big believer in fairy tales myself."

"I think you believe in relationships, though. And *I* believe that someday you'll probably find the perfect one."

"Oh, you do, do you?"

"Yeah."

"And what about you? Will you find the perfect relationship, too?"

"No," he said flatly. "And even if I did, I'd manage to ruin it, because I wouldn't know how to keep something like that alive. But you've got your aunt and uncle as an example of a marriage that works, and even I can see it's a good one."

"Yes, it is. But it's their marriage. I haven't had a relationship of my own work out."

"But you deserve to." An unamused laugh rumbled against her back. "You deserve someone a helluva lot better than me."

Something twisted in her stomach. But her own tone was every bit as cynical as his when she said, "You think so? Or is this just a more tactful way of kissing me off?"

His arms tightened around her. "I don't want to kiss you off." He bent his knees and pressed an erection she'd been too upset to notice before against her bottom. "I'd like to make love to you until you go cross-eyed and beg for mercy. But we've got to work together, Dru, and I also don't want a big mess when things between us get all screwed up . . . which they will sooner or later."

"Are you so sure of that?"

"Oh, yeah. Trust me on this. I'll do something to make you hate my guts . . . so let's be smart and just wind things up now before it comes to that."

Perhaps because he always came across as impervious to criticism and confident in the extreme, it had never occurred to Dru that J.D. might not think very much of himself. But that was what she was hearing now. He thought there was a relationship somewhere out there for her, but that a lasting bond wasn't even a possibility for him. He said she *deserved* someone better than him.

Where was what *he* deserved in all this? Why didn't he at least deserve to go into a relationship without feeling certain it would end up in tatters because of him?

She might be fooling herself and setting herself up for a world of heartache, but she thought John David Carver had a lot more going for him than *he* seemed to think he had. He could have let her walk away, left her believing he'd used her, but he hadn't. Instead, he'd laid his ego on the line for her to accept or slice into little pieces as she wished. He might never have seen examples of a functional, loving relationship, but he had some pretty decent values of his own, particularly for someone who had grown up without a nurturing influence.

Gripping her sheet, she turned to face him, and he allowed it this time, his arms dropping away. It was too late for her to walk away—the die had been cast last night. If he hurt her in the end . . . well, at least she would never have to be sorry she'd lacked the guts to go after a dream; would never have to regret having given up before she'd even tried.

"Tell you what," she said, reaching out to trail her fingers from the hollow at his throat down the clean white cotton of his T-shirt to his sternum, where she pressed her hand flat, fingers spread. "Why don't we risk it all instead."

He went very still, the sinew beneath her palm going hard as stone. His eyes were a hazel-green glint behind narrowed lashes as he stared down at her suspiciously. "What—do you want to gamble for my part of the lodge or something?"

"For Pete's sake, J.D. Of course not."

"Good. Because I said I was hot to have that sweet body of yours again and again, not that I'm a total—"

"I want to gamble on this need to know you that I

have burning here," she interrupted him, spreading her free hand against her stomach. "And here." She brought it up to her heart as she looked him squarely in the eye. The sheet began to slide, but instead of making a grab for it, she let it go. "I don't pretend to know what you feel for me, but I feel something for you, John David, and—"

She saw something flash across his face; then the next thing she knew, he had her pressed up against the dresser, his hands gripping her upper arms.

"Don't mess with me, Drucilla," he warned in a low voice.

"I'm *not* messing with you. I have feelings for you, and I want to explore what they are. I don't want to back away and pretend last night never happened just so we can work peacefully side by side."

He kissed her, and it was rough and on the verge of losing control. The sheet had disappeared somewhere, and she had one brief moment to register the softness of J.D.'s T-shirt and the rougher denim of his jeans against her bare skin before he ripped his mouth away and pushed himself back slightly, leaving her to stare up at him.

His breath sawed through parted lips as he looked back down at her. "Then that's what we'll do," he said with a clipped nod, and bent his head toward hers again. "But don't say I didn't warn you when everything goes to hell."

Butch was not the happiest camper in the universe when he watched J.D. walk the stacked Kewpie doll across the clearing. It had finally quit raining around five this morning, but he was cold and wet and hadn't gotten more than a snatch of sleep here and there all night long.

While his good buddy Carver had been tucked up nice and cozy, doing the horizontal shimmy-shake on a sweetly cushioned female.

The only good thing to come out of the miserable night was that he was now ninety-nine percent certain that this was indeed Loverboy's digs. He stepped into the clearing the minute J.D. and the woman disappeared down a trail he'd had plenty of time to explore last night. Holier-Than-Thou Carver hadn't gotten in his car and driven off, and from the looks of things and the few words Butch had managed to overhear just now, he'd say J.D. was walking the babe home. She was probably some chickie vacationing at the lodge or at one of the other cabins farther down the trail.

Butch eased up onto the porch and eyed the shiny red canoe resting upside down on a couple of sawhorses under the roof. Hell, that should have tipped him off right there. J.D. had had a thing for canoes ever since the time they'd thugged one out by the Arboretum when they were kids.

He tried the door, fully expecting to find it locked, but the knob turned smoothly beneath his hand. J.D. was slipping. This never would have happened in his Rat City crib. Living in the sticks was clearly causing him to lose his edge.

Which worked just fine for Butch. He opened the door, but then had second thoughts and hesitated.

He didn't have any idea how long it would take J.D.

to walk the woman to her room and get back here again. For all Butch knew, his old bud might fully intend to get himself another piece of ass. But he also might just dump her and come straight back to his own place.

And the last thing Butch planned to do was let J.D. know that he was here. His onetime friend was undoubtedly working a job around here—he never had known how to relax worth a damn and just have a good time. If this were a weekday instead of Saturday, Butch wouldn't have hesitated to grab the opportunity to go in and toss the joint. But he wasn't about to blow the element of surprise. Butch refused to even acknowledge the oily little roll he got in his gut at the thought of coming face-to-face with J.D.

He looked at the canoe again and then dug into his pocket. The idea that popped into his mind was pretty iffy, but what the hell—it was the best he could do with so little time to work with.

He pulled out his pocketknife and extracted the biggest blade.

Down in town, Kev propped his back against a stack of frilly pillows and watched Char, dressed only in his white shirt, as she bopped around the girliest bedroom he'd ever clapped eyes on. He'd never known so many pink stripes, flowers, and solids even existed—let alone coexisted in a halfway peaceful manner.

When Char leaned forward to peer into the big mahogany mirror that topped her fabric-skirted dressing table, he was torn between watching her fluff up that touch-me-Daddy bubble of blond hair, or the sleek little rump that played peekaboo with his shirttail every time she lifted her arms. A tent began to form in the patchwork quilt across his lap, and he grinned ruefully. You'd think the big boy would be worn out by now.

He couldn't get over how good it felt to be with her. While he was in D.C., he hadn't even thought of her—or at least he'd gone long blocks of time without thinking of her. But the minute she'd strolled into his father's store, he'd felt as if he'd been mule-kicked in the gut. It'd all come rushing back—the wanting, the not being able to have for fear she'd screw up all his plans—and he'd automatically reverted to his old push-away habits.

Now he couldn't get close enough. Rearranging a frothy little pillow that had slipped out from between his head and the knobby brass headboard, he smiled crookedly at the warm, jumbled disorder of her room. "I'm sorely disappointed in you, Char."

She whirled to face him, and the smile left his face at the stricken expression in her brown eyes. Hell. He would have thought that after last night she'd fully understand his intentions. He said lightly, "I thought for sure all you masseuse types surrounded yourselves with wind chimes, crystals, and whale music."

The stiffness left her spine. "Yeah? Well, I thought all you lawyer types slept in your power ties." One delicate shoulder hitched beneath the Egyptian cotton of his shirt. "Guess we were both wrong."

But her gaze remained uncertain, and he pushed himself a little higher among the pillows. To hell with keeping it light—if he was going to scare her off, let it be for the truth. "I'm here to stay, you know," he said. "There might not be enough work around Star Lake itself to set up my practice, but I plan to settle somewhere on this side of the state."

"And you're telling me this because . . . ?"

"Because I'm crazy about you and I think we've got the potential for something special. And because I don't want you to think I'm just killing time with you until I can make tracks back to the big city."

The small smile curving her lips caused more tenting action under the covers. "Take off my shirt," he commanded.

She looked at him from beneath her lashes. "I don't think so. I think I might just keep it for a very long time—maybe even forever." Kev didn't think she was talking about his apparel anymore, but before he could pin down the look in her eyes, she ran her hands under the collar, flipped it up, and gave him a flirtatious smile. "Besides, I bet a big-time lawyer like you has an entire closet full of boring white shirts."

"Maybe. But that one's my favorite."

"Pooh." She sashayed over to the bed. "One bland shirt's pretty much the same as another. What's so special about this one?"

He lunged, catching her around the waist and tumbling her onto the mattress. Propping himself over her, he brushed away a strand of hair that had flopped over one eye. "It has you in it."

"Oooh," she breathed and beamed up at him. "Good answer."

19

"Come *on*, Mom! We don't wanna be late—J.D. might leave without us."

Dru looked up from checking the contents of her beach bag to see her son standing by the front door, impatiently shifting his weight from one foot to the other. "He's not going to leave without us, Tate. Besides, we're nowhere near late. We've got a good fifteen minutes before he asked us to be there, and it's a five-minute walk, tops."

She could see by his continued fidgeting that her words had no effect whatsoever, and laughing, she snatched up her bag. "All right, okay—I'm ready, already."

Tate blasted through the doorway and out into the corridor as if a starter gun had been shot off. Dru's exit was more sedate, and by the time she'd locked the door behind her, her son was nowhere in sight.

She didn't catch up to him until she reached the clearing in front of J.D.'s cabin, and then it was to see Tate already on the front porch. He was all but dancing in place next to the canoe.

She smiled at his excitement. Then J.D. walked out of the cabin, wearing a raggedy pair of cutoffs, a black tank top, and flip-flops, and an extra throb was added to her heartbeat.

She hadn't seen him since late yesterday afternoon. Tate had arrived home from Billy's around five, and J.D. had hung around for only a short while before bidding them good night and taking off.

She'd known he couldn't spend the night—not with an impressionable boy in the house. But that hadn't helped to prepare her for how much she would miss him after he'd left. You wouldn't think a single night together could make such an impact on her life, yet it had.

It definitely had.

Seeing the anticipation on both male faces as she came up on the porch, Dru was especially glad the weather had turned nice again. J.D.'s eyes were alight, and while his smile wasn't quite as huge as Tate's, he was clearly just as pumped up about the maiden voyage of his canoe.

"Give me a hand here, buddy," he said to Tate as he assembled boating paraphernalia. "Help me check this stuff off against my list. I want to make sure I've got everything we need for the big event."

"Let's hope you do." Dru glanced at the stuff stacked on the porch floor. "If you add anything more, your boat will probably sink beneath the weight."

J.D. flashed her a smile that was every bit as brilliant as her son's, and Dru felt her heart squeeze at seeing such unrestrained joy on his normally guarded face. He looked as happy and lighthearted as a teenager cutting school to hit the local swimming hole.

But he pretended indignation. "Hey," he protested. "I don't have all that much stuff. Do I, Tate?" He didn't even hesitate to enlist her son's support, and when it was unreservedly given, the wattage on J.D.'s smile cranked up a few degrees higher. "See?" he demanded. "Your kid agrees. We've simply got us a few flotation cushions to sit on, a paddle, and a cooler that's so small it's hardly worth mentioning. That's it. Except for lunch, of course, but as any guy will tell you, that's not an extra; that's essential." He gave her beach bag a nod. "It's that big ol' satchel of yours I'm worried about. What've you got in there, anyway, primping stuff?"

"Primping stuff!" She swung the bag at his lean hip, but he neatly sidestepped it. "I'll have you know I've got the bare minimum of necessities in here. Well, except for the lunch part. We did duplicate that, because I didn't know you were packing one, too, but aside from—"

"You brought *lunch*?" His eyes lit up. "What'd you pack? Chicks always do so much better than guys in the food department, but that's only because they belong in the kitchen."

"Oh!" Her bag hit the porch floor. "You are really asking for it now, buster." She launched herself at him, but before she knew what was what, she was flush up against his body, his arms wrapped around her, pinning hers to her sides.

"*Mom*!" Tate's tone of voice said he was not amused. "Leave J.D. alone—we've got a boat to launch." He shook his head in disgust and looked at his hero. "You know what else she's prob'ly got in there?" he asked in a long-suffering tone that implied cod-liver oil at the very least.

J.D. cocked his head at Tate in a solemn, you've-got-my-fullest-attention-buddy gesture while he subtly rubbed his pelvis against Dru's. "What's that?"

"*Sunscreen*. She never lets me go anywhere without sunscreen. And towels, I bet. Like we couldn't just drip-dry."

"Hey!" Dru stuck her nose in the air. "I don't need this abuse. Maybe I'll just take my fried chicken and go home."

J.D.'s arms tightened around her for a second before he turned her loose. "Now, let's not be too hasty. Whaddaya think, Tate? I mean, girls don't really belong on boats, since they lack the proper reverence and appreciation. But still, fried *chicken*."

"Yeah, Mom makes awfully good chicken—'specially the drumsticks. And I suppose towels aren't really all that bad. Maybe we'd better let her stay."

"It's a sacrifice on our part," J.D. agreed. "But I think we should."

"You're both much too kind." But Dru couldn't prevent the grin she felt tugging up one side of her mouth. This teasing J.D. was new and totally surprising—she couldn't have stopped herself from being charmed to save her soul.

J.D. handed Tate the lunch he'd packed and asked him to put it back in the refrigerator. Then he divided the gear into two piles for Dru and Tate to carry, and hauled the heavy wooden canoe out into the yard. Once it was clear of the porch roof, he hefted the vessel to balance it, upside down, upon his head.

"Wouldn't it be easier to just stack all the stuff inside and have us each take an end?" Dru questioned.

J.D. gave her a purely male look that seemed to demand, *Do I* look *like I need help?* as he did something that caused his biceps to leap into prominence. Dru snorted, but she felt heat spread not only up her throat and onto her face at the silly macho display, but also downward from her stomach.

Tate came barreling back, and he and Dru gathered up their loads, then followed J.D. down the trail. A few minutes later they were on Ben and Sophie's private dock.

As J.D. squatted down to stow everything in the canoe, which he'd tied alongside, Dru stripped off her T-shirt and shorts, which left her in her new bathing suit. After digging her sunscreen out of the beach bag, she slathered some on herself, then passed the bottle to Tate and oversaw its application. She handed him his life vest, then tucked her clothing and the shirt Tate tossed her into the bag with the towels. Giving both males an ironic look, she said, "I think I'll just leave this here. I wouldn't want it taking up too much precious cargo space."

Tate shot her an unrepentant big-toothed grin and clambered into the canoe.

J.D.'s gaze tracked her suit from its low-scooped top to its high-cut bottom as he motioned for her to follow her son into the canoe. Instead, Dru stopped in front of him.

"If you think you're getting out of wearing sunscreen like the rest of us, buster, you're dead wrong," she said. "I don't care how big and bad you think you are, your skin can be damaged just as easily as Tate's."

He went still for a minute, then slowly reached over his back to pull his tank top off over his head. Dru shook lotion into his hand for him to apply to his front, then did his back herself. "Get your face, too," she directed as she carefully tucked his shirt into her bag alongside her own and Tate's.

Then she stepped into the canoe, and J.D. uncleated the line and pushed off, stepping into the stern as the boat moved sleekly away from the dock. From beneath her lashes, Dru observed the pure contentment that came over his face when he settled onto his seat and commenced to paddle with strong, smooth strokes.

And her lips curved up in a contented smile of her own.

J.D. couldn't remember the last time he'd felt this mellow. The sun was warm on his shoulders, and the lap of water against the hull and the call of birds flying overhead and roosting in the trees that crowded the shoreline began to supplant the sound of kids' voices on the swim float. The canoe handled effortlessly as it cut smoothly across the placid water toward the less populated end of the lake.

He watched Tate where he knelt on the forward seat, gripping the sides of the canoe with both hands. Head into the breeze like a happy pup thrusting its nose out the window of a moving car, he bobbed his rump up and down against his heels and chattered with excitement. And Drucilla, who had bullied him into wearing sunscreen so his tough hide wouldn't be damaged, gave him a soft smile every time he looked her way. Add a picnic of home-fried chicken to anticipate and—J.D. grinned—it just didn't get much better than this.

A little over halfway across the lake, he noticed Dru's eyebrows abruptly draw together. She frowned down at her feet, then looked back up at him.

"J.D.? We're taking on water."

He looked down and saw that lake water was indeed seeping up through the floorboards beneath Dru's feet. His eyebrows snapped together. What the hell? Had he somehow missed seeing some gaps in the bent cedar planking? He didn't see how that was possible, considering the way he'd gone over the craft again and again during the past week and a half. Yet he'd clearly missed something, for already water was beginning to pool up and down the keel line.

He whispered a curse and sank his paddle deep in the water, pushing it forward to stop the canoe and swivel it around. He looked at Dru. "There's a cup in the cooler. Start bailing, will you?"

"J.D.?" Tate turned from his perch in the front of the canoe. "How come we're turning back? Hey! There's water all over the bottom!"

"Yeah, we seem to have sprung a leak." J.D. spared him a quick glance. "Be sure your life vest is fastened, Tate." Then he returned his attention to putting as much power behind his strokes as he could to get them back to shore before the canoe filled.

But it was starting to take on water at an accelerated rate, and because he far outweighed Dru and Tate, it rolled down to his end, which rapidly began to fill up. The bow lifted up, while the stern settled lower and lower in the water.

And he knew they weren't going to make it.

"Whoa!" Tate yelled, as if he were on a carnival ride that had just taken an unexpected twist.

To even out the weight distribution, J.D. moved to kneel by the mid-boat thwart in front of Dru. "It's taking on too much water too fast," he told her quietly. "I think it'd be safer for us to go into the water now, before matters get critical. I'm sorry." He'd clearly failed to do something or had overlooked an important step when he'd restored the boat, and his mistake had put her and Tate in danger as a result.

"Ah, no," she said and leaned forward to cup his face in her hands. "*I'm* sorry, John David. Your beautiful boat." She gave him a swift, hard kiss, then turned in her seat as the stern sank deeper into the water. "Tate, come here."

He slid down to them, staying low, and shot J.D. a calm look. "We jumpin' ship?"

"I'm afraid so, kid. Let me help you over." J.D. rose up on his knees and reached past Dru to slide his hands beneath Tate's armpits. He carefully lifted the boy over the side and lowered him into the lake. "Tate," he said seriously, looking down at the child whose flotation vest kept him bobbing upright in the water, "I want you to swim well out of range of the boat."

Then he reached for Dru, but she bent forward and gave him a soft peck on the lips. "I can do it," she said. "You just concentrate on saving your canoe." And she rolled over the side with a soft splash.

He wanted to get the boat turned over while there were still pockets of air in it to keep it afloat. But the stern had swamped fast and was already beginning to sink. J.D. bailed into the water, then turned to see what he could salvage from the situation.

The stern was going under and the bow was rising straight up in the air, and it was a toss-up whether the craft would simply sink straight down or continue over and come down upside down. He hoped for the latter—until he saw it would happen exactly that way . . . and that Tate was right in the descending bow's path.

"Tate!" he yelled. "Get back!" He launched himself forward.

Dru screamed her son's name at the same time, and the pure terror in her voice sent Tate, who had started to turn at J.D.'s yell, paddling back around to face her. He was blind to the danger headed his way, and J.D. put on a burst of speed, swimming faster than he'd ever swum in his life.

He knew he wasn't going to make it in time to push Tate beyond the rapidly descending bow's path, so he threw all his energy into one last powerful butterfly stroke that brought his shoulders rearing up out of the water. With only seconds to spare, he landed on top of Tate, and his hands shoved the boy deep beneath the surface of the water. Red-hot agony exploded between J.D.'s shoulder blades in the next instant as the point of the bow hammered down on top of him; then he too was submerged, driven underwater several feet to a place both cool and dark. Nerves sang up to his neck, across his shoulders, and down both arms, and inhaling sharply through his mouth in an involuntary response to the pain, he swallowed a copious amount of lake water.

It rushed down his windpipe and up his nose, and he sank deeper beneath the surface. His lungs burned with the need to cough, and for just a moment he couldn't tell up from down.

Then he realized that his body mass had pushed Tate's skinny little frame deeper underwater and blocked the boy's life vest from doing its job. Wrapping his hands around Tate's waist, he scooped him out from under him and thrust the boy toward the golden-greenish light that sent shafts through the lake's uppermost strata. He shot toward the surface in Tate's wake.

Both sucked in great gulps of oxygen the instant their heads broke through water into fresh air. They were immediately racked by harsh paroxysms of coughing, which forced brackish water out of their lungs. Then Dru was there to pull Tate into her arms and support him until he quit coughing.

One arm hooked desperately around her neck, he turned to glare at J.D. through red-rimmed eyes full of baffled anger and betrayal. "You tried to drown me!"

The accusation hit J.D. like a fist in the gut, and the little bit of breath he'd managed to regain stopped up in his throat. In the small corner of his brain still functioning on logic, he understood that Tate had been facing away from him and knew only that one minute he'd been treading water, and the next J.D. had shoved him under and held him down.

Emotionally, though, the I've-been-double-crossed look in the boy's eyes went straight to his heart, and he stared back mutely without a word to say in his own defense.

"No!" Dru cried with heartfelt passion. She grasped Tate's chin and tugged it around until he looked at her. "*No*. The canoe flipped over and was just about to hit you in the head! He had to push you out of the way, Tate! He saved your life." She sidestroked the two of them toward J.D. "Oh, God, John David, thank you for saving my baby's life!"

Reaching him, she released one of the arms that fiercely hugged Tate to her breast and wrapped it around J.D.'s neck, turning it into a three-way embrace. She pressed frantic kisses of gratitude against his throat, his chin, his jaw. Then she drew back and studied him with worried eyes. "You were hurt," she said. "I saw the canoe slam down on top of you." She tried to turn him to see. "Show me where you're hurt."

He'd never had anyone mother him in his life, and he shrugged uncomfortably. "It's nothing," he said roughly. "I'm fine." A spot between his shoulder blades ached like a sonovabitch, but there was nothing that could be done about it out here in the middle of the lake. Besides, he was a grown man; he didn't need to be fussed over.

Even if it did feel kind of nice.

Then Tate's arm snaked around his neck, too. "I'm sorry, J.D.," he said in a small, tremulous voice. His chin wobbled and tears rose in his eyes. "I shouldn't have said . . . I didn't mean"—his voice suddenly cracked—"I just wanna go home!"

J.D. had once been ten years old himself and remembered what it felt like to cry in front of others, so he pressed Tate's head down onto his shoulder to give him some privacy. "Your mama and I are going to get you home real soon, buddy," he said into the child's ear and rubbed his jaw against Tate's sleek, wet crown. "I promise. And I'm sorry I scared you. I wouldn't have done that for the world if I could've avoided it."

" 'Kay," the boy said with a sniff.

Then J.D. heard the whine of an outboard motor, and he looked up to see one of the lodge speedboats racing across the lake toward them. The driver throttled back when he was a hundred feet away and the boat gently rode the wake that continued to push it forward, easing to an expert stop alongside them. J.D. recognized the driver as one of the young men who worked in the sport shop and saw with surprise that Sean, the bellhop, was with him.

"Are you guys all right?" Sean demanded, leaning over the side. "We saw the canoe come down on top of you. Is everybody okay?"

J.D. felt Tate's hand go up to hastily knuckle the tears from his eyes, and to give him an extra minute to compose himself, he gently urged Dru forward. "Why don't you go first?"

She glanced at Tate, then nodded and raised her hands to Sean for a boost up.

J.D. watched her come out of the water and hook a

leg over the side of the speedboat. He figured he couldn't be injured all that seriously when he found himself admiring the way her wet suit molded to the lush curve of her bottom as she tumbled over the side into the craft.

Tate wiped his nose on J.D.'s shoulder and J.D. tucked in his chin to look down at him. "You ready, buddy?"

"Yeah."

He tightened his arms around the boy for a second. "You were one brave kid throughout this whole ordeal and handled yourself like a pro. I'm proud of you." He lifted Tate up to Sean, who swung him into the boat.

Then he took one last look around. He knew the tip of the canoe was most likely bobbing somewhere just beneath the surface, but there wasn't so much as a ripple on the water's surface to show where. For an instant a despairing sort of sickness sat heavily on his gut. Then, with a mental shrug that helped shove the feeling aside, he reached up to grab hold of the speedboat's side and lever himself up out of the water.

20

Sophie and Ben were waiting on their dock when the boat pulled up alongside it, alerted by a call from the boat's cell phone.

J.D. rose stiffly to his feet and stood back to let Dru and Tate climb out first. Thanking the two young men for their prompt rescue, he stepped up onto the dock and watched as Ben uncleated the line he'd looped around a piling and tossed it to Sean. Then he braced himself for the older man's condemnation. He didn't doubt for a moment it would be swift in coming.

Sophia swooped down on Dru and Tate before the boat even had a chance to back out of its mooring. She wrapped her arms around her chicks and hugged them to her. "Are you all right?"

"Yes, we're fine," Dru said. "J.D.'s hurt, though."

"He pushed me under the water, Grandma," Tate said excitedly, and J.D. had to marvel at the kid's ability to bounce back so quickly. "I thought he was gonna drown me, but he was getting me outta the way of the canoe when it came down. Then POW! It got him instead."

Dru disengaged herself from Sophie's embrace. "Uncle Ben, there are towels in my bag over there. Could you get them out?" She crossed over to J.D. "Turn around. I want to see your back."

"Let it go," he said brusquely. "It was a minor pop, nothing worth fussing over." Even if it did throb like a bitch in heat.

It was no more than he deserved, anyhow. He rolled his shoulders guiltily, then had to bite back a groan at the pain.

Dru narrowed her eyes at him. She was chock-full of unspent adrenaline and in no mood for his stubbornness. He'd take care of her and Tate in a red-hot minute, but just let the tables be turned and it was "nothing worth fussing over."

"You don't seem to understand, Carver," she informed him with a levelness she was darn proud of, considering she really wanted to yell *Listen up!* and shake some sense into him. "That wasn't a request for permission. Turn around!"

To her amazement, he did. He looked less than happy about it and he muttered beneath his breath as if it were just one huge waste of time, but he actually humored her and presented her with his back.

She sucked in a shocked breath. The skin between his shoulder blades was scraped raw in an inverted V, and additional scrapes trailed down his back. The skin around the point of impact was badly swollen, and a dense purple bruise had begun to bloom from it, spreading across his shoulder blades like the wings of a malignant butterfly.

"Oh," she said in a tiny voice that not only wavered but was several notes higher than normal. She cleared her throat. "Uncle Ben! Come quick."

She felt J.D. stiffen in resistance, but she didn't give a damn. If anyone would know what to do about this, it was her uncle.

Ben looked at J.D.'s back and winced. "Ouch. Looks like it did a number on him, all right."

"And this would have been Tate's head if J.D. hadn't thrown himself between him and the canoe."

"It was my damn canoe that put him in that position in the first place," J.D. growled.

Dru ignored that remark for the idiocy she felt it was. "Do something!" she demanded of her uncle.

He'd been gently pressing the skin around the worst of the abrasions, and he nodded. "Let's go up to the house." He squeezed J.D.'s shoulder. "I'm sure it hurts like crazy, but I don't think we're looking at any serious or permanent damage."

"That's what I've been trying to tell Dru," J.D. said and turned to face them. His posture was wary, his expression shuttered. "Look, I'll just go home and wash it off in the shower."

"No," Ben said firmly. "You'll come up to the house and let me clean and dress it properly."

"Grandpa was a medic in Vietnam," Tate informed J.D. proudly. "So you better do what he says." He darted around to see J.D.'s back for himself. The sight of it froze him in his tracks. "Jeez." He swallowed hard, his expression miserable. "Aw, dang, J.D., I'm sorry."

J.D. turned to look down at him in surprise. "You've got nothing to be sorry about, bud. None of this was your fault."

"Uh-huh. You told me to swim out of range, and I didn't go far enough."

"*No*," J.D. insisted. "You were a trouper from beginning to end. If anyone's to blame here, it's me. I never should have had you in the canoe until I'd made sure I hadn't missed something."

"Oh, *please*," Sophie said with brisk impatience. She scowled at J.D. "I've always regarded you as an intelligent man, so don't go getting stupid on me now."

She picked up a towel and wrapped it around Tate's shoulders, tossed one to Dru, then walked up to J.D. with the last one. She offered it to him along with a stern stare.

Dru was surprised to see him shift beneath that drilling gaze as uneasily as Tate ever had whenever he'd found himself its unlucky recipient. But J.D. obviously hadn't yet learned to duck and run for cover. Accepting the towel, he slung it around his neck, met her gaze head-on, and stubbornly maintained, "I still shouldn't have risked their safety like that."

"Don't piss me off, boy," Sophie began hotly, but Ben deftly inserted himself between her and J.D.

"You're pushing some real hot buttons here, son," he said, and herded the younger man toward the trail. "Soph is real big on personal accountability."

"I'm *trying* to be accountable!"

"And you're doing a damn fine job of it. But what

you're not doing is allowing Dru and Tate to be responsible for their own actions."

Drucilla, following them up the switchback, watched J.D. turn a blank expression on her uncle. His dark brows gathering over his nose, he demanded, "What are you talking about?"

"Hell, son, think about it. Both of them knew before they ever stepped foot in your canoe that it was an old wreck whose seaworthiness was iffy at best."

"Okay, I'll buy that," J.D. agreed. "But they also knew I'm good at fixing things. They trusted me to fix the canoe so it *was* seaworthy." He stopped and faced Ben. "And I thought I had. I swear to you, Ben, I went over that boat with a fine-tooth comb. I read everything on the subject I could get my hands on, and I could have sworn she was watertight."

"So something slipped by you." Ben shrugged and got them moving again. "It happens."

"Not to me it doesn't. Not usually."

Dru held her breath, expecting to hear her uncle lambast J.D. for his arrogance.

Instead, he merely said with gentle sincerity, "I'm real sorry about your boat, son. I know you were crazy about it. But sometimes shit just happens. If it's any solace, though, it's a wooden craft, so it's probably already surfaced. We can retrieve it when you're feeling better."

J.D.'s shoulders were stiff with repudiation. "What's the point? Like you said, it was a wreck and I obviously didn't know jack about fixing it."

Ben opened his front door and stood back to let J.D. and then Dru precede him into the house. He directed a level look at the younger man. "Still. Unless we pull it out, you'll never know exactly what went wrong."

"Yeah, I suppose." Then J.D. nodded. "You're right."

Ben led them to the kitchen, where he pulled out a chair from the table. "Here, sit down," he directed J.D. "I'll go grab my kit."

J.D. swung the chair around, set his towel down on its seat, and straddled it. He folded his arms across the backrest and stared glumly into space.

Dru came up behind him and curled her hands over the rounded muscles where his shoulders met his arms. Careful to avoid contact with the growing bruises, she gently kneaded them. "I'm real sorry about your canoe, too, J.D."

He craned around to see her. "Why the hell is everyone being so nice about this? I came *this* close to killing your kid!"

"No, darn it, you did not!" She sank to her heels next to him, her hands gripping his thigh. She gave his leg a fierce shake. "Tate and I weren't *about* to be left on shore while you had all the fun of taking the canoe out on her maiden voyage. And Uncle Ben is absolutely right—we knew the risks involved. You don't have to assume responsibility for the world here, John David. Let us be accountable for our own actions."

J.D. got a wild look in his eyes, but before he could say a word, Ben returned with his first-aid kit. An instant later Tate burst into the house, with Sophie a mere second or two in his wake. For several moments then, confusion reigned and the noise level climbed as

Ben cleaned and bandaged J.D.'s back and the rest of them fussed over him.

It didn't occur to Dru to find anything odd in that. This was what Lawrences did when a disaster happened to one of them. They rallied around and tried to make things better. And as far as Dru was concerned, J.D. had behaved in a truly heroic fashion.

But she could see that he didn't view his actions in the same light, and she finally distanced herself a bit to give him a little room to breathe. She watched uneasily as the wild, hunted look in his eyes grew more pronounced and tension made his posture more and more ramrod-still.

She couldn't tell exactly what ultimately spooked him. Uncle Ben had finished patching him up, Aunt Soph had supplied coffee, and all of them were actually giving him a little more room. Perhaps it was Tate, deep into his hero-worship mode, who pushed him over the edge. Or it might have been the admiring comment Sophie made.

Whatever the reason, J.D. abruptly shoved to his feet. "I've got to go," he said, his eyes feral. "Um, I have to get out of these wet jeans." His gaze darted left, then right, settling briefly on each of them. "I'm sorry, okay? I just . . . have to go."

And with her heart down around her knees, Dru remained mute as he turned and strode from Ben and Sophie's house.

J.D. slammed into his cabin, then simply stood in the middle of the living room, his chest heaving as he struggled to draw a decent breath.

He rammed all ten fingers through his hair and scraped it back from his forehead, elbows jutting forward as he stared blindly at the wall across the room. Christ. What were they *doing* to him?

He'd learned a long time ago neither to expect nor to want what he couldn't have. A Lawrence had taught him that, and it was a lesson he'd taken to heart.

Now here was a whole new batch of Lawrences, tripping all over themselves to treat him as if he were some freaking prince—and he could see they weren't mocking him, even though they must know damn well the sort of background that had spawned him.

Damn them. They were making him think he could *have* some of those things. Making him want what he'd been denied his entire life—and want it bad.

Fuck.

Well, he wasn't about to fall for that chump's game—not this time. It hurt too much when it all fell apart, which—sooner or later—it inevitably did; that was simply the nature of the beast. So the Lawrences could just forget about getting him to lower his guard. He wasn't going to expose a soft underbelly so they could stick it full of knives. He hadn't survived this long by being stupid.

"J.D.?"

He jerked around. Dru stood on the other side of the screen door, staring back at him. If she'd worn any makeup today, it was no longer evident. She still had on her damp bathing suit and her hair hadn't yet fully dried. The portion that had was flyaway, sticking up here, clumping there, and straggled over one eye.

And, damn her, he'd never seen a prettier, more welcome sight in his life. It scared the hell out of him.

"Go away, Drucilla."

"No." The screen door creaked as she opened it and stepped inside. "You've had a lousy day and are clearly upset, and I'm not leaving you like this."

Anger coursed through him and he embraced it with his whole being. Was it asking so damn much to have one lousy afternoon to pull himself together? He stalked over to her and bent to thrust his face aggressively close. "Go home, dammit!"

She touched a soft hand to his jaw. "No."

All his emotions pushed to the surface. Ignoring the discomfort in his back at the sudden move, he crowded her up against the arched support that divided the living room from the dining area and penned her in by slapping his hands flat on the wall on either side of her head. He lowered his face until they stood nose to nose. "What is it with you?" he demanded, furious with her for the way she kept pushing—and with himself for giving a damn. "You think just because I bounced you around my bed for one lousy night it gives you the right to come barging in where you're not wanted?"

She stared up at him, all soft determination and gas-flame blue eyes. "Yes."

Alarmed, he stiff-armed himself away. "Go home. I don't have a goddam thing to offer you."

"Oh, boy," she breathed. "That's the biggest lie I've ever heard. You have *so* much to offer."

"I've got *this*." He lowered his head once again to kiss her roughly, and it was all probing tongue and hard dominance. Then he jerked back and glared down into her flushed face, his heart pounding, pounding, pounding against the wall of his chest. "I've got the Natural Wonder and a few moves guaranteed to make you scream," he said harshly and ground his pelvis against her to demonstrate. "And that's *all* I've got."

"Then I guess that's what I'll take."

Blood roared in his ears. "Haven't you heard a word I've said, Drucilla? I've got nothing for you that hasn't been offered to a dozen other women before you."

She winced slightly but met his gaze steadily. "You're not going to drive me away, John David."

"Damn you," he said hoarsely, and slammed his mouth down on hers. If she wouldn't listen to reason, he'd just have to demonstrate once and for all that he wasn't the man she thought he was.

He kissed her with a hot, rough lack of control that was long on frustrated passion and short on finesse.

But rather than be repulsed, she went up in flames. Her hands fisted in his hair to hold him to her, and she kissed him back every bit as roughly as he kissed her. The last of J.D.'s control hit the skids.

He couldn't keep his mouth or his hands off her then, and between one moment and the next, without a clue to how he'd accomplished it, he had the top of her suit scrunched up beneath her armpits and the bottom stripped off and discarded. Without once removing his mouth from hers, J.D. reached between them to fumble with the button and zipper of his cutoff jeans. Once they were undone, the garment needed only the smallest push before its damp weight and gravity dragged it down around his ankles. He hadn't bothered with underwear and he sucked in a sharp breath when he felt Dru's hands slide around his hips to grip the bare flesh of his buttocks. He lifted her against the wall and sheathed himself inside of her with one strong, smooth thrust.

She wrapped her legs around his hips, and her breath began to hitch in her throat almost immediately. J.D. ripped his mouth away and leaned backward from the waist as he felt her orgasm approach. Pumping his hips with steady, emphatic thrusts, he greedily observed every expression that crossed her face.

She opened her eyes and saw him watching. Color burned with feverish heat high on her cheekbones. "Oh, God, J.D.," she whispered. "Oh, God, I'm going to, I want to . . ."

"*Come*." Hands against the backs of her thighs, he pressed her legs high and wide while he bent his knees and pushed up into her from a slightly different angle. Deeper and harder, until her head dropped back and she stared blindly into space. Frantic sounds climbed her throat and the wet satin tightness that clasped his sex like a Chinese finger puzzle tugged and contracted around it as she climaxed.

He felt his own orgasm gathering momentum in his testicles and pulled back for one final thrust . . .

Only to remember a small but pertinent fact, and yank himself out of her entirely.

"*No*!" she protested. "Not yet; you haven't—" Her hips moved against his in a bid to get him back inside her, and when he instead pressed himself between silky, down-covered folds of feminine flesh outside the danger zone, she wailed, "*Why?*"

"No condom," he panted and saw her eyes go wide in horrified comprehension. He stroked his erection along the slippery length of her cleft once, twice, three times.

Then, with a groan, he spilled his seed against her lower stomach.

When the last pulsation had faded, he took a deep, shuddery breath and let his forehead thump down on the tongue-and-groove wall next to her head. He sagged heavily against her, compressing her between his torso and the wall's solid surface. He felt logy and boneless and full of a perfect contentment such as he'd rarely experienced—as though he'd just been welcomed in front of a roaring fire on a bitterly cold day.

"Jesus Jake," he whispered and carefully scooped his hands beneath her butt to both protect it from the roughness of the wood and support her weight. "It's a wonder you don't have a backside full of slivers."

She kissed his throat. "You know what, J.D.?" she whispered. "You're a great big fraud."

His heart seemed to stop for an instant, then kicked like an enraged mule against the wall of his chest. Warily he pulled back far enough to look into her face. "You wanna give me a clue to what the hell you're talking about?"

"This," she said, tightening her legs around his hips. "I'm talking about this. There is no way in hell that what you and I just shared is the same thing you've offered to a dozen women before me."

21

J.D. carefully straightened and, with Dru's arms still looped around his neck and her legs gripping his hips, walked into the bathroom. He eased her onto her feet, ran hot water to wet a washcloth, and cleaned them both up.

"No comment?" she inquired.

He shrugged. "What do you want me to say?" That he had a sinking feeling she might be right? He'd learned young never to hand over the kind of power such an admission would endow.

Dru stared at him in frustration. "I don't get you at all," she said and reached for a towel to wrap around herself. Even though she'd known he wouldn't welcome her with open arms, the stony expression she faced now made her long to shake him until he opened up to her once and for all.

She stared up at him in mute frustration, and he simply returned her look in that cool, contained manner he seemed to adopt so easily.

"What's not to get?" he said with a shrug. "I'm a fairly simple man."

"Oh, yeah, simple." She nearly choked. "That must be why you ran from Sophie and Ben's house like all the demons from hell were nipping at your heels."

"I don't have any idea what you're talking about," he said stiffly and reached for the other towel. Maintaining aloof eye contact, he wrapped it around his hips.

"Oh, yes, you do, and don't you dare pretend otherwise! Uncle Ben patched you up, and Aunt Soph and Tate and I fussed around you a little bit, and you couldn't take it. Why is it so damn difficult for you to admit that we might actually have something worthwhile to offer you? Or that you and I could possibly have something special growing between us? I know you feel something for me, J.D."

"Yeah? And what makes you think that, Drucilla? The fact that I pulled out to keep you from becoming an unwed mother—*again*?"

For just an instant she froze. Even suspecting it was a calculated ploy to keep her at arm's length, it hurt to have him throw that in her face.

She thought she might understand his reasoning—but it filled her with impatience.

She stepped close and thrust her chin up at him. "You want to know the details of that, John David?" she demanded. "All you have to do is ask."

"I don't give a rip one way or the other."

"Oh, like hell. I bet you're just dying for every nasty

little detail." Watching with satisfaction as a dull, angry red climbed his throat and onto his face, she said, "I was eighteen years old when I met Tate's father. I was in college, away from home for the first time, and I thought he was my one true love. It turned out to be nothing but a fantasy, though, because the minute I told him I was pregnant, he disappeared."

"Aw, hell." J.D.'s face registered contrition. "Listen, you don't have to—"

"It wasn't my first rejection," she interrupted without compunction. He'd started this; he could damn well hear her out. "My folks were a lot more interested in chasing adventure than in parenting, and they dumped me on Aunt Sophie and Uncle Ben every chance they got. Which in the end was undoubtedly a huge favor, but I sure didn't see it that way when I was a little girl." She ran a hand through her hair and realized for the first time what a mess she must be, then shrugged. "Obviously I decided to keep my baby. And having gotten to know Tate, you can appreciate that I've never once regretted that decision. What might not be quite so evident is that I also decided to forgo love from that point on, because love hurts and I had no desire to be hurt again. I managed to keep my heart inviolate for years. Then you came along."

He went very still. "And—what?—you suddenly find yourself in love with me?"

The sneering tone shot straight to her heart. Did he think it was *easy* to open herself up like this? But when she looked at him closely, she saw his tense jaw and watchful eyes. They didn't quite pull off the cynical amusement that Dru suspected had been his aim.

If she were the least bit smart, she'd listen to that tone of voice and protect herself by flat-out denying her feelings. But his expression gave her the courage to say truthfully, "Yes. Exactly."

A myriad of emotions flashed across his face but were stifled so rapidly, so completely, that she was left wondering what she'd seen. All he showed now was a faint impatience.

"You don't even know me," he said flatly. "Hell, we've only known each other a few weeks."

"That's perfectly true," she readily agreed. "And I'll tell you truthfully—if Tate ever comes to me when he's eighteen and tells me he's crazy in love with some girl he's known for as short a time as I've known you, I'll do everything in my power to talk him out of rushing into anything foolish."

"Well, thank God for that."

"I wouldn't thank Him quite so quickly if I were you." She smiled at the immediate wariness that flashed across his face. "Because I *do* know you. And I'm a long way from that naive eighteen-year-old who fell for Tate's daddy. So while I plan not to rush blindly into anything, neither do I find my feelings the least bit foolish."

J.D. snorted. "Hell, no. You just fancy yourself suddenly in love with me. Nothing foolish about that."

She smiled reasonably. "What exactly do you find so outlandish about it?"

He had that hunted look in his eyes again. "Like I said, sweetheart, you don't know me."

"I know the important stuff—that you're a hard worker, sweet as can be to Tate, and so honorable it moves me to tears. God knows you take the word 'responsible' to a whole new level. Give me some credit, John David. I've worked with the public my entire adult life—I do recognize a good man when I see one."

"Yeah, right," he scoffed. "Didn't you learn anything from this afternoon, Drucilla? I'm not a man you want to put your faith in."

"Oh, what rot! We've been over this and *over* this." She reached out to touch his bare stomach, her fingers tracing lightly down the hard, warm muscles above the low-slung, knotted towel. "I don't get it, J.D. Why do you persist in pushing away every single person who wants to get close to you?"

"Because it saves time!" Staring at her in frustration, he thrust an impatient hand through his hair. "You think I haven't wanted to get close to anyone before? You think I haven't tried? Well, think again, because I've not only wanted it, I've given it my best shot in the hope that I'd somehow find what a few lucky others seem to have found. But it's been my experience that while things may start out promising enough, it goes downhill from there."

"Where is it written that it *has* to, though?" she demanded.

"For chrissake, Drucilla—grow up!" Then he shook his head and looked at her with regret, reaching out to smooth her hair away from her face. He buried his fingers in the thick fall behind her ears and traced the slopes of her cheekbones with his thumbs. "No, forget I said that; you deserve to keep that wide-eyed optimism as long as you can. But I'm warning you right now: if you hang around me long enough, you'll lose it. And you'll sure as hell change your mind about me. If there's one thing I've learned, it's that folks always do."

"Well, I'm not 'folks,' and I don't plan on changing my mind."

Hating the cynical disbelief in his eyes, she raised up on her toes to press a tender kiss against the muscle that bunched in his jaw. She grasped his forearms for balance, and felt them as stiff as porch posts beneath her hands. She drew back to look into his eyes. "If there's one thing I intend to do, Carver, it's stick around. You might as well get used to it."

If the look on his face was anything to go by, that was precisely what he was afraid of. She laughed ruefully—since it was either that or cry—and patted the rigid muscles beneath her hands. "You needn't look so alarmed."

"Dammit, Dru, one of us had better be! I've done things in my life that would turn your stomach."

"When?" she demanded. "When you were a *kid*? Because I know you haven't been arrested for anything as an adult."

"How the hell would you know that?"

"When Edwina left her share of the lodge to you, we ran a background check on you just like we'd do on any applicant applying for a top position. And you don't have an adult record, so quit trying to convince me what a badass you are." She rubbed her knuckles against his hard abdomen. "I don't plan to push you, J.D. And it's not as if I'm asking you to waltz me down the aisle. I just want to spend some time with you, okay?"

"Yeah," he agreed cautiously. "I like spending time with you, too."

Warmth spread in Dru's breast. "Okay, good. Then just consider this while we're together: perhaps I haven't known you for long, but I'm a pretty decent judge of character, and I've come to appreciate your value as a man. I'm willing to wait until you can appreciate it as well."

Then you'll have a long wait, was all J.D. could think. It wasn't that he didn't want to believe every word that came out of her mouth. But there was something about him that ultimately drove people away. If he bought into her fairy tale now and had to watch the disillusionment in her eyes later on—and in the eyes of her family—when they all discovered whatever that something was, he didn't think he could stand it.

So all he said aloud was, "I'll keep that in mind."

Butch glanced around to make sure no one was near enough to observe what he was up to, then crouched down by the back fender of J.D.'s Mustang and removed the gas cap. He was tired of screwing around—he wanted to get the hell out of Nowhereville and back to the life he knew.

Threading a length of hose down into the gas tank, he considered maybe giving up his plans to eliminate J.D. and simply lighting out for home. If his old bud had seen anything on the news, he sure as hell hadn't made any mad dash to Seattle to blow the whistle. J.D. seemed all wrapped up in the brunette with the big blue eyes and the bodacious ta-tas. So maybe he oughtta just pack it up and head for home.

Then he thought, *Yeah, right.* Like J.D. had ever been interested in any woman for more than a few days running. And the damn news reports in Seattle were still running the sob story put out by the store clerk's family.

With renewed purpose, he sucked on the free end of the hose, then stuck it into the mouth of one of the two five-gallon cans he'd brought along to hold the Mustang's siphoned gas.

After Dru left to check on Tate, restlessness rode J.D.'s back like the Devil himself. He wandered from room to room looking for something to occupy his attention—*anything* to prevent him from thinking. But he couldn't find a single thing to settle on, so the thoughts he'd tried so hard to keep at bay kicked in. He'd give his left nut to avoid them, because the way he'd felt when Dru had professed her love disturbed him. It disturbed the hell out of him.

He wasn't a man who feared much; that was the upside of having been brought up rough. If you'd managed to survive the foster system with all its pitfalls and miseries, you could survive damn near anything else life had to throw at you.

But if he were honest with himself, he'd have to admit he was afraid of the love Dru offered. Afraid of the strength with which he wanted it. Afraid that if he brought himself to accept it, he'd grow to depend upon it.

And he was especially afraid of what it would do to him if, when—no, *if*, dammit—it was taken away.

Maybe his fears were irrational, but being able to give and accept love came down to a matter of trust—and he just didn't know if he had it in him *to* trust.

And yet . . .

A big part of him already did trust Dru. If anyone deserved his faith, it was her. She was genuine and honest and so damn squeaky-clean—utterly untainted by the sort of squalor that had marked so much of his life.

Now he was actually considering the idea of a relationship—and with a decent woman. Seriously considering it, giving it the honest-to-God benefit of the doubt. She had him thinking *if* instead of *when*. *If* it fell apart.

And if that wasn't trust, he didn't know what was.

Hell, he didn't know whom he was trying to kid, anyhow. There was no way he was walking away from this. Doing so would hurt every bit as much now as it would if he stuck it out and in the end she walked out on him anyhow. He was a practical man, so he might as well enjoy what she had to offer while he could.

His pacing brought him back for another pass through the bedroom, and he paused to give the closet door a considering glance. He turned to leave the room but stopped before he reached the door. A moment later he crossed the room to the closet and pulled his duffel bag off the shelf, where he'd flung it the day he'd arrived.

He sat down on the bed and for several long moments simply stared at the bag in his lap. Then he reached inside and pulled out the stack of letters from Edwina.

He fished Edward Lawrence's watch out of his pocket and rubbed his thumb over its etched gold lid. He regarded it soberly for several long moments. Then he returned it to his pocket, set the empty duffel next to him on the quilt, and pried open the first sealed letter.

It was similar to the few he'd read when he'd first left Edwina's care, and his jaw tightened. It forgave him for a transgression he'd never committed.

Didn't it?

Reading the letter once again through the eyes of a man, rather than those of a hurt and bitter boy, he realized that, no, perhaps that wasn't precisely what it said. He stared down again at Edwina's spidery, old-fashioned handwriting.

I've always believed in maintaining the highest standards. But I now realize that we all make mistakes, and that an error of judgment can be made in the space of a second—and haunt us from that moment forward. Come home, J.D. Please. Give us the chance to put this all behind us.

As a youth, he'd taken her words to mean that while she maintained the highest of standards for herself, she didn't expect him to adhere to such lofty standards. He'd concluded that Edwina was saying he didn't quite measure up, but that she'd allow him to come back nonetheless.

As an adult, he saw that there were a number of ways in which her words might be construed. The tone seemed much sadder and more remorseful than he remembered. Filled with an odd, aching regret for what had been so precipitously thrown away and could never be retrieved, he reached for the next letter in the stack. He ripped the envelope open and fished out the single piece of expensive parchment.

My dear J.D.,

I would not have believed it was possible to regret the manner of our parting more than I already do. Then this morning my dear father's watch was discovered deep in the cushion of his office settee. Darling, I am so sorry I doubted you—even if only for a moment. Please, please forgive me and come home. Or at least call me. We need to talk.

Yours truly,
Edwina

Stomach leaden, J.D. went through the remaining letters, missives that had followed him from one foster home to another. Some of them had caught up with him right away; others had collected a number of forwarding addresses before they'd finally reached him.

He sorely regretted not opening them now. For himself and for Edwina. He'd spent a lot of years resenting her . . . unnecessarily, it seemed. Her letters were full of apology and love, and sitting here in the bedroom of a place she'd bequeathed to him, he acknowledged the possibility that he himself might have left Edward

Lawrence's watch out on the arm of the settee that day, to be knocked into its depths.

Worse, with the arrogance of youth, he'd held Edwina to an impossible standard. He'd blamed her for not believing in him, but neither had he believed in her. When she'd asked him about the watch, he hadn't told her outright that he didn't know where it had disappeared to. And he sure as hell hadn't trusted her to work out their misunderstanding. Instead, his attitude had been screw-you combative, and he'd run at the first sign of trouble, rather than risk sticking around to be kicked out.

He found himself with a sudden need to be with Dru, wanting her warmth and her good humor, and he gently replaced the letters in his duffel bag and headed for the door.

It was a hell of a note to discover, after years of assuming he'd been wronged, that perhaps the person who had been wrong was himself.

22

When someone started banging on Dru's apartment door as if she were behind on the rent and they were there to collect, she expected to see J.D. on the other side. Instead, Char, looking sleepy and too boneless to have produced that authoritative rap, stood propped against the doorjamb.

She gave Dru a languid smile. "Hey, stranger."

Dru stared. Her friend looked . . . different. For a moment she couldn't put her finger on the reason why, then suddenly realized that Char looked as if she'd been thoroughly, utterly— "Omigod. You and Kev finally quit dancing around each other."

"It shows, huh?" Char laughed deep in her throat. With a fluid movement, she straightened away from the doorjamb and ambled into Dru's living room.

"Not at all; it was just a wild guess," Dru said dryly as she caught up with her friend. Then she gave her a poke. "From the look of you, I'm assuming it must have been—"

Char's eyelids went heavy and her lips curled up at the corners.

"—one *pret*ty darn satisfactory experience," Dru concluded. "I guess that explains why I haven't heard from you in a couple of days." She grinned. "Want some iced tea? Or I've got Pepsi, if you'd rather have something to give you a little oomph. Or there's"—she opened the refrigerator and leaned in to peruse its contents—"a pitcher of black cherry Kool-Aid."

"Who made the Kool-Aid, you or Tate?"

"Me."

"I'll have that, then. He always puts in too much sugar."

"Yeah, he follows the directions, silly boy. Grab a couple of glasses."

Char did and Dru dropped in the ice cubes she'd fetched from the freezer, then poured the Kool-Aid. They sat at the table.

Char propped her chin in her hand and gave Dru a dreamy smile. "Kev says he's been attracted to me since junior high." A wondering laugh escaped her. "Can you imagine? I thought he was an ass in junior high." Then her gaze sharpened. "But what about you? J.D. looked ready to chew your clothes off the other night at the bar. How did that go when he took you home?"

Dru was dying to lay out all her confusion, in the hope that her friend could help her make some sense of it. But before she could make up her mind whether to tell Char everything or keep it to herself until she was surer of her situation, there was another knock on the door.

"Now, who the heck can that be?" Char asked with a lazy smile. "All your friends are here."

"Cute." Dru rose from the table and went to see. She opened the door and stared in surprise at the man in the hallway.

"J.D.!" It wasn't that his appearance on her doorstep was so startling, but he didn't look at all his usual wary self. What *was* it with everybody today?

Staring back at her a little wild-eyed, he reached out and pulled her against his chest, then wrapped his arms tightly around her, burying his nose in her hair.

"What?" she mumbled against his shoulder. "Has something happened, John David?" She tried to pull back to get a look at his expression, but his arms tightened further and she subsided against the hard plane of his torso and simply held him in return. "Are you all right?"

Soft laughter, abrupt and lacking in humor, erupted from his throat. "I've just had a twenty-year belief turned upside down—"

"Did I hear you say J.D., Drusie?" Char's voice floated out from the kitchen, and J.D. stiffened. "Come on in here, big fella, and join us," she invited. "We were just getting set to go wild on black cherry Kool-Aid."

J.D.'s arms dropped away and he stepped back. "I'm sorry," he said. "I didn't realize you had company."

His expression had turned cool and noncommittal, and Dru got the impression he was ready to turn right around and head back out the door. She reached for his hand, gripping it between both of hers.

"Char's not company; she's a friend. To both of us, I'd like to think." She tugged on the hand within her grasp. "Come in. Have a glass of Kool-Aid with us. Or if you prefer, I'll even provide you with an actual grown-up drink."

That drew a slight, lopsided smile from him. "It's been a few years since I've had Kool-Aid, but I used to think it was pretty hard to beat." He followed her into the kitchen.

As their Kool-Aid klatch progressed, J.D. appeared to relax a bit. He talked easily with her and Char, and if he didn't laugh often, he at least smiled in the appropriate places. Dru nevertheless got the feeling he was waiting for Char to leave. His expression might be contained once again, but she sensed the turmoil beneath and was anxious to know what had put that earlier look in his eye.

She never got the opportunity to find out, though. For, just about the time Char started making noises about taking off, Aunt Sophie and Tate showed up.

J.D. greeted them civilly, but Dru detected frustration in the stiff set of his shoulders. She could relate. The fact that he'd come to her with whatever troubled him pleased her, but she wanted to talk to him about it, and it didn't look as if that was going to happen any time soon. And as Sophie told them about her plans with Uncle Ben for the evening, Dru realized she wouldn't even have the opportunity to go back to J.D.'s place to talk to him there.

She could only watch helplessly as, looking at her as if he wanted something from her that she couldn't define, J.D. finally said his good-byes, backed out of her kitchen, and headed back to his cabin in the woods.

By ten that night, Dru was going crazy. Tate was in bed and she found herself restlessly prowling the apartment. Finally, uttering a sound of disgust, she picked up the phone and called the front desk. The lodge provided a baby-sitting service, and if ever there was a good time to utilize its services, this was it.

She identified herself when Reception picked up and inquired about the availability of a sitter. When assured that one was free, she said a heartfelt "Good. Would you ask her to come up, please? Tate's asleep and I have to go out for an hour or so."

Fifteen minutes later she crossed J.D.'s clearing and climbed his porch. Moths fluttered against the light fixture overhead, casting huge, erratic shadows as she tapped on the screen door.

J.D. appeared silently on the other side. "Hey." The door creaked as he pushed it open. "I didn't expect to see you tonight."

"I hired a baby-sitter for an hour or two." She swiftly pressed herself against him, looping her arms around his neck. Raising up on her toes to give him a peck on the lips, she then drew back to look into his face. "You were upset this afternoon. Tell me what happened."

He hesitated, as if he'd had second thoughts since he'd left her apartment. After a moment, however, he led her to the Mission-style rocker in the living room, where he pulled her down to sit on his lap. He wrapped his arms around her, and pushed off with his foot to set the chair in motion.

Then he told her about Edward Lawrence's missing pocket watch, his belligerent flight from Edwina's house, and the letters that had followed him from foster home to foster home.

"And you never read them until today?" she asked when he lapsed into silence.

"After I'd read the first couple, there didn't seem much point. I was so certain I knew what they said."

His tone clearly tried and found himself guilty, and Dru rubbed her cheek against the hollow between his chest and collarbone as she looked up at him. His hazel-green eyes had narrowed as he stared stonily at the opposite wall.

"Don't do that to yourself," she commanded softly. "Edwina did that, too. I remember her talking about you when I was a little girl. Except I didn't know it was you at the time—you were just some boy she kicked herself for handling all wrong."

"Ah, damn." He gazed down at her. "I was really crazy about her, you know? She must have been close to sixty when I met her—I remember she seemed incredibly old. But she knew about things I'd never even heard of, and she treated me nicer than anyone I'd ever met."

"You loved her," Dru said softly, and had to blink away the tears that rose at the look flashing across his face.

"Yeah. I guess I did. She was the first person I ever knew with actual standards. She thought that things like table manners mattered, and she talked with a perfectly straight face about the importance of personal honor—which, believe me, was not a concept I'd ever heard anyone in my part of town discuss before. That's what made it so tough when things between us suddenly turned to shit. But at least I had my sense of injustice to keep me warm." He laughed without humor. "Now it turns out I'm probably the one who threw it all away. What am I supposed to use when things turn cold and lonely now?"

"Me." Dru stretched up to press a soft kiss on his mouth. Settling back, she cupped his jaw in both hands, looked him in the eye, and reiterated firmly, "You use me—I'll keep you warm. I love you, John David."

An indefinable light flared in his eyes and his grip on her was almost painful as he pulled her up and fiercely returned her kiss. His hands went to the buttons on her top. "You don't have to say that, you know," he muttered against her lips.

A moment later he demanded in a low voice, "Tell me again."

Midmorning the next day, J.D. let himself into his cabin and headed straight for the bathroom. Bits of grass stuck to his T-shirt and in the sweaty creases of his neck, and grease smeared the knuckles of his right hand and his forearm. He pulled his shirt over his head, tossed it on the floor in the corner, and washed up. Snatching a towel off the rack as he passed by a moment later, he headed for the bedroom.

While he dried off, he thought of Dru last night saying *I love you*. He approached the memory warily from every conceivable angle, shying away from it one moment, only to immediately turn around and edge right back up to it. No one had ever said that to him before, and when he finally sank his teeth into the fact that she had, he found himself worrying it like a hound with a knotted rag—particularly the part where he'd kept demanding to hear it over again. He couldn't believe he'd made love to her with such agonizing slowness, dragging it out until he'd thought the top of his head would blow off before either one of them found satisfaction. And all to hear her say, "I love you, John David. Oh, please, *please*, I love you."

Christ. Talk about a needy bastard.

Standing stock-still in the middle of the room, blindly tuned in to the thoughts and images in his head, he shook them impatiently aside and grabbed a clean T-shirt out of the drawer. Enough, already. He had a job to do and this wasn't getting it done.

He'd just pulled the shirt over his head and was stuffing his arms into its sleeves when he heard a clatter of feet on his porch and a knock on his door. Tucking the shirt into his waistband, he went to answer it.

Through the screen door he saw Sophie, Ben, and Tate standing on the porch.

"Hey," he said in surprise. "What's up?" It was the middle of the morning and he was scheduled to be out with the gardening crew, which he assumed they knew. So what had brought Dru's family here?

Dru's family. His heart kicked hard against the wall of his chest and he snapped straight-backed. "Is it

Dru?" He shoved the door wide and took a tense step out onto the porch. "Has she been hurt—"

"Dru's fine, son," Ben said.

Sophie looked stricken and said, "Oh, darling, *no*." She reached out to squeeze his forearm. "I'm so sorry," she added contritely. "We certainly didn't intend to scare you."

"Yeah, we just came to getcha because they're bringing in the canoe," Tate said excitedly.

"What?" He'd heard the words perfectly clearly; he was just having a difficult time changing mental gears. Drawing several deep breaths to get his heart rate back down where it belonged, he said more calmly, "Someone found my canoe?"

"A couple of the lifeguards had today off and decided to amuse themselves diving for it," Ben explained. "It didn't present much of a challenge, apparently, since the bow had surfaced, but they called a minute ago to tell me they're towing it to our dock. We thought you'd like to be there to check it out."

The depth with which J.D. wanted exactly that took him by surprise, and he took an eager step forward, ready to go. Then he remembered his errand and halted. "Damn. I can't. I've got to get back to work."

"One of the perks of being an owner, son, is that you get to take an hour off here and there when something important comes up."

"Yeah, and I'd do it in a minute, too. Except one of the riding lawn mowers quit cutting properly, and the supervisor assigned me to take the blade assembly in to be sharpened at a place called McCready's."

"I'll take it," Sophie volunteered. "You go with Ben and I'll run the assembly into town."

Yes! His first inclination was to make a headlong dash for the dock, but the pesky sense of fair play that Edwina had instilled in him dictated that he offer her an opportunity to change her mind. "You sure?"

"Yes. I think it's more important that you check out your canoe than it is for me to see it."

"Thanks, Sophie. Do you know how to drive a stick shift?"

"Sure. It's been a while, but I cut my teeth driving my father's pickup truck, and that's not a skill one ever forgets."

"If you don't mind taking my car, then, I've already loaded the blades in the trunk. No, hell, what am I thinking?" Disappointment weighed heavily as he took a step back and shoved his hands in his jeans pockets. "You can't carry it into the shop. The assembly's not particularly heavy, but all those blades are darn awkward—not to mention greasy."

"I'm not helpless, J.D.," Sophie snapped. "And I respond to soap and water every bit as well as you do." Then the short-tempered impatience left her expression. "Sorry."

"Grandma, you having a menopause moment?" Tate asked, leaning against her side.

She gave him a one-arm hug. "No, darling. Much as it pains me to admit this, sometimes I just have plain old, garden-variety cranky moments." She turned a gentle smile on J.D. "Mike McCready will give me a hand. You run along with Ben. Tate, would you like to ride into town with me?"

"Huh-uh. I wanna go with Grandpa and J.D."

"All right, then." She kissed his forehead, looking past him to J.D. "Where are your keys, dear?"

J.D. fetched them and walked her out to the car. "It has power brakes and steering, and the rest is pretty standard," he said. "Actually, for an old car, it's amazingly free of quirks. Ignore the gas gauge, though; it'll read 'Empty,' but it's not. The gauge has been broken for as long as I've had the car, so I always keep the tank filled."

Sophie slid in and started the car, holding the accelerator down briefly and making the engine roar. She gave him a cheeky grin, buckled up, and familiarized herself with the Mustang's controls. Then she put it in reverse and carefully backed out of his slot. With a wave at the three males, she slid the stick shift into first gear and drove down the road.

"Let's go!" Tate said the moment the car disappeared from view, and he raced back around the cabin.

As they headed out after him, J.D. looked over at Ben. "Thanks," he said. When Ben regarded him questioningly, he added, "For coming to get me. I appreciate it."

"No problem. You deserve to know the reason your canoe sank like that. If it was my boat, I'd sure as hell want to know why."

"Yeah, I do want to know. I didn't realize how much until you told me someone had brought it up." Hands thrust in his pockets, he rolled his shoulders uncomfortably. "I owe you."

"Good." Ben reached into his chest pocket and fished out a cigarette. "Then you won't bitch if I light up before we catch up with Tate."

"Hell, I don't owe you *that* much."

Ben laughed and lit up, moving downwind.

Tate and two young men in wet suits were on the dock when J.D. and Ben arrived. One of the divers was securing his rowboat to a piling while Tate peppered him with questions. The other hauled in the line they'd used to tow J.D.'s canoe. J.D. stepped up to help him lift the boat out of the water and they carefully set it, bottom up, on the dock.

He thanked the two young men and shook their hands, then turned his attention to the canoe while Ben talked with them. Squatting on his heels mid-thwart, he stroked his hand over the canoe's curved side.

The boat was a little waterlogged, but in surprisingly good condition for having been underwater twenty-four hours. He rolled it over to examine its length.

The cedar was so swollen from having been immersed that he couldn't visibly locate a problem area, and after several moments of searching, he blew out a frustrated breath and tipped the boat back over. Then, starting at the stern, he kneaded his fingers along the keel line.

"Found anything yet?" Dru's voice caused J.D. to start in surprise, and he looked up to see her stepping onto the dock.

She walked over and gave his shoulder a squeeze. "Uncle Ben called to let me know Jake and Collin had brought your canoe up. Have you learned anything to help you figure out why it sank?"

"Not yet." He went back to palpating the keel line inch by inch, aware of her moving off to greet Tate and her uncle. Aware, too, of a warmth that spread throughout his chest at the steadfast support shown by this confusing Lawrence family.

The wood beneath his two middle fingers suddenly depressed, and J.D. backed up and kneaded the area again. He felt definite sponginess, and a smear of candy-apple red paint rubbed off in a tacky curl beneath the press of his fingertips. "What the hell?" he murmured.

"Find something, son?" Ben squatted down across the canoe from him.

"Yeah, but I'm not sure what." He felt a little farther along the keel line. "Damn, here's another one." He rubbed at the new spot with his fingers and paint scrubbed away there, too. "I wish I had my tool belt on me. I could use a knife or a chisel."

Ben fished a pocketknife out of his khakis and handed it over. "Will this help?"

"Yes. Thanks." He glanced up at Dru as she joined her uncle, then extracted a blade and began scraping the paint away from the first area.

"What is it, J.D.?" Tate demanded, pressing against his back to peer over his shoulder.

"I'm still trying to figure that out. Back up a little, will you, buddy? You're casting a shadow."

"But I wanna—"

"Tate, back up," Dru said firmly. "Come around to our side. You can still see what's going on, but you won't block J.D.'s light from over here."

J.D.'s gut churned uneasily as he cleared a patch of paint away from the first site. Hoping his suspicions were wrong, he moved up to the other depression he'd located and scraped the paint away from there, too. Then, swearing under his breath, he sat back on his heels.

"What is it, son?"

J.D. met Ben's gaze across the width of the boat. "It's subtle, but it sure looks as if these leaks were deliberately carved between the ribs here and here"—he pointed out the spots with the tip of Ben's knife—"and then painted over."

"The hell you say. You think someone's deliberately—?"

"Yeah, and there are probably more, because I remember the water coming up through the bottom in several places."

"Why would anyone want to hurt your boat, son?"

J.D. shrugged, because it *didn't* make sense. Yet he was still uneasy, and his gut urged him to go with his instincts.

"Okay, let me put it this way," Ben said. "Why would anyone want to hurt *you*?"

J.D. stilled, thinking of the Lankovich trial and Robbie Lankovich's threats. For some reason, his thoughts then segued to his car, and to—

"Shit!" He surged to his feet and stared at Ben in horror. "Sophie!"

23

Ben swore too, then said, "My car is closest." The two men took off at a dead run for the switchback trail up to Ben and Sophie's house.

Dru and Tate ran behind them, although she didn't have the first idea what was going on. *What* about Sophie? she longed to demand, but she was conscious of her son well within earshot as he raced along the trail ahead of her.

Ben headed straight for his Buick when they reached the garage, but J.D. put out a hand to stop him. "If my car suffered a failure of any kind, we might need some basic equipment for a rescue. You've got a well-stocked garage and workshop—help me find what I need."

It took only moments for them to do so and to throw the gathered items into the trunk. Then all four of them piled into the car and Ben cranked the engine over and rapidly reversed the car out of the garage. Slamming the gearshift into drive, he turned and roared off down the road.

When they took the first curve on what felt like two wheels, J.D. reached across and gripped Ben's arm. "Slow down," he ordered firmly. "You won't do Sophie any good if you end up wrapping your car around a tree."

From the backseat Dru heard her uncle take a deep breath and blow it out. The car slowed to a more reasonable speed as he let up on the gas.

Leaning forward between the men, she sank her fingernails into J.D.'s hard shoulder and demanded, "What's going on?"

His face was carefully expressionless when he turned to face her, but she saw the uneasiness in his eyes, and her anxiety escalated tenfold. J.D. wasn't the type to worry unnecessarily.

"It looks as if someone sabotaged my canoe," he said flatly. "And if they did that, it stands to reason they might have messed with my car, too."

"*Why*?" she demanded in outrage, but then immediately waved the question aside. "Never mind that for now. What does it have to do with Aunt Sophie?"

"Your aunt drove my car to town." Succinctly, he explained why she'd done so.

When he'd finished, Ben took his gaze off the twisty road long enough to shoot a rapid glance at J.D. "Dru asked a valid question," he said. "Who would want to sink your boat or sabotage your car?"

"I've been racking my brain over that very question, and the only person who comes to mind is Robbie Lankovich," J.D. said.

"The guy you sent to jail? His kid, right? The one who considers himself a wise guy?"

"Yeah. When I blew the whistle on Lankovich senior, Robbie made a lot of threats. Idle threats, I thought at the time."

Then he swore beneath his breath and hunched in on himself. "This doesn't make sense. If Robbie had wanted to get me out of the way, it would have been a helluva lot smarter to attempt it *before* his old man came up for trial. But that's pretty much Robbie all over: he's such an ineffectual fu—screwup—you can discount three-quarters of what he says." Arms folded across his chest and hands tucked into his armpits as if he were cold, he said, "Still, he's a crazy son of a bitch—and the only person I can think of who might have a grudge against me."

Dru glanced over at Tate, who had been unnaturally quiet, and saw him sitting tensely, straining against the shoulder harness that held him in his seat as he stared out the window.

Suddenly he grew alert. "Grandpa! There's J.D.'s car!" Then he grew still. "Oh, man," he whispered. "That's not good."

Dru's stomach gave a lurch. Dear God. It looked as if Sophie had tried to turn onto a cutoff road, but had taken the last sharp curve too widely to make the turn. The car had overshot the cutoff and listed crookedly off the shoulder just beyond. The front tire on the driver's side had gone clear over the verge, and the back tire had nearly done the same. Sophie sat stock-still clutching the steering wheel, seemingly frozen by the sight of the hillside that dropped steeply away just outside her window.

Ben swore softly beneath his breath, but J.D. said in a cool, commanding tone, "Pull up behind her, but stay off the shoulder so you don't disturb anything that might shake loose."

Then he turned and pinned his gaze on Dru and Tate. "I need both of you to remain very quiet and to stay away from the Mustang until we've pulled your aunt to safety. Can you do that?"

Dru said, "Yes, of course." Eyes huge, Tate stared at J.D. and nodded.

"Good."

Everyone climbed out of the car as soon as Ben shoved the gearshift into park and yanked up the emergency brake. Then he headed directly to the Mustang to assure Sophie they'd soon have her out of there. Dru wrapped her arm around her son and, stoically resisting the siren voice within that urged her to race over there to add her reassurances, started to lead him across the road. J.D.'s voice calling her name halted her.

"I know you want to help," he said, striding up to them. He thrust out a handful of flares. "So maybe you could set these up for me around the bend. Hopefully they'll slow down anyone speeding down the hill, which will prevent us from compounding our problems."

Tate's face lit up at the prospect of something constructive to do, and Dru suspected her own expression mirrored her son's. She accepted the flares and Ben's disposable lighter, then rose on her tiptoes to give J.D. a quick peck on the lips. "Thanks."

It didn't take her and Tate long to position and activate the flares above the sharp curve. They returned to see J.D., lying on his back with a metal hook gripped in one hand, wriggle his way beneath the Mustang's back end. The hook was attached to a length of chain that disappeared beneath Ben's Buick.

Dru's breath caught in her throat as she watched. The car was in an extremely precarious position. She was almost afraid to expel the air in her lungs, for it seemed as if one strong exhalation might send the Mustang crushing down on top of J.D.'s chest or tumbling over the hillside, sweeping him and Aunt Sophie along with it.

J.D. was equally aware of the Mustang's insecure grip on the mountainside. But if it took him out before he could hook the chain to the car's axle, it was no more than he deserved for putting Sophie in danger. He sucked in a deep breath and focused on his task. It went without a hitch, and a moment later he crawled out from under the car and signaled to Ben, who returned to the driver's seat of the Buick.

"Okay," J.D. called, pushing to his feet. "Take it nice and slow." Bending, he looked through the passenger window at Sophie. "When you feel the tires grab the road, turn the steering wheel to the left," he instructed her. "We'll have you out of there in two shakes."

She stared at him with tension-widened eyes and tipped her chin infinitesimally to acknowledge that she'd heard.

Ben reversed the Buick at an angle across the road, and the chain between the two cars rose up off the ground and grew taut. Gravel crunched beneath the Mustang's back tire as it inched away from the verge. The front tire spun uselessly in space for several stomach-dropping moments, but then caught on the shoulder and grabbed. Sophie followed J.D.'s instructions.

Ben didn't stop the Buick until the Mustang was well away from the edge of the drop-off and back on the road. Then, with a shout, he jumped out of the car and raced to his wife as J.D. assisted her from his car.

Ben swung Sophie into his arms and held her fiercely. A moment later he pushed her back far enough to peer into her face. "Are you all right?" he demanded. Instead of waiting for an answer, however, he immediately jerked her back in his arms and pressed his cheek against the top of her head. "Jesus, I was scared," he confessed. His grip on her tightened further. "It feels so good to hold you. *Are* you all right?"

"Yes. No. I'm not sure." Near-hysterical laughter escaped her. "I still don't know exactly what happened, Ben . . . but for a while there, I thought I was dead for sure." Her teeth chattered and she pressed herself nearer, as if to absorb as much of her husband's body heat as possible. "Everything was okay when I set out, but then the engine started to cough and cut out, and suddenly it just plain quit—there was no power at all. The steering and brakes barely functioned, and it was like trying to maneuver a hippo with sheer muscle power." Her shivering increased and she burrowed closer, clutching Ben's sides. "Ah, God, don't let me go, okay? I was so scared."

Dru and Tate threw themselves into the huddle, and

J.D. watched the family hug and kiss and touch for a moment before he turned away to disengage the chain from the two cars. He tossed it in the trunk of the Buick, then moved Ben's car out of the road in case a vehicle suddenly came whipping around the curve. Once it was safely to the side of the road, he walked over to his own car to see if he could determine what had caused it to lose power.

It didn't take him long—Sophie's description of the way it had coughed and cut out made him check the gas tank first thing. It was empty, with no discernible leak.

The group hug broke up, and with an arm slung around Sophie's shoulder, Ben urged her toward their car. "Let's get you home," he said gruffly. He turned to J.D. "Did you get a handle on what happened?"

"Looks like my tank was siphoned dry."

Ben swore beneath his breath, then gestured toward the car. "Climb in. We'll talk about it once we've gotten Soph settled at home."

J.D. was silent on the ride back to the Lawrences' house, but he knew what he had to do. Acid churning in his gut, he leaned forward to tap Ben on the shoulder as they neared the lodge. "Can I borrow the work truck to get gas for my car and drop off the blade assembly?"

"Sure." Ben pulled into the drive that swept past the lodge's big front porch and brought the Buick to a halt. "You can pick up the keys at the front desk."

J.D. climbed out of the car and leaned down to study Sophie's pale face through Ben's open window. He cleared his throat. "I'm really sorry I got you mixed up in this mess," he said sincerely, then widened the scope of his glance to include Dru and Tate in the backseat. "Sorry I involved all of you. Give me an hour or two to get my stuff together; then I'll clear out."

Sophie and Tate exclaimed in startled protest and Ben said, "Now, son, don't make any hasty decisions. Let's talk about this."

But it was the shock on Dru's face that struck J.D. to the bone. He'd made a valiant attempt not to look at her, but he hadn't been able to help himself. What he saw was betrayal staring out at him through laser blue eyes, in a face drained of color.

It was tempting to let guilt chew on him, but then a healthy dose of anger came to his rescue. Dammit, it wasn't like he *wanted* to leave—he was doing this to keep her and her family out of the line of fire! Slapping his hand down on the window opening, he straightened. Then he turned away and strode into the lodge.

He should have known he couldn't simply drive off into the sunset. When he opened the driver's door to the truck a couple of minutes later and swung up into the cab, he found Dru already inside, waiting for him.

She met his gaze head-on. "You didn't really think it was going to be that easy to just walk away, did you?"

He rammed the key in the ignition and turned it, then slammed the shift stick into gear practically before the engine had roared to life. He spared her one brief glance before he pulled out onto the road. "Trust me, sweetheart, there's not a damn thing that's easy about any of this."

She didn't respond, and he determined to hold his

tongue as well. It took him less than three minutes to cave, though. "I'm getting gas for my car, then I'm packing up and getting the hell out of here."

He fully expected her to argue with that, but she crossed her arms over her breasts and turned her head to stare out the side window. She was silent when he pulled up behind his Mustang a few minutes later to transfer the blade assembly unit into the bed of the truck. She wasn't any chattier the rest of the drive down to town. But instead of continuing to stare out at the scenery, she swiveled in her seat to stare at him. He was highly aware of her gaze on him every second of the ride, but still she didn't say a word.

It made him jumpy as a cat.

It didn't help that he was also uncomfortably aware of her lightly tanned thighs, which he caught glimpses of every time he shifted gears. The temptation to reach across the stick shift and wrap his hand around the sweet curve of the nearest thigh was damn near irresistible. He wanted to press his palm against the warmth of that velvet-smooth skin of hers one last time and feel the fit, firm muscle beneath.

But this was hard enough as it was. Touching her now would be like driving nails into his own coffin.

And that was assuming that she wouldn't smack him upside the head should he attempt it.

Dru waited until he'd dropped the lawn-mower blades off at the machinist, filled up a gas can at the service station, and was headed out of town before she spoke. She'd been mentally assembling her arguments for the past twenty minutes, but in the end she merely said, "Don't go, J.D."

Muscles in his arms leaped to prominence beneath his skin, then went rigid, and his knuckles turned white where he gripped the steering wheel. His eyes were hot as coals as he swung his head around to stare at her, and what she saw in their depths didn't reassure her.

"I have to," he said.

"That's ridiculous. Of course you don't."

"Yes, dammit, I do!" Releasing the steering wheel with one hand, he raked his fingers through his hair in frustration and looked over at her as they left the town behind. "You think this is easy for me?"

"Yes. I do. If it was so terribly difficult, you wouldn't be so damn quick to pack your bags."

"I don't have a choice, Drucilla! I thought I could start a new life here, but that's clearly not going to be possible. And I'll be damned if I'll let shit from my old life explode all over you or Tate or your aunt and uncle."

A mishmash of anxiety and resentment tightened a knot in her stomach. "So you're saying you're leaving because you *care* for us?"

He looked reluctant to admit any such thing, but finally gave her a terse nod. "Yes."

She snorted. "Please. People who care for each other stick together."

"People who care for each other see to it that those they care for don't get hurt!"

"Which only proves my point. *We* don't appear to be the target here, J.D. Your Robbie person is gunning for *you*, not us, so why do you need to go anywhere? You might as well stay right here, where we can make sure you don't come to harm."

"Oh, yeah," he scoffed. "Like a bunch of hotelkeepers are going to be any kind of defense against a lunatic with a grudge."

"And who do you fancy yourself to be in this scenario—GI Joe?"

"Of course not," he said stiffly, but Dru rode right over him.

"I think you do. I think *you* think that because you lived in a few foster homes while you were growing up, it somehow makes you worlds tougher than me."

That brought his hard-angled jaw up. "There's no 'think' about it—I *am* worlds tougher than you!"

"You are so full of it, John David! You think your life was so much harder because your mama didn't want you? Well, big deal—my parents didn't have time for me, either. I've learned to take care of myself just fine, thank you very much, and I neither want nor need you to sacrifice yourself for me."

He pulled the truck up to its parking space outside the lodge and looked across at her. "I'm leaving, Drucilla."

"And how do you figure that will help us—help *me?* Just how will your leaving to make yourself a moving target, and us never knowing what the hell happened to you, help me or Tate or Aunt Soph and Uncle Ben?"

"It'll take all of you out of target range."

"And what about the fact that I love you, J.D.? Doesn't that count for anything? It seems to be something you like to hear—but I guess when it comes right down to it, my love really doesn't matter to you at all, does it?"

For a second he looked as if he were going to

explode, but then his expression went blank. Dru fully expected him to look her in the eye and agree that it didn't. Instead, he said flatly, "It matters. But I'm still leaving."

Frustration erupted and she jumped out of the cab. Holding the door open, she stared up at him across the length of the bench seat. "Then you're a fool," she said. "Because you could have had me, but you threw me away for the stupidest reason in the world: to satisfy your damn fatheaded, macho pride."

She closed the door and refused to drop her eyes before his turbulent dark-eyed gaze. "I hope it keeps you warm at night."

24

"*I hope it keeps you warm at night,*" J.D. mimicked sourly as he shouldered the gas can and tramped down the hill to his car. *Keeps you warm, keeps you warm, keeps you warm.* The words echoed in his mind, and no matter how hard he tried to shut them out, they accompanied him step for step down the road like a choir of tinny voices from a fever dream, repeating endlessly.

You could have had me, Dru's voice whispered, *but you threw me away for the stupidest reason in the world: to satisfy your damn fatheaded, macho pride.*

He swore and ruthlessly clamped a lid on the voices, to shut them down—especially that last one. Dammit, who needed pride to keep him warm? He had his indignation. Star Lake Lodge was as close as he'd come to a home in twenty years, and Drucilla and Tate,

Sophie and Ben, the nearest thing he'd had to family. To hear Dru tell it, though, you'd think he was about to stroll out the door swinging his pocket watch and whistling a happy tune, when he felt like his guts were being ripped out without anesthesia.

He'd never known anyone remotely like Dru, had never realized it was possible to feel about a woman the way he felt about her. He'd done his best to shroud the truth from himself, to cloak it behind lust, but now that Lankovich had made it impossible to stick around any longer without putting Dru and her family in danger, J.D. could no longer dodge the facts. Sure, he wanted to make love to Drucilla day and night; that was a given. But more than that, he wanted to move in with her and her kid. He wanted the right to protect her, to raise Tate as his own, to be the guy who maintained upkeep of the lodge. He wanted the kind of life he'd believed only other people got to have, the kind of life that Dru had shown him could possibly have been his, too.

"Possibly" being the operative word here, Boscoe. J.D. arrived at his Mustang and swung the gas can to the ground. The fact was, if Lankovich hadn't stepped in to trash that particular dream, something else probably would have come along to mess it up. Face it: he wasn't cut out for a Disney family kind of life. He hadn't believed it even existed, until he'd met the Lawrences.

That he now knew better—too late to do him a damn bit of good—left a bitter taste in his mouth, but J.D. swallowed it and buckled down to the business at hand. He popped the car's hood and unfastened the gas cap. Then he poured the contents of the can into the gas tank, except for the last cup or so, which he dumped into the carburetor.

As he slammed down the hood, tossed the empty can into the Mustang's trunk, and then walked around to climb into the car, he still found it hard to sink his teeth into the fact that Robbie Lankovich was the instrument of his leaving. He would have sworn the man was all talk and no action.

The car cranked over on the first try, and he smiled grimly. Didn't it just figure that this would be the one thing to work without a glitch today? He headed back up toward the lodge.

Dru had demanded to know what possible risk Robbie could present to her and her family, since J.D. was his target. And, hell, maybe she was right. Maybe he could—

He jerked the thought up short. No. *No*, dammit. *Don't* even *go there*. How would he live with himself if something happened to one of the Lawrences? He was doing the right thing by leaving. It was the only thing he *could* do.

It was just painful, was all. But he'd live.

He pulled up behind his cabin and climbed out of the car, slamming the door closed. He needed to throw his stuff into his duffel and hit the road before he could do anything stupid—like decide to stick around despite the risks to Dru and her family.

Indulging in a fantasy that he knew would never be realized, J.D. entered his cabin and was almost to the bedroom when he realized he wasn't alone. A man sat in the big Mission-style rocker in front of the window, the afternoon sun backlighting him so that his face was in shadow.

The gun in his hand, however, was clear as day as it pointed straight at J.D.'s chest.

Char took one look at Dru's face as her friend walked through the lobby, and excused herself to the activities clerk with whom she'd been checking her schedule. She caught up with Dru just as the elevator doors were closing between them.

"Hey, Dru. Hold up."

Dru appeared not to hear her, and Char dove for the doors, thrusting her hand between the closing panels to trigger the opening mechanism. She slid through as the doors once again bounced apart.

Dru turned her head then and looked at her through stricken eyes that didn't quite track. Char had the distinct impression her friend hadn't any idea who stood in front of her. "Dru?" she said gently. "What happened?"

When there was no reply, Char reached out to rub her hand up and down her friend's upper arm.

Dru started. Then she blinked and, focusing, discovered her best friend standing in front of her with a look of concern on her face. "Char?"

"Where's Tate, Drusie?"

"With Aunt Sophie. I don't want him to see me like this." She felt her chin wobble and gave her best friend a helpless look. "I can't seem to hang onto my Mom face."

"What happened?"

The pain struck anew and, wrapping her arms around her waist, Dru hugged herself. "He's leaving, Char."

"Who's leav—J.D.?"

"*Yes*." Tears rose in her eyes, but she blinked them back furiously. "The shit. The lousy, lousy *shit*."

"But why? He's crazy about you."

"He says it's to *protect* me. And Aunt Soph and Tate—to protect all of us."

"Protect you? From what?"

"Some guy who sabotaged his canoe and his car." Drawing a deep breath, Dru gathered her scattered wits enough to relate what had been happening.

"And he thinks that by leaving he can protect you from this fellow? Why, that's actually kind of romantic." Dru's feelings must have been written across her face in screaming neon, for Char immediately scowled. "Romantic for a guy who's basically a lousy shit, that is." Then she looked Dru in the eye. "So what did you have to say about all this?"

"I tried to change his mind. I argued with him until I was blue in the face." A niggling voice in her head whispered, *Not really,* and tried to tell her that she'd been reeling from the shock too much to debate effectively, but she shook it aside. "I told him this Lankovich person was clearly gunning for him, not us, so there was no reason for him to leave. But he's got it in his mind that removing himself is the only answer and he won't listen to reason." The elevator doors opened on the top floor and they stepped out into the corridor. Skirting a Housekeeping cart outside one of the rooms, Dru stalked over to the private staircase that led up to her and Tate's apartment, but turned to face her friend, her arms still crossed over her waist in an attempt to hold in all the hurt. "So I told him it was the stupidest decision I'd ever heard in my life, and I hoped it kept him warm at night."

"And?"

"And what?"

"What do you mean, and what? That's *it*?" Char demanded incredulously. "You hope it keeps him warm at night? I'm embarrassed for you, Lawrence. You've been able to argue me into a corner since we were ten years old, but now that you've got a fight on your hands that matters more than any you've ever had, you hope *it keeps him warm at night*? I've never heard anything so feeble in my life!"

Dru's misery was replaced by a red-hot flash of anger. "I felt like I was being broadsided out of the blue by a two-ton truck, McKenna. What was I supposed to do, beg him to stay?"

"Hell, yeah, if that's what you really want. And if you truly do believe he's a lousy shit, then at the very least you were supposed to lay into him. If he's leaving anyway, don't you at least want to tell him exactly how you feel?" Tilting her head to one side, she raised her eyebrows at Dru. "How *do* you feel?"

"Like a fool. Like once again I let my hormones sucker me into believing I'd found my One True Love, when what I'd actually found—*again*—was just another man looking for a little temporary satisfaction. I took the biggest risk of my life with him, Char. I knew better, but I did it anyway—I opened myself up to the possibility of falling in love again. And even though he never said so, I thought it was a real love for *both* of us. Not just a flash-in-the-pan sexual attraction, but the honest-to-God real deal." She glared at Char. "But only on my part apparently, if he can just walk away this easily."

"I think you ought to tell him that."

That struck a chord with the resentment beneath Dru's hurt, and she straightened her spine. "Yes. Absolutely. He doesn't get to do this—he doesn't get to set me up for a fall, then just walk away with that mealymouthed rationalization." She pivoted and walked back to the elevator, where she jabbed the Down button. When it didn't immediately arrive, she turned on her heel and set out for the stairs.

"Now, that's more like it," Char called. "You go get him, girl."

"Hello, J.D." The man with the gun stood up and took a step forward, away from the blinding backlight. The gun in his hand remained doggedly aimed at J.D.'s chest.

"Butch?" Recognizing his friend's voice was like taking a swift kick to the solar plexus, and J.D. scrubbed his fingertips over the spot as if it had taken an actual blow. Another corner of his mind, however, promptly breathed *Aha*. "Well, I'll be damned," he said, eyeing the man he'd always thought of as his closest friend. "I *knew* Robbie Lankovich didn't have the stones for this."

Butch's laugh was full-bodied and robust. "You thought *Junior* was behind these little incidents? Jesus, boy, spending so much time in Pissville U.S.A. has clearly cost you your edge. Not only does Robbie lack the balls, he's a mite too busy to concern himself with Big Daddy's woes. He's spending all his time trying to explain himself to the IRS."

"Is that so? Well, excuse my lousy judgment, but I was working without the facts." J.D. sat down on the edge of the couch. Bracing his hands on his knees, he looked up into Butch's smiling face and tried to reconcile his friend's grin with the gun that hadn't wavered. While part of his mind refused to believe Butch would ever pull the trigger, another part rapidly selected and discarded a multitude of ways to get out of this situation.

Knowing just what the hell the situation *was* would be a real help. "I can honestly say it never once occurred to me that my best friend would want to remove me from the picture. Care to share why?"

"Don't pretend you don't know, Carver."

"Sorry, bud, but I *don't* know. What, did you find out about the lodge and it pissed you off for some reason?"

"This place?" Butch looked sincerely baffled. "What's this place got to do with anything?"

"I inherited part of it. Remember Edwina Lawrence? She owned part of this resort, and she left it to me."

"Well, hell, if that isn't just perfect." Butch shook his head in disgust. "I mean, is that goddamn typical, or what? How is it that you can always wade in the same shit as the rest of us, but somehow come out smelling like a fucking petunia?"

"Just good, clean living, I guess."

"You think this is funny, you pious jerk-off? You closed down Lankovich's entire operation and put two dozen men out of work. But do you have to scramble for a job like the rest of us? Hell, no. You end up owning a swank lodge."

"You can go to hell before I'll apologize for that again," J.D. snapped. "*I* didn't put you out of work, Lankovich did! If I hadn't blown the whistle on him, that building would have collapsed like a fucking house of cards. Innocent people would've died."

"So? It wouldn't have been our fault. We did what we were supposed to."

"Christ, Butch, you never change, do you? *It's not my fault*—what is that, your freaking anthem? Who the hell's fault is it that you're standing here pointing a gun at me, if not yours?"

"Yours. If you hadn't taken my job away, none of this would have happened."

"And I suppose if I'd drowned or gone off a cliff, that would have been my own damn fault, too." Gripping his knees to keep from lunging for his friend's throat and giving him the excuse to fire his gun, J.D. marveled, "I'd actually forgotten your convoluted way of reasoning. This must be the Dickson version of that old if-a-tree-falls-in-the-woods thing, huh? If someone dies because of what you set in motion, but you aren't actually looking, does it really count as murder?" Disgust welling up, he gave Butch a contemptuous once-over. "Frankly, I gotta wonder how you can sneer at the size of Junior's balls. I sure as hell never would've expected you to show up to confront me face-to-face like this. Face it: the leaks in the boat and the siphoned gas tank are more your speed. Head-on like this, you can't pretend it isn't really happening."

"Shut up, J.D.!"

"Or what?" he demanded, nodding at the gun. "You're gonna shoot me with that thing?"

"Yes."

"And you don't plan to shoot me if I stay nice and quiet?"

Butch shifted restively and his gaze cut to the side for a second.

J.D. laughed bitterly. "That's pretty much what I thought. Since it looks like you plan to shoot me either way, what possible reason do I have to keep my mouth shut?"

"I'll give you a goddamn reason," Butch snarled and leaned forward intently, his eyes narrowed to cold slits. "I can make it quick and painless, or I can blow your goddamn kneecaps off before I take you out."

"You're right; that is incentive." The proposed violence surprised him: Butch had always been a hothead, but he'd never been vicious. J.D. kept his face impassive, however, for Rat City rules decreed that the guy with the best poker face usually won. "You want to tell me why, first?"

"You really don't know, do you?" Butch rubbed the back of his neck with his free hand as he stared down at J.D. "Great—don't that just freakin' beat all? I coulda stayed home and saved us both a shitload of trouble."

J.D. shrugged, although his curiosity was roused.

"Nobody's pointing a gun at *your* head to make you stay. Go home now."

"Too late for that. I know you: now that you've got a whiff of the scent, you'll start sniffing around, and you won't quit until you dig up the truth. That's what brought me here in the first place—your threat on the phone to hunt down my secret. You're a fucking pit bull, J.D. You always have been." He gestured with the gun. "Stand up."

J.D. stood. *Threat on the phone?*

"Now turn around."

A bark of laughter escaped him. "Are you crazy? You want to shoot me, you can damn well do it face-to-face."

Butch shook his head in quick, agitated movements. "You think I *won't*?"

"I think doing someone when you don't have to look him in the eye is a lot more your style."

"Yeah, well, guess what, pal? I've changed my style."

J.D. really didn't want to believe that Butch truly could kill in cold blood, and not just because his butt was on the line. "I'm sorry to hear that. Since when?"

Butch looked him straight in the eye. "Since the clerk at the One Stop forced me to shoot him."

25

Dru had one foot on the front porch step and was all set to barge into J.D.'s cabin and give him a piece of her mind when she heard the voices within. Caught up in her own furious inner dialogue, she didn't pay strict attention at first to what was being said. But when a voice she didn't recognize said something about shooting someone, she froze. Oh, God, what was this?

She eased off the step, knowing she should go for help. But curiosity drew her to the window at the far end of the living room instead. The cabin was set up off the ground with a crawl space underneath, so even standing on her toes, she could only see a tiny portion of the room. It afforded her a partial view of J.D. and the backside of another man.

The screened window was open, and when J.D.'s voice suddenly broke the charged silence, it was with a clarity that made her jump skittishly.

"Ah, Christ, Butch," he said. "You actually did hold up that convenience store, then?"

"Gina was giving me a rash," the other man said sulkily. "You know how she is—I couldn't keep asking her for beer money."

"So you walked into a store that you frequent all the time and robbed it at gunpoint instead?" J.D. demanded incredulously. "Do you ever stop and listen to yourself, for chrissake? You *shot* a man."

"It didn't have to be that way! He forced my hand. All the idiot had to do was fork over the money, but *no*, he just had to play the hero. You would have thought it was his own money, he was so damned determined to hang onto it. You ask me, he was begging to be killed."

Dru's jaw dropped and she felt her skin literally crawl, as if she'd just brushed up against something scaly that rustled in the dark.

Disgust laced J.D.'s tone when he muttered, "Holy shit."

"Fuck you, Carver!" Butch snapped. He took a threatening step forward and Dru's muscles tightened, but then he paused, and she saw some of the tension leave his posture.

"You know, I always liked you," he said. "But I'm sure as hell sick of your holier-than-thou attitude. Like *your* shit don't stink, J.D."

Abruptly, he laughed, and it was not a jolly sound. "Come to think of it, you're in this right up to your self-righteous neck. You were my alibi, bud—that makes you an accessory. How do you like that for irony?"

"Well, I'll tell you, Butch—I've actually been thinking quite a bit about what passes for friendship or loyalty in our neck of the city. And I've come to the conclusion that holding or calling in markers isn't it."

"Close enough, bud."

"You think so? Just look where it's gotten us now. When you told the cops that you were with me, I agreed because I felt I owed you a debt."

"Damn straight you owed me. I saved your neck when we were kids."

"Yeah, you did. And don't think I don't appreciate it. But ever since I left Seattle I've been around people who truly love and watch out for each other, and you know what? They don't seem to keep score. I think that maybe the mark of real friendship is doing the hard thing and refusing to lie for your friend when he's screwed up. Maybe if I'd done that when you first told the cops you were with me, you wouldn't find it so damn easy to stand here now, fully prepared to kill again."

Oh, God, oh, God. She should have run for help the minute she'd figured out the man in J.D.'s cabin was most likely the one who'd damaged his canoe and car. She was scared to death that if she went for help now, something dreadful would happen to J.D. while she was gone. Looking around, she spotted a large rock half buried in the dry, hard soil beneath the window. She squatted to pick up a smaller stone and started digging the large one free.

She heard a definite sneer in Butch's voice when he said, "So what you're saying here is that if you'da turned me in then, your butt wouldn't be in a sling now."

"No, dammit! I'm saying I think it's downright sad that you're finding it easier each time to pull the trigger. Hell, I don't know, Butch. Maybe you wouldn't have felt a drop of remorse one way or the other. But at least I wouldn't have contributed to how easily you seem to be turning into a stone killer."

When Butch laughed, Dru paused to stare up at the window, her temper commencing a slow burn.

"Good ole J.D.," Butch sneered. "Christ, you are some throwback, you know it? You've got *way* more conscience than's good for a person. Doesn't it ever get inconvenient?"

"All the time."

"But you always do the right thing anyway, don'tcha, bud? Maybe this little Pissville burg is the right place for you, after all." A rumble of amusement sounded in his throat. "Well, hey, I can arrange it so you'll never have to leave. Turn around."

J.D. made a rude noise. "Forget it. Like I told you already, you can damn well look me in the eye when you shoot me."

"And like I told you, asshole, that's doable."

No! Dru rocked the stone beneath her hands back and forth with frenzied strength to loosen the last bit of earth that held it firm.

"Of course, leaving a bullet-riddled corpse in the middle of my living room might mess up your chances of escaping some," J.D. said. Dru, who was fast descending into a hot, sweaty panic, marveled at his coolness. "You want to actually get away with this, Butch? Then your best bet is to take me out into the woods somewhere far away from here."

What the hell are you doing? Dru surged to her feet, the rock now clenched between her hands. Was he *crazy?*

"What are you, crazy?" Butch echoed her thought, but he didn't sound horrified like her—he sounded suspicious as hell. "Why would you help me?"

"Because the people around here have come to matter to me, and I don't want them involved in this. There's a ten-year-old kid who visits me all the time, and I don't want him to find my moldering remains. Hell, Butch, they think I'm leaving today, anyway. Let's just pack up and get the hell out of here, and no one will ever be the wiser."

"Fine," Butch said flatly. "But you mess with me, and I'm telling you right now that I'll come back to take it out on the brunette with the sweet tits that I saw you with the other night."

"What the hell has she got to do with this?"

"I'm not sure. But she's got something to do with it. I can feel it in my bones."

"As usual, Dickson, your bones are full of shit. But, whatever—I'm not going to mess with you."

"Fine, then. Get your stuff."

Dru raced on tiptoe to the front of the cabin and crept up onto the porch. Flattening herself against the wall to the side of the door, she tried to slow down her breathing. She felt perilously close to hyperventilating.

She could hear the men's voices but caught only a few words over the thundering pulse in her ears. It felt like a decade before she heard them approach the front door.

She saw the screen door open. Gripping the rock in

both hands, she pressed back hard against the wall in an attempt to become invisible.

J.D. walked out first, duffel bag in hand, and the sight of his wide shoulders and long back, clad in one of his ubiquitous white T-shirts, steadied her slightly. The sight of the ominous black gun in the other man's hand when he followed J.D. through the door made her realize she could actually go through with this. If she failed, he'd sounded far too willing to shoot J.D.

And she was damned if she'd let that happen.

Drawing in a deep, silent breath, she eased her arms up over her head, then took a giant step forward and swung the rock as hard as she could at the back of the man's head. She tried to visualize the porch post beyond him to fool herself into believing she wasn't *really* hitting a living, breathing human being. Even so, she pulled her punch slightly just before the rock connected with his skull.

And still it made the most horrid sound she'd ever heard in her life.

The rock tumbled out of her nerveless fingers at the same time that the gun in the man's hand clattered to the porch floor. Then, between one heartbeat and the next, he dropped like a sack of cement.

J.D. whirled around, and he felt his jaw drop at the sight that greeted him. Butch lay sprawled at his feet, out cold, and Dru stood behind him with the whitest face he'd ever seen, swaying slightly and looking as if it wouldn't take more than a puff of air to blow her away.

The big rock at her feet was self-explanatory.

"Damn, sweetheart." He bent down and picked up

the gun, gingerly sliding the very tip of his index finger through its trigger guard. She moaned low in her throat, and he looked up at her. "Shhh. It's okay. Don't faint on me now."

"Did I kill him?"

Pulling his T-shirt out of his waistband, he used it to keep his fingerprints off the gun and hopefully still preserve Butch's as he gingerly tucked the weapon into his waistband. Praying that he wouldn't end up shooting his own dick off, he double-checked the safety.

Then he pressed his fingers to Butch's carotid artery and felt the steady thump thump of a pulse. "No. He'll live."

"Oh, God, John David, did you hear the sound his head made when I hit him?"

"Can't say that I did. I was kinda expecting to be shot in the back at any—"

"Have you ever dropped a watermelon?" She shuddered. "It sounded like that. Exactly like a ripe melon breaking open."

"Try to think of something else." He rose to his feet and stepped forward to pull her into his arms, his eyes closing. He hadn't expected to ever hold her again. He could feel her shaking, and realized she needed more than a hug. He stroked a soothing hand down her braid. "It's okay now, sweetheart. Shhh. You saved my life." He'd had his own plan to get his dick out of the wringer, but she'd taken care of matters much more expeditiously. "Easy, now. It's going to be all right."

"I think I'm gonna throw up."

"Whoa." He whipped her away from his chest and hustled her over to the porch railing. She braced her hands against the balustrade and bent forward, her head hanging limply between her shoulders. J.D. rubbed small circles between her shoulder blades.

She gagged numerous times, but finally raised her head. "False alarm, I guess." Breathing deeply, she looked over her shoulder at J.D. "I think I'm okay now."

He tugged her back into his arms. "Poor darlin'." He tilted his chin to look down at her, relieved to see a faint wash of color back in her cheeks. "I'd better go call the sheriff's office before Butch comes around."

Dru pulled back far enough to stare up at him, her eyes a blazing blue. "Who the hell *is* he?"

"He used to be my closest friend. He killed a man in Seattle." J.D. wasn't in any big-time hurry to tell her that *he'd* provided the alibi that allowed Butch to nearly drown her son, kill her aunt, and terrorize her. "I'll go call the sheriff," he repeated. "You want to come inside with me?"

"Yes." Then she hesitated. "No. My stomach's still kind of rocky. I think I'd better stay outside where I can breathe real air."

He hated the idea of leaving her alone with Butch, even if he was unconscious. Yet he understood her need to be out here, where the scent and sight of the surrounding evergreens could settle her nerves, so he held her at arm's length for a moment to stare down into her face, then reluctantly let her go.

He stopped on the way into the cabin to squat down next to Butch and double-check his condition. Oddly,

J.D.'s primary emotion was a deep regret. They'd shared a lot of good times and had a long history that was impossible to discount.

He'd have to work on doing exactly that, though—because Butch had been perfectly serious about killing him. J.D. rose to his feet. Jesus Jake. What a mess.

In the cabin, he walked straight to the telephone, dialed the sheriff's office, and related the situation succinctly. Then he dialed the Lawrences' number to let Ben and Sophie know what was going on.

The phone on the other end had only rung once when Dru's scream split the air.

J.D.'s blood turned to ice and, dropping the receiver, he raced out onto the porch, yanking the gun from his waistband as he ran. He'd never moved so fast in his life.

Butch had come to and had Dru by the ankle. He'd clearly caught her by surprise, for she stared down at him in absolute horror and was screaming her head off. J.D. skidded to a halt and kicked Butch in the forearm, breaking his grip on her.

He wanted to break more than that. Filled with a vicious anger, he squatted down and shoved the gun into the angle where Butch's neck met his jaw. "Breathe wrong, you son of a bitch, and I'll blow your head off."

Butch just moaned and cradled the arm J.D. had kicked, and J.D. looked up at Dru, who was gulping in air. "Are you okay, sweetheart?"

Her teeth chattered and, hugging herself, she simply

stared at the two of them as if they were a couple of wild animals who might rise up at any moment to rip her throat out. She was hollow-eyed and as white-faced as she'd been right after she'd cold-cocked Butch with the rock.

Despite the rage that he wasn't certain should be directed at Butch or himself, he said gently, "Okay, I can see that you're not. Listen, I was just calling your aunt and uncle and I don't think I hung up the phone. Why don't you go see if anyone's on the line."

The minute she disappeared into the house, he gripped Butch's hair and pulled his head back, pressing the barrel of the gun a little more tightly against Butch's carotid artery. "Give me one good reason why I shouldn't just pull the trigger now and save us all a lot of trouble."

"Christ, man," Butch croaked. "You don't wanna do that—"

"That's where you're wrong, amigo. Because I do." He drilled the gun deeper yet into the vulnerable skin beneath Butch's jaw. "I *really* do."

Butch's nostrils flared wide and his eyes showed the white of panic all around his irises. "Think about this a minute, J.D.," he urged. "You're not the type of guy to commit cold-blooded murder."

"I didn't think so, either," J.D. agreed. "But that was before you messed with my woman." He lowered his head and murmured in Butch's ear, "It would be the perfect solution all around, don't you think?"

Butch's eyes sliced in his direction. "What are you talkin' about?"

"Killing you would be a big favor to the world at

large, and get me off the hook for providing your alibi. The more I think about it, in fact, the more I like the idea. Wanna hear what I'm going to tell the sheriff when he gets here?"

"J.D. . . ."

"I don't know *why* he wanted to kill me, Officer," J.D. said in a sincere tone imbued with a hint of hurt confusion. "I thought we were good friends, but he kept saying he was going to drag me out into the woods and blow my head off. Luckily, before he could, Ms. Lawrence hit him with a rock. That's when I called you. Only he wasn't out cold and he grabbed Dru. I kicked him, but then he tried to grab the gun I'd taken off him, and we struggled. Then the gun just . . . went off. God, I sure didn't mean to kill him." J.D. smelled a sharp ammonia smell and looked down to see a patch of wetness spreading across the fly of Butch's jeans. He felt a fierce satisfaction, and the rage consuming him suddenly drained away. "Whoops. It's not nearly as much fun to be on the receiving end of these threats, is it, buddy?"

Butch's eyes narrowed. "You're not going to pull the trigger, are you, Carver?"

"Nope." He eased the gun's barrel back a fraction. "Not unless you force my hand."

"That's the difference between us, you know," Butch said contemptuously. "When it comes down to the wire, you're nothing but a pussy."

"That a fact? You might want to note that it wasn't me who pissed my pants. And the real difference between us, you dumb shit, is that I know what's important in life and you *still* haven't figured out what the hell that is."

"Oh, I know what's important."

"Yeah, that's why you killed some poor schmuck rather than have to ask your wife for beer money. Or—here's a concept for you—get up off your ass and actually hit the pavement to find a job so you could pay for it yourself."

"You self-righteous prick. At least I'll have the satisfaction of knowing you'll go to jail, too."

"We'll see. Another difference between us is that I understand that killing you isn't the answer to keeping me out of it. But you don't quite grasp that, do you, Butch? You still don't get that it's wrong to kill a man just because he stood between you and a six-pack."

The screen door squeaked and J.D. looked up to see Dru staring out at them from behind it. For just a second he froze, trying to see her expression through the mesh. Then gravel crunched in the drive behind the house.

He returned his attention to Butch. "Looks like your ride is here, ace."

Sticking the gun back in his waistband, he reached down with his free hand and hauled Butch to his feet. A moment later the sheriff's deputy came around the corner of the house.

Yet as glad as J.D. was to see him, he couldn't help but feel that the man's appearance spelled the end of not only Butch's dreams, but his own as well.

26

The minute the deputy bundled Butch into his cruiser, Dru turned to J.D. She hauled off and smacked his chest with the flat of her hand. "*Just take me out into the woods somewhere and shoot me?*" she demanded, then wrapped her arms around his waist to hold him with desperate strength. God, she'd been so afraid. Pressing her cheek into his chest, she glowered up at him and said, "*I* ought to shoot you."

"I know." His arms closed around her and he held her close for a moment. Then, too soon for her peace of mind, he pushed her back to hold her at arm's length. The regret in his expression started butterflies dancing in her stomach.

"I'm sorry, Dru," he said, gently brushing his thumbs back and forth in the hollows above her collarbone. "Sorry you heard that. Sorry you were forced into an act of violence. Hell, I'm sorry I involved you in this whole sick mess in the first pla—"

"Drucilla!" At Sophie's anxious voice, Dru looked around to see her aunt and uncle emerging from the spur trail.

The sheriff's car was just backing out of the drive, and she could see Butch staring sullenly at them through the side window. She shivered. The last thing she wanted was for her son to be in that man's sights—even if it was merely a glimpse as they hauled his murderous carcass off to jail. Pulling free of J.D.'s embrace, she took an anxious step toward her aunt and uncle.

"It's all right," Sophie said as they approached, and her uncanny ability to read her niece's mind immediately comforted Dru. "We sent Tate to act as spotter for a group of water-skiers that Joe's taking out. He'll be occupied for another hour at least. What *happened*, darling? You weren't very coherent on the phone."

"Maybe I can explain," J.D. said, and gave them an abbreviated rendition of the past hour.

When Dru saw he planned to leave out every bit of his own heroics, she interspersed some commentary of her own. But she felt like a split personality as her mind worked on two separate levels at once. She was torn between admiration for J.D. and a guilty anger that she kept stuffing down. She wanted to provide her aunt and uncle with a more well-rounded version of what had happened, yet at the same time—

"J.D. told Butch if he killed him in his cabin he'd probably be caught—then he advised the guy to take him out into the woods somewhere far away from here so Butch could kill him in peace instead!" She simply couldn't wrap her mind around that.

"For chrissake, Dru!" J.D. snapped, and Dru blinked at the ire in his voice. "I wasn't about to have you or Tate discover my body if things went wrong, but you're making it sound as if I offered myself up like some sacrificial lamb."

"Considering that's exactly what I thought you were doing, John David, how else *would* I put it?"

"I'm sure J.D. had a plan to rescue himself," Ben interjected tactfully.

"Damn straight I did." But J.D.'s mouth crooked up on one side. "Which is not to say that I wasn't mighty grateful to you and your rock."

To Dru's utter horror, all of the emotion of the past couple hours caught up with her and she burst into tears.

"Damn! Aw, damn, sweetheart." J.D. pulled her into his arms. "Don't do that. Please. Don't cry." He snuggled her a little closer, rocking them side to side. "I'm sorry you had to hit him. I know that violence isn't exactly an everyday event for you."

The way it is for me. That was the unspoken inference, and that was what Dru truly cried about—because she knew the way J.D.'s mind worked by now. "You're planning to leave, aren't you?"

"Of course he isn't, honey," Ben answered for him. "You're still upset, but once you have a minute to catch your breath, you'll realize the threat has been removed. There's no reason for J.D. to go now."

But Dru could feel J.D.'s stillness against her. And

she'd seen that regret in his eyes. She knuckled the tears from her eyes and looked over at her aunt and uncle. "Could I have a little time alone with J.D.?"

"Yes, of course." Sophie hooked her arm through Ben's. "Come along, darling."

"But—"

The look she gave him made him snap his mouth shut in mid-protest. She turned a gentle smile on Dru. "We'll be at home if you need us."

They disappeared down the trail a moment later, and J.D. gazed into Dru's flushed face. He realized that the next few minutes were bound to be about as difficult as it gets, when she extricated herself from his arms, took a huge step back, and faced him with her arms crossed over her breasts.

The look on her face said, *Explain yourself, buddy*, and he felt his own defenses kick in. He crossed his arms over his chest also. "Don't give me that look."

"You're planning to walk out of my life—you don't get a say about my expression, too."

He took a giant stride toward her, tempted to snatch her up and shake her . . . or to hold her still long enough to kiss that stubborn you're-the-slime-on-the-bottom-of-my-shoe look from her face. Instead, he stopped inches shy of actually touching her, his hands fisted at his sides.

Touching her would *not* be a good idea. Not if he planned to get out of her life so she could go back to the one she'd had before he'd crashed into it.

The one she deserved to have back.

He thrust his nose next to hers instead. "You suddenly a mind reader?" he demanded, refusing to feel guilty. He was going to do the right thing if it killed him. "What the hell makes you think you know my plans?"

That stubborn chin of hers cranked another notch higher. "You plan on sticking around, J.D.?"

Well, shit. That went to the heart of it, didn't it? He looked her straight in her big baby blues and said, "I provided an alibi for Butch the day he killed a convenience-store clerk. Until today, I didn't know he'd shot the man, but that's no excuse. Neither is the fact that I owed Butch a debt for saving me from falling off a building when we were kids. I want you to know, though, that I honest-to-God believed him when he told me he was with a girlfriend while that store was being robbed. I swear to you that I never would have lied for him if I'd believed for a minute he was involved in the robbery." It was crucial she believed that much, at least.

"Of course you wouldn't," she agreed. "But why didn't you just let the girlfriend provide his alibi?"

"Because he's married to the meanest woman in the Western Hemisphere, and I knew she'd slice his balls off and serve them for dinner if she'd heard he was stepping out on her." *Oh, good, Carver*. He'd provided an alibi for a murder suspect so the suspect's wife wouldn't discover her husband was cheating on her. He just kept on sounding more and more heroic, didn't he?

He swore. "I don't have a decent excuse, Dru. I just allowed myself to be talked into it—which is another reason I have to go to Seattle and turn myself in."

"What'll happen to you when you do?"

He shrugged. "I could get off with a slap on the

wrist, I suppose. Or I could go straight to jail without passing Go." He thought the latter more likely, but didn't say so aloud.

Dru's arms slid from their militant pose, and she wrapped them around her waist to hug herself. "Either way, you don't plan on coming back, do you?"

He didn't look away, though the pain in her eyes made him want to. "No."

Dru felt something inside her crack in two. She'd heard enough of his conversation with Butch to know that she meant something to him. And *still* he was willing to simply walk off and throw it all away.

Willing to throw her away.

Anger flared up like an inferno exposed to fresh oxygen. Its fiery fury burned hotter and stronger than her pain, and she welcomed its cleansing heat.

"Well, that works out very nicely for you, doesn't it?" she demanded coolly.

He stilled. "What?"

"You get to stroll away from a sexual arrangement that was probably beginning to bore you, anyway."

"Jesus, Dru. You can't possibly believe—"

"Why, did I miss some declaration of undying love? But no—you did warn me you weren't a man who believed in love ever after, didn't you?" She hugged herself tighter, but arranged her features to convey indifference. It seemed vitally important that he not know how hurt, how *furious*, she was. "So feel free to leave with a perfectly clear conscience. I'm *used* to being discarded like a used Kleenex once a man gets his fill of me."

The anger in her stomach churned hotter. She

wanted to lash out, to make him hurt the way she hurt. "But just for a change of pace, John David, I'll tell you what I'm going to do. As soon as the dust settles from the back of your car disappearing over the rise, I think I'll head down to the Red Bull and pick me up a nice cowboy. Dance a few slow dances, have a couple drinks. And who knows? Maybe I'll just take him home with me at the end of the evening. I have it on good authority, after all, that I have the perfect little slut dress to entice—"

He grabbed her arms and hauled her up onto her toes. Thrusting his face close to hers, he snarled, "You'd wear *my* dress to seduce another guy?"

"In a red-hot minute, bub. Maybe I won't bother with underwear this time. That way my new squeeze won't have to waste time getting to the main event."

"The hell you say! No shit-kicking cowboy lays his hands on you. You're *mine*."

"Your woman." That was what she'd heard him tell Butch.

"Damn straight! And nobody touches my woman except—" His face suddenly went blank and he let her go, stepping back. "Oh. Very clever. But it's not going to work, Dru. Besides, you'd never do that."

"Says who? You aren't going to be here, so why shouldn't I?"

"I guess there is no real reason, but I know you, lady. I don't doubt that somewhere down the road you'll make love with someone, but you'd never roll right into bed with the first man you saw just because you're pissed at me."

"But sooner or later I *will* roll into bed with someone's who's not you, J.D." She watched his jaw muscles bunch and flex. "And you don't like that idea at all, do you?"

"No."

"Why?" She wasn't sure whom she was torturing more by pursuing this, him or herself. "What do you care? You're gonna be gone."

"You just don't get it, do you, Dru?" He thrust his hand through his hair and stared at her. "I'll probably be in *jail*. Christ, could we possibly *be* more different? You've got your Mayberry U.S.A. life, with your family and your friends who want nothing but the best for you. I've got a best friend who wants me dead, and the prospect of hard time. We don't have a damn thing in common for any kind of lasting relationship."

"You are so wrong! God, I've never seen a man work so hard to cut himself out of the picture!" Determination replaced her anger. "Just answer me this, okay? What are your feelings for me?"

Staring at her with shuttered eyes, he stood there without speaking for so long that her heart sank down to her toes. Damn him, he was determined to "save" her from his big bad influence, no matter what.

To her surprise, he finally said haltingly, "I . . . care for you."

"You care for me," she repeated. "Like you *care* for crème brûlée? Or rebuilding broken stuff? Or, no, wait! I'm probably a little more important than either of those. Like you'd care for a puppy, maybe?"

His eyebrows gathered like storm clouds above his nose. "Like I care for the air I breathe, all right?"

Yes. Despite his don't-screw-with-me scowl, her

heart began to lift. "*Very* all right. Though your delivery could stand a little work." She reached out to trail her fingertips down his forearm. "I love you, John David. Do you love me?"

"What if I do, Drucilla? It's not gonna change any—"

"Do you love me?"

"Will you listen to me, dammit? It doesn't make any difference if I do or I don't—"

"Do you love me?"

"Yes! But it's more complicated than that—"

"No. No, it's not. We love each other, and that's the bottom line."

Shoving his hands into his pants pockets, he hunched his shoulders. "I wish that were true. But the real bottom line is that I have to go back to face the music, and I've gotta do it alone."

"You don't, though. You say we're so different? The only real difference between you and me, J.D., is that I've had a support system my entire life and you haven't. But you have one now."

"Dru—"

"So you made a mistake," she said, wanting desperately to see some softening in his expression, needing a sign she was getting through to him. "I know the man you are, and so do Tate and Aunt Sophie and Uncle Ben. You don't deserve to go to jail over this, and we'll fight it to the Supreme Court if we have to. And if that doesn't work and you do have to go away, then I'll simply wait for you to get out."

His face went hard. "No," he said in a tone that brooked no argument. "You won't. Go back to your life, Drucilla. And leave me to mine."

There was no compromise in his eyes, in his voice, and all Dru's fierce convictions and arguments drained out of her.

God. Would she never learn? She should know by now that she couldn't force someone to love her, that she couldn't compel anyone to stay if he didn't want to. People had left her behind all her life, no matter how desperately she might yearn otherwise. The sooner she accepted that, the better off everyone would be. She stepped back, her hands dropping limply to her side.

"I don't know why I thought you'd be different from everyone else," she said dispiritedly. "You know what? I give up. Go back to your life, John David." She studied him one last time, collecting memories for the cold nights to come. Then she sighed, feeling nothing but tired. Tired and worn down to her soul. "I hope it will turn out to be everything you ever wished for."

Pivoting on her heel, she headed for the spur trail, leaving him standing in the clearing.

J.D. stared across at the empty trail head, nausea roiling in his gut. One minute Dru had been looking up at him with those vivid eyes of hers burning with conviction as she'd assured him she'd support him right up to the doors of the Supreme Court, and the next, he found himself standing in front of the cabin all by himself.

Again.

"Well, good," he said, staring at the void where she'd disappeared down the trail. Then he turned away to climb the porch steps. "Fine." He bent and picked up his duffel.

She'd done exactly what he'd told her he wanted. And that was for the best. He'd been alone all his life, and that was how he liked it. He headed down the steps for his car.

I hope your life will turn out to be everything you ever wished for.

His duffel hit the ground as everything inside of him went motionless.

The one thing he'd wished for his entire life had been a home to call his own. So why, now that he'd been offered one, had he just thrown it away?

He'd been afraid of disillusioning Dru somewhere down the line, so instead, he'd disillusioned her now. Somehow it had seemed better to hurt her a little now than to hurt her irreparably later.

But he'd never seen defeat in Dru's eyes before. He'd seen her angry and aroused; he'd seen her contemptuous, happy, and hurt. But he'd never seen her defeated. Until today.

He'd put that look in her eyes. He'd pushed her away and refused to let her be responsible for her own decisions. What had Ben said about accountability—how it sometimes meant allowing others to make hard decisions for themselves, instead of trying to spare them future pain by removing all choice from their hands?

He'd taken Dru's choices away from her. And for what? Because he might be penalized for his role in Butch's deception?

What if they didn't sent him to jail? Did he really want to spend the rest of his life in one rented room after another, without a place to truly call home? Did he really want to be an outsider getting his family fix by looking into other people's lives?

"Damn. I'm an idiot."

But an idiot whose gut had finally quit churning.

He hit the spur trail at a dead run.

Dru heard footsteps pounding down the trail and wearily moved aside. She could hear kids yelling and splashing in the distance and assumed this was another on his way to join their ranks.

Instead, she heard her name spoken in a hoarse voice, and her arm was suddenly gripped just above her elbow. Head whirling dizzily for a moment from being swung around, she stared in shock into J.D.'s face.

He latched onto her other arm and studied her intently. For the longest time, he didn't say a word. He simply stood there breathing heavily, gripping her arms tightly, staring down at her. She closed her eyes, not sure she had the strength to go another round with him.

Then he shook her once and her eyelids snapped open. She saw him swallow hard. "Drucilla Lawrence," he said. "Will you marry me?"

"W-what?" But she'd heard him; she knew she'd heard him. The heaviness that had weighted her soul lifted, and her heart took flight. "You want to marry me?"

"Oh, yeah."

It seemed suspiciously easy after his consistent

refusals to let her into his life, and she narrowed her eyes, unsure what to trust. "Why should I believe you now? Five minutes ago, you wanted to do everything all alone, without any help from me."

"Five minutes ago, I was a moron. I'm a whole lot smarter now. I want to spend the rest of my days with you, Dru. I want to grow old with you, to raise Tate and have other babies with you."

He lowered his head, and Dru's heart stuttered to a halt as his lips bestowed a gentle benediction upon hers. Then they lifted and his eyes blazed down at her.

"You mean so much to me," he said fiercely. "I love you in ways I didn't realize were even possible. I know I've been bullheaded about keeping you out of my problems, but I couldn't stand the thought of anything bad ever happening to you. I guess nobody makes it through life without taking a direct hit or two, though, huh?"

"No one," she agreed. "The trick, I think, is to make the good times count and to hang onto the people who love you with both hands so you have a support system when the not-so-good times hit." She cupped his jaw in her hand. "Are you ready to let me be your support system, John David, come good times or bad?"

A wild light flared in his eyes. "*Yes.*" He hauled her into his arms and held her so tight she could barely breathe. "Jesus God, yes. I still can't wrap my mind around the vision of you sitting across from me in a prison common room, but if you say you want to help me fight this thing, then that's what we'll do. I love you so much, Dru. Let me be the person who sticks with you through life. Don't make me go back out in the cold alone."

"You don't ever have to be alone again if you don't want to be," she said softly. Then she tilted her head back and gave him a slow, sly smile. "So long as you let me win every argument and grant my every wish."

He froze for a moment. Then the I'm-bad-and-don't-you-forget-it expression she was accustomed to reappeared. "You just keep waiting for that to happen, sweetheart," he advised. He rubbed his hands down her bottom and did something wicked with his pelvis that made her catch her breath. "You just keep on waiting for about the next fifty years."

Epilogue

It had been an eventful week and a long drive home, and J.D. pulled Dru away from Ben and Sophie's front door before she could rap on it with her usual don't-expect-me-to-wait-before-I-come-in rat-a-tap-tap. The sun was beginning to set earlier these days, and kamikaze moths dashed their brains out against the overhead porch light as she turned an inquiring gaze his way. Tenderly, he crowded her against the log wall and planted his hands, palms flat, next to her shoulders.

"This will probably be our last minute alone before Tate goes to bed tonight. How 'bout a kiss before we go in?"

With the immediate responsiveness that got him every time, she looped her arms around his neck and tilted her head up, her lips pursed in invitation. He lowered his head and kissed her softly.

Then he kissed her a little less softly.

Pulling back a moment later, he skimmed the pad of his thumb over the faint flush that stained her cheekbone. "It's good to be home," he said, stepping back. "I'm looking forward to the peace and quiet." He reached over and rapped on the door, then reached for the doorknob.

"Um, about that, J.D.," Dru said as he slid a hand onto the small of her back and ushered her ahead of him into the house. She looked at him over her shoulder. "Maybe I should've warned—"

"*Surprise*!"

J.D. stopped dead in the doorway as people popped up from behind Ben and Sophie's living room furniture. There seemed to be dozens of them, but he soon saw it was actually only Dru's aunt and uncle, Tate, Char and Kev, and a few of the staff he'd gotten to know from the lodge. He looked over at Dru, who shrugged and gave him a sheepish smile.

"You knew, I take it?"

She fluttered her eyelashes with exaggerated innocence. "Aunt Sophie might have mentioned something about it when I called to give them the good news."

"Congratulations, darling," Sophie said, coming up to them. She kissed him on the cheek and gave his arm a squeeze. "I was certain the prosecuting attorney would do the right thing, but you must be so relieved it's all over."

"Yeah, I am." He and Dru had just spent the past week and a half in Seattle straightening out his legal standing. The police and the D.A. had deposed him, scrutinized his background, work record, and current situation, and in the end had declined to press charges against him. Except for his having to go back to testify at the trial, that part of his life was closed.

Sophie chatted for a couple of minutes before drifting away to check on refreshments, and from that point on, J.D. was never alone. One by one everyone at the party stopped by to congratulate him. Dru ambled in and out of his orbit, and Tate was never far away, hovering like a hummingbird, darting and bobbing with excitement.

During a momentary lull the boy came up and hung on J.D.'s arm. "You and Mom can get married now, huh, J.D.?"

"Yeah." With the black cloud of his possible incarceration hanging over his head, J.D. had hesitated to make solid plans. Dru, however, had felt no such compunction, and she'd already booked a small church in town, arranged for the flowers, and bought her wedding dress. Char had bought a maid-of-honor dress and Sophie had claimed rights to the wedding cake. They were like a force of nature, and J.D. and the rest of the menfolk had pretty much just gotten out of their way.

He grinned down at Tate. "In less than a month now, buddy."

"Uh, J.D.?" Tate hesitated a moment, looking uncertain. Then he firmed up his jaw, squared his narrow shoulders, and met J.D.'s eyes head-on. "When you marry Mom . . . can I call you Dad?"

Blown away, J.D. stared down at his stepson-to-be. "You want to call me *Dad*?" he blurted, then could have cut his tongue out when he saw Tate flush.

"Forget it." Pride clearly smarting, Tate started to move away. "It was a dumb idea."

"Hell, no, I'm not going to forget it." J.D. hooked his elbow around the back of the boy's neck and hugged him to his side. He gave him a gentle noogie. "It's an *excellent* idea. I'd be honored, Tate. I can't tell you how honored I'd be."

Face tilting up at him from the crook of his arm, Tate gave him a dazzling, big-toothed smile. "Yeah?"

"Oh, yeah. Absolutely."

"Cool!" He tugged at J.D.'s arm. "Leggo. I wanna go tell Mom!" He raced off.

J.D.'s old neighborhood hadn't encouraged sentimentality, and he didn't quite know what to do with the huge lump in his throat. He slipped away from the party and went out onto the front porch.

God, he had so *much* these days that it sometimes scared him. He kept expecting to wake up and discover it was all just a great dream, and he was actually still back in his studio apartment in Seattle. Alone again.

"J.D.?" Dru stepped out onto the porch. "Are you okay?"

He slid his arm around her as she drew near and pulled her to him. Holding her close, he absorbed the heat of her plush curves and rubbed his jaw against her shiny, silky hair. "Tate asked if he could call me Dad," he said, and had to clear his throat.

"I know; he told me." She snuggled against him. "He also told me your answer. That was sweet."

"It wasn't *sweet*; it was true. I really am honored that he'd want me for his father."

"I think he's the one who feels honored." He felt her cheek rise as she smiled against his chest. "Only three and a half more weeks to go, John David. Then you're mine, all mine."

"*Only*, she says. Seems like a pretty long time to a guy who has to wait for an opportunity to sneak off before he can get a little."

"Aw, poor baby." She executed a little wiggle against him and slid her hands into the back pockets of his jeans to give his cheeks a squeeze. Rubbing her breasts against his chest as she raised up on her toes, she whispered in his ear, "It'll be worth the wait. I promise."

"Ah, man." His hands pulled her closer. "How'd I get so lucky, Dru? I feel like I won the lottery."

"Yeah? You like having part ownership in the lodge, huh?" she teased.

"I like having part ownership in your life. The rest is just gravy." He massaged his hands up and down her back. "It just doesn't get much better than this."

"Now, *there* I have to disagree." Dru gave him a smile that turned him to butter. "Because this is merely the beginning, John David. And from now on, it's just going to keep on getting better and better."

"I need to get away from it all!"

How many times have you cried out these words? The chance to change your life and maybe even be swept away by romance is so tempting . . . And as everyone knows, there's nothing like a good vacation . . .

The Avon Romance Superleaders are your passports to passion. As you enter the world created in each book, you have the chance to experience passion you've only dreamed of. Each destination is different—you might be whisked into Regency London, or perhaps to a secluded mountain cabin. But at each stop along the way, an unforgettable hero awaits to take your hand and guide you on a journey into love.

Imagine long, lazy summers in the country—the sun caresses your skin by day as you bask in its warmth in your favorite hammock . . . and each evening you curl up by the fire as contented as a cat. But something—or someone—is missing . . .

Then a compelling stranger comes striding into your life. And suddenly, a fire of a different sort begins to keep your nights hot. He's all-male, he's all-trouble . . . and he's got you . . .

All Shook Up

COMING JANUARY 2001

by Susan Andersen

"Are you planning on stalking me around my office?" Dru asked. Then she lost it. "Who taught you your manners, anyway? It certainly couldn't have been Great-aunt Edwina."

A muscle ticked in his jaw. "No, the lesson I learned from Edwina was that talk is cheap, and in the end there's only one person I can depend on—myself."

"Indeed? You'll have to excuse me if I don't cry big, sloppy tears over how misused you were. Because it seems to me that Edwina's talk wasn't all that cheap—for here you are, aren't you? Half owner in our lodge."

He took another step closer. "And that bothers you, doesn't it, sweetheart?"

She deliberately chose to misunderstand. "That you're bad-mouthing the woman who made it possible?" She ignored her reaction to his proximity this time and thrust her chin up. "Yes, I can honestly say I find that rather tacky."

For a moment his eyes went hot with some emotion Dru couldn't pin down, and she felt a burst of triumph that she'd managed to push one of his buttons. It was only fair, considering he seemed to have a natural facility for pushing all of hers.

Then his eyes went cool and distant. "Well, see, that's the thing about us lowlife types," he growled, stepping forward again. "Tacky is mother's milk to us, and we live for the opportunity to get something for nothing." He ran a rough-skinned fingertip down her cheek, leaving a streak of heat in its wake.

Dru jerked her head back, but he just moved in closer. "And we don't particularly care who we have to step on to get it either," he said in a low voice. "You might want to keep that in mind." His thumb rubbed her lower lip open, but he drew his hand back before she could slap it away. Giving her a slow once-over, he smiled insolently, and she saw that he didn't have bad teeth at all. They were maybe the slightest bit crooked—but very white and strong-looking.

The moment she dragged her gaze back to his eyes, he lifted an eyebrow. "The books?"

Blood thumping furiously in all her pulse points, Dru stalked over to the cabinet and pulled out the ledgers. A moment later she slapped them in his hands. "Here. These cover the past three years. Don't spill food on them and don't lose them."

"Guess that means I'd better not eat my peas with my knife again, huh?"

Embarrassed by her own snide rudeness, she resumed her seat, snatched up a pencil, and tapped it impatiently against the desktop, hoping to give the impression of a woman too busy for this nonsense. "Just be careful with them."

"Yes, ma'am." He gave her a bumptious salute and, with surprising grace for someone wearing several pounds of boot leather on each foot, strode out of the office.

Dru remained fuming at her desk long after he had gone. Things between her and J.D. were shaping up like Trouble with a capital *T*, but she had a bad, bad feeling that his being aggravating as all get-out was the *least* of her problems. She was more worried about the way she felt every time he was near.

Oh to be a Regency debutante . . . to wear beautiful gowns and to waltz (with permission, of course!) with a handsome nobleman, hoping he'll steal a kiss—and more—once the ball is over . . .

But what if your London season doesn't end in a spectacular match? Would you take the chance of traveling to the romantic Scottish Highlands and marrying a man you've never met? Who would want to be someone's poor relation anyway? After all, every woman needs a husband, and that's reason enough to sign . . .

The Marriage Contract

COMING FEBRUARY 2001

by Cathy Maxwell

"That is a wedding ring on your finger, isn't it?"

Anne had an unreasonable desire to hide her hand in the folds of her skirts. She clenched her fist. She wasn't ready for the confession, not ready at all.

He misinterpreted her fears, his gaze softened. "Your husband will be happy to know you are safe after such a bad accident."

"I hope he will," she managed to say. *Tell him,* her inner voice urged. *Now.*

Her husband looked down at the way he was dressed and laughed in agreement. He had a melodic, carefree laugh, for such a large man. Anne knew he would have a fine singing voice, too. And he didn't sound mad at all.

"It's a ritual I have," he explained with a touch of sheepishness over his peculiar dress. "Based on Celt customs. Well, actually, they are customs of our own. They make the sport more enjoyable. Adds to the game of the chase."

"Game?"

"Aye, a little danger is a healthy thing." He shrugged with a rueful grin, like a overgrown boy who couldn't help himself from pulling a prank.

Relief teetered inside her. Her husband didn't sound *raving* mad—just unconventional. He had a reason for being blue. Of course, she didn't know what to make of a man who considered it a game to fight a wildcat with his bare hands, a man who *enjoyed* danger—but then, this was Scotland.

And as long as he wasn't howling at the moon, her marriage might work.

Heat rose in her own cheeks. She attempted to make her interest a purely medical one. "Perhaps someone should put a salve on your scratches."

"They can wait." He abruptly changed the subject. "I'm sorry, I don't know your name."

She had to tell him before courage deserted her. This imposing man, clad only in a kilt, could overpower her merely by his presence. And they were alone together in the beautiful, but desolate Highlands, where no one could protect her. Still, she had to tell him . . .

"My name is Anne. I've come from London, sent by your sister. And I am your wife."

Most women would do anything to get out of wearing a hideous bridesmaid dress. Of course, leaving town is one thing—but leaving this century *is quite another! But that's just what Kelly Brennan does . . .*

And she ends up in sultry, steamy New Orleans, landing in the arms of a dashing, wealthy, and tantalizing man, who woos her like a lady by day . . . and someone quite different by night. But is it too extreme to marry someone from another era, even if he proves that he loves you . . .

Time After Time

COMING MARCH 2001

by Constance O'Day-Flannery

"Mr. Gilmore! Please."

Kelly heard him breathing heavily and, even through the darkness, she could see his shocked expression.

"Oh my god! I beg your pardon, Miss Brennan. I . . . I am mortified by my own actions."

Kelly pushed her hair back from her face. What could she say? She couldn't condone what had just happened, yet she was still reeling from the kiss, the first kiss in many years that felt as though it had awakened something in her she thought had died when she was twenty-three.

"I . . . I saw you standing there in that nightgown, and for a moment I thought . . . well, I thought you were someone else." He took a deep, steadying breath.

Kelly knew he meant his wife, his dead wife. This was becoming too uncanny, for in the darkness, he again reminded her of Michael. She couldn't help it. She giggled in nervousness. "You certainly surprised me, Mr. Gilmore."

"Please call me Daniel. And again, I implore your forgiveness. I most certainly am not the type of man who accosts his houseguests in the middle of the night."

"I didn't think you were." Now, why in the world did she want him to take her back into his strong arms? Craziness. Would it never end?

"I guess I shouldn't have been wandering around your home in the dark." She was rambling now, but who could blame her?

He'd kissed her! Just like that. *Kissed her and she'd liked it!*

"This is a most awkward situation, Miss Brennan."

"Call me Kelly," she whispered. "My husband died when I was much younger. I sympathize with your loss."

"You were married?"

"Yes. He died when I was twenty-three. Honestly, I don't know that I've ever really gotten over it."

"Was it the war?"

"The war . . . No, it was an accident. Something that never should have happened. Well . . . I guess I should say good night."

"Good night, Kelly."

He said her name . . . and she loved how it sounded coming from his lips. Lips that had felt so inviting, so impassioned . . . what was wrong with her?

"Good night," she whispered again and quickly opened the door to her bedroom.

Closing it behind her Kelly leaned against it and sighed heavily. She looked around and sensed a familiarity she hadn't felt before. How could she possibly know this place . . . this house and, somehow, him?

If a proper young English lady finds herself having the ill fortune to be confined with a stranger in a public conveyance, she must take special care not to engage this person in any way—either by speaking or staring.

It is true that a carriage can be rather small, making it difficult to avoid speaking to a handsome stranger—even if he might not be a gentleman. But as everyone knows, conversation can lead to so much more. And a woman can be ruined if it's known she's committed . . .

The Indiscretion

COMING APRIL 2001

by Judith Ivory

She stared at his black hat tipped over most of his face. If he ever should play in a Wild West show, he'd be a stagecoach robber, she decided. Or a gunfighter with a "quick temper and a quicker trigger finger," which was a line out of one of her brother Clive's Buffalo Bill novels. She entertained this fantasy for a few minutes, smiling over it. Yes, something about him, a leanness, "a build as hard and dependable as a good rifle" (she, in fact, had pilfered one of Clive's contraband American novels just to see what they were about), not to mention something in his brooding attitude, spoke of a possibly harsh, very physical existence.

Her imagination put him in a big, tooled-leather saddle on a horse caparisoned in silver stars down its breast. To his black hat with silver beads she added silver guns in holsters at his hips and American spurs that jingled as he walked. She remembered what such spurs looked like and, more memorable, what they sounded like: a lot of metal to them, a silver band low on each heel, silver chains underneath, with jagged, spinning wheels at the back. Nothing like an English riding spur with its single, neat point affixed to an English gentleman's boot.

Something about his posture, his attentiveness, made her call over the road noise. "Are you awake?"

After a second, he pushed his hat brim up enough with a finger so that his eyes were visible, if shadowed. "Yes, ma'am."

He had a nice voice when polite, like a bow being pulled slowly over the lowest groaning strings of a bass. He took his time saying things, slow-talking his way over sliding consonants and drawn-out vowels. His diction was full of *ma'am*s, *thank-you*s, and *you're-welcome*s. A politeness that turned itself inside out when he used it to say surly things.

"Who's Gwyn?" she asked.

Sam sat there slouched, watching a lady he'd been sure wouldn't utter another word to him, while he chewed the inside of his cheek.

Why not tell her? he thought. "The woman I was supposed to marry this morning." He sighed, feeling blue again for simply saying it. Hell, what sort of fellow left the woman he'd courted for almost two years at the altar in front of all their friends and family? He expected a huffy admonishment from Miss Prissy Brit now—

"I'm so sorry," she said.

The coach turned sharply, and they both leaned to counter the force of the motion, him stretching his leg out to brace himself with the toe of his boot, her swinging from the handgrip.

Over the noise of their travel, she asked, "What happened?"

Sam frowned. Now where had this little lady been five hours ago? Because that was the one question he had been dying for someone to ask all day, though not a soul till now had thought to. Her concern and his needy longing for it from someone, anyone, shot a sense of gratitude through him so strong he could have reached out and kissed her.

He said, "I was on the way to the church, when out the window of my hackney, I saw the robbery I told you about. The fellow stopped the woman on a Plymouth street and grabbed at her purse. She fought him. He was puny but wiry and willing to wrestle her for it. It made me crazy when he dumped her over. I figured, with me being a foot taller and sixty or so pounds heavier, I could hop out, pin the punk to the ground, then be on my way with very little trouble. I wasn't prepared for his four friends." Sam sighed. "I spent the morning at the doctor's when I was supposed to be standing at the altar."

"But your bride—"

"My bride won't talk to me long enough to hear my explanation."

Their eyes met and held. Hers were sympathetic.

And light brown. A kind of gold. Pretty. Warm. He watched her shoulders jostle to and fro as she said, "Well, when she saw you like this, she must have—"

"She didn't see me. She only called me names through her front door. No one would let me in."

"How unreasonable."

"Exactly." What a relief to hear the word.

"You could send her a note to explain—"

"She returned it unopened."

"You could talk to someone, get a friend to tell her—"

"No one will speak to me. I had to bribe the stable-boy to get me to the coach station."

Her pretty eyes widened. "But people have to understand—"

Exactly what he wanted to hear, the very words he'd been telling himself all day. And now that he heard them, he realized how stupid they were. "Apparently not. 'Cause not a person I know does."

Bless her, her mouth tightened into a sweet, put-out line. "Well, how unreasonable," she said again. Oh, God bless her.

"Yes." But no. He looked down. "It is unreasonable. Until you realize that I left Gwyn at the altar once before, eight months ago."

She straightened herself slightly in her seat, readjusting her wrist in the leather strap. Aha! her look said. Maybe it just wasn't the right woman.

There's something about a man who works with his hands . . . his self-reliance and ruggedness—along with his lean, muscled body—make him oh, so appealing.

So if you're seeking a strong, silent type—a man of the land—you might want to check out Wyoming. Yes, this is someone who seems like he's only willing to speak when he's asking you out to a Saturday night dance—but once he takes you in his arms, you'll know he'll never let you down . . . and he'll probably keep you up all night long. Because this is the place you'll find . . .

The Last Good Man

COMING MAY 2001

by Kathleen Eagle

She heard the scratch of gravel, turned, and caught the shift of shadow, a moving shape separating itself from a stationary one. It was a horse.

"Where did you come from?" Savannah asked, approaching quietly, assuming it had wandered up there on its own, and she was all set to welcome the company. Then she got close enough to make out the saddle.

"The Lazy K."

The deep, dearly familiar voice seemed to issue from the mouth of the cave.

"Clay?" She jerked the hem of her skirt free from its mooring in her waistband and let it drop. Another shadow emerged, bootheels scraping with each step as though they were taken reluctantly. He looked bigger than she remembered. "Clay, is that you?"

"The real me." He touched the brim of the cowboy hat that was pulled low over his face. "Are you the real Savannah Stephens?"

She laughed a little. "I was hoping it wouldn't matter up here."

"It matters to me." He reached for her hand. "Welcome home."

He seemed to surround her entirely with a simple squeeze of the hand. She stepped into the shelter of him, her nose a scant inch below his square chin. She had yet to see his face clearly, to assess his life by counting lines, but it didn't matter. She knew Clay Keogh. Reflexively she lifted her free hand, her fingertips seeking something of him, finding a belt loop, a bit of smooth leather. All she wanted was a proper greeting, a quick embrace, but she heard the sharp intake of his breath, and she knew she had the upper hand. She'd turned the surprise on him. He was big-man sure of himself one minute, shaky inside the next, simply because she'd stepped a little closer than he'd expected.

A power surge shot through her.

She lifted her chin, remembering times gone by and aiming for a little humor with her old dare. "You can do better than that, Clay," she purred. Her own throaty tone surprised her. Having no humor in her, she couldn't help but miss the mark.

He touched his lips to hers, tentative only for an instant. His hunger was as unmistakable as hers. His arms closed around her slight shoulders, hers around his lean waist. He smelled of horsehide and leather, tasted of whiskey, felt as solid as the Rockies, and kissed like no man she'd ever known, including a younger Clay Keogh. She stood on tiptoe to kiss him back, trade him her breath for his, her tongue for his.

"Savannah . . ."

She couldn't understand why he was trying to pull away. There'd been a catch in his breath—she'd heard it distinctly—and it was that small sound that had set her insides aflutter. The surprise, the innocence, the wonder of it all. Good Lord in heaven, how long had it been since she'd been kissed?

"Shhh, Clay," she whispered against the corner of his mouth. "It's so good, finding you here."

"Glad to see—"

"But don't talk yet. Just hold me. It feels so good. You're not married or anything, are you?"

"I'm something." His deep chuckle sounded a little uneasy, which wasn't what she wanted. She wanted him easy. "But not married."

"Let me see you," she said, reaching for his hat. He started to duck away, but she flashed him a smile, and he stopped, looked at her for a moment, then bowed his head within her reach. "Girlfriend?" she asked as she claimed his hat and slid her fingers into the hair that tumbled over his forehead.

"No."

"Me neither."

"How about boyfriends?"

She laughed. "Completely unattached," she assured him, learning the new contours of his cheek with her hand.

"Well, I've never been to New York, but I hear there's a lot of variety there."

"There's variety everywhere, Clay. Don't tell me you've turned redneck on me. I won't have that."

"You won't, huh?" His smile glistened with moonlight. "Not much has changed here."

"That's what I was counting on."

It's one thing to get away from it all . . . and it might be another to visit the town of Gospel, Idaho. Still, even though it's not near very much, you can always have some eggs at the Cozy Corner Café and get your hair done at the Curl Up and Dye Hair Studio.

And there's the added attraction of Gospel's sheriff. He's easy on the eyes and not above breaking the laws of love to get what he wants. Before you know it, you'll have plenty to talk about in the way of . . .

True Confessions

COMING AUGUST 2001

by Rachel Gibson

"Can you direct me to Number Two Timberlane?" she asked. "I just picked up the key from the realtor and that's the address he gave me."

"You sure you want Number *Two* Timberlane? That's the old Donnelly place," Lewis Plummer said. Lewis was a true gentleman and one of the few people in town who didn't outright lie to flatlanders.

"That's right. I leased it for the next six months."

Sheriff Dylan pulled his hat back down on his forehead. "No one's lived there for a while."

"Really? No one told me that. How long has it been empty?"

"A year or two." Lewis had also been born and raised in Gospel, Idaho, where prevarication was considered an art form.

"Oh, a year isn't too bad if the property's been maintained."

Maintained, hell. The last time Dylan had been in the Donnelly house, thick dust covered everything. Even the bloodstain on the living room floor.

"So, do I just follow this road?" She turned and pointed down Main Street.

"That's right," he answered. From behind his mirrored glasses, Dylan slid his gaze to the natural curve of her slim hips and thighs, down her long legs to her feet.

"Well, thanks for your help." She turned to leave, but Dylan's next question stopped her.

"You're welcome, Ms.—?"

"Spencer."

"Well now, Ms. Spencer, what are you planning out there on Timberlane Road?" Dylan figured everyone had a right to privacy, but he also figured he had a right to ask.

"Nothing."

"You lease a house for six months and you plan to do nothing?"

"That's right. Gospel seemed like a nice place to vacation."

Dylan had doubts about that statement. Women who drove fancy sports cars and wore designer jeans vacationed in nice places with room service and pool boys, not in the wilderness of Idaho. Hell, the closest thing Gospel had to a spa was the Petermans' hot tub.

Her brows scrunched together and she tapped an impatient hand three times on her thigh before she said, "Well, thank you gentlemen for your help." Then she turned on her fancy boots and marched back to her sports car.

"Do you believe her?" Lewis wanted to know.

"That she's here on vacation?" Dylan shrugged. He didn't care what she did as long as she stayed out of trouble.

"She doesn't look like a backpacker."

Dylan thought back to the vision of her backside in those tight jeans. "Nope."

"Makes you wonder why a woman like that leased that old house. I haven't seen anything like her in a long time. Maybe never."

Dylan slid behind the wheel of his Blazer. "Well, Lewis, you sure don't get out of Pearl County enough."